THE DIVINE SHOT

Betty Mann

iUniverse, Inc.
Bloomington

The Divine Shot

iUniverse books may be ordered through booksellers or by contacting:

iUniverse
1663 Liberty Drive
Bloomington, IN 47403
www.iuniverse.com
1-800-Authors (1-800-288-4677)

ISBN: 978-1-4502-7105-9 (sc)
ISBN: 978-1-4502-7107-3 (ebook)
ISBN: 978-1-4502-7106-6 (dj)

Library of Congress Control Number: 2010916422

Printed in the United States of America

iUniverse rev. date: 1/03/2011

PROLOGUE

I t had taken months for the three young men to travel from Iraq to this heavily forested area of Canada. They huddled under a canopy of trees near the Canadian—U.S. border as they awaited transportation to their final destination inside the United States. They had searched for hours for this pickup location—a tree with a wide, silver reflective band around the trunk.

They shivered from the frigid early morning air and were nearly hugging one another just trying to stay warm. The fog was so thick they could hardly see the person next to them. The cold, damp air was something they had not experienced in their country. The three men wore lightweight clothing and traveled with very little in their back packs and, up until now, it had been sufficient. They had not anticipated the need for heavy clothing for only one day's journey. And, if things had stayed on schedule, there would have been no need for warm clothing.

Their pickup was to have taken place at nine PM. It was now two AM and the men were concerned some unforeseen circumstance was causing the delay in their pickup. They prayed to Allah that the Canadian authorities had not captured their fellow countrymen. There was no contingency plan and returning to Iraq was not an option. The information they plan to gather while in the United States was vital to future operations. They were expected to do this successfully, regardless of what happened to them, or what they had to go through.

Details and arrangements to get these men into the United States had taken their superiors thirteen months to complete. And in the months the three men had been traveling, all the pre-arranged plans had gone smoothly. Every contact was on time; each leg of the journey was well organized and executed without a hitch. The most grueling part of the operation was the long, agonizing journey from Turkey. In Turkey the three men boarded an old fishing boat for the trip to Canadian waters. They knew the crew of the boat was involved in all types of shady deals, which was the reason this particular vessel had been chosen. The fishing boat was small, had meager accommodations, and not nearly enough rations for the long trip across the ocean. Although they made several stops along the way for fuel and supplies, they always seemed to run out of food long before the next destination. All the stops were made in small out of the way locations, and were so quick their feet hardly hit dry land before they were off and running again. The men understood and accepted that these poor conditions were necessary to insure their safe passage to the United States.

The three traveling companions bunked on the floor in the storeroom off the kitchen. The floor space was just large enough for the three men to lay side-by-side with their shoulders nearly touching. The only toilet was located in mid-ship, but the cramped space and foul odor made conducting necessary bodily functions hardly worth the effort. As a result, the boat's rails were more frequently used as a toilet, provided the boat wasn't bouncing thirty feet into the air. Rough seas made it hard for anyone to keep anything on their stomach. The rails were good for that, as well. But, often the sickness overwhelmed them before they could get to the side of the boat. This left them no choice but to upchuck wherever they found themselves. After several days of this, it was hard to walk anywhere on the boat without stepping in vomit, and the smell permeated the small vessel. The few deck hands seemed oblivious of the poor conditions, and for the most part could care less whether their guest travelers were upchucking all over the boat, or if they died in some secluded dark corner.

Food rations rarely lasted more than a few days after each stop. So, the menu consisted mainly of fish and any other edible creature that was brought up from the sea. The meals were prepared in one of three ways—fried, steamed or baked. Fish, fried in rancid oil, was served most often and contributed to the sea sickness they all experienced. They had eaten worse while on previous missions in the desert, but never in their lives had they been so sick. Before the journey's end, all three men had had their fill of seafood and would rather die than to ever eat another bite of the horrid creatures.

By the time they reached their contact near the Canadian border, all three men had lost nearly twenty pounds each. They had allowed their beard and hair to grow long again to grow long again and now looked and smelled like they had on past missions in the desert.

The contact met them in a rowboat three miles off the Canadian coast, just north of the border with the United States. After they came ashore, three of the men carried the small boat into the woods while the other man covered their tracks. They carefully piled small branches, limbs, and leaves around the boat in an effort to conceal it. The rowboat would be used again at another time for this same purpose. The contact then led the three men through the dense forest for two long grueling days. They were sick and weak from their ordeal on the boat from hell, and the hike through the cold, damp forest, with very little rest or food did nothing to improve their physical health. It just made matters worse. And, after finally arriving at their small camp, they slept for three days straight. Here they remained for three months while they recovered from their traumatic boat experience and learned details of their upcoming mission.

It was a small camp located deep inside the dark, heavy forest where no one, except those with hidden agendas, would dare enter...a perfect hideaway. Twelve of their countrymen were already there; men who had previously made a trip similar to the one they had just made. They lived in two small shacks made of logs nestled under the deep shade of the thick canopy of trees. The shacks were hard to see even during the day. Each shack was furnished with three sets of triple bunk beds made of small logs which rested along three of the outer walls. A table with benches, made with the same materials, was placed in the center of the room on a floor of hard, packed soil. A wood-burning cook stove provided enough warmth for the small space. The accommodations were meager at best, but they had everything they would need for their stay in the forest.

This small cell was responsible for retrieving new recruits from incoming boats and providing new identities and documents. They were to see that the new recruits were well rested, clean-shaven and their hair cut short so they could blend into the American scene. The three men were given new identities, U.S. driver's licenses, U.S. passports and any other documents an American citizen would possess. They would also provide them with instructions and a map to the next contact point, where they would cross the border into the United States.

At daybreak, with directions in hand, they left the camp on foot for their new destination. They knew they would have to keep a good pace if they were to be at the rendezvous by nine PM. They would not have a guide for this part of their journey and were on their own until they reached their next pickup point.

The day's hike through the dense forest was long and tiring. According to the hand-written directions, the pickup point should be near. They were having a hard time locating the tree with the wide silver band wrapped around it, so they spread out in different directions in search of the tree. It had to be in this area. Everyone moved quickly in their search, as it was almost dark. They had flashlights, but were given instructions to use them only in case of an emergency or for the contact signal. Lights were too easily seen at night in such a dark forest. After traveling this far, what they didn't need now, was to be caught by the Canadian Mounties. They spread out and met back in a central location every fifteen minutes. Then they'd branch out in different directions again.

When it became too dark to see, and the tree still had not been located, they turned on one of the flashlights. This time the three men stayed together while they continued the search for the tree in the darkness. They located it thirty minutes before the scheduled pickup time. This would give them an opportunity to rest for a short while before their new contact arrived. He was to escort them the remaining ten miles to the U.S.-Canadian border and smuggle them across, avoiding customs and border patrol agents.

The men waited patiently but were becoming very concerned about the delay in their pickup. Plus, they were freezing in the cold, damp night air. The contact was hours behind schedule. If he didn't show soon, an alternative plan would have to be found. They had no automobile, so they would have to cross the border on foot. They had a map but it contained no details about foot travel beyond where they were. They had only limited information about their travel and contacts in case they were captured. Besides directions to this pickup point and the name of the man meeting them, they also knew the name and location of their next contact in the United States. This information was committed to memory and the handwritten map given them at the camp was to be destroyed once they arrived at the rendezvous location. They had no cell phone and returning to the camp was out of the question. The mission had to go forward. With the limited information they had, and their lack of knowledge of the surrounding area it would be a challenge to reach the next contact point. They knew their country well and often traveled on foot for weeks at a time, but this country was strange to them. The intense geographic study they completed on the United States and Canada didn't include foot travel through the countries. Even though things had not gone as planned, they all had faith that Allah would send the pickup contact soon.

They had never been so cold and seriously considered building a small fire. But, they reconsidered after looking around at all the wet vegetation, and besides, a fire might bring unwanted attention. They were becoming restless and wanted to leave, but agreed to stay two more hours to see if the contact showed. It would be near daybreak then and they could see where they were going if they had to proceed on foot. Everyone was tired and sleepy. One of the men volunteered to keep watch while the other two huddled close together on the wet ground and napped.

The lookout had been watching for the flashing light signal for one and a half hours when he saw the signal in the distance. The lights of the automobile flashed twice and then three times. He shook his friends awake in time for them to see the next series of flashes. He removed his flashlight from his back pants pocket and returned the signal. The automobile slowly approached the frozen, exhausted men.

The three men watched the beat-up, late model, four-wheel drive Jeep approach them. They were tired, hungry, and eager to get out of the cold, damp air. Although they were glad their pickup had finally arrived, they were also agitated that he was hours behind schedule. And they were in no mood to extend the usual friendly greetings that they were so accustomed to.

"It's about time you got here. We have been freezing our tails off for hours waiting on you. What caused you to be so late?" one of the men said, as the driver opened the door of the automobile.

"Just get in the car," snapped the driver. He had had his own difficulties getting to the pick-up location and wasn't in such a great mood himself.

The passenger who came with him said nothing, as he exited the passenger side of the automobile to allow the three men to enter the back seat. Not another word was said, as they sat crowded together for the slow, bumpy ride though the dense forest and fog. The sun was clearing the horizon by the time they made the ten mile trip to the border.

For one of these men this journey will lead to a series of events that will change the lives of people he is yet to meet. His actions and quest for revenge will result in tragedy for some, but for others it will lead to new relationships and new beginnings.

CHAPTER ONE

Edna was already considered a senior citizen, but you would never convince her of that fact. Her tall, slender body and stylish haircut made her look twenty years younger than most women her age. The fact that she never missed an appointment with the hair colorist contributed a great deal toward her youthful look. Style and fashion had not been important growing up in her large family, but Edna had a flair and creativity with clothes that had blossomed as she grew older. Her fashionable clothing, quick step, and bright attitude also added to Edna's youngish appearance.

She had known her husband, Grady, for forty-seven of the sixty-three years of her life. But, even he couldn't talk her out of taking this solo road trip to visit distant relatives in Mississippi twelve hours away. Still thinking she could do the things she did when she was twenty, she loaded the late model, GMC Suburban with a few personal belongings, placed the strap to her yellow carry-everything purse over her shoulder, and kissed her loving husband goodbye on the way out the door at precisely 5:00 AM.

She didn't make a habit of going on extended trips without him, and when she did, it was bittersweet. She loved traveling, but knew she would miss Grady tremendously. Watching him now in the rearview mirror waving goodbye, gave her a sick, lonely feeling—almost making her regret taking this solo trip.

After a quick stop at the 7-11 for her favorite traveling breakfast, she eagerly returned to the highway. With music blaring in the CD player, a mug filled with blueberry crème coffee in one hand and a sour cream donut in the other, Edna was ready for the long ride northward. It doesn't get much better than this, she thought.

As she settled into the rhythm of the highway, the joy of travel and the beauty of the countryside began to drown out the lonely feelings she had initially felt. It was a cool, autumn morning and, even in Florida, the beginnings of a new season could be seen. This heightened Edna' excitement about the trip and, with each mile she pushed any regrets a little further away.

When she took long road trips, getting an early start always added to the excitement. And, for Edna, it was especially thrilling now to watch the sun peek over the horizon. The cloudless early morning sky was streaked with vibrant orange and blue colors. She didn't see this sight often, as she and Grady were retired and slept every morning through this wonderful gift from God. They did, however, see the moon a lot. Both of them were night owls; if they went to bed before midnight, it was too early.

The twelve hour drive she was facing would be a challenge without someone to share the driving. Edna's sister, Louise, usually traveled with her, but couldn't make this trip. Grady was never fond of visiting distant relatives, hers or his, so she decided to make this trip alone.

Edna had planned her trip so she could leave on a Saturday and avoid the heavy weekday traffic on the interstate. Now as she breezed down the highway, she could see very little traffic. "So far, so good," she said out loud. "I haven't seen any highway patrolmen. I hope all of them have the weekend off."

Although Edna had never been stopped for speeding, she had, on numerous occasions in the past, exceeded the posted speed limit. It was in her blood to drive fast...but not by much. After all, she was a safe drive. Even her driver license was stamped "Safe Driver". Ten miles over the limit was a comfortable speed for her but twenty over invigorated her and made her more alert. Well, at least that's what she would tell Grady when he cautioned her about driving fast. Having the power over the big machine was what she really loved. Grady was always after her to use the cruise control. But, that was his thing, not hers. He seldom drove over the speed limit, as he was never in a hurry. Nor, did he get the thrill of speed like she did. Often he'd set the cruise control when they traveled together and would sit back and enjoy the scenery. She would never tell him, but this often annoyed her and, whenever possible, she would jump behind the wheel first and wouldn't relinquish it until she was too tired to drive anymore.

She had been driving for three hours and her Bob Seiger CD had been played and replayed. Enya had now taken over the CD player. Edna thought *"A Day Without Rain"* would be a little easier on her ears; especially after listening to three hours of *"Roll Me Away"* with Bob. Plus, she had also managed to acquire a sore throat as a result of the boisterous backup performance she and the Silver Bullet Band had been giving Bob. Edna wasn't much of a singer, but she loved to sing along, usually very enthusiastically, at least as long as no one else was around to hear.

Grady had given her a karaoke machine for Christmas two years ago. She never thought about karaoke or ever thought she wanted a karaoke machine, but it turned out to be a great gift— one she still enjoys today. He put it in the spare room where they keep a second television and their much underused exercise equipment. Almost every night for a year, she closed herself in the room and selected the songs she enjoyed singing the most from the large array of songs in her CD notebook. She would pretend no one could hear and sing her heart out. It was great entertainment for her. She often lost track of time and would sing into the wee hours of the morning. As with any busy schedule, things would crop up that would keep her from spending as much time with her karaoke as she would like. As a result, a couple nights a week was about all the time she had now for this special pastime activity.

She looked at the clock on the dashboard; it read 9:00 AM. She glanced at the radio and her thoughts wandered to her favorite weekday talk radio programs and she knew she would miss them greatly. She enjoyed listening to Gary Bratt in the mornings, followed by the Rusty Howard show, and then Gary again on television at 7:00 o'clock. Their nationally broadcast programs, on the most part, were politically structured, but both men had a great sense of humor and their playful manner took the edge off the serious topics they would sometimes talk about. She liked both men, but was really partial to Gary, the *Brattman*, as he had dubbed himself. The nickname had stuck, and his radio and television programs were now referred to as the *Brattman Show*.

Although she enjoyed the music in the CD player she would rather be listening to her favorite radio programs. "Oh well, you can't have everything. This is Saturday, after all. My two favorite guys have to rest sometime." She shrugged her shoulders and decided this would be a good time to take a break to top off the gas tank, stretch, and visit the restroom.

Almost every exit on Interstate 95 had gas stations, but she really hoped to find a 7-11, so she could refill her mug with blueberry crème coffee. No other stations had that flavor, and if she couldn't get it, she would forgo coffee. Edna didn't consider herself a coffee addict; she seldom drank coffee. Drinking coffee was something she did when she was away from home, or when she was on a road trip such as this. Somehow, blueberry crème coffee relaxed her and made driving a lot more fun. The truth be known, she just loved the flavor.

Ten minutes up the road she saw the exit sign. Not knowing which stations she would find, she took the exit and, to her dismay, there was no 7-11. She saw four gas stations in the area. The prices were all within one cent of each other, so she pulled into the closest one. Boy, it will be good to get out and move, she thought. She couldn't imagine why she was so stiff. It wasn't like she had been exercising for three hours; she had only been sitting behind a steering wheel enjoying the scenery. She had never gotten this stiff from her daily four mile walks through the wildlife sanctuary adjoining her neighborhood.

She exited the Suburban, gave her body a quick stretch, and then began the process of fueling the truck. She locked the gas nozzle so that it would fill the tank without her assistance. Then, she stepped a few feet away and did some serious stretches. It felt as if every muscle in her body ached. She didn't see anyone around within hearing distance, so she said out loud, "If I feel this bad now, what am I going to feel like by the time I get to Hattiesburg tonight?" Refueling completed, she locked the Suburban then went inside the station to use the restroom. She knew she wouldn't find her blueberry crème coffee at this place and didn't bother to look.

Edna was on the road again and soon became preoccupied with thoughts of her first cousin. Even though she didn't know Linda Ann well, she was greeted enthusiastically when she had contacted her the previous month to make arrangements to visit her Mississippi family. Hattiesburg, Mississippi is where Linda lives and this was to be Edna's destination by nightfall. The plan was to visit Linda in Hattiesburg for two days. Then, they would visit other family members throughout the state. Even though most of their older relatives had long passed away, there were, however, numerous first, second, and third cousins whom neither of them had met. She hoped to meet most of them in the course of her two week visit. Linda Ann was also looking forward to this trip since it had been some time since she had visited the ones she did know. Both women were eager for the opportunity to meet the others.

Edna last saw her cousin Linda twelve years ago, when she and Louise took a road trip through Mississippi to visit family. Louise and Edna had made several road trips together in the past forty years—usually to visit family in Mississippi or Georgia. Their road trips were always short because a week was about all

Edna could stand being away from the love of her life, Grady. They'd do things like most women traveling alone would do... shop and chitchat all the way to their destination. Talking wasn't all that necessary, however, since they already pretty much knew what the other was thinking. But, when it came to Edna's deep feelings for Grady, she couldn't share them with Louise. Her sister might have understood her feelings, but Edna knew for sure she would think her silly for desperately missing him. This was a part of her that she wouldn't let her sister see. It occurred to her, *you never really know everything about a person, no matter how close you think you are.*

Edna really missed her traveling companion. They were from a large family of fourteen children. Louise was eleven months older than Edna—so they felt almost like twins. In high school they were often mistaken for each other. They were now approaching their golden years and lived in different cities. Talking endlessly on the phone and visiting on special occasions was about the extent of their relationship now. Years pass and people change. Those changes have been different for each of them, and although the family resemblance still remains, people no longer mistake them for each other.

Caught up in her reminiscing, she totally lost track of time. An hour had passed and she had hardly felt it. She put aside all thoughts of her family, removed the CD from the player, and switched on the radio in search of some kind of talk show she could listen to.

It took some searching through the radio channels to locate a program that wasn't full of static. Even the station she settled on wasn't static free, but she could at least understand what the host was saying. The program had already started and she wasn't sure who the host was but the subject sounded interesting. He was talking about gun rights and gun control. This particular subject hit home with her, because Grady had insisted she get her concealed weapons permit before her road trip to Mississippi. She had traveled with a weapon on her past road trips. But, it had been stuffed so far back under the seat of the automobile she was driving, that it wouldn't have been accessible if danger had presented itself. For the most part, she forgot all about the gun. It wasn't until the permit class she recently attended that she learned how illegal and potentially dangerous traveling across state lines with a gun could be. In some states a gun forgotten under the seat of an automobile could land a person in prison. She and Grady owned two guns, but she knew very little about them and had only fired at a few cans years ago. She had a healthy respect for guns and hated being around them. In spite of her fears, she did, however, like a 25 cal. 1954 Beretta semiautomatic she saw at the gun show where she and Grady attended the permit class.

The gun permit class was not that long ago, and she remembered all the mixed emotions she experienced during the class. The instructor illustrated how to handle a weapon properly and described how to safely use a gun. But, the most thought provoking part of the lecture was the ramifications of using a gun. With all the complicated laws, it made you afraid to even think about a gun, much less own one.

In spite of Edna's fears and concerns, Grady still wanted a small gun she could carry in her purse on her road trip. They didn't buy the Beretta from the gun show that day, but found one at a gun shop later that week. This was the gun she now had tucked somewhere deep inside her yellow carry-everything giant purse. *If I should happen to need that gun to defend myself, I'll have to ask the attacker to give me time to locate it.* In her whole life, she had never used a weapon against another person, and she hoped to exit this world without having to do so.

The static on the radio had gotten louder than the talk show host. Edna became agitated and tired of searching for a station with less noise. The static won in the end; she turned the radio off. It was just as well because her sour cream donut breakfast was long gone and she was starving. It was almost time for lunch and she felt like a long walk. She and Grady often went for long walks several times a week; she knew she would miss them on this trip.

Thinking of Grady and walking gave her the urge to call him. She knew he would be wondering how she was and how far she had traveled. It wouldn't surprise her if he called her at any moment to remind her to stop for lunch. She decided to save him the trouble and reached for her cell phone which was sitting on the passenger seat. Seeing the battery was low, she plugged the phone into the lighter to charge, and then called home.

CHAPTER TWO

Grady had a heavy feeling in the pit of his stomach as he watched Edna drive away. Normally when she went on road trips one of her sisters would go along for company and to help her drive. No one could go with her this trip, and visiting distant relatives wasn't his cup of tea. He didn't especially like the idea of her traveling the long distance alone, but she loved driving and could drive endlessly whenever the two of them traveled together. He wasn't worried about Edna's driving abilities, but unforeseen things such as mechanical problems or illness could crop up at any time. *I hope I'm worrying unnecessarily. She isn't even out of sight and I already miss her.*

Grady knew family was a big part of Edna's life. She has such a large family. He remembered, at the age of sixteen, the first time he came to her home to pick her up for a date. He pulled up on the grass in her front yard in his used, but well maintained 1952 Plymouth. As he got out of the car, he noticed three little barefoot children running across the yard in his direction. They ranged in ages, he guessed, from three to seven. He remembered thinking at the time how cute they were with their dirt smudged, smiling faces. They had been playing with toy trucks and trains in the sand when he drove up.

The three children practically tackled him, tussling for a position on both legs. He walked across the yard toward where Edna waited for him, dragging all of them on his legs. Edna opened the screen door to the front porch and welcomed him inside. She seemed highly amused, but not surprised, at the children's behavior. She told him some time later that any man who wanted her would have to accept her family. As Grady entered the small living room that day, more children materialized. He thought the space looked exceptionally tidy and clean, considering all the children who apparently spent a lot of time there. His first impression after seeing all the young children was...*her family must run a child care center*. He was amazed when Edna introduced them as her sisters and brothers.

He had had great admiration for Edna the first moment he saw her in the small living room with the children that day. She laughed and teased with them and made them feel as if they were part of their date. He hadn't minded though and rather enjoyed watching the interaction with the children. She'll make a wonderful mother some day he remembered thinking at the time. She had already begun to win his heart, though she did not know it.

Grady thought about his family. He remembered when he was very young, and his mother told him a little brother or sister would be coming to live with them. When it was explained to him that he would have someone to play with, he became very excited and couldn't wait for the baby to arrive. He'd ask his mother several times a day about where the baby was. He couldn't have known at the time that his life was about to change forever. Grady was his parent's first child and his grandmother's first grandchild; so he had been the center of attention for two years. Between Alma, his grandmother on his mother's side and his twelve year old Aunt Virginia, and nine year old Aunt Ubadene, Grady's feet hardly ever hit the floor.

Grady was the oldest of three boys and had often wanted to eliminate two of them; especially when they invaded his small private space. Wes was two years younger, had a head full of bright red hair, and was as mischievous as any human he had ever seen. His brother Lee was four years younger. He and Wes called him "Cotton Head" because of the very light blonde hair on his head. Lee was always happy to join in any mischief, but he was more of a follower than an instigator.

Grady loved his brothers and wouldn't give them up for anything. However, there were times he had wondered what it would have been like to be an only child; *just to have my own room would have been a dream.*

The small two bedroom house where Grady had lived in Florida was cold in the winters and hot in the summers. It was a wood frame house and the interior walls had no insulation. There was no air conditioning, and the only source of heat was a kerosene heater located in the living room. Grady had often felt confined in the small bedroom he shared with his two younger brothers. He thought about Edna and the living arrangements she shared with all those children; her home wasn't any larger than his. "Heck, I still can't imagine seven boys and seven girls in one family. I wonder how Edna kept her sanity with all that activity around her every day," he muttered to himself.

Grady knew Edna truly loved her brothers and sisters. He asked her once if she loved one more than another. She said she loved them all the same, but felt closer to her sisters. She thought it was because all the girls had shared so many duties. Coming from a migrant background, the family would leave for work in the fields before daybreak and return at dark. The girls in the family had the cooking and household chores added to the end of their workday in the fields. She said that's how all seven of the girls became close—by rotating and sharing their duties so that no one carried a heavier load than the other. It was to her older brother, Henry, that she gave all the credit for this rotation schedule, which they called "*The Detail*".

Grady was very familiar with the events which had led to *the detail*; Edna had told the story many times. While Henry was

home on his first furlough from the Air Force, he overheard some
of the girls bickering over who was going to clean up the kitchen
after dinner. Henry thought he could help them settle their
dispute. He gathered all the girls in front of the warm fireplace
located in the small living room. In his mild mannered tone, he
said he wanted to set up a detail for them. Then he explained what
a *detail* was. In the military everyone is assigned a task they're
expected to complete. They are assigned this task for a week or
two and then rotated to a different one, he had told them. This
type of detail can work for you, too. He then explained how it
would work. He paired the girls, an older one with a younger one,
and included anyone old enough to lift a broom. Chores were
assigned for a week for each pair. At the end of the week the chores
were rotated among the pairs of children so they did something
different each week. The schedule was made a month in advance
so everyone knew what they were supposed to be doing and when
they were to do it. Henry set up the first month's schedule and
the girls faithfully continued on with this system as long as they
lived at home.

Edna was in the second grade when her brother settled the
dispute over chores. After *the detail* the girls stopped their constant
bickering, which made their mother eternally grateful to her son.
Grady once asked Edna why they followed *the detail* for all those
years. And, why didn't they just tell their brother to take a hike
and go on about their business? She said he was much older than
they were, he was in the military, and they were scared to death
of him. They were sure if they fell out of line he would find out
about it…and, none of them wanted that.

Henry had been retired from the military for years, when
Edna mentioned *the detail* to him one day while she and Grady
were visiting him. He remembered setting it up, but he thought
at the time they would forget all about it as soon as he was out
of sight. He was shocked when Edna told him they had followed
the detail for more than twenty years. Edna had also remarked at

the time that it was unfortunate he hadn't set up a detail for the boys in the family as well.

Grady went to the kitchen and poured himself a cup of hot coffee and sliced off a piece of the homemade pound cake Edna had left for him on the counter. He walked out the kitchen door to the adjoining sunroom to enjoy the view of the lake. He watched a flock of black ducks land in the lake and knew it wouldn't be long before they were up in his back yard eating the grain he had placed in a bowl for them earlier that morning. As he relaxed in the overstuffed white wicker lounge chair and sipped his coffee, his mind drifted back to Edna. He couldn't believe how lonely he was without her, and he had two whole weeks of this to endure. He couldn't blame her for wanting to see her family, though. After all, it had been years since her last visit. She talked often about visiting them and even made plans to do so many times, but something always seemed to come up. When she mentioned a road trip to Mississippi this time, he tried to discourage her. He felt a little guilty about that now. But, he had finally given in to her wishes because he knew it would probably be the last opportunity she would have, as they were both aging and might not be able to travel too many more years.

Grady had an odd feeling about this trip though, because it was a long distance and she was alone. He wondered how far she had traveled and prayed nothing bad would happen to the old Suburban she was driving. He made sure the truck was in good working order before she left. But it was, after all, old—anything could go wrong at anytime. *Perhaps I wouldn't be feeling quite so apprehensive if she wasn't driving the old Suburban. I guess I should've traded it in for a new one before she left on this trip.* It wasn't in Grady's nature to get rid of something that was in good working order. *That truck has several more years of life left in it yet.*

Before she left, he made sure she had the recently acquired gun permit and gun; not that she would ever find them in that big yellow carry-everything purse she insisted on carrying with her. He could never understand women and their purses; purses that could hold enough stuff to fill a barrel. *No wonder Edna has back problems.* However, the variety of items in her purse never ceased to amaze Grady. If they were out somewhere and needed something, Edna would rummage around and eventually drag it from "*The Purse*".

Grady missed her now and needed to hear from her. In ten minutes, he'd call. It would be close to lunch time and she could stop and talk a while. But, knowing Edna, she would probably drive through a fast food restaurant for something she could eat while driving down the road. On every road trip they ever went on, her challenge was to race the clock. She would save a minute every way she could in order to get to their destination quicker. "I'll have to remind her to stop, actually get out of the automobile, and sit inside a restaurant to eat when I speak to her," he said, as he lifted himself from his comfortable chair to open the porch door for Chatty, their little tabby cat, who kept meowing to get outside.

Grady said a quick prayer for God to keep Edna safe while she traveled, and then sat back in his chair until time to call her. The home phone rang, shaking him from his thoughts. *Maybe it's Edna.* He ran inside to pick up the phone and saw on the caller ID that it was her. He answered the phone with an expectant "Hello".

CHAPTER THREE

E leven months had passed since their arrival into the United States and the three men from Iraq were well settled in their roles as upstanding American citizens. Meanwhile, they gathered vital information from their workplaces for their leaders back in Iraq. The transition was much easier than they originally thought it would be. The United States was such a multi-cultured country that no one paid much attention to the differences in their appearance and speech. When they were out and about they'd get an occasional second glance or a stare, but it wasn't anything they couldn't tolerate. It didn't take them long, though, to realize just how complacent the American people really are. They couldn't see danger if it hit them in the head. If an American walked into Iraq, there would be talk of it throughout the country by nightfall. An American would not be able to move as freely in Iraq and do the things they were about to do in this country.

They didn't like Americans, and it was a challenge to pretend to be one while living amongst them. Their assignments sometimes took years to complete; so, they would have to endure whatever it took. Many of their countrymen had been living in the United States for years. Some had married American women and had children in order to establish their roles for a mission. When their missions were completed, they'd disappear, leaving the family behind, never to be seen by them again. Immediately, new identities were provided and they were given a new assignment in another location.

Most aspects of their lives were controlled by their handlers. Accommodations were provided and jobs were arranged according to the requirements of their mission. As a result, some members had better living accommodations than others, some had easier jobs, and some were placed in lower socioeconomic conditions. Each man understood, however, that they all had important roles to play. Their network was well established and each member had access to any supplies they needed, including guns and explosives, if necessary. No expense was spared. But, always, the main concern was the mission, and this remained the foremost concern in the lives of these men.

The terrorist cell the three men were assigned to included three others—a cell leader and his lieutenant, who both lived in Alabama, and one other man who lived in Tallahassee, Florida.

The three new recruits were sent to the state of Florida. One was placed in Tampa where he lived in an older neighborhood and worked as a clerk in the county court house. One was placed in Miami where he lived in an apartment and worked as an independent computer expert. The other man shared a condo in Tallahassee with one of his countrymen who had arrived four years earlier.

This recruit was placed in a night job doing custodial work at the Florida state capitol. His roommate, Butrus bin Fareed, was already established in his job in campus security at Florida State University. During his four years at the university he had gained his supervisor's trust and now helped set up security for Florida State athletic events.

Jobs for the new recruits were selected and arranged by their cell leader based on the workplace's potential to provide information or to further a possible attack at some time in the future. Once the leader assigned a task, no matter what it entailed, it was accepted and completed without question. Questioning the authority of the cell leader would lead to severe repercussions.

All the men were very intelligent and capable of doing any type of work. They weren't interested in the amount of money the jobs paid, because their living expenses were paid by their organization. They were placed in their positions for the purpose of the mission only.

Ahmed Bin Hamzah was the new recruit assigned to do custodial work at the Florida state capitol. During the brief time he had been employed there, he had become well acquainted with the two guards who work the night shift with him. One of them made routine checks through the halls and the other patrolled the grounds. So, the place was basically empty. This gave Ahmed the opportunity to access computer files and collect valuable information from desks and file cabinets which were often left unlocked. Ahmed is an expert at hacking into computer files. He believes Americans are too trusting and careless with things that should be locked up. It amazed him how much vital information was left on desktops at the end of the day. Cleaning an office never took much of his time; so, he would linger in the offices at night gathering information, sometimes for hours. Ahmed knew what type of information to gather for the mission and had no problem gathering it. He had done this type of operation many times before, but this time he was becoming restless and bored.

Ahmed had been promised a more challenging task when he arrived in the United States. More importantly, however, he harbored a personal reason for seeking this assignment. For nearly a year, he had gathered various types of information vital to future missions from computer files and papers left on desks. While the information proved to be helpful to his network, he was eager to fulfill his real purpose for being here—*to get even with Bush and the Americans.* And he was eager to do this...*Now!*

Ahmed's wife and two sons had lived with his parents and his nine year old brother and twelve year old sister in a modest home on the outskirts of Baghdad. All of them had been killed in the bombing raids Bush ordered. Ahmed was away on a mission when the raids took place. The bombs demolished everything they owned. Very little of his family's remains were ever found. He planned to see that Bush and his family paid for murdering his family.

He was told he could have his revenge if he came to the United States. Yet, after all this time, the cell leader had made no progress toward fulfilling this promise. He knew it was dangerous to oppose his leader. To do so, could incur the man's wrath. However, he didn't care about angering the leader, nor, did he care about living. Everything he lived for was gone. Ahmed had no home or family to return to in Baghdad; what friends he once had were killed in various missions gone wrong. Most of them died as the result of suicide bombings and other kinds of war related missions during the past several years. He would approach the cell leader soon about the promise...*very soon.*

CHAPTER FOUR

Ahmed's fondness for American cuisine had grown immensely since his arrival in the United States. Southern cooking, often referred to as home cooking, was his favorite. *Cornbread* was the best thing he had ever eaten. He couldn't understand why it was called that. To him, it tastes more like a sweet treat or cake. Some of the vegetables he was fond of had strange names like okra, mustard greens, squash, collard greens, pinto beans and kale. They have green beans in parts of his country, but they're prepared differently here. He loved green beans no matter how they were prepared.

Iraq doesn't have drive-thru restaurants and Ahmed was amazed at the vast numbers of them here in this country. They seemed to be everywhere. He had grown accustomed to the fast food way of eating and rather enjoyed his frequent visits to them, especially Burger King. Beef was practically unheard of in his country. There was a distinct difference in the taste of the lamb he was accustomed to eating, and the red meat of a cow. It was impossible to find lamb in any fast food restaurant in this country; therefore, he took a chance and ate a hamburger. He had heard of hamburgers before, but had never eaten one until this trip to the United States. He was pleasantly surprised at the smoky flavor of the beef. It was very tasty and the lettuce, pickles, onions, tomatoes, mustard, mayonnaise and ketchup added different textures, and all the flavors blended well together. His first hamburger dining experience was quite enjoyable. The twenty-five pounds he had put on since his arrival in the United States, he attributed to his love of the burger and home cooking. He had more than made up for the weight he had lost on the fishing boat on his way over from Iraq. To have the ability to drive-thru and pick food up at a window is an ingenious idea, thought Ahmed. Since he had no one to dine with, it was more convenient to drive-thru, and then eat on the move. He hated eating alone in a room full of strangers and seldom did so.

There was only one restaurant where he didn't mind sitting alone. He made his weekly visits there on Tuesdays before reporting to his night job at the capitol. He chose Tuesdays, because the restaurant wasn't very busy on that day. He had been there on other days when the wait would be up to an hour. Ahmed hated waiting for anything. But, there wasn't much he disliked more than someone writing his name on a list, handing him a black disk, while saying…*that will be forty-five minutes.* However, he would tolerate the wait for his southern food fix at his favorite restaurant, if it wasn't too long. The Pickle Barrel was the only restaurant where he would wait to eat, though. *What kind of name is that for a restaurant anyway? Typical Americans—not much they do makes sense. Although, food was one thing they did get right… except for those darn sour pickles this place always put on his plate, even after he'd ask them to leave them off.* Thinking about food and the Pickle Barrel was making him hungry.

He had plenty time before he had to be on his night job. He seriously considered going to Burger King or to one of his other favorite drive-thru restaurants. But, his craving for home cooking at the Pickle Barrel was too strong to resist. He thought about what day it was; it wasn't Tuesday, it was Friday. He knew it was the night before that stupid Florida State University football game, and people would be coming in from everywhere to watch it. That was another thing he hated and didn't understand about Americans. *Didn't they have anything better to do than to waste hours of time watching a field full of grown men falling all over themselves chasing after a ball?* Ahmed considered all sports unproductive and a total waste of time. He checked his watch once more and decided to take a chance on beating the crowd to the Pickle Barrel.

Immediately upon arriving at the Pickle Barrel, Ahmed knew he hadn't beaten the crowd. The parking lot was nearly full. His first reaction was to turn around and go to the Burger King, but thought he would at least check to see how long the wait would be. After all, it had taken him thirty minutes to get there from across town. He hated to waste time waiting for a table to eat. It wasn't that his time was all that important, or he didn't have the time to wait. He had hours before he had to be on his job.

There was something else he noticed about the American people. At times, they would wait for hours to eat at their favorite restaurant. Yet, when they were in their cars on the highway, they'd fly down the road like the world was coming to an end. *Maybe they're rushing to their favorite restaurants so they can wait for a table.*

Ahmed pulled into the first empty parking space he saw, and then walked through the crowded porch into the restaurant. Judging from the parking lot and crowded porch, he figured the inside shop would be crowded, as well...*it was.* He quickly became agitated as he worked his way through the crowd to the back of the shop where the podium was located.

Ahmed approached the podium and asked, "How long is the wait for a table?"

"How many are in your party?" the hostess asked.

What a stupid thing to ask. Can't she see that I'm alone? He replied, "One."

He watched her stick the dreadful black disk toward his face as she said, "*Forty-five minutes—your name please.*" He was becoming more agitated by this whole process—the disk—giving his name to be put on a list in order to eat—but the forty-five minute wait was pushing him to the brink. Also, there was something about the hostess, but he couldn't quite put his finger on what it was. Judging from her body language, he got the feeling she resented him. *Maybe she doesn't like Middle Eastern men. A woman in my country could be severely punished if she were to act in this manner toward a man.* He knew he had to use some self-control and not allow his frustrations to be seen. Unnecessary attention was something Ahmed tried to avoid.

Ahmed gave the hostess a fictitious name and took the disk from her bony hand. He would wait the forty-five minutes for the table this time. But, he won't waste one minute of it in the shop with all that useless stuff surrounding him. He could see shelves of pickle memorabilia lining the walls. Mixed in with the local university attire were racks of pickle designed tee shirts, sweaters, blouses and the like. Scattered through the large room were jars of various kinds of pickles and relishes stacked high on round tables shaped like pickle barrels. Candy of all types was sitting around in display cases. Small inexpensive toys, trinkets, china cup and saucers, and dolls were everywhere. It was just too much stuff. *Do people really spend their money on that junk anyway?* He charged through the double doors out onto the porch.

The porch held no interest for him either. He had no intentions of striking up a conversation with a total stranger while rocking back and forth in a high back chair. The thought of rocking brought back the sick memories of his ride from hell on the small boat which brought him to this country. No, he wouldn't waste forty-five minutes of his life on the porch. He walked across the parking lot to his automobile and reclined in the front seat while he waited for the flashing red lights to go off on the black disk. He closed his eyes and tried to nap.

Ahmed was unable to sleep. He had slept most of the day and didn't need any more sleep. Instead, he passed the time by reading a newspaper he had brought with him. This was one thing all the agents were taught during their training—*to read all newspapers and to listen to television news in order to keep up with what's happening in the world.* Occasionally, secret messages were televised. Reading the newspaper calmed him down somewhat. But the time he was promised was up and the lights hadn't begun to flash. He could feel the agitation building again.

An additional ten minutes passed. Still the lights on the disk don't flash. So, Ahmed decided to return inside to check on his table. In spite of the strong irritation he was feeling, he approached the hostess and politely inquired about the table.

"A table is being cleaned for you now, sir," she informed him, as she retrieved his disk and picked up a menu. "This way, please."

She sat him at a table for two in the back section of the dining room. He often sat in this area on Tuesday when he came to the restaurant.

"Your server will be May. She'll be with you shortly," the hostess said, and then walked away.

Ahmed watched the hostess walk back to her podium. He couldn't get over his dislike for her. *Tuesday must be her day off.* He had never seen her before and was certainly grateful she didn't work on *his* day.

As promised, May came by momentarily to take Ahmed's order. She was an attractive middle-aged woman. *She's tired*—he judged from looking at the dark circles under her eyes. And, from the way she shuffled her feet when she walked, it appeared she had been on them for awhile. Her mannerisms were pleasant, but he sensed something was troubling her. Ahmed had always been good at reading people, and he was sure his assessment of the woman was correct.

Ahmed ordered country fried steak, mash potatoes, mustard greens, cream corn, fried apples, with a large sweet ice tea, and of course, cornbread. He hadn't eaten anything since the sausage and egg biscuit that morning and could hardly wait for his dinner to arrive.

May returned shortly with his drink order. As she reached across the table to set his drink down, the short sleeve of her blouse crept up her arm, displaying a large bruise. *Bruise—just as I suspected.* Ahmed had seen this type of bruising on many women in his country. His wife, while she lived, carried many bruises; most of which couldn't be seen under the clothing which covered her whole body.

Seeing the bruise on May's arm sparked a lot of memories of his relationship with his deceased wife. He had really loved her. If it hadn't been for the macho image he had wanted to present to his peers, he probably wouldn't have beaten her at all. Thinking back on it now made him realize how cruel and selfish he had been. He had done a lot of bad things in his life, even killed many people without question or regret. However, the one thing he regretted now, more than anything, was how he had physically abused his wife. It wasn't until she was killed that he realized the guilt he felt for his actions.

Bush was the reason he was here in this strange country he didn't even like. If he hadn't ordered the attack on Baghdad, his wife and family would be alive today. He missed them more than anything and longed to see their faces. The hurt was still fresh in his mind. It seemed as if it were only yesterday that he received the news about the destruction of his entire family. It was unbearable for him to know he would never see or touch them ever again. All the family pictures and mementoes were destroyed in the blast. He felt a deep anger at having been deprived of *even a picture.* Without even a small remembrance he was having trouble remembering what they looked like. *Yes, I'm going to get even with Bush—one way or the other. He's going to pay, and soon, for the grief he has caused me.*

A short time later May shuffled across the dining room floor carrying his food on a heavy tray. She sat the tray on the edge of his table while she placed each item in front of him. "Is there anything else I can get for you?" she asked before she left him to eat.

He responded, "Everything looks good. Thank you." Just for an instant, Ahmed felt compassion for her. He wondered what she went home to at night. His guess was that she had to work many long, hard hours at the Pickle Barrel just to pay her bills. She didn't appear to have a lot of joyous moments. *This woman probably has never been on a vacation in her whole life.*

As always, Ahmed enjoyed his Pickle Barrel meal; except for the pickle, which he wrapped in a napkin so that he wouldn't have to look at it. He hadn't bothered to tell May not to put it on his plate because he knew it would be there anyway when his food arrived.

When he exited the dining room and entered the gift shop on his way to pay the bill, he passed the podium where the waiting list was located. He noticed the hostess still adding names. She saw him looking in her direction and said, "Have a good evening." This pleasantry tended to irritate him even more and he walked by her without responding.

As Ahmed approached the cashier to pay his bill, he was taken aback by her curly carrot-red hair. In his whole life he had never seen hair that red. The freckles across the bridge of her nose weren't that uncommon. He had seen quite a few Americans with such freckles, but the hair color was new to him. Another thing stood out about her. She looked as if she were about to deliver at any time. Pregnant women in his country were seldom seen in public, and here this woman was working right up to delivery time. He paid the bill, and then charged through the doors to the parking lot.

As he crossed the parking lot to his automobile, he thought about the comment the hostess had made as he was leaving. *She had some nerve speaking to me. I don't need her to tell me what kind of evening to have. It's none of her business what kind of evening I have.*

Although Ahmed had enough time to get to his job, he didn't want to get caught up in the rush hour traffic. And, given his mood, he knew sitting in traffic would only aggravate him further. So, he took the interstate around to the state capitol exit. This way he would arrive early.

The longer he drove the more agitated he became. For the life of him, he couldn't pinpoint why the hostess affected him this way. He became angrier by the minute. Finally, he reached the boiling point. His anger also spilled over onto his cell leader. *He hasn't fulfilled his promise to help me seek my revenge. Regardless of the consequences, I'll call him tonight about my vendetta against Bush.*

As Ahmed drove toward the capitol his cell phone rang and about scared him off the road. His phone seldom rings and he couldn't imagine who would be calling him. Opening the phone, he answered with a brusque, "Hello."

His roommate and cell member, Butrus bin Fareed, was calling. "Ahmed, this is Butrus. Something's come up; I can't make it for breakfast in the morning like we planned. I've just been told we're going to institute our highest security measures and I'll have to be at the stadium early in the morning."

"What's going on, Butrus? I was really looking forward to those pancakes."

"I've just learned Governor Bush and President Bush and their families are going to attend the football game tomorrow night. I'll be busy all day with the additional security."

Suddenly it came to Ahmed how he can achieve his personal vendetta. "Butrus, this could be great news. Let me call you back when I get to the capitol."

Ahmed's heart began to race at the prospects of taking out the whole Bush family, *just like they took out mine.* He knew security would be tight, but he felt certain he could come up with a plan to accomplish this. Racing toward the capitol in a better mood, he began to mull over the possibilities.

As he pulled into the parking lot on the capitol grounds, the final pieces of the puzzle fell into place. This is a brilliant plan, he thought. Tonight, while Butrus is off work, he can assemble a bomb large enough to do the job.

They have the necessary bomb making materials in their arsenal located in the attic of the garage. Ahmed was confident his roommate could smuggle the bomb into the stadium and would know where to place it. *However, I intend to be the one to put it in that place.*

It was a cool autumn evening, so he sat in the car with the windows up and dialed Butrus.

CHAPTER FIVE

Butrus thought the plan was brilliant and knew the perfect spot to place the bomb. He had spotted this location many months before in case it was needed for such an occasion as this. In a corner below the floor of the skybox was a small ledge with just enough space to conceal the bomb from view. It was too high for the dogs to smell and no one would ever think to sweep up there. If he placed the bomb inside the skybox he knew it would be found during the sweep—he wouldn't make that mistake.

Butrus knew the security team would go over the skybox with a fine tooth comb. Not one inch would be overlooked. The usual sweep would take place and the bomb sniffing dogs would perform their duties. This would be done early in the morning, and then all entrances would be locked down and special guards posted until the final sweep which would take place just minutes before the families enter the room that evening. Security would be tight while they enjoy the game—*until the blast.*

Seldom was there anyone around the stadium in the early morning hours, so he would arrive earlier than usual for work and place the bomb. The chances of him being seen were slim. He would need a long ladder in order to reach the high ledge. But, he often carried a ladder around for various types of jobs. No one would be suspicious if he were seen with one.

However, as great as this plan was, there was a problem with it. In order for Ahmed to receive the satisfaction he so desperately desired, he insisted he be the one to place the bomb. Although Butrus was well liked by his co-workers and had a high security clearance with the freedom to move about without question, he was concerned. If they were seen, someone might question the two of them walking the stadium grounds.

While Butrus was finalizing the plans for the bomb, Ahmed entered the capitol building. He was aware of all the locations of the surveillance cameras and knew they were only used during the day to watch the comings and goings of people who frequent the halls and rooms every weekday. With confidence he walked the halls and entered rooms as he had done nearly every night for almost a year. Tonight he would by-pass cleaning the floors, as he often did. After collecting the trash and doing a little light dusting, he would call the cell leader in Alabama and present the plan he and Butrus had already discussed.

Ahmed knew he was overstepping his bounds by proposing a plan of any kind to the cell leader. But, a plan to assassinate two presidents of the United States, the Florida state governor and their families by tomorrow night was really too good an opportunity to pass up. The cell leader might think it a brilliant idea or he might have him killed by nightfall for ever coming up with such a plan in the first place. *This is my big chance and they owe me this opportunity to revenge the death of my family. I may never get another chance like this.* To him, it was worth risking insulting his cell leader.

He positioned a chair in the hallway to sit on so he could see anyone who might come his way while he was talking on the phone with the cell leader. He knew the two night guards very well, but didn't want anyone to overhear him plotting the assassination of the president of the United States. He was familiar with the guard's routine, and he wasn't due on this floor for another twenty minutes. Ahmed stayed vigilant as he dialed the cell leader in Alabama.

Husam al Din, the cell leader, listened to Ahmed as he went into the details of his plan to assassinate the Bush families. In the beginning, Husam was reluctant to even consider such an idea. But, he had been stringing Ahmed along since his arrival in the United States nearly a year ago.

Husam was aware that Ahmed was one of their best soldiers. All soldiers were highly trained in many areas, but he was brilliant when it came to hacking into computers. Ahmed had shown patience in the field in previous missions, always vigilant and wary of enemy movements. He exhibited an analytical mind when devising tactics for attacks. He was ruthless and backed down from no one. But, he was also respectful, showing Husam the respect he commanded as the cell leader. Husam wondered why Ahmed hadn't been appointed a cell leader.

However, after the death of his family, Ahmed had changed somehow. He seemed restless and easily provoked. Husam was aware of the promises made to Ahmed in exchange for coming to the United States. This plan was brilliant and well thought out. It could be accomplished without much manpower. Maybe it was time for Ahmed to have his revenge. And, since only two men would be physically involved, there would be little chance of being discovered. Also, there would be no connection to the rest of the cell members, thought Husam. He would talk this over with his lieutenant and get his views before committing to a final decision. Husam promised to call Ahmed back with their decision later that night.

Ahmed was pleased the cell leader was considering his assassination plot and quickly called his roommate to inform him of this progress.

His roommate was already into the assembly of the bomb. He anticipated having everything ready in time to pick Ahmed up after his night shift. They would drive to the stadium the next morning, leaving Ahmed's car in the capitol parking lot. After placing the bomb, Ahmed would walk back the few blocks to pick it up.

Shortly after Ahmed concluded his conversation with his roommate, the phone rang. Husam was calling to give his go-ahead for the assassination and asked if they needed anything.

"Everything has been taken care of," Ahmed said with pleasure.

CHAPTER SIX

Saturday at exactly seven-thirty AM, Butrus was at the state capitol when Ahmed's shift was over. He had his favorite hard rock music blasting on the radio. "Can you turn that thing down?" Ahmed snapped, as he settled himself into the front seat. Butrus turned the radio off, pulled out of the parking lot, and accelerated toward the stadium.

Ahmed was almost trembling with excitement. *There is nothing that can disrupt my good mood today. Even the loud music on the radio wasn't that bad.* He could hardly believe he was finally going to exact his revenge. Butrus had a plan to get him into the stadium and would then show him where to place the bomb. *This is surely a glorious day for me.*

"You have the bomb ready to go?" asked Ahmed.

"Yeah, it's in the trunk.

"Since security is so tight, you don't think we'll have any problems getting in, do you?"

"Not this early. The security team isn't even expected to arrive until nine o'clock. We'll be in and out before they drink their coffee. Have you thought about what time you want to set the timer?"

"Oh yes. I think I'll give everyone time to get settled in their seats with their attention glued to what's happening on the field. I want everyone in their seats so they can witness the blast. I think they should be settled in real good by the second quarter. Don't you?" Ahmed laughed loud and hard.

Butrus joined in the laughter. "I think that'll be a good time. You certainly don't want to set it during half-time while everyone's at the concession stand. Half the stadium would miss out on the big explosion. Are you going to watch the game?"

"You really don't think I would miss watching the soon-to-be, most-talked-about game in history…do you? Too bad you can't watch it with me."

"I didn't really think you'd miss the game. After all, this is your *get-even-time*. But, I'm sure I'll not only witness the fancy skybox go up in the big blast; I'll probably have to help clean up the mess afterwards. I know one thing, though; I won't be anywhere near that skybox during the second quarter."

"I appreciate you doing this, Butrus. This really means a lot to me. Allah has surely blessed me today."

"Allah-be-praised," they said in unison.

As Butrus approached the stadium, Ahmed could almost taste the sweet revenge. His heart was racing with anticipation.

Butrus pulled up to the security gate at the side of the stadium parking lot and entered his pass code. The gate didn't open. *What's happening now?* He entered the code again and the gate didn't open. Puzzled, he made a quick survey of the grounds near the stadium. He couldn't believe his eyes; the place was crawling with bomb-sniffing dogs and agents searching every inch of the place, including the few cars already in the parking lot. *They must have decided during the night to add additional security measures and to get started much earlier than they had originally planned.* Butrus had not been informed of these changes. *Ahmed is not going to like this. Now I'll have to enter through the main gate at the front of the stadium. Every automobile…including mine…will be searched by officers and their bomb-sniffing dogs.*

Butrus drove a few blocks down the street and pulled over on a quiet side street and killed the engine.

Ahmed suddenly became uneasy. "Why didn't the code work, Butrus? Why are you stopping here? What's happening!" he snapped.

Butrus paused for a moment. He took a deep breath. "I can't take the bomb inside."

"*What?* What do you mean you can't take the bomb inside? We had this planned. I have to kill the Bushes today. I have waited a long time for this. You have to get that bomb inside that stadium!" shouted Ahmed.

"Hold it...hold it, just calm down, Ahmed. I know how disappointing this is for you. You had a good plan, and this should have worked out. But, I was not told of these changes. The sweep was to have taken place later this morning. It was to be confined to the stadium. The automobiles in the parking lots weren't part of the sweep. I'm sorry this didn't work out for you. You'll have to take the bomb back with you to the condo."

"This can't be happening! My plans are made! I want to kill all of them!"

It enraged Ahmed to think his mission had to be called off. He wanted revenge and he wanted it...*NOW*!!!!

Butrus became concerned for his friend and didn't know what else to do to calm him down. He had never seen him so upset.

Ahmed was red in the face, flailed his arms all over the place, and wouldn't listen to reason.

"You really need to settle down, Ahmed. Don't worry; you'll get your revenge. We'll plan another attack and get them," Butrus assured him. His attempt at calming his friend didn't work. He glanced at his watch and suddenly felt the need to get to work.

"Ahmed, let me take you back to your automobile. Since it looks like everyone else is already on the job, I think I need to get going."

"Don't bother. I'll walk back. Maybe the walk will do me good."

"I'm sorry about all this, Ahmed," Butrus said, as they exited the car.

Butrus popped the trunk and removed the backpack which held the bomb and gave it to Ahmed to take back to their arsenal in the attic.

Ahmed threw the backpack over his left shoulder and crossed the street in the direction of the state capitol. He hoped the walk back to his automobile would take the edge off his rage. He realized there was no other choice; the mission had to be aborted. However, he didn't fault his friend for the mix-up. *It's the fault of the stupid Americans. They're always messing things up for people.*

The few blocks he walked back to the capitol did nothing to calm Ahmed. It just gave him more time to stew in his juices. He was angrier now than ever. He opened the trunk of the car, threw the backpack inside, and then slammed the lid close. He sped out of the parking lot and headed toward the condo. Ahmed was geared up and ready to kill. As he drove, he searched his mind for an alternative plan for his failed assassination attempt.

He shouted into the windshield, *"I'm going to kill somebody today, and if I can't kill the Bushes, then it'll have to be someone else... preferably a lot of someone else's. If I kill a lot of stupid Americans, then that'll make up for what Bush did to my family!"* And, by the time he arrived at the condo, he knew exactly who it would be, where it would be, and the when...was *NOW*. Ahmed proceeded directly to the arsenal located in the garage attic for the necessary equipment to arm himself for *HIS* new mission.

CHAPTER SEVEN

E dna heard Grady's sweet hello on the other end of the phone and knew at once he had been thinking about her. It made her miss him even more now that she was so far away. She would talk just long enough to give him a progress report and to ask about the pets. Of course, the usual *I love you* and *miss you* would be exchanged. Grady would understand the minutes on her cell phone were limited and won't expect her to talk for a long time; she may need them for the rest of the trip.

The phone call was short but it was good to hear Grady's voice again. *Good heavens, I just left him a few hours ago. How am I going to survive the next two weeks? It isn't as if I have never been away from him during our forty-three years of marriage. Maybe I miss him so much because I'm traveling alone. Get a grip*, Edna, *or you'll be turning around and heading back home. Surely, my mood will change when I see Linda in Hattiesburg tonight.* It wasn't uncommon for Edna to talk to herself when she was alone. Though, she had never let anyone know she did such a thing; they might think it odd or something.

At the moment, she was hungry. It was sweet of Grady to remind her to stop for lunch. However, a reminder wasn't necessary this time. A cooler full of drinks and a large paper bag full of goodies were within reaching distance on the passenger seat. But the junk food she brought from home didn't appeal to her, nor did any drive-thru eatery. She wanted real food. She wanted *"Home Cooking"*.

Traveling now on Interstate 10, she had been driving a little more than six hours and was near Tallahassee. *Go Noles!* She had a lot of fond memories of this city. Grady attended Florida State University and they spent their first year of marriage here while he completed his last year of college in preparation for dental training.

At the 80 miles per hour she was now driving, the exits were flying by. She hardly had time to focus on the signs before she passed them. She would have to slow down in order to read the signs if she expected to eat today. She eased up on the accelerator. Her friends entered her mind. They always called her "Lead Foot Edna" when she drove with them. Edna would laugh and tell them she was a *safe driver* and she had the driver's license to prove it, and then she would continue driving her comfortable speed. With that comment, they usually backed off the subject of speeding.

Ah, there it is. The sign said, Pickle Barrel. Edna knew the Pickle Barrel was an up-and-coming new chain of restaurants throughout the state. She and Grady often ate at the one located near them. She loved eating at *The Barrel, as she always called it,* but, shopping at *The Barrel* was even better. *If I have time after lunch, I'll walk around and do a little shopping before I get back on the road. Maybe I'll buy a jar of those dill pickles to take to Linda Ann.*

Edna could feel her mouth salivating just at the mere anticipation of biting into the crispy long pickle she knew would be served on her plate. She liked a lot of things on *The Barrel's* menu, especially vegetables and cornbread. But today, she wanted meat. Country fried steak; mash potatoes, gravy, green beans and cornbread, with a large ice tea were calling her now.

She took the exit and saw the Pickle Barrel off in the distance to her left. She made the turn onto the back road which led to the parking lot. As she entered the lot it looked as if everyone in Tallahassee wanted to eat there as well. You would have thought it was the only place in town to eat. Every parking space was taken. Plus, every patch of grass had a car parked on it. Then it occurred to her—*this is Saturday*—*the big football game between Miami and Florida State University will be played this afternoon. No wonder this place is packed with people. Every eating place in this city will be crowded today.* After making three rounds of the parking lot, there was still no parking space opening up. Just as her blood was beginning to boil and thoughts of leaving entered her mind, a car pulled out five slots in front of her. *"God, you must have known I would starve to death in this parking lot if I didn't find a parking space soon. Thank you for the space."*

Now parked, after driving more than six hours with only one short break, she realized why she shouldn't be on this trip *ALONE.* While driving around for so long, she really thought she might die of starvation in the parking lot. Now, she felt sure she would die in the front seat of her late model Suburban. She couldn't move! All ten fingers were locked on the steering wheel. It was too painful to release them. Her shoulders, back and legs weren't feeling all that great either. After a moment she managed to release the right hand just long enough to switch the ignition off. The pain was so dreadful; she couldn't even rest her hand on her lap. Slowly, she replaced her hand back on the steering wheel. She felt as if rigor mortis had surely set in while sitting there in the front seat. *Should I call 911? How embarrassing! I can see the next day's newspaper headlines now—**OLD WOMAN FOUND FROZEN DEAD IN FRONT SEAT OF OLD SUBURBAN AT PICKLE BARREL—NO FOUL PLAY—POSSIBLE STARVATION—TEMPERATURE OUTSIDE 79.***

GET A GRIP EDNA! If she could have pried her hands off the steering wheel, she would have slapped herself around a little. Edna couldn't remember where or how she came by the phrase *"GET A GRIP"*. But, she always used it when she though she was losing control of a situation. It usually brought her back to her senses. Slowly, she leaned her head against the headrest and closed her eyes, allowing herself to rest for a moment. When she opened her eyes, she felt better. She looked down and was surprised to find both hands resting painlessly in her lap. Slowly she tried moving her feet and legs. They too, moved without pain. She leaned over the steering wheel to test her back and felt no pain. *What happened? I must have fallen asleep causing my body to relax.* A glance at the dashboard clock confirmed she had indeed fallen asleep. The time was 12:30 PM. She had arrived around 11:30 AM. An hour of precious travel time had been lost. *I will have to call Linda after lunch to let her know I will be arriving later than expected. It feels good to be able to move again.* She reached across the seat to retrieve her all important carry-everything purse. With purse in hand, she opened the door to the Suburban and painlessly stepped outside.

Halfway through the parking lot Edna could see approximately fifty people outside on the porch of the Pickle Barrel. It looked like a sea of garnet and gold. People were dressed in all sorts of university attire. Edna spotted a young man about twenty years old who had a Mohawk haircut. One side of his head down to his neck, chest, arms and hands was painted garnet, while the other side was painted gold. Of course, he wore no shirt and his pants had fringe down the legs resembling something a Seminole Indian would have worn. *It takes all kinds.* Families with children all dressed in Florida State colors were sitting and standing around rocking chairs. Some were playing checkers on the giant wooden checkerboard beside their chairs. Three little girls had pulled up the small rocking chairs into a huddle and were rocking and singing *"Jesus Loves Me"*. Almost every teenage girl had some form of logo like *FSU, NOLES* and *GO NOLES*, painted on their cheeks or forehead. Some had spiked hair colored garnet and gold. She noticed very few Miami fans standing around. But the few who were there, proudly displayed their university colors. *Things have certainly changed a lot since Grady attended school here.*

Edna was almost upon the porch when she remembered the gun she carried in her carry-everything purse. Although the gun wasn't loaded and couldn't hurt anyone, it made her uncomfortable carrying the weapon around where there were so many people. The gun permit she carried didn't make her feel much better about it either. *I really should return to the Suburban and leave the gun behind, but since I'm already here, I'll go ahead and put my name on the waiting list.*

She stepped inside the restaurant and saw another sea of people looking much like the others outside waiting on the porch. They were rifling through racks of clothing, trying on *FSU* caps and holding *FSU* tee shirts up to see if they fit. A little boy was in the toy area holding a small stuffed animal crying at the top of his lungs because his mother wouldn't buy it for him. People were all over the place. The restaurant had put out a tray with a variety of pickles and a bowl of cheese dip for people to sample while they waited to be seated. Several people waited in that area for a chance to grab a pickle, or to dip a cracker in the bowl of cheese. Edna felt like joining them but thought better of it and continued toward the back of the shop where the podium was located.

As she approached the podium, she was thinking the wait was going to be long. The young woman who assisted her appeared to be waiting on tables up front as well as being in charge of the waiting list. Her name was Jenny. The apron the hostess/waitress was wearing had her name and three stars embroidered on it.

"Approximately one hour", Jenny said while placing a round black disk in her hand.

Edna knew this would be another hour of lost travel time. But, she would make good use of the time and forgo shopping for a long walk. She was told not to worry about the range of the black disk; it would reach anywhere outside.

Rather than hauling her yellow carry-everything purse on the walk with her, she took it back to the Suburban. Her walking shoes were packed away in her luggage, so the shoes she had on would have to do for this walk. She took a few minutes to stretch and warm up, and then quickly surveyed the area and saw there were no sidewalks around the restaurant. All the green areas were occupied with parked cars; which left the road as the only place to walk. *Oh well, the road will have to do. I'll have to be careful not to get caught up in my thoughts and forget about the traffic.* Another newspaper headline flashed before her—*OLD WOMAN HIT BY CAR WHILE WALKING IN STREET AT PICKLE BARREL—LONG WAIT FOR TABLE CUT SHORT.*

It felt good walking outside. However, she didn't want to go too far from the restaurant in case the red lights went off on the little black disk. She needed a little cool down time and she would have to retrieve her carry-everything purse from the Suburban and that would also take some time.

She began to relax as she settled into her walk. The fresh cool autumn air was invigorating and made her walk a little faster than she normally would have. The air was crisp and smelled fresh—much like the air she remembered when she lived in upper state New York.

Her thoughts wandered back to that pleasant time when she and Grady were stationed at Plattsburgh. It was his second year in the Air Force. They lived in a small duplex on base and enjoyed the neighbors and co-workers. It didn't matter to them where they lived. They were always happy and it was always home. What stood out most in her memory now, about living there, was the weather. Being from the South, she had never experienced such cold weather. The smells of the cool, crisp, autumn air were unforgettable, like today.

Several cars slowly passed her during the course of the thirty minutes she had been walking around the Pickle Barrel perimeter. She would probably have enough time for another round before she stopped to cool down. Well into her last loop around the building, she felt strange about something that caught her eye. It wasn't so much strange, as it was the feeling she had about what she saw. She saw a man dressed in dark slacks and a light blue dress shirt. He was walking at a fast pace from the back of the restaurant's loading area. What stood out most to her and caught her eye, was the fact that he didn't appear to be a Florida State fan, and he was half running. *My active imagination is on overdrive again. He looks well dressed. His black hair is clean cut. Surely, there is a good explanation for his actions. Maybe he's an employee on his lunch break, hurrying off to meet someone for lunch somewhere else.* She ignored the strange feelings and continued her walk. *It's none of my business where he was rushing to.* Her mother had taught her—if it doesn't concern you—stay out of it.

Suddenly the red lights on the black disk went off. She had not expected it so soon. Now she would miss her cool down time. *Well, at least I'm close to the Suburban.* She ran to the automobile and quickly unlocked the door to retrieve her carry-everything purse. Then she ran back inside the restaurant to return the disk in exchange for a table. Just in time; her name was being called for the last time. Politely she asked the hostess/waitress, Jenny, if her table could be held long enough for her to wash her hands.

"Of course," Jenny replied.

Food! Finally, I'm going to get some real food. Edna charged through the restroom door.

Quickly, she washed her hands. She knew she should hurry back, but she just couldn't resist a few pumps of the goat milk hand lotion sitting there on the counter. It was, after all, there to be sampled.

Flying out the door of the lady's room while rubbing the lotion between her hands, she was anxious to claim her table. Heaven knows, she didn't want to lose the table she had waited so long for. As she rounded the corner, she heard a disturbance coming from outside. The sounds were faint. It sounded like people shouting, but she couldn't make out exactly what they were saying. *It's probably those Florida State fans doing some kind of chant, or maybe I'm imagining things again.* She disregarded the strange noise and took a few more steps toward the dining room. She was now standing close to where she had last seen Jenny. She glanced through the restaurant once more looking for her. What Edna earlier thought was merely commotion on the porch had now turned into chaos. It was clear to her now that the disturbance she heard moments ago was not her imagination. But, it also wasn't the Florida State fans having a group cheer. The sight she saw when she turned in the direction of the disturbance was beyond belief.

A man was standing in the small hallway between the exterior and interior double doors. He appeared to be loaded down with weaponry. He paused just long enough to insert fresh magazines into the guns he had just emptied on the porch. As he pulled a high powered rifle over his shoulders, he opened fire while charging through the interior doors. It was obvious he wasn't there to take hostages. He was shooting at anything and everything.

This man was the cause of the disturbance outside. *He must have shot everyone on the porch.* Edna's eyes were automatically drawn to the exterior windows. Disbelief overpowered her. Suddenly, feeling faint, she fell to her knees. She was sickened by the sight she saw through the half drawn sun shades. Blood ran heavily down the gift shop windows where bullet riddled bodies had fallen into the glass.

CHAPTER EIGHT

P eople having lunch inside the dining room, thought they heard something out of the ordinary, but weren't sure. Jenny came from the kitchen toward the gift shop area. She too, was unaware of the events taking place inside the shop. As she approached the gift shop, she was shocked by the sight of the gunman shooting his way through the doors. Jenny urgently turned back into the restaurant and shouted for everyone to "GET OUT!"

As Jenny ran toward the emergency exit, she continued to shout, "Everyone come to the exit...go to the kitchen...hurry, hurry, he's shooting everybody!"

At first there wasn't much movement in the dining area. On the most part, the people who saw Jenny running and shouting through the restaurant thought she had gone stark raving mad. But when they finally realized what the waitress had said and what was taking place in the shop, customers began to react—screams could be heard—chairs were knocked over—dishes crashed to the floor—as frightened people stampeded in all directions. While frantically looking for a way out of the dining room they saw Jenny struggling to open the only fire exit door in the area.

Jenny couldn't understand why she was having such difficulty opening the exit door. It always opened for her during the fire drill exercises. She felt around the doorframe looking for anything that might prevent the door from opening. There were no visible obstructions. Once more she gripped the handle of the door and pushed her one hundred twenty pound body against it with all her might. The door would not budge. Two men came to assist her, but all their efforts didn't budge the door. It appeared to be blocked from the outside. They quickly gave up their efforts and rushed toward the kitchen with hopes of exiting through the back door. Jenny ran to stand by the kitchen door and shouted and motioned for everyone to *come this way.*

People eating in the back part of the restaurant weren't sure exactly what the waitress had shouted. But, they saw a crowd of people in the front area of the restaurant running toward the kitchen. Feeling an increasing unease they began to think...*why were they running to the kitchen? Why weren't they exiting through the gift shop? Was something bad going on in the gift shop that caused the people in that area to flee in a different direction? Something was happening!* They too began to gather their belongings and lunch companions and joined the race in search of an exit.

Edna glanced through the doorway into the dining room. She could see the panicked look on the people's faces as they rushed the kitchen with protective arms around their loved ones.

A small group of about twenty people started toward the doorway into the gift shop near where Edna was crouched. They hadn't entered into the shop area yet, so she motioned and shouted "KITCHEN" to them. They quickly turned and ran toward the kitchen. Others behind the group followed their lead. Running to the kitchen was not an option for her. There was too much distance between where she was and the dining area. If she moved in that direction, she would be in plain view of the shooter. He was shooting at ANYTHING THAT MOVED. For now, she had no choice but to stay low and look for some kind of protection in some other area. *Dear, God, have mercy...send help soon.*

CHAPTER NINE

Jenny had arrived for work that morning at 6:00 AM, and her feet were killing her. It was always chaotic in the restaurant on the big game days. Florida State and Miami was the biggest game of the year. But, today was especially busy for some reason. In her three years working there, she had never seen it this busy. What made matters worse, two waitresses were sick with a very bad case of flu and had been out of work for days. She was sure, since they were short-handed, this would be a twelve hour day for her. The tips and overtime pay would certainly be a big help to her, though.

Jenny was twenty three years old and had pretty much raised herself. She never knew her father. And, being an only child, she was often left alone to fend for herself while her mother was off somewhere, or being rehabilitated. Ever since she could remember, her mother was in and out of some rehab center. When she was very young, an elderly great aunt would take her in until her mother reappeared. After several years of this routine, her aunt became tired and refused to keep her anymore. Jenny was old enough at that point to take care of herself.

In spite of the many hardships at home, Jenny was determined to do the right things in life. Not that she ever had anyone around to teach her right from wrong, but she was a quick learner and learned by watching the good things that others did. She also learned a few things about her mother in the short periods of time in her life when she was around. The important thing she learned was that she desperately did not want to be like her mother.

Her dream was to go to college someday. She had made very good grades in high school, but she just couldn't afford to go to college at the moment. Basically, she was just trying to survive and, day by day, she could feel her aspirations for college slowly, but surely, drifting away.

Jenny had never been married and didn't even have time to date. By the time she completed her shift at the Pickle Barrel, there was no time for a real life that included dating. She rented a room in an old Victorian house that belonged to an elderly woman who needed a few extra dollars of her own. The woman also wanted company. It was the company part that was now keeping her in residence. Jenny's rent was a month in arrears, and her home phone had been disconnected for three months. She was always taking on extra shifts at the Pickle Barrel when one became available. Lately, with the flu going around, she had been working a lot of overtime. She hoped to get her bills caught up, but she was afraid she might die from exhaustion first.

Jenny was doing double-duty today. She was keeping track of the waiting list, seating people, and serving the four tables closest to the front entry. She promised to hold a table for a single lady while she washed her hands. When the lady returned her disk earlier, she looked as if she had been on a long walk or run. There were beads of perspiration on her forehead and her eyes were red and tired looking. Jenny figured she had a couple minutes before the lady's return—that would give her enough time to visit the kitchen to check on the order for table two.

On her return from the kitchen, Jenny saw the lady she was holding the table for on her hands and knees at the corner of the front counter. Panic was in the air. She heard loud shouts and screams, but from where she stood, she couldn't see what was happening. She took a couple more steps in the direction of the gift shop. As she peeked through the entryway she could see the gunman and the destruction in the gift shop. People in the gift shop were running in all directions—fleeing the front where the gunman was standing. The beautiful displays her fellow co-workers spent so much time arranging were being mown down by gunfire. As she watched, incredulously, people fell wounded as they tried to escape. Blood was everywhere.

Panic stricken, Jenny turned back and ran through the dining room shouting as loud as she could: "GET OUT! HURRY! HURRY! HE'S SHOOTING EVERYBODY! GET TO THE KITCHEN! GET TO THE EXIT EVERYONE! GET OUT!"

CHAPTER TEN

verything was happening so fast. The shooter was on a rampage. Edna guessed ten to fifteen people had already been shot in the front area of the gift shop where the shooter had entered. It was a bloodbath. People were screaming and fleeing for their lives. They were running in all directions seeking any type of cover to avoid the hail of bullets. She saw several people attempting to open the fire exit. But for some reason the door wouldn't open. When shells started slamming into displays near them, they gave up all hopes of opening the door, and fell to the floor. They scattered in all directions looking for cover under displays or any other place that might give them some protection. People and beautiful displays were being mown down like they were nothing. Everything was being destroyed by the rapid gunfire.

The shooter appeared to be enjoying his rampage. As he fired his weapon he shouted "DEATH TO AMERICA—ALL AMERICANS MUST DIE—ALLAH WILL REIGN OVER YOU" and several other Arabic phrases that Edna couldn't understand. *This is unreal…No one could be this mad. Please help us, God.* Edna knew this man meant to kill everyone there.

Edna fell from her crouched position onto the floor. Laying flat on her belly with her hands covering her ears, she wished she could melt into the woodwork where she couldn't be seen. Her head was turned to her right side. Thank heavens her eyes were open. She could see an open space recessed under the nearby counter. The counter rested on legs which could not be seen from the front. It looked as if the space was high enough for her to crawl through. She thought being behind the counter would offer her more protection and buy her a little more time here on earth. She shoved her carry-everything purse through to the other side. Then she dragged her one hundred thirty pound slender body through. Now on the other side, she quickly turned back around to face the opening. Lying flat under the counter, she had a fairly good overall view of the room.

Edna could see the shooter was approximately six foot tall. His hair was black and clean cut. He appeared to be well dressed underneath the arsenal he—*Oh, my good heavens! This is the man I saw running from the back of the restaurant while I was walking earlier!* She recognized his clean cut black hair and the dark slacks. She could see only the long sleeves of the blue dress shirt which peeked from the black sleeveless military style vest he wore. Now she understood the reason for the strange feelings she had when she first saw him. If she had only listened to those feelings and sought help, maybe this could have been prevented. With her eyes closed, Edna's face fell flat to the floor as she cried, "Oh my dear God in heaven—what have I done?"

Edna lifted her head and looked in the direction of the shooter; focusing on the weapons the man carried. She was no expert on guns. But the ones this man carried definitely did not qualify under the laws for a concealed weapons permit. She suspected the weapon he had strapped across his shoulder and was now firing was an AK-47 assault rifle. She remembered seeing one on the nightly news not long ago. There were also two mean looking pistols clipped to a swing belt at his waist. *Uzi's*, she thought. They appeared to have silencers on them. *He must have wanted to surprise everyone on the porch, giving them no time to flee. The noise from the guns would've alerted everyone inside the restaurant, and most likely, they would've charged the front door as they ran for safety. Maybe he wanted time to shoot everyone quietly on the porch, and then reload before he charged the inside where he'd have everyone captive and he could take his time and enjoy shooting them.* She noticed the vest he wore was bulging with what she also suspected was additional ammunition. This guy had come prepared to kill.

Edna shook all over. Her heart felt as if it were jumping out of her chest. She felt sure she was taking her last precious moments of breath. Somehow, she felt responsible for this. She wanted to pray to God, but she had never prayed much and wasn't sure if she even knew how to say a proper prayer. But, if there ever was a good time to learn, this was it. At the moment she was shaking so badly she didn't think she could even talk to God. *Maybe God can hear my thoughts.* She considered this and quickly thought her prayer. *God, please hurry…he's killing everyone.* Her thoughts rushed to Grady and her family. *What effect will my death have on them?* She knew this would be devastating for all of them and she hated being the cause of such grief.

Bullets zoomed overhead and all around the room breaking displays of pickles, jams, jellies, lotions, special homemade jars of various sauces, and anything else that was in the line of fire. Edna felt sure this would be the day of her death. *I'm not ready to die yet. God, please don't let me die now.* There was so much unfinished business. She longed to hear Grady's voice. She wanted to tell him goodbye.

CHAPTER ELEVEN

J enny ran through the restaurant rounding up people and giving orders for them to exit through the kitchen. "HURRY, HE'S SHOOTING EVERYONE!" she kept saying as she rushed them along. Moments later she noticed people hanging out the kitchen door. They were standing still. *Why aren't they moving? The back door should've been opened by now. Everyone should be charging outside.* She wanted to see what the holdup was. As she worked her way through the crowded kitchen she saw panic and confusion on everyone's faces. At first the crowd was reluctant to let her pass to the front. Then they recognized her as the woman who was helping them. Thinking she was in charge, they stepped aside to let her pass. When she made it to the back door, she found three chefs trying to force the large double doors open with anything they could get their hands on. It wasn't working... THEY WERE TRAPPED!

Jenny asked the chefs why they couldn't open the door.

"It's blocked from the outside," one of the chefs answered.

Some customers overheard the exchange of words, and then panic spread throughout the crowd like wildfire. About one hundred people turned back into the dining room shouting and screaming for everyone to *go back, the door is blocked!* As word spread about the locked door, chaos erupted.

Everyone who could began to pick up chairs to break out the large windows. The fixed, double-paned windows were not easily broken. Urgency turned to panic when the unruly crowd realized they may not be able to break the windows and escape. As more people from the kitchen reentered the dining area, they also began to pick up chairs to smash against the windows. The chairs were not strong enough to do the job. Some people were searching the area for something more substantial to use. The tables were the most substantial objects in the room, but they were bolted to the floor or into a wall. The longer it took to break a window, the more panicky the crowd became. Six strong men with chairs were hitting one large window as hard as they could. The window did not give. After several hard tries with the chairs, they gave up and started ramming the window with their bodies.

The crowd fell silent and watched the six men in their last ditch effort to break the window. This was their last hope for escaping the madman in the gift shop. Six fresh bodies replaced the first six. Their attempts at breaking the glass didn't work either. It was obvious the window couldn't be broken using the meager objects around them. They felt trapped and watched as their hopes of escaping the building diminished.

Survival instincts overcame the crowd. Shouts, screams and crying started up again, as they realized this may be their last moments of life. They picked up anything that had any weight to it and charged all the exterior windows. As they fought their way toward the windows, small children were torn away from their parents and trampled by the mob. They showed no regard for anyone in their path as they charged the windows with chairs and items they had pulled from the walls. A few bystanders frozen with fear, stood and watched while the large mob rammed the windows with shovels, rakes, bats, sling blades, crates, boat ores, and chairs. Several people had fallen to the floor after being sliced by a blade or hit in the head with a bat or crate—only to be injured more seriously as they were trampled by the anxious mob.

An elderly woman seated on the floor held the head of her deceased husband in her lap. The old man's heart couldn't take the stress of the events happening around him. Devastation and tears were evident on the grieving woman's face.

The need to escape was becoming crucial. No one wanted to face what was coming from the next room. The peace loving people who came into the restaurant for a quiet meal had now turned into a mob intent on survival.

Screams from the gift shop and rapid gunfire were louder now and sounded like it was closing in on them.

Jenny had watched the panicked crowd turn and run back into the dining room after they discovered the back door was blocked and couldn't be used for their escape. She was powerless to help anymore, and she knew there was no other way out. The windows were double-paned with mullions, making them very resistant to breaking. They were very large and designed to keep anyone from breaking in. In this case, no one could break out, either. There was nothing that could stop the shooter from killing everyone in the building.

Earlier when the disturbance first started, she saw a young man on his cell phone talking with a 911 employee. He was giving a step-by-step description of the events taking place and pleaded for them to send help soon. While she was gathering people into the kitchen area, she noticed many other people using cell phones to make what they believed was their last call to loved ones.

Help was surely on the way. But would it arrive in time to save any lives? At the moment, Jenny couldn't hear any sirens and was suddenly terrified at the realization that she was going to die at the hands of a madman. Her life flashed before her eyes. She thought of all the things she wanted to do: college, fall in love, have children, and die an old woman were but a few of them. Jenny looked around the kitchen and saw that she was alone. It occurred to her that this was the way most of her life had been—*ALONE*. No one would care whether she was alive or dead. Actually, she was the only person who cared if she lived. Her cell phone was in her purse, which was in the employees' locker. But there was no one to call who could comfort her in these last moments. There was no one to hear her last goodbyes. Suddenly the sound of screams became louder and gunfire sounded as if it were closing in on her. *It won't be much longer now.* Knowing this would be the first and last prayer she would ever say, she fell to her knees. *Please, God…don't let me die this way.*

CHAPTER TWELVE

T he counter Edna was hiding behind was twenty-five feet long, four feet high and made of wood. There was a corner at each end where the counter wrapped and connected to the back wall. A thirty-six inch wide opening was located in the center area for easy access. A cash register sat on either side of the opening along with various types of small displays. The wall behind the counter displayed many items such as small collector's dolls, cups and saucer sets, and collectables of all types. The wall above the counter where Edna was hiding displayed various kinds of candies.

Edna drew her head from underneath the counter and looked toward the opposite corner. She saw the cashier sitting there with her knees drawn up to her chin. Strands from her long, curly, red hair fell over her young face. She had freckles across the bridge of her lily-white nose and rosy cheeks. Edna loved red hair and freckles. But, what stood out most about the young woman was the fact that she was pregnant. The corner where the waitress sat was nearest to the shooter and Edna feared for the life of the young mother-to-be. The two women glanced at one other. Edna no more than turned her head back, when several shells penetrated the wooden counter. They ripped through the woman's body, cutting her nearly in half and were now lodged in the wall three feet behind her. The young woman sank to the floor in a pool of her own blood. Edna could only stare in disbelief at the gruesome sight. *Oh, dear Lord, I'm going to be next. Don't let this happen...please; please...I don't want to die like this.*

Edna could see the woman's blood gushing from her body and rolling toward her. She sat with her hands tightly covering her mouth, trying to suppress the much needed scream she wanted to release. Her scream probably wouldn't have been heard over the gunfire and screams already taking place. But, for some reason, she felt the need to keep silent and to stay put. *Please... please, God—help us.* She focused on the blood which was rapidly approaching her. Dying in a pool of another person's blood didn't appeal to her. Actually, it was downright disturbing. The wooden floors must have been slanted a little in her direction because the blood was coming toward her at a fast pace. Knowing she couldn't leave her hiding place, she mentally prepared herself to allow the blood to seep around and under her own body. The smell of blood preceded the flow and a sick feeling overpowered her. She didn't know if anything was left of the donut and coffee she had eaten that morning, but something was coming up for sure. She leaned to one side and dry heaved a few times.

The flow of warm blood had now caught up with the smell and began to soak up around her. As she wiped her mouth with the back of her hand, it occurred to her...*maybe, just maybe, this woman may save my life.* She mentally prepared herself for what she was about to do, and then reached her hands into the pool of blood she was now lying in. She spread it all over her upper body, arms, and the back of her hands. She put a large handful in her hair, and then she smeared it all over her face to make it appear she had been shot. If the shooter came close to her, she would play dead. To Edna, this was a chance worth taking. She said a quick prayer for the young woman...And, *thanks for this chance to live.*

After covering herself in blood, Edna crawled back under the counter. From where she lay she could see a few people crawling across the floor toward the back of the gift shop. There was nowhere else to go from there, except to the restrooms. The restroom doors had no locks. It would only be a matter of time before the shooter made his way there. To make it to the dining room and kitchen without being seen was impossible. A mother with a baby in her arms, holding the hand of a little boy about four years old, suddenly stood and charged toward the nearest restroom. Other people in the group huddled out of sight next to a display of quilts.

"AMERICANS MUST DIE—ALLAH WILL SEE JUSTICE IS DONE—I WILL HAVE MY REVENGE NOW!" shouted the gunman. His loud voice seemed to vibrate over the gunfire and throughout the room.

Her imminent death and Grady were all Edna could think about. She always thought when it came her time to leave this earth; Grady would be at her side to help her through it. It was apparent now; this was not going to happen. She needed to let him know what was happening to her. She wanted to tell him what a wonderful husband he had been and what a terrific life she had experienced here on earth because of him. She wanted him with her when she took her last breath. *It might be a selfish and cruel thing to do to you, Grady, but I have to talk to you.*

Edna backed from underneath the counter once again, and then reached across the floor and pulled her yellow carry-everything purse close to her. She opened it to search for her cell phone. The woman's blood she had dipped her hands into earlier lay thick and slick on her hands making it difficult to handle things. She glanced at her blood-stained clothing for a clean spot to wipe her hands and didn't see one. Giving up, she plunged her hand inside the purse. As she felt around, her hand ran across a pack of tissues. She retrieved them, pulled out a few, and wiped the blood from the palms of her hands. She plundered around again for the phone. *Maybe Grady was right—there's too much stuff in here. Come on…come on where's the phone. I must hurry.* She was having a hard time finding the phone. "Oh my!" she screamed. It hit her like a ton of bricks. She remembered plugging the phone into the lighter; it was charging in the Suburban. "This can't be! I can't die without Grady by my side!" Tears started flowing down her bloody face. She knew she would never see her beloved Grady, or hear his sweet, gentle voice again.

Drowning in tears and despair, Edna felt sure this was the end for her. Then suddenly, she remembered…the little Beretta pistol was in the purse. She pulled herself together, then quickly grabbed the purse and held it upside down to empty the contents onto the bloody floor. Sifting through the scattered contents, she located the gun case. She picked it up and attempted to open it. The case had a zipper which ran completely around the outside edge. She was having trouble unzipping it with her trembling hands. *Stop shaking…Stop shaking…Stop shaking.* She closed her eyes and took a few deep breaths in an effort to calm herself down. When she finally succeeded, and everything was laid out before her, it all looked so strange to her. It was like she was seeing all this for the first time. She was terrified of the gun and wasn't sure she could remember how to load it.

The gunman was closing in on her and she knew she needed to work fast. But she was having a hard time controlling the shakes. She lowered her trembling hand and picked up the gun, but afraid she might drop it, she eased it back to the floor until she could retrieve the single shell from the case. The shell would have to be placed inside the chamber and the clip placed inside the grip. Her elbows and arms were sore from leaning on them. And it was difficult trying to maneuver while lying on her stomach. She decided to sit up and lean her back against the wall in hopes of steadying her shaking hands long enough to load the gun. She thought about the dead cashier and hoped bullets wouldn't come flying her way while she sat there. She closed her eyes momentarily and took a few more deep breaths, as she willed herself to calm down. She picked the gun back up and released the barrel designed to hold the single shell. Her initial attempt at loading the shell into the chamber failed.

The pressure was more than she could stand. She could hear the loud THUMP—THUMP—THUMPING sounds of her heartbeat pounding in her head. It was difficult to concentrate on any one thing. Her whole life flashed before her. Fear had caused her to lose all self-control. She wanted to talk to Grady—she wanted to visit relatives in Mississippi—she wanted to see her sisters and brothers—but, she wanted to live more than anything. To kill another person—she DID NOT want to do this.

Edna placed the gun and shell on the floor beside her. With her free hands she began slapping both sides of her face. "*GET A GRIP! GET A GRIP! GET A GRIP!*" she whispered to herself. She closed her eyes briefly…the tension eased. The shaking had let up somewhat and she thought she could manage to load the bullet into the chamber now. Suddenly, rapid gunfire started hitting the wall behind her. She fell flat on the floor until the gunfire traveled to another location, and then she sat back up. The shooter was very close to her now. Quickly, she picked the gun and shell up once more—this time they met. Edna closed the loaded chamber. Again, shells whizzed overhead and lodged into the candy wall. Debris from various types of candies fell to the floor and showered her body. Sheer fear overcame her. She fell flat on the floor, then repositioned herself under the counter in front of the opening and looked for the shooter.

She didn't want him facing in her direction when she aimed the gun, as he might see her. The real truth was she didn't want to be looking at his face when she pulled the trigger. She also had doubts about her small caliber shells penetrating the front of the bulging military style vest the shooter wore. The back of the vest was flat. It didn't appear to be filled with ammunition. She would use his back as the target. Edna knew her little Beretta was no match for a madman with machine-guns, but it was the only other gun in the building. She would have to try to take him out. *He's going to kill me anyway. But, I have seven chances in this little gun to get him before he gets me. I have to at least try. I can't die without trying,* she cried into the palms of her hands.

She had a full, open view of him now. He was very close and his back was to her. He was busy shooting in the opposite direction. It's now or never, she thought. She rested her aching elbows on the floor and brought up both hands with the gun in the aim position...*Oh dear heavens, I can't do this.* She lowered the gun and held it in her left hand. Lying in the cramped space was causing a great deal of pain in her neck and shoulders, but that was the least of her worries at the moment. She swiped her right arm across her face to wipe the bloody tears from her eyes. She was able to see more clearly now. *God, I really need your help now.* Like it or not, it was up to her. She knew everyone there was going to die if she didn't shoot this man.

Edna was squeezed under the counter and had very little maneuvering space, but she managed to raise the gun back up. This time the gun felt light in her hands. Her body even felt lighter than it had moments ago. Although she was afraid, she knew what had to be done. The gun was fixed on the man's back and she hoped her aim was in the location of his heart.

Out loud, Edna began to pray a *real* prayer for the first time in her life: *"Dear God, Our Heavenly Father...I do NOT want to take my brother's life. Only YOU know the right thing to do here today. Guide my hands, Dear Lord, and use this weapon to do Your will."* She pulled the trigger and did not let up until there was *silence*.

She saw the gunman jerk and stumble slightly and then begin to fall, almost in slow motion, face down onto the floor. As she realized what she had done, Edna dropped her small gun and a calming darkness overcame her. The shooting had stopped.

CHAPTER THIRTEEN

✝

It was mass hysteria in the restaurants dining room. People climbed over one another trying to reach the windows that wouldn't break. Suddenly, shouts came from near the gift shop. "THE SHOOTING HAS STOPPED! THE SHOOTING HAS STOPPED!" As the good news quickly spread, everyone began to settle down. Someone whispered…*maybe he's reloading.* Distant sounds of sirens could be heard. Help was on the way.

A young father of two slowly peeked around the wall into the gift shop to see if the shooter was reloading, and was surprised when he saw him sprawled on the floor in a pool of his own blood. There was no movement of any kind from the man. He appeared to be dead. *How could that have happened! No one else had a gun in the shop. Maybe a shell ricocheted and hit him.* The young father thought it strange, but gave no more thought to how it happened. He was just glad the shooting had stopped. He turned back into the dining room and shouted, "HE'S DEAD! HE'S DEAD!"

Jenny was in the empty kitchen on her knees praying her first prayer and what she thought was her last, when the shooting stopped. At first she thought it was wishful thinking on her part. She held her breath…listened carefully. There was very little sound coming from the dining room, and there was no shooting. He must be reloading, she thought. She closed her eyes and made a plea to God…*PLEASE LET THIS BE OVER.* At that instant someone ran through the dining room shouting—HE'S DEAD! HE'S DEAD! HE'S DEAD! Joy and disbelief swept over her. Needing to see for herself, she ran to the gift shop entrance. It was true! There he was on the floor in a pool of blood. As tears of joy rolled down her cheeks, all she could say was…"THANK YOU, GOD."

The crowd was confused and extremely anxious after receiving the news about the dead gunman. What were they to do now? The exit doors were blocked and no one wanted to exit through all the blood and dead bodies they knew were in the gift shop. But they were more than ready to flee the building, jump into their cars and disappear to anywhere else but there.

Jenny noticed the confused crowd and knew they were eager to leave the building. She knew exactly how they felt, because she wanted to flee the building herself. But, she was smart enough to know they weren't going anywhere anytime soon. She picked a fallen chair up from the floor and stood on the seat so that she could be easily seen over the crowd.

"May I have your attention, please?" she shouted over the noise. "Please folks, let's settle down. Let me have your attention." She could see them beginning to settle down…*they're actually listening to me.* "The police have arrived and everything will be alright. Everyone, please find a place to sit down and wait for the officials to tell us what to do next. I'm sure they'll want to talk to all of us. So, please find a place to relax until they can get to us. You know the shooter is dead and you're safe." She pointed, "Let's all gather in this back section of the dining room and sit down and wait. I know this is a nightmare for all of us. But, it's all over now. The shooting has stopped. You're ok now. You know you can do this. So, please, everyone find a place to rest until the officials come."

From her vantage point on the chair, Jenny could see the crowd had settled down and was working their way in the direction she had pointed. Jenny couldn't believe they had listened to her and were actually following her instructions. In her whole life, no one ever thought what she had to say was important enough to hear. She stepped down from the chair and walked with the crowd to the back corner of the dining room.

As they walked, Jenny noticed people had stopped to assist others who had fallen earlier during the stampede. Some of the injured people appeared to have broken bones, while others had large cuts which bled freely. Jenny noticed an elderly lady sitting on the floor crying while cradling the head of her deceased husband in her lap. Jenny stopped and sat beside the woman. She placed her arms tenderly around her, consoling her as gently as she could. Jenny had been holding the brokenhearted woman in her arms for a brief moment when the woman pulled away, and through a cracking, tearful voice she said, "Thank you."

While Jenny sat there, she saw a group of five people cautiously entering the dining room from the gift shop. It was obvious from the look on their faces they were terrified; just like everyone else in the building. Jenny asked the elderly woman if she would be alright while she left her to assist them. The woman said she would be alright and thanked Jenny again for her kindness.

Jenny went to the small group and instructed them to join the others in the back of the room. It then occurred to her, there may be other people hiding and afraid to come out. She passed through the doorway of the gift shop and announced, "Everyone come to the dining room. The gunman is dead. It's o.k. to come out." Then, she entered both restrooms and coached everyone out.

Small groups began to appear, and then more and more people surfaced from their hiding places. As they appeared, Jenny directed them to join the others in the back corner of the dining room. She caught sight of a young mother with one hand holding tightly to her toddler son. She held an infant in the crook of her other arm. Both children were crying. The mother looked as if she were about to collapse. Jenny was afraid she would drop the baby, so she asked if she could carry the child until they were settled in the dining room. The mother placed the baby in Jenny's arms. Jenny then wrapped her free arm around the mother's waist and escorted them to a quiet location.

After settling the mother and children in the dining room, she hurried back to the gift shop to assist others who had made their presence known. She reentered both restrooms and opened each stall. No one was left there. She glanced around the area once again. She hadn't physically searched the front of the gift shop and had intentionally delayed that search until last. It looked as if everyone was out of the area, but she wanted to be sure. The destruction which lay in front of her was indescribable, and the thought of walking on the bloody floor and stepping over dead bodies was very disconcerting.

Taking small steps, Jenny was careful not to step in pools of blood. As she walked, she bent over to check under riddled displays for anyone who might be injured, or too afraid to come out. She calmly repeated as she walked, "If you can hear me, the gunman is dead. It's safe for you to come out now. Everyone is in the dining room where it's safe. You can join them. Come on out now."

Thus far, she hadn't found anyone else alive. She had gotten as far as the very front of the shop and was about ready to work her way back to the dining room when she heard faint whimpering sounds coming from under a heap of clothing on the floor. The clothing display had been mown down by gunfire. She approached the mound and began to peel back the articles of clothing to reach the source of the whimpers. She spoke softly, as she peeled back the clothing and exposed two little boys. One of them appeared to be about five years old and the other one looked to be about four. They were wrapped tightly in each other's arms, and were covered in blood. They don't appear to be injured; so how did they get blood all over them? Jenny thought. She opened her arms, welcoming the children into them. The two children rushed into Jenny's arms. Their bloodstained bodies crushed against her dark green Pickle Barrel apron, as they latched onto her. She told them to lay their heads on her shoulders and close their eyes. She held them tightly, as she carefully stepped over bodies and avoided walking in blood while she made her way out of the shop. There were no other signs of life in the gift shop, so she walked quietly over and sat next to the grieving elderly woman. The two children clung tightly to her as she sat down.

Everyone stayed seated and remained relatively quiet as they awaited their rescue. Although there were no visible signs of police or rescue, they knew it wouldn't be long. Many 911 calls had been placed. Faint sounds of sirens in the distance and motor vehicles gathering at the back of the restaurant could be heard. They also could hear low, muffled sounds of radio communications. Even though help had arrived, no one made an attempt to leave the dining room.

The two little boys whimpered, as they held tightly to Jenny. Emotionally drained, the grieving elderly lady now lay on the floor beside her dead husband with her right arm stretched across his chest.

Jenny glanced around the room. She knew there were many dead and wounded people in the gift shop and probably even more on the porch. She wondered how many immediate family members were killed or wounded, and how will this tragedy affect all of these people's lives. Without parents, what would the future hold for the two children she now held in her arms? The elderly woman lying beside her deceased husband probably didn't have many more years of life left, but would she spend them reliving this nightmare?

Everyone had settled down the best they could. Concerned loved ones were crouched or sitting near crumpled bodies that lay on the floor. There would be much grieving tonight, Jenny thought. *No one will be concerned about me, though. No one has ever been concerned about me. My landlord might wonder where her renter had gotten off to, but will forget about me in a few days and then rent the apartment to someone else.* After what she had experienced here today, she no longer cared about having relationships with people who didn't care for her. She had learned that life was precious and could be wiped out at any time. She planned to start her new life with a different attitude and new goals. Her new life had just begun, here and now.

While awaiting their rescue, the room had become unusually quiet. The only sounds that could be heard now in the dining area were occasional whimpers and low voices talking to loved ones on cell phones. The Pickle Barrel's phone could be heard ringing in the gift shop, but no one made a move to answer it. Probably the usual call to see how long the wait would be for a table, Jenny thought. She wasn't about to drop two clinging children, leave a grieving widow woman, and step over bloody bodies in order to answer the phone. There were other Pickle Barrel employees waiting with the surviving customers in the dining room and none of them were interested in the ringing phone either. After about ten rings, it went silent. After a few minutes, however, it began its shrill ringing again. No one made a move to answer it.

CHAPTER FOURTEEN

I t was 1:40 PM and Detective Eugene Brewer was in his patrol car driving to Quincy, Florida, to teach a training class which was to begin at 3:00 PM. There would be enough time to grab something to eat along the way. He'd only had a light breakfast and he was hungry. Since the class he was teaching today would be a long one, there would be no opportunity to eat until late that evening. So, he began scrolling his mental list of drive-thru restaurants in the area for one that appealed to him. He was traveling Interstate 10 and knew every restaurant on every exit for fifty miles in either direction. Thomasville Road was the next exit coming up. He knew Arby's and Burger King weren't far off the exit. Either of them would be quick and easy enough, he thought, as he glanced at the exit sign that read—Thomasville Road one mile. Then his thoughts of food were shattered by a dispatch from the Leon County Sheriff's Department requesting assistance.

◄*Anyone in the vicinity of 23122 East Monroe Street— respond—automatic gunfire in progress—possible casualties— proceed with extreme caution.*►

Oh shit, there goes my day, Eugene thought, while turning on his siren and flashing lights. He radioed dispatch with his location and informed them he was responding to the call. Passing up the Thomasville Road Exit, he proceeded to the next exit which was East Monroe Street. Knowing this address very well, he couldn't imagine why there would be automatic gunfire at the Pickle Barrel. *Nothing would surprise me, though.* He had seen a lot of strange and crazy things during his fifteen years on the force. Knowing he really needed to teach his class today, he hoped it would be nothing very serious which would require a lot of his time. But, he felt deep inside; it was going to be a long night. It was always serious when automatic gunfire was involved.

He was off the interstate and on East Monroe Street in a matter of moments. Although the Pickle Barrel was partly obstructed from view by other businesses and trees, Eugene didn't have to see it to know its location. He killed the siren as he exited the interstate, and then turned onto the side road which led into the parking area at the back of the building. Eugene noticed immediately that he was the first responder. The front porch was not visible from where he entered the parking lot. Not knowing what he would find, he slowly drove from the back of the building toward the side where the porch was partially visible, and then he stopped. There were no windows on this side of the building, so he felt confident his car could not be seen by anyone inside. But, from where he sat, he could see there was destruction on the porch and bodies were lying everywhere. They had fallen in the bushes, on the lawn, and halfway to the parking lot. At the moment, he didn't hear any shooting, and a quick survey of the premises showed no signs of movement. He picked up his mike and reported a 1097 (*arrived on scene*) to dispatch and reported his findings at the scene. He confirmed casualties and requested a supervisor, homicide, crime lab, and medical examiner. Eugene could hear sirens rapidly approaching and waited in his concealed location for the backup to arrive.

Within minutes backup had arrived. The supervisor, homicide detective, crime lab, and medical examiner were all on location. Crime scene tape was being stretched to cordon off the area, and emergency personnel were waiting for the scene to be secured so they could enter and tend to the wounded. Two attempts at calling the Pickle Barrel went unanswered. A command post was quickly being set up down by the main street...a safe distance from the shooting. Eugene knew for a fact the media would be on the crime scene in no time. The P.I.O. (public information officer) would deal with the public and media at the command post location.

Most people called Eugene, Gene for short, but in police circles, he was known as "The experienced one", because of his many years on the force and his leadership abilities. He had worked his way up through the ranks and was now a highly respected senior officer. Standing now with three fellow officers, Gene would lead the operation to secure the scene inside the building. With guns drawn, they made their way across the parking lot. They took cover behind trees, bushes, and automobiles and tried to conceal their approach the best they could. While Gene and his group cautiously worked their way to the front of the building, another group of officers were removing the steel braces which blocked all the exterior doors. There would be no radio contact between the two groups of men until the area was safe and secure. Only silent communications, such as hand signals would be used. Everyone knew the routine and what was expected of them.

After the officers had removed the braces which blocked the exits, they gathered at the loading dock by the kitchen door. They slowly opened the double doors just enough to slide a small camera connected to a long rod inside. The camera would show any movement inside the room on a monitor the officer held in his hands. They could see no activity on the monitor. The three men drew their guns, eased the doors open and quietly entered. They spread out in different directions in the kitchen and surveyed the area for any threat. When they saw no obvious danger, they gathered at the only doorway to the dining room. The team stood with their backs against the wall while they waited and listened for sounds of voices or movements. There was no gunfire taking place at the time but the shooter, or shooters, may have hostages at gunpoint. The officers would hold this position until Gene and his team had enough time to enter and secure the front of the building. Then they would make their presence known.

With increased awareness, Gene and his team worked their way along the side of the building toward the front porch. The front of the building had large windows which stretched across the length of the porch. Gene noticed the window blinds had been pulled down, as they often were this time of day to block the morning glare of the sun inside the restaurant. The four men stayed close to the wall as they crawled under the windows. They inched their way down the porch while easing turned over tables, rocking chairs, and checker boards from their path. They couldn't move the fallen bodies out of their way; they had to crawl over them. By the time they reached the front entry, the elbows and knees of the clothing they wore were stained with blood.

The four men huddled together on their knees in front of the entry doors. They watched and waited while Gene held the small camera on a rod up to the window of the door. The camera would show what was happening in this area. Then, they could evaluate whether it was safe to enter. Cameras were used routinely in cases such as this and proved to be instrumental in saving officers' lives. Gene carefully watched for movement on the monitor he held in his hand. He could see no movement. He repositioned the camera to a different location, and then watched the monitor for movement again. When he was satisfied that there was no threat in the area, he brought the camera down and placed it with the monitor on the floor beside him. He gave the all clear hand signal to the other officers and slowly eased the double doors open.

They continued to crawl on hands and knees through the first set of double doors. Gene noticed empty high powered magazines lying on the floor. When they reached the second set of doors, Gene rose up slightly and peered inside the gift shop. He could see the destruction. Blood and bodies were scattered throughout the room. But, he saw no movement. Two officers held the doors open while the other two crawled inside the shop. Then, they moved inside to join them. All was quiet in the building. Gene gave the hand signal to stand. They all slowly and silently rose to their feet. With their guns stretched out in the aim position, they spread out in all directions in pursuit of the shooter, or shooters.

Gene walked the center isle with his hands held high in the aim position. He focused in the direction of the center and back areas of the room, taking special notice of any areas where someone with a gun could be hiding. He saw no opposing threat. As he made his way to the center of the shop, he glanced down and saw a heavily armed man lying in a pool of blood. Gene approached the man with his gun aimed at his head. He then signaled to his fellow officers he had found a gunman. The three men quickly cleared the rest of the gift shop and made their way to where he stood. Their aim never left the man on the floor, as they approached and surrounded him. One officer pinned the shooters arms to the floor with his foot while the other two disarmed him. They checked his vital signs and discovered he was dead. He had been shot in the back.

There's another gun here somewhere, Gene thought. They would have to be vigilant until they found the other gun and shooter. At the moment, securing the building was their first priority. If they found no other accomplice, then they would have to determine who shot this madman.

They spread out again to complete their sweep. With one hand, an officer eased the door to the lady's room open, while shielding his body against the solid wall near the opening. There appeared to be no one in the restroom. He entered the room and cautiously checked each stall. No one was there. His partner checked the men's room at the same time and the results were the same.

Gene continued his search for a possible second shooter—one who might be holding hostages in the dining area. He knew other officers were securing the kitchen, so he concentrated on the dining room. With his back pressed against the wall of the gift shop, he peered around the wall into the dining area and didn't see anyone. Where is everyone? Gene thought. Is someone holding them at gunpoint in the back area of the dining room which is out of my sight? He saw the disarray of the place and noticed blood on the floor. This Pickle Barrel was unusually large and had four partitioned areas. He had now entered the second one. Still, he saw no one. He saw his small team cautiously surveying the area as they followed up behind him, and then spread out into the room.

As Gene eased his way toward the last section of the dining room, he caught sight of a young woman sitting on the floor amongst fallen chairs and items that had been pulled from the walls. She had two small children in her lap. The children appeared to be covered in blood. There was no movement or noise coming from that area. *A gunman might be holding them at gunpoint.* The young woman turned her head slightly in his direction—they made eye contact. Gene could see she was freeing one arm which had been holding one of the children. He stood still and looked into her eyes and mouthed...are you o.k.? She held her hand up and gave him the o.k. sign with her finger and thumb and mouthed back...everyone is o.k.

He breathed a sigh of relief. He slowly walked to the edge of the small area to evaluate the situation. His gun was still in the aim position. He now lowered it and then locked it back into the holster. He couldn't believe what he saw before him. There were approximately one hundred fifty people huddled in the far area of the room. Most of them were sitting on the floor. He could tell from the disarray of the place this group of people had not been so orderly a short while ago. He could see expressions of relief on their faces as he made his presence known. Yet, they sat in silence. No one spoke or made any attempt to leave. "What has gotten into these people?" he said to himself as he walked closer to the group. He couldn't understand why they weren't rushing to leave the building.

Gene reached for his hand radio and reported the area secure. He knew the paramedics needed to assist the injured. All the other departments had their duties to perform, as well. He was sure it would take a while to sort all this out. Gene noticed that all the officers who had entered the kitchen area had also made their presence known. They were now standing around the perimeter of the dining room. Gene gave them a *"thumbs up"* then turned back to face the people in the dining room. He advised the group of people what they could expect next. Still, after he gave them their instructions, no one made any attempt to leave, nor did they ask him any questions. This was highly unusual. Normally, he would have a riot on his hands. Why was this group of people so different?

Gene stood about twenty feet from the young lady he had communicated with earlier. He wanted to talk with her away from the children and motioned for her to join him. As he watched her make her way across the floor in his direction, he felt drawn to her. He couldn't take his eyes off her. There was something about the way she carried herself. Her tall, slender body looked so delicate. She had a certain charismatic style which appealed to him in a way he couldn't explain. She appeared confident and in control.

Now that she was standing before him, it was hard for him to remember why he had called her over in the first place. He was having a hard time concentrating on the business at hand while looking into those sky-blue eyes. Her shoulder length, sleek black hair, only enhanced her eye color. He felt like a love sick high school kid. He could see from the blood smeared apron she wore, her name was Jenny. The apron had three stars embroidered above her name. He had eaten at the Pickle Barrel chain of restaurants scattered all up and down the state of Florida, and he was familiar with the star recognition program they used. A star was given for each time the employee was recognized for their good services. The chain had very high standards and expected a lot from their workers. To earn a star wasn't an easy thing to do. This meant that

Jenny had been decorated on three different occasions. She must really be a valued employee, he thought. In all the times he had eaten at this very Pickle Barrel he had never seen her. Suddenly, he wanted to know more about this Jenny with three stars.

CHAPTER FIFTEEN

Jenny didn't hear movement from the gift shop area, but her eyes were drawn in that direction. As she glanced toward the entry, she saw a plain clothed person, wearing what looked like a bulletproof vest with his gun drawn. He was inching his way along the wall toward the dining room. She suspected he was a police officer, and that he had already surveyed the gift shop and restrooms. He didn't speak as he entered. He probably couldn't judge the situation in the dining area from his angle. He may be looking for another gunman, Jenny thought. She was unsure what to do to alert the officer that there was not another shooter. She didn't want to make any sudden moves, or noise, that might cause panic again in the dining room. It seemed no one else in the room had spotted the officer.

Jenny slowly readjusted one of the little boys to free her arm. The officer had made several more small steps into the dining room. She could tell he was unsure if there were survivors and if they were safe. She made eye contact with the officer and watched as he mouthed...are you o.k.? While shaking her head up and down, she gave the ok sign and mouthed back...everyone is o.k. The officer holstered his gun, and then made his presence known to everyone. Suddenly other officers materialized throughout the room.

Jenny noticed the look of surprise on the faces in the crowd when the police officers suddenly materialized before them. They hadn't heard them enter the room. It was as if they had come out of the woodwork. No one made any attempt to move from where they sat, and listened while the officer in charge radioed outside to report that the area was secure. He told everyone what to expect next.

The officer said each of them would be questioned and for them to stay put until the arrangements were made. There would be a police officer placed at the entrance of the dining room, and no one would be permitted to enter the gift shop. He informed them that paramedics would be in shortly to see to the wounded.

The officer in charge was standing about twenty feet from where Jenny sat with the two children. The elderly woman, who lay on the floor with her dead husband, was not easily seen from where he stood. She saw the officer motioning for her to come to him. He apparently wants to speak to me alone for some reason… why me? she thought. She gently removed the clinging children off her lap and sat them beside the elderly woman. The children cried and reached for her. She gave them both a quick hug and assured them they were okay and that she would be right back. Jenny rose to her feet, and then walked across the room to face the officer.

As she walked, she noticed how tall the officer was. He had to be over six foot, she guessed. Now standing before him, she had a clear view of his handsome face. She stared into the most beautiful dark brown eyes she had ever seen. It was as if they were the windows to his soul. They looked like kind, loving eyes. She wondered what had transpired in his lifetime to make them appear this way. She always felt you could tell the nature of a person by their eyes. He must have loving parents who were always there for him. That was something she had never had in her life. She noticed the kindness in his mannerisms earlier as he gave instructions to the frightened people sitting around the room. Jenny saw the name tag on his bulletproof vest. It read, Eugene Brewer. His name even suits him, she thought. She suddenly felt embarrassed, and hoped he couldn't tell she had been admiring him. For some reason she couldn't pull her eyes away from him and continued looking up into those dark brown eyes as he questioned her.

"I appreciate you leaving the children to speak to me. I won't keep you from them very long. I just wanted to thank you for your help earlier," he said.

"I thought you may be having a hard time judging the situation in this area."

"We were concerned you were being held as hostages by another gunman. Things seem a little odd considering what has happened here."

"I'm not sure I understand what you mean"

"It's highly unusual for people to be so cooperative in a situation like this. Do you know why? Did the manager or someone settle them down?" As he questioned her, he found himself staring into beautiful blue eyes surrounded by long, dark lashes.

"The manager had an errand to run on his lunch break and hadn't returned when the shooting started. I asked them to have a seat in the far corner of the dining room and to wait for further instructions from the authorities. I'm sure they're eager to get away from here."

"Well, we'll get everyone out as soon as we can. You've certainly been very helpful here today. I appreciate what you've done. I'll be in touch with you later for more details."

Gene noticed Jenny had no wedding rings on her hand and wondered if she were married. She had been holding in her lap two children covered with blood. Were they her children? Why were they covered with blood and she wasn't? He knew he wanted to get to know this Jenny better. He slowly walked with her back to where she had been sitting with the two children. *This is not the proper time to ask personal questions. I'll wait and talk with her when the time is right.*

Jenny sat down and pulled the children into her lap. The elderly woman lying on the floor with her arm around her dead husband then came into view. Gene focused in on the woman and the body. His hands flew up to his face. He rubbed his eyes to clear his vision. Then he shook his head to clear it, and then rubbed his eyes again. What he was seeing couldn't be real! *What were they doing here?* He fell to his knees and pulled his grieving mother into his arms. They wept beside the body of the man they both loved so much.

CHAPTER SIXTEEN

aramedics were busily performing their duties outside on the porch. Fire rescue and ambulances were being located closer to the building where it would be quicker to load and transport the wounded. Occasional shouts could be heard from paramedics—*I have a live one over here. This one needs the hospital now.* They worked their way through the porch area, checking each body as they looked for signs of life. If vital signs could not be found, they would leave that body and go on to the next. Paramedics administered aid to each survivor, as needed. They started I.V. fluids, stabilized broken bones, dressed wounds, administered C.P.R., stopped bleeding, and reassured survivors. After each wounded person had been examined by a paramedic and given the care needed to stabilize them, they were then loaded into an ambulance and transported to a local hospital for further treatment.

Three paramedics worked on the porch, while three more were inside the building caring for the wounded. Ambulances had been summoned from all the local hospitals; they were lined up in front of the building waiting for patients to be rushed back to the emergency rooms.

The mobile command post located at the entrance was completely surrounded now with curiosity seeking people and reporters, hoping to get a better view of the events taking place. Police officers were posted to keep the spectators from breaching the crime scene. A television helicopter circled overhead, while other media vans gathered near the interstate exit. Reporters were eagerly waiting for an opportunity to talk to someone in charge about the shooting. The side entry road, which leads into the building, had been blocked by the police when they first arrived on the scene. Only essential officials and emergency personnel were permitted to enter the secured area.

Gregory Lowe, the P.I.O. (*Public Information Officer)* was busily gathering information to be announced to the public. He could see the helicopter circling and media vans lining the roadway. "Boy! This is going to be a big one," he said to no one in particular. "I'll have to choose my words carefully. If they get wind of a possible *terrorist* involvement, panic will spread through the community like wildfire." Gregory knew this case was going to consume a lot of his time—possibly for days or maybe weeks. That's why he had called his wife Anita Kay earlier to tell her he wouldn't be able to be with the family at their church program that night. Anita Kay had always understood when it came to his official duties. She was also capable of running the household and managing the children in his absence. He felt very fortunate to have a woman like her to share his life with. Throughout his seventeen years on the force, he had known many men whose wives couldn't change a light bulb without assistance. Most often, the marriage ended in divorce. Gregory plowed his way through the crowd then stepped inside the command post and began preparing a statement from the notes he had taken.

CHAPTER SEVENTEEN

L arry was a lead homicide investigator. He and Gene had known each other all their lives and were really more like brothers than good friends…their birthdays were only a few months apart. From kindergarten to high school seniors they attended the same classes in the same schools. When they were little boys playing cops and robbers, they always said they wanted to be police officers when they grew up. Upon completion of their police training, they requested to be assigned to the same department. After several years as partners, they decided to pursue different fields within the department. However, certain cases would allow them to work together. Both men were single and often socialized outside work. Their socializing usually consisted of attending the Florida State football and basketball games. Occasionally they'd take in a movie, and in the summers, surfing was high on their list of things to do. Often on their comings and goings from work, they'd meet at this very Pickle Barrel for a meal. They both had dated some nice women, but neither of them had found the one to take home to meet the parents.

Larry was standing across the dining room opposite where Gene had been instructing the crowd sitting around the room. He had seen Gene motion to a young woman sitting on the floor twenty feet from him. She had been holding two children in her lap. She sat the children aside and joined him. They spoke briefly before they both returned to where she had been sitting. Larry saw Gene suddenly fall to his knees, pull someone into his arms, and begin embracing the person. But, he couldn't make out who it was. Gene appeared to be very upset. Feeling something was wrong, Larry rushed across the room. As he approached the small group of people, he recognized Gene's father lying on the floor. He also recognized Gene's mother.

The young woman was now standing over Gene, looking down at the grieving pair. As she picked up the two young children, Larry saw tears rolling down her face. It was obvious, she felt their sorrow.

Larry also felt their sorrow. He knew the close relationship Gene had with his parents, and didn't want to disturb them while they wept in each others arms. Larry introduced himself to the young woman and offered to assist her with the children. He informed her that the dead man was Gene's father and the woman he held was his mother.

Jenny had suspected as much when Gene pulled the woman into his arms. She thanked Larry for the offer to help with the children, but they held tightly to her and refused to let go.

It quickly became apparent to other police officers in the area that someone close to Gene had been involved in this shooting. The officers fell silent as they approached the small gathering. They knew and loved Gene's parents and couldn't believe they had become victims of this terrible tragedy. One of the officers radioed for a gurney to be sent to their location immediately. "Officer's family member is down," he sadly said.

Moments later a gurney was at their side. The team stood by silently, while Larry knelt and placed his arms around Gene and his mother. "I'm so sorry for your loss," Larry said. "Let's get your mother out of here, Gene. She needs to rest. Take her to the hospital and have her checked out. I'll see that your father is taken care of. We have a gurney waiting. He'll be taken out as soon as we complete the preliminaries. You know he's in good hands.

Take your mother to your car and I'll have someone drive you to the hospital. Mrs. Brewer, are you able to stand? You need to go with Gene to the hospital now. We'll see that Mr. Brewer is taken care of. Come; let me help you to your feet."

"I have to get back to my duties," Gene said as he sobbed and brushed the tears from his face with the bloody sleeve of his shirt.

"No. Your mother needs you now. You should go with her," said Larry. "Everything here is under control. I'll call headquarters and let Captain Hall know what has happened to your father."

Gene stood, and then turned into the open arms of his fellow officers. Each of them expressed their condolences. Moment's later two officers helped escort Gene and his mother out the fire exit door toward his car. Mrs. Brewer was halfway across the parking lot when she noticed Jenny was not by her side. She stopped where she was and told Gene she wanted Jenny and the children to join them.

"Mother, this is not procedure. She has to stay for questioning," he informed her.

"I don't care about procedure. She can be questioned later. This young woman has been through a lot today, and those children need to get out of that place. I wouldn't have made it through the day, if it hadn't been for her kind support. I want to repay her for her kindness. I want her with me now."

"Alright then, but if I get into trouble, I'm going to have you bail me out." He knew she wouldn't leave without them. He turned to the officer walking next to him and asked him to return for Jenny and the children.

Jenny sat in the back seat of the unmarked police car with the two children still clinging to her. Gene and his mother sat in the front seat next to the driver. Gene had his arm around his mother's shoulders and their heads were together. Jenny could hear soft, soothing sounds being exchanged between them. She was still puzzled why she and the children were asked to join them. She really expected to have to stay at the Pickle Barrel and be questioned with everyone else. However, she was very grateful they were away from all the turmoil. The children had settled down and were sleeping in the crook of her arms. She was exhausted and desperately needed to stretch her arms, which had become numb. She knew the movement would disturb them… something she didn't want to do.

Gene removed his arm from his mother's shoulder and gave her a quick, loving kiss on the cheek. He took the cell phone from his belt and dialed the family doctor. He briefly told the doctor what had happened at the Pickle Barrel and about the death of his father. After a short pause, he asked the doctor to meet them at Tallahassee Regional Hospital. Dr. Murray had been their family doctor and friends of the family for most of Gene's life. Gene had gone to school with his children. Occasionally, they still socialized with one another. So, when it came to this tragedy, Gene had no reservations about asking their family friend for help. Gene also knew the doctor would have it no other way.

When they pulled into the emergency entrance, wheelchairs were already waiting for them. Gene helped his mother from the car and settled her into one of them. The officer helped Jenny pass the sleeping children into the arms of two Red Cross volunteers. They grunted as they were being shuffled around, but they didn't wake up. Jenny was seated in one of the wheelchairs and pushed inside. She asked to be placed beside the children's bed in case they woke up—she would be there to comfort them. Mrs. Brewer was placed in the cubicle next to them, and Jenny could hear Gene reassuring her. Then he asked if she would be alright while he stepped outside for a moment.

Jenny could sense him standing on the other side of the cubicle and walked to the opening and drew back the curtain.

He was about to ask if he could enter when she opened the drape. He said, "I'm sorry, I don't mean to intrude. But, I just realized, I haven't introduced myself. My name is Eugene Brewer, but most people call me Gene. I see from your apron, you are Jenny, with three stars."

"I'm pleased to meet you, Gene. I saw your name on your vest earlier." She thought it was funny the way he had said… *with three stars.* "I'm so sorry for the loss of your father. How are you doing? How is your mother holding up? I have been terribly worried about her since I found her earlier today sitting on the floor with your father."

"I think we're still a little numb at this point. No one ever expects this type of tragedy to happen to them. One thing for sure, I know we'll miss him. He was the bedrock of our family, and everyone who knew him loved him deeply."

As he talked about his father, Jenny could see fresh tears forming in his beautiful brown eyes. The urge to take him into her arms and comfort him was strong. She held back and listened while he continued to speak.

"I'm sure it'll take some time for us to adjust to not having him around. How are your children? I saw them covered in blood. Are they injured?"

"They have no injuries that I can see. However, I'm really worried this tragedy might affect them for the rest of their lives."

"Do you need to call your husband or family to let them know where you are and that you are o.k.?"

"I appreciate you asking, but I don't have a husband or any family. These children aren't mine. I pulled them from underneath a collapsed display while I was searching for survivors in the gift shop. There was no adult with them when I found them. My first thought was the parents had been shot, and before they died, shoved the children under the clothing display in an effort to save their lives."

"Well, it was a good thing you searched the area and found them. I would hate to think they had to stay under a pile of clothing until help arrived. I'm sure their parents will be found during the investigation. Hopefully they'll be found alive."

Jenny heard the children on the bed behind her waking up. They sat up and looked around the strange room. Jenny saw the frightened look on their faces and heard their cries. She rushed across the room to gather them into her arms. Gene followed her into the room. He stood by and watched her comfort the children. Jenny waited for the children to settle down, and then turned in his direction and softly said, "This is Mr. Gene. He's here to help you find your mother and father. You are at the hospital now. A doctor will be in shortly to check on you and ask you some questions. Do you think you could answer a few questions for Mr. Gene before the doctor arrives?" Jenny dabbed at the tears which ran down their cheeks. The boys shook their heads up and down, indicating their approval to speak with Gene. "Everything will be alright. I promise," said Jenny.

Gene traded places with Jenny so that he could be close to the children as he spoke to them. "Hi, how are you? Are you hurt anywhere?" he said.

They turned their heads from side to side and said, "No."

"Can you tell me your names?"

They looked at each other and began to tear up.

"It's o.k. I'm a police officer. I only want to help you. If you'll tell me your names, I can find your family for you. Then you can go home."

They stopped crying, and the older of the two said, "Danny."

"Rossi," said the younger child.

"That's good. Now, can you tell me your last name?"

The boys looked puzzled. He could tell neither of them knew what a last name was.

"Can you tell me your mommy and daddy's name? What do people call your mom and dad?"

They were silent, as they studied the question Gene had asked. Then, Danny answered, "Mama."

"Daddy! I want my daddy!" Rossi cried, which set Danny off.

"I want my mama! Where is my mama?" Danny screamed.

Gene knew he would get no more helpful information from the boys. He stepped aside and looked on as Jenny pulled the boys into her arms to comfort them. Gene leaned in close to her and whispered, "Jenny, I'm going to check on Mother. I want to see if the doctor has arrived. I'll talk with you again in a few minutes."

Gene eased the curtain back to his mother's small examination room. He saw her slumped in the wheelchair. Her head had dropped to one side as she napped. She appeared so fragile, and looked much older than he had ever seen her. He wondered what she would do now that his father was not there to care for her.

His mother sensed his presence in the room and woke up.

"Are you o.k.?" he said. "The restrooms are just outside if you need to go."

"Thanks sweetie, but I'm alright for now," she said.

"How are the children and Jenny?"

"The boys are upset and want their parents. And, you don't have to worry about Jenny, Mother. She can take care of herself, and everyone else."

"That's good. What will happen to the children while their family is being located?"

"Typically, a social worker will take them and place them with foster parents until the family is found. It shouldn't take very long. Everyone at the scene should be identified within a day or two."

"Hello...Pauline. Hello...Gene," Dr. Murray said, as he entered the small cubicle. He made his way over to Pauline and embraced her as he conveyed his condolences. He shook Gene's hand and asked what he could do for them?

"Mother has had a very traumatic day," Gene said. "I would like you to check her out. I'm sure the next few days will be trying for her, as well. She may need something to help her rest."

"Well, I think I can handle that. How about it, Pauline, you want to sit here on the side of the bed and I'll have a look?"

Both men helped her to the bedside and waited while she made herself comfortable.

"Dr. Murray, there is one more thing I'd like to ask of you," Gene said. "We brought with us, a young woman and two children. They're in the cubicle next to us. Would you mind examining the children? They are covered in blood, but I don't think they have any wounds. I'm really more concerned about their mental state."

"I'll be glad to check them out," Dr. Murray replied.

Dr. Murray completed his examination of Pauline and found nothing out of the ordinary. She was physically and emotionally drained. He gave her a few sleeping pills from his medical bag to take home with her. "You're in great shape, Pauline. You just need to get some rest. If it's alright with you, I'll stop by your place and check on you in the next few days."

"Please do," she said.

"Why don't you lay back and rest while I go next door to see the children. Close your eyes and try to relax. This won't take long." He eased her back until her head reached the pillow. He then pulled a sheet up over her.

Gene stepped next door with Dr. Murray. He introduced Jenny and the children. Dr. Murray noticed the blood soaked clothing the children wore. He knew they had been traumatized the moment he saw the distraught look on their faces. It'll take a very long time for these children to recover from this, he thought. His only hope was that their parents hadn't been killed.

Jenny had crawled up onto the edge of the bed next to the children. They clung to her, as if she were their only lifeline. Jenny knew the doctor was there to evaluate the children and began to reassure them. "Danny and Rossi," she said. "Dr. Murray is the doctor I told you about earlier. He is here to make sure you are not hurt. He wants to listen to your heart and check your body for any cuts or scratches. Will that be o.k. with you? I promise he won't hurt you. I'll be right here beside you."

Dr. Murray was impressed with the way Jenny communicated with the children.

The boys held tightly to her when she made a move to step down from the bed. "It'll be alright. I'll be right here. I won't leave you," she assured them again. "Let the doctor check you over. Then we can leave."

They let go of her and allowed her to leave the bed without further resistance. They sat still as Dr. Murray approached them. He spoke softly, as he reached for his stethoscope.

"Now, this won't hurt a bit. Tell me, Danny, how old are you?"

Danny hesitated, and then he said with a tear-filled voice, "Five."

"Boy! I could tell you were a big guy. Do you have any pets?"

"Yes. I have a dog."

"What's his name?"

"It's a girl dog. Her name is Sally."

"Did you name her?"

"Me and Rossi named her. She is going to have puppies and we get to keep one of them. Mama said we could choose."

Dr. Murray had finished his examination of Danny and could find nothing visibly wrong. He then turned his attention toward Rossi.

"Okay Danny, you check out pretty good. Now let me look at Rossi."

Rossi was ready and waiting. He figured, if it didn't hurt his big brother, it wouldn't hurt him.

"Well now, Rossi, how old are you?" the doctor probed gently for information.

"Three—no, four."

"Oh! So, you're another big boy, like your brother. Do you or your brother go to school?"

"I'm in preschool," Danny spoke up.

"Is that right? What's the name of your school?"

"Lee Street Preschool."

"That's sounds like a great school. What's your teacher's name?"

"I have two teachers—Mr. Fisher and Miss Shaw. Mr. Fisher plays games outside with us."

"I bet they are really good teachers."

He finished the exams on both boys and was satisfied they were o.k. physically. But, he was concerned about their mental state.

Dr. Murray thanked the boys for allowing him to examine them. Then he stepped back to talk with Gene and Jenny. The doctor knew what he had to do next. He would have to call the social worker to pick up the children. He dreaded the thought, as this might cause further trauma to the boys.

Gene didn't like the idea of turning the children over to a social worker, but it was procedure. So much for following procedure, he thought. I broke procedure when I took Jenny and the boys from the crime scene. He said nothing as the doctor left the room to find the hospital social worker.

"Is this the only recourse these children have?" Jenny asked Gene when the doctor was out of sight.

"I'm sorry, Jenny. I don't make the policies. We have to follow the procedures that have been set up for cases such as this. I don't like it anymore than you do."

They had been talking with their back to the children. Now, Jenny turned to face the two small boys sitting on the bed. She began to sob; the tears wouldn't stop coming. She couldn't take the pressure anymore. It just wasn't right for them to take the children from her.

Gene felt her pain, but, his hands were tied. He turned her around to face him and quietly asked her to stop crying in front of the children, as it would upset them again. He watched her brush the tears from her eyes, and then she asked him to stay with the boys while she visited the restroom to wash her face. After she left the room, he walked over to the bed and sat with the boys.

As Jenny returned from the restroom, she saw Dr. Murray with a woman she assumed was the social worker coming down the hallway. Her heart sank to her feet...she began to cry again.

Gene could hear Jenny crying through the curtain. He asked the boys if they could stay alone just for a moment while he stepped outside. "You'll be alright until I get back, okay?"

Both heads bobbed up and down.

Gene found Jenny leaning against the wall crying uncontrollably. "What happened? I thought you were going to be alright with this." He no more than got the statement out of his mouth, when he saw Dr. Murray and the social worker. He knew then, she had seen them, too. "Oh, dear!" he said. "Jenny, they have to take the children. Seeing you upset will only upset the children even more." He pulled her close to him and looked into her bloodshot blue eyes. He pleaded for her to pull herself together for the sake of the children. "Please don't make it harder for them."

Jenny covered her face with the wet paper towel she had gotten from the restroom. She took a few deep breaths, and pulled herself together just as the doctor and social worker walked up beside them.

The foursome entered the small room where the children sat on the bed. Jenny approached them with her arms outstretched. The boys flew into her open arms as if she were an angel from heaven who had come to take them to the safety of their home.

She held their small bodies close to her for a moment and, while they still clung to her, she eased upon the bed beside them. Thinking the separation from her would be traumatic for the children, she began to prepare them. "Danny, Rossi, this nice lady has come to help you until your family is found. You need to go with her for a little while," Jenny explained.

"No! No! No! We don't want to go with her! We want to stay with you," they shouted and held to her even tighter.

"But you'll be in good hands. She'll take care of you." Jenny found it hard to fight back the tears.

"No! No! Please don't make us go with her! We don't want to go! Please, please don't make us leave you!" the children shouted even louder. Tears rolled down their little red cheeks.

Jenny's heart could take no more of this. She turned to Gene with pleading eyes. "Please, can't something else be done?" she said while holding back the tears she so desperately wanted to release.

"Yes, why can't something else be done?" a voice echoed from the entrance of the room.

Everyone turned in the direction of the voice and saw Mrs. Brewer standing in the doorway. The shouting and crying had awakened her.

"Mother, why are you out of bed?" Gene walked over to her and took her arm to guide her into the already crowded room.

"I see no reason why Jenny can't take the children with her. The children trust her. It's obvious; they want to be with her. So, why shouldn't they?"

This hit Jenny like a bombshell. It wasn't as if she hadn't already thought of it. But after today, she may not have a place to live. She was sure she was out of a job. She had no money saved to fall back on. No matter how badly she wanted to take the children—she couldn't.

"May I talk to all of you outside for a moment, please?" Jenny said, while looking Gene straight in the eyes. Once they were out of the room, Jenny began reassuring the children again.

"I want you both to listen carefully to me. I need to step outside the room just for a little while, and I need for you to stop crying. If I can talk them into letting you stay with Mr. Gene and Mrs. Brewer, would that be o.k. with you? It'll only be for a couple of days. You can pretend it's a vacation."

"No! We want you to stay with us," said Danny.

She held them close to her and softly said, "I know you want to stay with me. But, you see, I don't have a home to take you to. I would love to stay with you, but I can't.

Both boys studied what she had said, and then Danny softly spoke, "Its o.k. Miss Jenny. We can stay with Mr. Gene."

"Thank you, sweetheart. Then I'll go talk with him. I'll be right back."

Jenny stepped outside the small room to join the others. She noticed Mrs. Brewer sitting in a chair someone had brought in for her.

"What did you want to talk to us about? Doctor Murray asked.

"I hope I have an alternative solution for the children. It's impossible for me to take the children. After today, I have no job, I have no transportation, and when my landlady hears that I'm unable to pay the rent again this month, I'll be out on the street. I'd love to help the children. But, there are too many things working against me right now. I spoke with the children and they have agreed to go with Gene and Mrs. Brewer, if it can be worked out."

"Gene is a police officer and well thought of in the community," his mother stated. "I see no reason why anyone would object to him watching the children for a few days."

"But, Mother, the next few days are going to be very busy for us. I have my job. I don't see how I can manage to care for two children."

"How much managing do you think two little boys will need?" she added.

"I just don't see how I can manage this. And Mother, you certainly can't care for the needs of these children."

"Well, Jenny can come and help. The children already trust her. Would you do that, Jenny? You can move your things in and take care of the children. You can tell that landlady of yours to take a hike. What do you say, Jenny? Will you do that?"

Jenny couldn't believe how the conversation had turned. This was a lot to absorb all at once. She had been awake since five o'clock that morning and was so tired she could hardly think. She knew she would be out on the street looking for another place to live soon anyway. This would provide her the opportunity to help the children. Plus, it would give her a couple days to adjust to all these new changes, while she figured out what to do about another job.

"I'll stay with the children until their family is found, if it's okay."

Gene turned to the social worker and said, "Could that be worked out?"

"It sounds like a great idea to me," the doctor commented.

"Considering the circumstances, I see no reason why temporary guardianship shouldn't be turned over to Gene and Pauline. I'm sure it'll only be for a short while. Dr. Murray and I will have the necessary papers drawn up for you to sign before you leave the hospital. It shouldn't take long," said the social worker.

Jenny bent down and gave Mrs. Brewer a quick hug and said, "Thank you." She turned and reentered the room to inform the children of the decision that had been made.

The children were sitting in the middle of the bed with their legs crossed and their little hands holding their crotch area. A grimace was on their faces. They were practically jumping up and down. "We have to go pee," Rossi said.

"Okay. Hold on just a minute," she said. Quickly turning back around, she peeked outside the curtain. Gene was still standing next to his mother.

"Gene, may I speak to you?" she whispered. When he came close to her she told him the boys needed to use the restroom. "Would you mind taking them?"

Moments later, Gene lifted Rossi off the bed and stood him on the floor. "There you go big boy. Just stay right there while I get your brother." He then placed Danny on the floor beside Rossi. "Do you two big boys think you can walk with me to the men's room?" They reached up and took Gene's hands and eagerly began to walk. Gene smiled, as he let the boys lead him from the room.

The men's room was just a short walk to the right of their cubicle. The children dragged Gene along in their rush to get there. He released their hands when they reached the door and watched as they ran to the urinals. A linen cart was parked next to the men's room. He reached inside the cart and pulled out a couple washcloths and hospital gowns.

Jenny joined Mrs. Brewer in the small waiting area. She wanted to take advantage of the quiet moment to express her condolences. "I'm so sorry for the loss of your husband," she said. "I understand he was a very fine man and loved by everyone. Mrs. Brewer, I know you don't know me, but I'm here for you if you need me. Please don't hesitate if you need to talk to someone."

"Oh, Jenny, you've already done more than you'll ever know. Earlier at the Pickle Barrel, I think I would have died beside my beloved husband if you hadn't been there for me. I was ready. I couldn't foresee another day without him. He was the first thing I wanted to see in the morning and the last thing I wanted to see at night. I didn't know how I could survive without him. But, I know now that I must try. It's because of you, Jenny."

"What did I do? I really didn't do anything except try and comfort someone who had just lost a loved one."

"You did that, and much more. While you sat on the floor beside me with the two children clinging to you, I thought of Gene at their age. I couldn't help but think what it would have been like for him to go through what these children have gone through today. I suddenly wanted to live. I want to spend more time with Gene. I want to see my future grandchildren. I know I'll miss my beloved husband for the rest of my life. But, I also know I'll see him again in the *Hereafter*."

"Do you really believe in the *Hereafter*?"

"Yes, I do. Don't you, Jenny?"

"I don't know, Mrs. Brewer. I've never really been to church to learn about these things."

"Oh, my dear child, we'll have to do something about that. You must get to know the Lord."

They heard the door to the men's room open and both women looked in that direction. They saw Gene carrying the boys in his arms. He had cleaned them up and dressed them in hospital gowns which were ten sizes too large. Jenny really wanted to laugh. What a picture this would make, she thought. She could tell Gene and the boys had bonded. As they drew near, Pauline and Jenny heard the boys whispering in Gene's ears; "I'm hungry, Mr. Gene," Rossi said. "I want something to eat," said Danny.

"I could use something to eat myself," stated Gene. Then it occurred to him; he had been looking for a place to eat this afternoon when all hell broke loose at the Pickle Barrel, and it was almost dark outside now. Suddenly, he was starving.

"Tell you what, partners—why don't I see about breaking us out of this joint. Then we'll ride through a drive'em-thru and snatch up some grub. Let's take these two good-looking women sitting here with us. How's about it, boys—you want to take 'em with us?"

The boys looked puzzled. They weren't sure what to make of this funny-talking man.

Gene noticed their reaction and said, "Come on partners, are we gonna snatch up these pretty gals and drive'em-thru for some grub or not?"

Pauline and Jenny were about to burst with laughter. The boys saw the women trying to hide their laughter, and then they began to smile. "Yes," they said in unison.

"Okay then, partners. You guard the womenfolk while I find a way to break us out of this place."

Before he left to speak with the receptionist, he sat the children down beside Jenny and his mother. He said to the boys, "I'll be right back. Now, be sure to take good care of the womenfolk."

As Gene approached the front desk he saw the Captain of the precinct standing there. He appeared to be asking for directions. Gene walked up beside him and said, "Hello, Captain Hall"

"Oh, there you are. I was just asking where I could find you."

"Why are you here, Captain?"

"Larry called from the crime scene and told me about your father. He said you were here with your mother. The precinct was a madhouse, but all the officers had everything pretty much under control, so I thought I would make a quick visit to check on you. How's your mother?"

"She checked out o.k. But, she's had a traumatic day. She's taking my fathers death pretty hard."

"Gene, I'm so sorry about your father. Is there anything I can do for you and your mother?"

"I can't think of anything at the moment, but I'll let you know if something comes up. Captain, I'd like to take the rest of the night off. I'll be back to help with the investigation tomorrow."

"That's one of the other things I want to talk to you about. I want you to take some time off, Gene. You need time to make funeral arrangements for your father and, your mother needs you to be around for awhile. All this hasn't fully hit her yet, and the next few days are going to be very hard for her. You're all she has left. You should be there."

"I understand what you're saying, but pre-arrangements have already been made for the funeral. I'm sure mother will spend a lot of time resting. And, if I'm around, she may feel she has to do her motherly duties. I don't want her catering to me."

"Well, maybe it'll do her good to stay busy. This is a hard time for both of you. You need each other to get through this."

"But the department will need all the help they can get on this investigation, and I'm a senior officer. We've never seen a massacre like this in this city. My team needs me."

"I understand; however, your father has just passed away at the crime scene. You are emotionally attached and I can't permit you to work on this case."

"I'm sure my emotions concerning my father will not interfere with my work on the investigation."

"Gene, I'm ordering you to go home, be with your mother, and don't let me see you on the job for three weeks. Oh, one more thing. I'll send an officer to take statements from your mother and the young woman. Questioning the children might be too traumatic. We'll hold off on that for now. I saw Dr. Murray on his way out and he filled me in on the children. It's a good thing you're doing—taking the kids in like that. I'm sure some of their family will be located soon."

"Captain, I'm sorry, I know I wasn't following procedure when I took Jenny and the children from the crime scene. Mother wanted them with her, and I couldn't say no to her."

"I understand, Gene. At least we know where they are. And, like I said earlier, we'll get their statements later."

"Thank you, sir. I appreciate that."

"Well then. Report to work in three weeks," the captain said, as he turned to leave the building.

Gene turned his attention to the desk clerk and inquired about being dismissed. "Yes sir, Dr. Murray said you can leave anytime you're ready."

"In that case, I believe we're ready."

"Oh, Mr. Brewer, I have the papers from the social worker for you to sign."

Gene signed the paperwork. He had taken a few steps from the desk to leave. Then he turned back when he remembered the hospital gowns he had taken from the cart. "I forgot to tell you I borrowed two hospital gowns from the linen cart. I'll see that they're returned to the hospital."

"That's alright. There's no hurry for you to return them," said the clerk.

Gene walked back to where the small party was waiting for him. As he walked, he put aside his frustration at being pulled off the murder investigation. It was, after all, the cause of his father's death and he wanted to help with the investigation. As he approached the small group, he could see how tired and hopeless they looked. His mother looked old and drawn. The children appeared lost in the large hospital gowns. Jenny looked tired, but couldn't have looked more beautiful. The children's eyes brightened when they saw him approaching.

"I broke us out of this place," Gene said. "Are ya ready to high-tail it, partners? Snatch up these women here and we'll ride 'em through the drive'em-thru and get some grub."

The children displayed a big grin and reached for the hands of the women. Jenny took Danny's small hand and let him believe he was pulling her up from her chair. Gene helped his mother to her feet. Everyone held hands, as they began walking toward the exit door. "Here we go, partners," Gene said. The children took two steps and stumbled. Everyone had forgotten about the oversized garments the children were wearing. Gene and Jenny looked at each other and broke out laughing. They each picked up a child and continued walking.

Ben, the police officer who drove them to the hospital, was still sitting in the parked car outside the emergency room. He saw the small group coming out the exit door and ran to assist them.

"Are we riding in the police car again?" Rossi asked Gene.

"We sure are. Do you want to ride up front with me?"

"Will it be okay?"

"Can I ride up front, too?" Danny asked.

"I think we can work that out. Mother would you mind riding with Jenny in the back seat?"

"I wouldn't mind at all, if it's okay with her. It'll give us a chance to talk along the way."

"I'd like that very much," Jenny said. Then it occurred to her, she had no idea where they were going. She knew they were going to a drive'em-thru to grab some grub, but had no idea where they would be going after that. She needed to get her things from her rented room. In her hasty flight from the Pickle Barrel, she had forgotten her purse which was locked in the employee's locker. She had nothing but the clothes on her back and a blood stained Pickle

Barrel apron. She had no driver's license, no identification of any type, and no money—*not that I ever had very much money anyway. What have I gotten myself into? I don't even know these people. They seem like nice people. Murderers seem like nice people, too.* Of course, she didn't think Gene and his mother were murderers. But, who are they, really? Jenny thought. *I'll have to ask Mrs. Brewer a lot of questions when everyone is settled in the automobile.*

Gene was aware of the seat belt law and car seats for children. He also was aware that the patrol car wasn't equipped with either car seats or enough seat belts for everyone up front. But, he knew he would bend the rules once again for the sake of the children. They needed something to distract them from the horrors they had experienced that day. Gene watched Rossi and Danny's eyes fill with wonder and curiosity, as they explored the buttons and lights on the instrument panel.

A blast of communications came over the radio and the children jumped. When they realized what the sound was, they began to giggle.

"Did you make it do that, Mr. Gene?" Danny asked.

"Make it do it again," said Rossi.

"No, partners. I didn't make it talk. Someone at headquarters made it talk."

"Can you turn on the flashing lights and sirens?"

"Tell you what, boys, let's get some food. Then, we'll drive out of town and turn the lights and sirens on. I can only leave them on for a short time though. Would you like that?"

"Oh yes, that's great. I'm hungry," Danny announced again.

"Me, too," Rossi said.

"There's a Burger King just up the street. Do you like Burger King? How about it—you want to stop there?"

"We like Burger King," Rossi spoke up.

"Well then. Maybe we should ask the womenfolk if they'd like that. How does Burger King sound to you ladies?" Gene said over his shoulder to the women in the back seat.

"Burger King sounds great," they said.

As their car pulled away from the hospital grounds, two ambulances, with sirens blaring, rushed into the emergency entrance. Gene was sure they were delivering the wounded from the Pickle Barrel.

CHAPTER EIGHTEEN

F riends and family members gathered around the Pickle Barrel, outside the cordoned-off area. They were on cell phones communicating with people inside the building and were aware of the tragic event that had taken place there. It was becoming more difficult for officers to keep the people from charging the restricted area. Reporters were among the people outside. They could be heard shouting—how many shooters are there? How many casualties are there? Have the shooters been arrested yet? Police officers guarding the perimeter could only assure them that everyone was being cared for. They would be given any new information regarding the matter as soon as it became available.

Ambulances had been coming and going for some time. There were still several more injured people lined up waiting to be transported to hospitals. Their injuries weren't life-threatening. Larry could see that all the injured bodies had been removed from the porch area. Only the deceased bodies still lay where they had fallen. Nightfall was upon them and he wanted to clear the crime scene, especially on the outside, while it was still daylight. The crime lab officials and medical examiner had been working as quickly as they could and were nearly finished in the porch area. Larry made a quick turn and almost collided with the P.I.O., Gregory.

"The spectators out there are becoming frantic. I'm afraid they're on the verge of charging the area," Gregory informed Larry. "I've tried my best to reason with them but they won't listen. I have to come up with something to say to calm them down. Rumors are spreading about a terrorist attack. If a rumor such as this spreads, there'll be sheer panic in the streets. Can you suggest anything that might ease the situation?"

"I really can't blame them for being anxious. We've never had a tragedy like this before. I don't know. Just try to get through to them that everything's under control. Tell them the lone shooter has been taken down and inquiries are being made about his identity. Also, tell them we will update them with any new information as it comes to us."

"I've already tried to reassure them, but I'll try again. Do you have a count on the wounded and dead?" asked Gregory.

"Not at this time. But it shouldn't be too much longer before we'll know."

"A lot of family members out there don't have cell phones to communicate with their family members who are inside. And, some of the ones who do aren't getting any answers when they call. They see ambulances coming and going. They know something terrible has happened and they're afraid for their family members."

"Yes, I know. It has to be hard for all of them. Just tell them the wounded are being seen after and will be sent to the local emergency rooms. They can call there to check on them. The survivors who haven't been injured will be free to leave after they've been questioned at the precinct. Ask family members to go home so their loved ones can contact them once they're released. Try to convince everyone else to go home so we can do our job."

"Okay, I'll do what I can. I'm preparing another statement for the late night news. Is there anything you want to add? I issued a short bulletin about the shooting to the media earlier."

"That's good. I'm sure you have everything covered concerning the media. I don't have anything to add. It would be a big help though, if you can keep the media off our backs for a while. We have a lot more work to do here tonight."

As Larry turned to reenter the building, a young police officer flew through the double doors almost hitting him in the head. "Whoa! What's the hurry?" Larry shouted.

"Oh! There you are, Larry. I've been looking everywhere for you. The paramedic came across this lady lying on the floor behind the counter—you have to come and see this. It's, it's remarkable."

The young officer led Larry behind the counter where a paramedic crouched on the floor beside a woman covered in blood. The woman appeared to be dead. He saw a large yellow purse at her side. The contents were spilled onto the floor, but he saw nothing out of the ordinary. As he surveyed the surrounding area he spotted the small gun. The men had freed it from her hand and kicked it aside before they checked her vital signs. Larry couldn't believe his luck. He knew at that moment—this case was pretty much solved.

"Is she alive?"

"Her vitals are weak, but she's alive. There are no injuries that we can find. We pulled her from underneath this counter. It appears she shot the gunman from under there." The paramedic pointed toward the opposite corner at the dead cashier and said, "She must have covered herself in this woman's blood to make it look like she'd been shot. It was really a very smart thing to do. If the shooter had stepped behind the counter and seen her all covered in blood, he might think she had already been shot and killed. Maybe he wouldn't waste his time shooting someone who was already dead. This is one very smart lady we have here."

"Do you have her personal information yet?"

"We were getting ready to check that when I sent for you."

"Well, get that done. Bag the gun and purse. Be sure to tag it. And bring it to me immediately. If she's not wounded, why isn't she responding?"

"I believe she's in deep shock, sir. We've done all we can for her on this end."

"See that she gets to the hospital right away, and make sure someone stays with her at all times. She's a murder suspect now."

Larry entered the dining area and saw the last few witnesses being escorted out to the waiting bus that would take them to the Sheriff's Department for questioning. He was grateful the crowd was finally out of the building. Now crime scene experts could spread out and do their investigation of the area.

Larry walked outside to check on the progress of the automobile investigation. Every tag number would be logged, along with the description of the automobiles. They would be identified and matched to the owners. Every automobile in the lot was part of the crime scene now and wouldn't be released to the owners until the cross references were completed and the crime scene cleared. The logging was almost complete. But, because of the large number of automobiles in the lot, it would probably be late the next day before the cross matches would be completed.

Larry was pleased with the way everyone performed their duties that day. Considering the magnitude of death and destruction, he was surprised the rescue and investigation had gone so well. However, more evidence had to be gathered before the night was over. He was confident it would be completed by midnight. Bodies would have to be photographed, identified, tagged, and then sent to the county morgue. The crime scene would also be photographed. Every inch of the shooter's body would be searched and his personal belongings and weapons sent to the crime lab. Most likely, the serial numbers had been removed from the guns the man used.

Larry's first thought when he entered the building and saw the Arabic man lying in a pool of his own blood was: *this was a terrorist act.* Of course, he would never express this to anyone who might spread the word. It was also possible this madman had a personal score to settle with someone. We may never find out what this vendetta was, he thought.

As Larry walked across the parking lot toward the porch to check on the progress there, he saw the young officer he had talked with earlier, running toward him with the bagged yellow purse in his hand.

"I have the information you wanted about the lady with the gun." The young officer passed him a plastic bag containing Edna's driver's license. He gave him the bagged purse and gun. "We also found this." He extended a plastic bag with Edna's gun permit inside.

"Good girl," Larry said when he saw the gun permit. "This is my kind of lady. What else do you have?"

"We found her name, address, phone number, and her husband's name, rank and serial number on her dependent military ID. There was a notepad with a phone number and an address with directions for a Linda in Hattiesburg, Mississippi. I have it all written down here for you." He handed Larry a sheet of paper with the information.

"This is very helpful. Thank you." He looked at the sheet of paper for her name. "Has Edna been sent to the hospital?"

"Oh, yes. An officer was sent with her in the next available ambulance with instructions to take *special care* of her." All the officers knew the hidden meaning of the words, *"special care"*.

"That was nice of you to think of that," Larry complimented.

"She deserves it, sir."

"Yes, I know she does. It's unfortunate she is considered a murder suspect now. Did she wake up before she was sent to the hospital?"

"No sir, she did not."

"Well, thanks again for the information."

Larry watched the young man walk back inside the building. This young man has a promising career on the force, he thought. He was really impressed with the officer's efficiency. Larry removed his phone from his waist belt. Then he called Captain Hall at headquarters.

Ω

Larry filled the Captain in on the details about Edna and the gun found next to her. "Yes Captain, I have the gun and purse in my hands. Edna's Beretta and the weapons belonging to the shooter were the only ones found at the scene. It appears this little lady took him out. Crime scene is working on all the angles as we speak. So, we should have a better picture of what took place very soon."

"Where is she now?" asked the Captain.

"She has been sent to the hospital with an escort and *special care* instructions."

"That's great. Let's let her rest tonight. Then, we'll see if she can answer some questions tomorrow. How is crowd control?"

"Helicopters are buzzing, trying to get a better look. News media of all kinds are lining the roadway. Friends, family, and spectators are eager to know what has taken place. You know how it is. But, everything's under control. Gregory has issued a statement to the media and I think that has calmed everyone down for now."

"Yes, I know. I have been following the newscasts on the tube. People are still concerned, though; the phones have been ringing off the hook all afternoon."

"Have the wounded been taken care of?"

"Everyone has been treated and sent to the area hospitals. C.S.I. (*crime scene investigation*) are identifying and taking the necessary photographs of the dead. It'll take several more hours before that's completed."

"Before you leave, I want you to set up two rotating teams to guard the perimeter. I want them there around the clock until this has been sorted out. I don't want any unauthorized person entering that crime scene. Be sure all the dead are sent to the county morgue before you leave for the night. Oh, send that gun and purse to me right away. And, keep this quiet. I don't want the media getting wind of this just yet.

CHAPTER NINETEEN

B us load after bus load of witnesses had been dropped off at the Leon County Sheriff's Department for questioning. The small building was bulging with people. Every inch of floor space was filled with people sitting, standing and lying on the floors. They were hanging out the entrance onto the sidewalk, as well. Every available officer had been called in to take statements. Questioning began as soon as the witnesses started arriving. After each person's identity was verified and their statements taken, they were free to leave. They were not permitted to return to the Pickle Barrel for their automobiles. Most of them understood and were too upset from their experience to return for their automobiles anyway. Family members or friends were called to pick them up at the station. Out of town visitors elected to stay in hotels until their automobiles could be released.

Upon completion of the questioning it became apparent that very few people had actually seen the shooter, and they were the ones who had been in the gift shop when he entered. One man, who had been in the dining room said he saw the shooter, but only after he had been shot and killed. Everyone in the gift shop gave about the same account of what took place. For the most part, only rapid gunfire and screams were heard by the others. However, everyone spoke of a waitress who had seen the shooter in the gift shop. They said she had taken charge and tried to help them escape the building. Also, after the gunman was killed, she settled everyone down. They said the waitress wore a Pickle Barrel apron with the name Jenny, with three stars embroidered on it. Nearly everyone had been questioned. But, so far, Jenny with three stars had not been one of them.

Captain Hall was back from his quick visit to the hospital and was now on the phone filling the Mayor in on the progress of the investigation. A young officer approached him carrying the bagged yellow purse and gun. The Captain took them from the officer, and then gave the young man a *"thumbs up"*

"Mayor, I have nothing more to tell you now. I'll let you know more as the results come in from the investigation. I'll call you tomorrow," Captain Hall said, and then hung up.

He turned his attention toward the bagged yellow purse and the small Beretta semiautomatic pistol. He retrieved them from his desk and stepped outside to find his personal assistant, Dee. He made his way through the busy room and saw her sitting on a sofa taking depositions from a distraught family. The time was 10:45 PM and the precinct was nearly empty compared to what it had looked like an hour ago. Dee kept her eye on the Captain as he approached her.

"I have finished with this family's deposition," she said. "Is there something I can do for you, sir?"

They waited for the family to gather their belongings and leave before the Captain spoke.

He held out his hand with the gun and purse and said, "I'd like for you to take these to the lab. Tell them this is evidence from a murder scene. I need to know any vital information they can find. This is top priority and I need the results as soon as possible."

Dee took the items from the Captain and then left for the lab.

Now back at his desk, he concentrated on the bagged identification cards and gun permit. He checked the name on the cards and saw the town, Palm Bay, Florida, on the address. *I know the Chief of Police there. Bob Rossman and I go back a long way. Since Edna is from his area, I'll call Bob directly when I find out more about her condition. Her family may be worried about her. Bob can have someone there let her family know where she is and her condition.* As he studied the permit in his hand it occurred to him what a heroic act this lady had performed today. Even though she is considered a murder suspect, because of her actions a lot of lives were spared. *The news media will have a field day with this one.* He would try his best to protect her, but the media always seemed to find the heroes. He reached across his desk for the phone and then dialed the hospital to check on her.

CHAPTER TWENTY

G rady was becoming increasingly worried about Edna. It wasn't like her not to keep in touch. He hadn't heard from her since lunchtime and had been trying to call her cell phone since six o'clock. He knew the phone was working because his calls kept going to voice mail.

Flipping through the television channels all afternoon, he was hearing different versions of the shooting at the Pickle Barrel in Tallahassee. One channel reported unconfirmed multiple shooters had shot everyone in the restaurant and then shot themselves. Another channel reported a terrorist holding everyone hostage. Every Channel seemed to have a different story, and it was hard to know what to believe. All the networks reported the Pickle Barrel was located off interstate 10. The interstate was closed in that area and was being used for emergency transportation only. Traffic had been rerouted to other streets. Now that the ball game was over, traffic had come to a dead stop on all roads anywhere near the Pickle Barrel area. Aerial shots showed traffic backed up for miles. Emergency vehicles could be seen running in both directions of the closed portions of the interstate. Whatever happened there must have been really bad, Grady thought. He was just glad Edna had been long gone from Tallahassee when this happened.

Grady knew Edna's love for outlet mall shopping and thought maybe she could've stopped at one along the way. *Maybe, she mistakenly left her cell phone in the Suburban when she went inside to shop. Time always got away from her when she was having a good time—especially when it came to shopping. I'm probably worrying unnecessarily.* He would give Edna enough time for the malls to close at nine o'clock. And then, he'd try calling her again. In the meantime, he'd try to put the worrying aside.

It was nearly nine o'clock and Grady still hadn't heard from Edna. He was very worried now. He thought about calling Linda, but wanted to try Edna one more time before he bothered her. He had the phone in his hand and was about to dial, when the phone rang. His heart fell to his feet. It scared him so badly; he almost dropped the phone. He checked the caller ID and saw it was Linda from Mississippi. *Oh good. Edna must have arrived and forgot to call to let me know.* He felt relieved and pressed the on button to talk with her.

"Hello, Linda. How are you?"

"I'm fine, Grady. But I'm worried about Edna. She hasn't arrived yet. I've been calling her cell number all afternoon and I get no answer. Have you heard from her?"

Grady suddenly felt faint. He couldn't believe what he was hearing. *Surely, she has to be there. Where else would she be?* He wouldn't let himself think the worst.

"Dear heavens, she should've been there hours ago. I haven't heard from her since lunchtime. I too, have been trying to reach her for hours. I thought maybe she stopped at a mall to shop or something. It isn't like her—not to stay in touch."

"You don't think she was involved in an accident, do you?" Linda asked.

"I sure hope not. I haven't been notified by any law enforcement about her involvement in any accident. But, have you been watching on TV about that shooting incident at the Pickle

Barrel? You don't think she could've been delayed or involved in some way with that? I don't understand why she hasn't called me. I'm getting really worried. And, I'm so sorry for the worry this has caused you. Hopefully, we'll hear from her soon. You'll let me know the minute she arrives, won't you?"

"Of course I'll let you know. Grady, I have been watching the news about the shooting. That happened around lunchtime. I believe she would've been long past Tallahassee when all that took place. It's just hard to believe she'd still be there. I hope she's alright. Do you think we need to call the police and report her missing?"

"Let's give her a little more time. If we haven't heard from her by midnight, then I'll do something. I'll call you one way or the other."

Grady hung the phone up. Suddenly, he felt sick to his stomach. He had been keyed up all afternoon and had skipped the dinner Edna had left him in the refrigerator. He ran to the restroom to vomit and to wash his face in cold water. He was at a loss and didn't know what he would do if he didn't hear from her soon. With the Pickle Barrel shooting fresh in his mind, along with not hearing from her, he was becoming increasingly worried that something was seriously wrong. He was scared and felt as if he were on the brink of losing control.

By ten-thirty Grady was beside himself. He still couldn't reach Edna on the cell phone, and hadn't heard anything else from Linda. He seriously needed someone to talk to. Someone who would sit with him and distract him from the dreadful thoughts he was having about her. He reached for the phone and called his neighbor and best friend, Bob. He was relieved when Bob answered the phone.

"Hi, Bob. I'm sorry for calling so late. You know Edna left for Mississippi today."

"Yes, I do. Is everything alright?"

"Well, no. She hasn't arrived yet, and I'm worried sick that something bad has happened. I haven't heard from her since lunchtime. She isn't answering the cell phone, which isn't like her."

"Grady, I'll be right over. Maybe we can call some local precincts along the route she was traveling. She could've been involved in an accident or something."

"Yeah, I thought about an accident, but no one has called me. I'm sorry to disturb your evening, but I'd really appreciate the company."

"You aren't disturbing anything. I'll be right over."

Within minutes his good friend was knocking at his door. Grady had never been so glad to see anyone. He welcomed Bob inside and offered him a cup of freshly made coffee—the leaded kind, not that decaf stuff Edna always makes. Grady was anticipating a long night and figured the caffeine would help. Both men helped themselves to a cup of coffee. Then they went to the family room to sit and talk.

Bob could see the worried look on Grady's face. He wasn't sure how to comfort his friend, or how to approach him about the possibility something bad may have happened to Edna. Bob had been in law enforcement all his adult life. He had seen this same scenario many times before. The outcomes weren't always good. Before he left home, he had gone to his desk and pulled out a list of law enforcement agencies throughout the state and brought it with him. He would use this list to make the calls to the precincts along the route Edna traveled. While they sat sipping their coffee, Bob thought he would take Grady's mind off Edna for a while. He asked if he had been watching the news coverage concerning the shooting in Tallahassee.

"Oh yes," Grady said. "From the coverage I've heard it's hard to know what really happened there. It seems every channel has a different version."

"I know what you mean. They can't seem to get their stories straight. I understand there's going to be a special press release from the Public Information Officer on the eleven o'clock news. Do you want to watch it?" Bob knew it was almost that time.

"If you haven't heard from Edna after the press release, we'll call some precincts along the route she took to see if they have any information," he calmly said.

"Sure. That'll be o.k. But Bob, you don't think Edna could've been held up by this Pickle Barrel incident, do you? He sat his coffee cup on the side table and reached for the TV remote control. "She should've been long gone from there by the time that took place."

Before Bob could answer his question, the home phone rang. Grady jumped from his chair and ran to the kitchen to grab it off the counter where he had placed it earlier. His hopes were shattered when he saw the caller ID…it was Bob's wife, Margaret.

"Hi, Margaret, I'm sorry to disrupt your evening by calling Bob out. I hope you weren't doing anything important."

"Don't worry about that, Grady. We weren't doing anything important. I'm sorry you haven't heard from Edna. If there's anything at all we can do for you, please feel free to ask. I'm just glad Bob could be there for you. Is he where I can speak to him?"

"He's right here. Thank you for understanding."

Grady gave Bob the phone. He then returned to his chair and picked up his cup of coffee. The feline queen of the house, Chatty, crawled into her familiar spot on his lap. She leisurely licked her paws a few times, and then curled into a ball for her usual long nap.

Bob spoke softly and Grady couldn't actually hear what was being said.

"Hi Maggie, what's up?"

"I don't want to alarm anyone, but Captain Hall just called from Tallahassee to talk with you. He didn't say what he wanted. But, he said it was important and wanted you to call him right away. I told him you were visiting a neighbor and I'd give you the message. Do you have his number?"

"Yes, I have a list of precincts and phone numbers. I'll call right now. Oh, Maggie, I may be here awhile."

"That's alright. I thought you would be. Let me know if you hear from Edna."

"Okay honey. Don't wait up. I'll talk to you later. Sleep tight. I love you."

"I love you, too."

He hung the phone up, and then asked Grady if he could make an important long distance call on his phone.

"Of course," Grady replied.

Bob looked up the phone number for the Leon County Sheriff's Department on the list he'd brought with him and then dialed the number. He couldn't imagine why Captain Hall would be calling him at this late hour, especially with the shooting that had just taken place there.

Captain Hall's personal assistant, Dee, answered the phone and asked Bob to hold while she located the Captain. Moments later, Captain Hall picked up.

"This is Captain Hall speaking."

"Hi Captain Hall, this is Bob Rossman returning your call. It has been a long time since we last spoke. Is everything o.k. with you? How's the family?"

"The family's doing well. I also hope all is well with your family. I called you because of this shooting that took place here today. I'm sure you heard about that."

"Yes, I've been watching it all afternoon on TV. I bet it's a madhouse there. I see traffic on interstate 10 is a big problem."

"It's been crazy alright. I'm sure it'll be a while before we get to the bottom of all this. You know how it is. But, nothing of this magnitude has ever happened here. It's hard to imagine how anyone could commit such an act. And, you know how it is with traffic jams—they eventually thin out. Besides, traffic is the least of my worries at the moment."

"I know what you mean. Well, good luck on the investigation. Maggie said it was important that I call you. What can I do for you?"

"I called you because there's a woman from your area here in the hospital. She was involved at the crime scene. I thought her family should know where she is. Do you think you could send someone over to her address to let them know she's in Tallahassee Regional Hospital?"

"That would be no problem. Give me her name and address. I'll see to it right away."

As soon as Bob heard the Captain say "Edna", his mind went blank, hearing no more. He was stunned and needed to sit down. Reaching for one of the rolling breakfast nook chairs, he sat down. After a brief moment, he recovered from the initial shock and heard the Captain as he finished giving the last part of the address. Bob didn't want to further upset Grady and tried to hide his emotions as he spoke. Choosing his words carefully, he continued his conversation with the Captain.

"What's the condition of the patient?" Bob asked.

"When I talked with the doctor a few minutes ago, she was unresponsive. All her vitals are good and there are no wounds or broken bones. The doctor said she's in deep shock and didn't know when she'd come to. It could be minutes, hours, days, or weeks—no one knows. She was unconscious when she was brought to the hospital. The doctor thinks a family member should to be at her side when she wakes up."

"Very well then, I'll see that the family is notified. Will you be around tomorrow?"

"Oh, I'm sure I'll be around for some time yet. I have a cot in the backroom where I lay my head when I have the time."

"Well, if there's anything else I can do to help, just let me know."

Bob hung the phone up. He took a few deep breaths, and then returned to his chair in the family room.

Grady sat sipping his hot coffee while he watched the television screen. He knew that Bob's capacity as Police Chief often required his attention at all hours of the night. So, when he had this important call to make, he thought nothing of it.

"Is everything alright? Are you ready to watch the press release now?" Grady asked.

"Not yet. Do you mind turning off the television—I need to talk to you about Edna. First of all…she's o.k."

Grady did as Bob asked and switched off the television.

When he mentioned Edna's name, Bob could see the shocked look on Grady's face and knew he was wondering how he knew she was o.k.

"What? What are you saying, Bob? How do you know she's o.k.?"

"The person I was just on the phone with was Captain Hall from Tallahassee. He said Edna was at the Pickle Barrel when the shooting took place."

Grady's face suddenly turned white. His hands shook as he attempted to place his hot coffee cup onto the side table.

If Chatty sensed anything amiss she didn't show it; she continued to sleep, still curled up in a big ball on his lap.

Bob wasn't sure how Grady would take the news about Edna and judging from this sudden reaction, he was now becoming very concerned about his friend. He reached over and helped Grady set the cup down.

"She wasn't hurt in any way, but she's in the hospital. The doctor said she's in deep shock and a family member should be with her when she awakens. I was thinking, I have tomorrow off and I'm sure I can arrange a couple more days off. We can take my car or we can fly up early in the morning—unless you—have someone else you would rather go with. You don't need to go by yourself."

A million things ran through Grady's mind: *Why was Edna in Tallahassee at that time? She should've passed through there hours before. Was she in the restaurant during the shooting? She must have been in the restaurant. Oh! My sweet Edna, no wonder you're in shock.* He could only imagine what she must have gone through. He had no idea which direction to take. He didn't care how he got there. All he wanted now was to be next to her bedside and the sooner the better.

"Bob, I couldn't ask you to leave your job and family for me. You're a great friend and I appreciate the offer, but this is too much to ask."

"You're right, we are good friends and that's why I want to do this. Maggie would insist that I go with you. And besides, I haven't taken any time off in a long time. It's about time I had a few days off."

"I need to get to her as soon as I can, Bob. I think flying would be the fastest way to go. The Suburban is there in Tallahassee. So, I can bring Edna back home in it when she's released from the hospital. And, I don't want any argument—I'm going to pay for your airfare and other expenses."

"Okay, then it's settled. You get your things together, and I'll go home and make the plane reservations. I'll try to get a flight out of the local airport by seven o'clock. Maggie can drop us off. Will that be okay with you?"

"That sounds good. I can't thank you enough for what you're doing. Let me get my credit card information for you to pay for the plane tickets." Grady placed the ball of fur to the side of the chair so that he could stand. Chatty came out of her ball just long enough to reposition herself into another ball.

"Don't worry about the credit card now, Grady. We'll settle up later. Try to get some rest tonight; you may not get much once you're at the hospital. So, do you think you can be ready in the morning by five o'clock?" Bob asked, as he walked to the front door to leave.

"I'll be ready. Thanks again, Bob."

Bob took a few steps down the front sidewalk. He then turned back and said, "Don't worry about the animals; I'll have Dixie feed them."

Grady watched Bob walk toward his home across the street. He felt blessed to have such a wonderful friend. He turned back inside his own house, and then locked the door behind him. The house suddenly felt empty, and he felt so alone. Remembering his promise to call Linda, he picked up the phone and dialed her number.

CHAPTER TWENTY-ONE

B en had driven them through the drive'em thru and everyone had eaten their fill of burgers, fries, cokes and shakes on their way out of town. After the boys finished their food, they were eager for Gene to turn the flashing lights and siren on. They were far enough out of town and Gene was sure the sound of the siren wouldn't disturb anyone, so he had turned them on briefly to please them. Both children now lay hard and fast asleep across his lap.

Jenny still needed to know what she was getting herself into. And, while things were quiet, she thought it would be a good time to ask Mrs. Brewer some questions. Up to this point, the conversation between them had consisted of small talk.

"Mrs. Brewer, do you mind if I ask you something?"

"Of course not, dear. What is it?"

"I haven't had a chance to ask where we're going. I know we're going to your place, but I don't know where that is."

"Oh, I'm so sorry, Jenny. How rude of me. I don't know what I was thinking. It never occurred to me that you didn't know where I lived. I guess you might say, I wasn't thinking. Can you please forgive me? It has been a very bad day for me. I'm so tired."

"I know this has been hard for you, Mrs. Brewer. You've been through a lot and I don't mean to cause any more stress for you. I just thought I should know where I'll be for the next few days."

"Yes, you're right, dear. You should know where you're going to be. I'm embarrassed that I didn't think to tell you before now." She reached over and gave Jenny's hand a little pat. "And, don't think for one moment that you're causing me any stress. You've been nothing but a comfort to me. I live in a remote area about forty-five minutes from Tallahassee. The reason we were in Tallahassee was because my husband and I have season tickets for the football games. Our plans were to eat at the Pickle Barrel before the game, and then to do our errands while we were in the city. As you already know, those plans didn't work out." Fresh tears began to pool up in her eyes.

"I'm sorry. I didn't mean to remind you of all that," Jenny said. "Is this a bad time to talk about this?"

"No...no, Jenny. I didn't mean to get all misty eyed on you. I just got carried away remembering everything. You go ahead and ask your questions. I don't mind, really."

"Well, alright. When will I be able to get my belongings from the apartment? I can call my landlady in the morning to let her know where I am. But, I'll need my things from there. I don't even have a change of clothes or anything to sleep in tonight."

"Don't worry about all that right now. We'll get you settled in, and then you can get your things from your apartment. I'm sure I can find something for you to sleep in tonight. It shouldn't be too much longer before we arrive."

Jenny felt more at ease after her talk with Mrs. Brewer. Away from the city lights, it was pitch-black, and she couldn't see a thing outside the windows of the car. Jenny had been born and raised in Tallahassee and had never had an opportunity to travel much farther than the city limits. And with no automobile, time, or money, her chances of seeing the world outside of Tallahassee were nearly nonexistent. The route she was now traveling was as far as she had ever been from home. Gazing out the window beside her, she thought about her mother. She hadn't seen or heard from her in several years, and wondered if her mother was traveling around the country seeing and doing the things she had always longed to do.

The car began to slow down. Jenny turned her attention toward the front window in hopes of seeing where they were going, watching carefully as the gleaming headlights illuminated the highway. Ben pulled off the interstate onto a two lane paved road. Mrs. Brewer had dozed off and the turn had awakened her.

"Oh, we're almost home," Mrs. Brewer said while sitting straight up and looking around. "I must have fallen asleep. I'm sorry, Jenny. I didn't mean to leave you sitting by yourself."

"That's alright. I was just relaxing and looking out the window." She saw that Mrs. Brewer had instantly gone back to sleep.

Jenny noticed there was very little conversation between Ben and Gene after the children had fallen asleep. And at one point, she thought she had seen Gene nodding off. She really couldn't blame him. After all, it had been a long, stressful day for everyone. If she weren't feeling so apprehensive about her immediate future, she could've fallen across the seat and gone hard and fast asleep herself.

After traveling on the two lane road for a few minutes, Jenny noticed a white rail fence lining both sides of the road. The bright white fence could be seen through the black of night, and it seemed to stretch out for miles. She longed for daylight so that she could see the land it enclosed. As they continued to travel the countryside, Jenny's imagination ran wild, picturing fields of wheat surrounding a farmhouse shaded by majestic live oak trees, and horses running through lush green grass while cattle grazed in the distance. Ben slowed the car down, made a left turn, which brought her back to reality. He drove a short distance, and then pulled up to a black box in front of a large wrought iron gate and rolled the window down. "Gene, what's the code?" he whispered to keep from disturbing the children. Gene whispered the code to Ben and he punched the numbers into the box.

Jenny admired the beauty of the wrought iron gate and the lush vegetation in the landscaped entry which lay before them. There were colored lights amongst the greenery and spotlights illuminated the tall palm trees. High above the arched gate was a lighted sign that read "Lucky Boy Stud Farm".

Mr. Brewer must have worked on the farm, Jenny thought. Maybe he was a horse breeder or something. It could be that Gene's family had worked here for many years and this would always be home to them. They probably live in a beautiful cottage surrounded by lush pastures out of sight of the main house. I can see his family in a place like that. Gene was probably born on this farm…how fortunate he was to grow up with all this around him.

The car pulled through the gate. Jenny's curiosity kept her eyes glued to the front windshield where she would have full view of what was coming. The paved road was lined on both sides with large, moss-draped oak trees which gave the illusion of driving through a tunnel. They drove slowly through the tunnel of trees for some time, but she couldn't see any signs of a residence. Later, as they rounded a gentle bend in the road, she saw the most beautiful sight of her life. The home, looking like an English castle, was surrounded by spotlights which illuminated trees, walls, fountains and statues. Small path lights lined walkways through lush tropical gardens near the house.

As Ben drove toward the back of the house, Jenny thought they were going to Mrs. Brewer's home, which she supposed, was located a distance from the back of the main home. They passed by a white pergola with grapevines draped over the top. In this area there were more lush gardens with lighted pathways that led to a large outdoor swimming pool. In front of her, she could see a two-story English tutor style home. It was a short distance from the main house. She assumed this was where Mrs. Brewer lived. Ben passed up the tutor home and pulled under a covered entry at the back of the main house. Jenny sat speechless. Her eyes were drawn to a beautiful covered walkway lined with tall white marble planters draped in greenery and red geraniums. A decorative curved wrought iron lamp gracefully spotlighted each planter. The dark gray flagstone pathway made the white marble planters stand out under the covered entry. Aromatic smells of fresh flowers permeated the crisp night air.

"Welcome to our home, Jenny dear," Mrs. Brewer said when Ben stopped the car.

"This is where you live?" Jenny said with a shaky voice. She suddenly felt out of place. She had never seen anything like this and couldn't imagine actually spending the night in such a grand place.

"Yes, Jenny. This is home. Now come on inside. I'll show you to your room and you can take a nice hot bath and relax a little. I'm sure you'll sleep well tonight after what you've been through today. Gene will see to the children. Won't you, son?"

Gene and Ben already had a child each in their arms and were exiting the car.

"Mother," he whispered. "Can you get out of the car without my help?"

"I can help her," Jenny answered.

Jenny's tall slender body towered over Mrs. Brewer's small frame as she helped her along—yet she felt so small and insignificant standing next to her. Jenny assisted the older woman down the walkway and through the heavy double doors, which had been propped open for them. Once they were inside, she released her hold on Mrs. Brewer then turned to close the doors.

"Thank you so much for your help, Jenny. I'm sorry the staff has already gone to bed. During all the turmoil we experienced today, we forgot to call and let them know about my dear husband's death. I'm sure we can get through the night without their help though. Come with me and I'll show you to your room."

Jenny was overwhelmed by the beauty of the home. This back area had a dark cherry wood spiral staircase which led to the upper floors. The staircase had to be at least twelve feet wide. She could see long stained glass windows at the top of the second floor landing. She wondered what the front entrance must look like. Jenny reasoned that the bedrooms were upstairs and started toward the staircase.

"Let's go this way, Jenny," Mrs. Brewer said, as she reached for Jenny's hand and moved in a different direction.

Jenny joined hands with the older lady and allowed her to guide her the short distance down the hallway to a double-door elevator. She was still looking around the area when the elevator doors opened. Mrs. Brewer stepped inside and pulled Jenny in with her. Jenny saw her push the button for the third floor. *They have an elevator. I've never been in a home with an elevator.*

"The stairs have gotten to be too much for me anymore. So, I have to use the elevator pretty much all the time now," said Mrs. Brewer. "That's why we came to the back entrance—it's closer to the elevator. You know, there was a time when I could run up and down every set of stairs in this whole building. Those were the days...what memories. Today, we actually use three floors of the home. The fourth floor and attic are livable, but we moved all furnishings from there after Gene grew up and went to police training. When he was a little boy, he had a lot of friends. They spent many hours up there playing. We left the playroom as it was, with hopes of having grandchildren who could play there someday. Maybe when the boys get settled, you can spend some time playing with them there."

The elevator stopped and the doors opened. "Here we are dear," said Mrs. Brewer.

Jenny stepped into a brightly lit lobby. The wall facing her had a large display of antique swords that crisscrossed to form a pattern. This gave her the feeling of walking through an English castle. She hadn't yet recovered her voice from the things she had seen downstairs. Now, she was even more amazed by the beautiful wallpaper, tapestries hanging high on the walls, majestic marble statues placed just right, antique oriental carpets scattered up and down the corridor, and lush floral arrangements sitting on beautifully carved wooden tables. A wide corridor branched off the hallway where she was now walking and exhibited the same elegant décor. The beauty was more than she could've ever imagined seeing in her lifetime.

Jenny was so mesmerized she hardly felt herself moving down the hallway. She saw Gene and Ben with the children in their arms entering a room a few doors down.

"Here we are, dear. This is your room," said Mrs. Brewer, as she stopped and let go of Jenny's hand in front of a set of double doors. She opened the doors, exposing the most elegant bedroom Jenny had ever seen.

Jenny stood motionless. Her jaw dropped.

Mrs. Brewer stepped inside the doorway and when she saw Jenny wasn't moving, she reached out and took her hand to guide her along. Then she looked up and saw tears rolling down her cheeks. "What's the matter, Jenny?" she asked with concern. "Are you alright dear?"

Jenny was overwhelmed and felt so out of place standing there in the beautiful bedroom. She found it difficult to find the correct words to express her feelings to Mrs. Brewer.

Mrs. Brewer sensed Jenny's unease and saw her struggling to speak. "Come and sit down Jenny. Let's talk." Mrs. Brewer guided Jenny to a settee inside the adjoining parlor and they sat side by side, still holding hands. She gave Jenny a moment to settle in, and then she asked, "What's wrong, Jenny?"

Jenny only held her head low and said nothing while teardrops fell to her lap,

"I want you to know you mean a lot to me. Please feel free to talk to me about anything. I want you to be happy and comfortable here. Please, Jenny, tell me what's bothering you," said, Mrs. Brewer.

Jenny fell into the arms of the older lady and wept until she could weep no more.

Mrs. Brewer had an idea what was bothering Jenny, because she herself had been faced with these same feelings when she first came here with her new husband many years ago. It had taken her some time to get over her insecurities and adjust to the wealthy lifestyle she had married into. She realized she had only met Jenny a few hours ago, but she felt she knew her spirit well enough, and she too would adjust. "You don't have to talk now, if you don't feel like it. Let me draw your bath and get a gown for you. We can talk when you're ready."

Jenny sat up and wiped the tears from her face with her Pickle Barrel apron. "It's nothing really, Mrs. Brewer. You're wonderful. Your home is like nothing I've ever seen. I feel so out of place here. I have nothing. I'm nobody. You don't need someone like me around here," she choked, as tears began to flow again.

"Oh, Jenny, you're so wrong. I do want you here. You shouldn't feel like you are nobody. You don't realize it, but you're a very special person. What you did today to assist those people at the Pickle Barrel was commendable. If you hadn't calmed them down, there might have been a riot and more people could've been killed. Jenny, dear, I don't want you to feel out of place here. I haven't always lived like this. I was very fortunate to have married a man I loved deeply, who just happened to be well-off. Having wealth wasn't always the case for me. I came from an honest, hard-working family. This is just a nice house, Jenny, with nice things. But, nice homes, land, and possessions are nothing, if you don't have peace in your heart. Being comfortable with who you are brings that peace to your heart. You just haven't been given the opportunity to find out who you really are. I can see the goodness in you, Jenny. Great things are waiting out there for you. Some day this peace will come to you. I know it will. Now come; let's get you settled for the night."

Jenny put her insecure feelings aside. She followed her new friend into the elegant bathroom and drew herself a bath in the oversized porcelain claw foot tub. She was tired and looked forward to relaxing in the luxurious hot bath. She hadn't realized it, but she still held the bloodstained Pickle Barrel apron in her hand.

"Jenny, go ahead and get your bath," said Mrs. Brewer, as she turned to leave the room. I'll get you a gown and leave it on the bench outside the bathroom door."

Jenny dropped the apron to the floor, dashed across the room where Mrs. Brewer was, placed her arms around her fragile body, and said, "Thank you so much for your kindness and understanding."

While Jenny soaked in the hot bath, she couldn't stop thinking about the events of the day. As horrible as things were, something good had come out of it—Mrs. Brewer and Gene. She appreciated Mrs. Brewer taking the time to comfort her and making her feel wanted and welcomed—especially, since her husband had just passed away in her arms. A sense of guilt crept over her. *I should have been comforting her.*

Jenny removed a large fluffy bath towel from the towel rack and patted herself dry. Then she wrapped the towel around her body and opened the bathroom door to retrieve the gown that had been left on the bench for her. She put the gown on and watched as the silky fabric flowed down and around the curves of her body and pooled up at her feet. She was surprised at how well it fit her. The silk champagne colored gown had delicate antique lace around the low-cut neckline and around the slinky hemline, which added a regal look to the graceful garment. It was beautiful. Jenny wasn't sure she complemented the gown, but it felt good against her body. She felt pretty wearing it. She hung the bath towel across the drying rack, and then took a hair turban from the shelf and wrapped her wet head. She thought of the children and wondered if Ben and Gene had gotten them settled into bed. After putting on the matching robe to the gown she wore, she walked down to the room where she had seen the men take the children.

Jenny eased their door open, and saw the boys hard and fast asleep wrapped in each others arms in the middle of a king-sized bed. Tears began to pool in her eyes, as she stared at their small, helpless bodies. She wondered what had happened to their parents. *Please, Dear God, let them find the parents to these children alive.* Rossi began to make small jerking motions and whimpered. Jenny wanted to comfort them and climbed in bed beside them. She pulled the boys into her arms and slept.

When she awakened the next morning, the boys weren't in the bed with her. Surely, they couldn't have gotten out of this big bed by themselves, she thought. *I must have been really out of it not to have heard them waking up and then leaving.*

Her hair was dry now under the turban. She knew it would be a job to untangle it. *I'll have to wet it again in order to get a comb through it,* she thought. She left the turban on and decided to check on the children before she tackled the issue of her hair.

Jenny saw the elegant home this morning with a different perspective. The talk she had had with Mrs. Brewer the night before changed the way she felt about things. All this still intimidated her, but she could handle it now. She remembered the way back to the elevator and took it to the main floor. When the elevator doors opened on the first floor, she caught the smell of breakfast. She followed the smell right into the kitchen where she found Mrs. Brewer sitting on a stool at the prep island, conversing with a middle-aged woman cooking at the stove. Jenny could see the woman had tears rolling down her cheeks. She figured the woman had just gotten the news about Mr. Brewer's death. The two women hadn't seen Jenny as she entered the kitchen and seemed startled when they noticed her standing nearby.

"I'm so sorry I startled you," said Jenny. "I hope I'm not interrupting anything?"

"Oh, no, you aren't interrupting anything. Please come and join us. I was just telling Mary Ann about what happened to us yesterday. By the way, this is Mary Ann. Mary Ann, this is Jenny. I told Mary Ann you would be staying with us to help with the children. Mary Ann is a longtime friend; she's like family to us. She is an excellent chef and has been preparing our meals since

Gene was what…nine, or maybe…ten. I don't remember, but a long time. So, if there's something special you'd like to eat, just let her know."

"I'm so glad to meet you, Mary Ann."

Wiping the tears from her eyes, Mary Ann laid the spatula down and came to the other side of the island where Jenny stood. She took Jenny's hands inside hers and gave her a kiss on the cheek. "I'm very pleased to meet you, Jenny. I've heard a lot of good things about you. I have made pancakes, eggs, bacon, fresh fruit, orange juice, and coffee. Are you hungry for any of that? If not, just tell me what you would like and I'll see that you get it."

"It all sounds delicious, and I'm really hungry. I can't believe I slept so late. Where are the boys?"

"Well, have a seat and I'll bring you a plate. Would you like a cup of coffee?"

"Yes, please."

The boys were awake when Gene checked on them earlier this morning. So, he got them up. You were sleeping soundly and he didn't want to disturb you. They're with him down at the stables tending to the horses. They've already eaten," Mrs. Brewer said. "So, have a good breakfast before we leave for church."

"*Church!* Oh, no…I can't go to church. I'm a mess." Jenny's hands flew around the turban on her head. "I haven't any decent clothes to wear. Mrs. Brewer, you have just lost your husband—don't you need to make funeral arrangements? Are you up to attending church today?"

"My dear, I can think of no better place to receive comfort than in the Lord's house with my brothers and sisters in Christ. My beloved husband would've wanted it this way. We made our funeral arrangements years ago—there isn't much to fuss with there. Don't worry about what to wear. Gene went shopping last night when he drove Ben back to the city."

"What about the children? They need clothing."

"That, also, has been taken care of. Gene bought church cloths as well as some casual clothing for them."

"How did he know our sizes? He never asked me for my size."

"He's pretty good about guessing sizes. Besides, he knows a few people in the boutique business. I'm sure they were a big help to him. Jenny, I wonder if you would mind calling me *Pauline*? You're going to be around for a while, and I think addressing me as Mrs. Brewer sounds a little too formal."

"I don't mind at all, if that's what you want. She placed her hand on the turban that covered her head and said, "Will I have time to eat and take care of this hair before church?"

"You have plenty of time. We'll just attend the church service today. It starts at eleven. So we need to leave by ten-thirty. Your new clothes are in your closet. I think you'll like what Gene has selected for you. You don't have to worry about dressing the boys—Gene can dress them."

After Jenny ate her breakfast she went back to her room to take care of the matted hair problem, and to get dressed for her first visit to church. She went straight to the bathroom shower to wet her head, not taking the time to check the closet to see what Gene had bought for her to wear. She knew she had to wear whatever it was, because Pauline was intent on her going to church. Besides, she had nothing else to wear.

Jenny finally got her hair styled to suit her. She then went to the closet to dress. The only thing hanging in the massive walk-in closet was a beautiful royal blue skirt with a matching jacket. She saw matching underwear, shoes, hand bag and jewelry lying on the bench inside the closet. Her heart began to race. She felt her face burning. *He bought underwear! I can't believe he bought my underwear!* She could tell they were expensive underwear. *Everything looks expensive.* For a long moment she stood nude inside the closet, as she wasn't sure how to act. In the end, she put on the garments which had been bought for her. When she was fully dressed, she admired herself in the full length mirror, and, for the first time in her life, she felt beautiful.

Jenny stepped outside her bedroom door and turned toward the boy's room. She saw Gene and the boys already dressed and walking in her direction. What a beautiful sight they were. Gene had on a dark gray suit with a blue shirt, which looked much like the color of the outfit he had bought for her to wear. He didn't wear a tie. The children were dressed in matching black suits with white long sleeve dress shirts. They wore black leather dress shoes. They looked like little men, and they both seemed relaxed and appeared happy.

Jenny smiled broadly as she walked up to them and said, "Well, well. What do we have here? Looks like I've run upon three handsome cowboys. Would you cowboys like to take a girl to church?"

The children displayed a big smile and put their hands up to their mouths and giggled. They had heard this kind of talk before.

"Well, what do you think, boys? This here is a mighty fine looking woman. You think we ought to snatch her up and take her with us to God's House?" The blue suit is perfect for her. She really is beautiful in it, Gene thought.

Still giggling, the children said nothing, but reached out and took Jenny's hands.

Jenny looked up into Gene's eyes and smiled.

He winked at her and said, "I guess we have the answer to that question. Let's be on our way then, partners."

The four of them held hands as they walked to the elevator.

Pauline was ready and waiting when they exited the elevator on the ground floor. "What a handsome bunch of folks you are," she said when she saw them.

"Jenny, would you wait here with Mother and the children while I bring the car around?" said Gene.

Moments later Gene drove up in a long midnight blue Lincoln. He came back inside and picked the children up in both arms and said, "I'll seat the children first and then come back for you two ladies."

"Are we going to ride in the police car again, Mr. Gene?" Rossi asked.

"Not this time, partner."

"Gene, I can help you with the boys," Jenny said.

"Thanks, Jenny. But I would rather you stay here with Mother. This won't take long."

Jenny noticed the tender loving care Gene gave his mother, as he later walked her to the car and helped her inside. He fastened the seat belt around her. Then he gave her a gentle kiss on the cheek. *This is like watching a romance novel unfold in front of me. Oh, how I would love to be a part of it,* she thought.

"There you go, Mother. You're all ready to go," he said before turning his attention to Jenny. She was standing beside the unopened back door of the car watching him. Gene caught her eye and reached in front of her to open the door. "You look beautiful, Jenny," he complimented.

"Thanks to you," she replied with a smiled. *Maybe I am a part of this unfolding novel after all.*

Jenny noticed the children were sitting in car seats as she settled in beside them. She wondered if Gene had also purchased them last night.

This was the first time for Jenny to see the ranch in the daylight. She marveled at the beautiful lush, green pastures as they drove through the tunnel of shaded oaks which meandered through the pasture land. She could see small homes and buildings resembling stables or barns at a distance. The weather was cool outside and horses with blankets across their backs could be seen grazing in the pastures. Jenny felt dazed, as if she were in a dream.

The children giggled as they pointed out the grazing horses.

"Danny, Rossi, I hear you went to the stables with Mr. Gene this morning to see the horses. Did you have fun?" Jenny asked.

"They were big, like giants," Rossi said excitedly.

"Yes, we saw two brown ones and one had big spots all over," Danny added. "Mr. Gene said they were boys and they are going to make baby horses."

Gene listened, as the boys talked about their experience at the stables. He couldn't help but smile.

Having the boys around brought back a lot of great memories for Pauline. She just sat back and enjoyed listening to the conversation.

"Did you touch the horses?" Jenny asked.

Rossi said, "Oh, yes. Mr. Gene let us touch the spotted horse. He said we could ride one sometime."

"Yes...maybe when we get back," said Danny.

"We can't do it today, Danny; Mr. Gene said we have things to do."

"Well, maybe we can ride the horse when mommy comes; she can ride with us."

Jenny's heart fell to her feet when she heard his comment. She glanced up front into the rearview mirror and saw the worried look on Gene's face as he looked back at her. Her mood had suddenly changed for the worse, but she felt she needed to present a positive appearance for the sake of the children.

"Tell Miss Jenny about the goat and ducks you saw in the barnyard," Gene said. He had seen the worried look on Jenny's face and wanted to cheer her up.

Danny couldn't wait to tell the story and began talking. "Oh! Mr. Gene gave us some corn and I was feeding the duck—she was eating out of my hand—a big goat came and ran her off and he took all the corn."

"Did the goat frighten you?" Jenny asked. She had never been around a live goat and wondered what it would be like to actually touch one.

"He kind of scared me a little. But, Mr. Gene wouldn't let him hurt me."

"How about you, Rossi—did you feed the goat?"

"He ate out of my hand and it felt funny. I thought he was going to bite me. I could feel his teeth and he had slobber all over his mouth. He got it all over my hands. Mr. Gene let us pet him. He felt scratchy."

Jenny looked into the rearview mirror again. And this time, she saw a smile on Gene's face. This was a great subject for the boys. They talked about horses and farm animals the rest of the way to church.

CHAPTER TWENTY-TWO

The Pickle Barrel investigation had gone on well into the early morning hours. Witnesses had given their statements. The dead had been sent to the morgue, evidence had been gathered, and automobile tags had been recorded. Cross-matching of automobiles was underway and would take a while longer to complete. Spectators began clearing away from the crime scene area around midnight and the media followed shortly thereafter. At two-thirty all official personnel went home, with the exception of two officers, who guarded the perimeter for the remainder of the night.

Larry was back at the precinct at nine the next morning. He and Captain Hall were going over the evidence collected the day before. The Captain laid down the paperwork he was holding in his hands, removed his glasses and said, "Let's walk around the corner to the café and get some pancakes. I haven't had a bite to eat since lunch yesterday and I'm starving. I just have to get out of here for a while."

"That sounds good to me," said Larry. "I haven't eaten since yesterday either."

Both men removed their suit jackets from the coat rack and exited the room.

"Dee, if you need me for anything, I'll be at the corner café having breakfast," Captain Hall said on his way out.

The change of pace and breakfast was just what the two men needed. They were ready to get back to work. "Let's see if we can piece this all together, Larry. Give me your assessment of what took place," Captain Hall said when they were settled back in his office.

"Judging from the evidence we've collected and my own gut feeling, I'd say this guy went off the deep end—and I don't think it was because he didn't like the food at the Pickle Barrel. Maybe he had something bigger planned and something got in his way. He was geared up to kill when his plan fell through and he took it out on these people. He probably knew the Pickle Barrel would be packed with people because of the big game in town. Apparently he didn't care about living, because he didn't try to conceal his identity by wearing a mask or any disguise. He knew he would be caught. And, judging from the high powered weapons he carried and the blocked exit doors, he planned to kill everyone there. Who knows, maybe he planned to turn the gun on himself—sort-of-like a suicide bomber. Only in this case, instead of blowing himself up and not having the thrill of seeing the mass of people die with him...he has the pleasure of watching them die before he kills himself. We may never know what drove him to do such a thing."

"I was thinking along those same lines myself. So, you think this was a random act, not premeditated?"

"More than likely it was. But, it would be interesting to find out exactly who this guy was and where he came from. There may be more to this than what we think."

"Let's find out everything we can about the man, Larry. There was a cell phone found in his pants pocket. Let's start there. I want every call he has ever made on it checked out. We got an address off his driver's license last night, and I sent someone over there to check it out. A little old couple has been living at that address for twenty-five years. All the other leads from the information he had on him also fell through. I figured all the identification was false, but we had to follow-up."

"Well, if he's connected to some kind of cell, I'm certain he communicated with his friends. His cell phone just might lead us to them. The judge has already given the court order for the phone company to turn over all his phone records. They should have them ready for us sometime this morning."

"Has his automobile been located yet? He must have driven himself. He was too heavily armed to take any type of public transportation to the Pickle Barrel. His car is probably in the parking lot or nearby."

"The automobiles are being cross-checked and should be completed sometime today. It's taking longer than usual, Captain, because of the number of people who were involved. Sorting through their personal belongings for identifications to match with an automobile and working with Department of Motor Vehicles is time consuming. Also, many people came from out of town and out of state for the ball game."

"Did you find any information on the shooter that indicated where he may have worked?"

"Nothing was found about his employment. But, there was something strange found in his pants pocket—a Pickle Barrel cash register receipt from where he had eaten there on Friday."

"Let's get a photo of him. Have someone locate the employees who were working at that time. Find out if he ate there often. Maybe someone will recognize him. They may know something about him—if he had an automobile. It could be that he lived close by the Pickle Barrel where he could walk back and forth."

Dee charged through the office door and approached the desk where the two men sat. "Here are the phone numbers you've been waiting for. I checked on the progress of the automobile cross-matching, and I'm told it should be completed sometime after lunch. Also, here are the lab results from the yellow purse and gun. Is there anything else you need before I leave for lunch— coffee or water, maybe?"

"Is it lunchtime already?" asked the Captain. "What happened to the morning? No, I wouldn't care for anything. What about you, Larry?"

"I'm good for now. But, thanks for asking"

Dee left the room and the men began to study the reports she had delivered. Captain Hall held the phone list up for Larry to see and stated, "This is strange—just look at this. There's only one page of calls in almost a year's service. Most people would have this many calls in a month."

"Maybe he was a recluse or something. Let's see how many different numbers there are on that list. He must have known somebody."

"Well, judging from this list, he didn't have a lot of friends. There appears to be only five numbers here and he made very few calls to them. Here, Larry, take this list and call off the numbers while I take some notes. Let's start with his last communication and work down. Did he talk with anyone Saturday before the shooting spree?"

"He didn't make any calls that day...no incoming calls."

"What about Friday?"

"It looks like he made three calls and received two. One of those calls he made was to Alabama, and he received one from Alabama."

"Give me that number. What about the Wednesday or Thursday before the shooting?"

"There were no other calls going or coming for the week before."

"Can you see if he called one number more frequently than the others?"

"Oh yes, he called one number quite often. Maybe he had a girl. He wasn't wearing a wedding band, so I figured he had a female friend."

"Let's start with that frequently used number; see who it belongs to, pay this person a visit, and ask a few questions," Larry said while turning his attention back to the report he had written the night before. "Captain, can you read off the shooter's billing address from the phone company for me, so that I can put it in my report?"

The Captain read the address for Larry, and then said "I need to get out of here for awhile. Why don't you and I take a little trip over there and see what kind of accommodations this guy had."

"Sure Captain, give me a minute to call the phone company to get the name and address for this number the shooter last called. It shouldn't take long."

While Larry was waiting on the phone for the information he needed from the phone company, Captain Hall studied the lab results on Edna's yellow purse and gun.

After a couple minutes with the phone company, Larry hung up. He began to compare the information he had just received with his notes. "Captain, look at this," he said. "The address for the cell phone number I just checked is the same as the shooter's billing address. It looks like he had a roommate."

"Let's get over there. Call for back-up, Larry. There's no telling what we'll find when we get there."

"You don't have to go, Captain. My men can take care of this."

"I know they can. But, I really need to escape this place for a little while. Seeing a little action will do me a great deal of good."

"Okay then, let's go. I'll call for backup from the car. What'd the lab find on the purse and gun?"

"They didn't find anything incriminating. I didn't think they would. This was just a little lady traveling alone with a gun permit and a gun in her purse that she had to use to kill a madman on a rampage. But, you know how it is…everything has to be checked out. I'm sure there'll be no charges brought against her. After all, if she hadn't taken him out, we would be cleaning up a lot more dead bodies."

"Have you heard how she's doing?"

"She was still unconscious when I talked with the doctor last night. He said she's in deep shock and didn't have any idea when she would come to."

They were about to exit the building when they heard Dee shouting for them to wait as she ran toward them. They stopped and waited for her. By the time she got there, she was out of breath. She took a moment to rest, and then she said, "They found his car. It was parked behind the building next door to the Pickle Barrel. It was hidden from view by some tall bushes. DMV matched the tag number with the name on his driver's license and registration. The car wasn't locked, and when they searched the trunk they found a backpack with a bomb inside it. The bomb squad is there now. They said there doesn't appear to be any immediate danger because the timer wasn't set. They're bringing it in. Oh! I almost forgot. They also found what looks like a janitor's uniform with his name on it. Apparently he worked at the State Capitol."

"That's great news," said Captain Hall. "Send someone to the Capitol to check him out. Larry and I are following up on the address from his phone records; so, I'll be out of the office for a while. Also, Dee, call the judge right away and get a search warrant for this address." He quickly jotted down the address. "We'll pick up the warrant at his chambers on our way over there. We might as well be legal while we're having a look."

CHAPTER TWENTY-THREE

Bob rang Grady's doorbell at five AM Sunday morning. He had made all the flight arrangements the night before. Lodging accommodations had been arranged for them in Tallahassee. He had also informed Dixie, their neighbor and Edna's close friend, about what had happened to Edna and the reason for their rush trip to Tallahassee. She was more than willing to feed the ducks, the cat, and look after Grady's place while he was away.

Grady answered the door holding his small piece of luggage in one hand. "Good morning, Bob," he said. "I feel awful. Are you sure I'm not asking too much of you? I'm sure I can make it to Tallahassee by myself if you have more pressing issues to take care of."

"It's no trouble at all, Grady. I'm glad to be here for you. Everything has been arranged, and Maggie is waiting in the car to take us to the airport."

"Did you get in touch with Dixie about feeding the ducks and Chatty; what about the mail? I forgot to stop the mail."

"I have taken care of all that. You don't have anything to worry about while you're away. What's important now is for you to go and take care of Edna."

"I feel so lost—like I'm forgetting something," Grady said while locking the front door.

"The flight is only forty-five minutes; you'll be there soon. I'm sure you'll feel better once you see Edna. Let me help you with your bag, Grady."

The flight was quick, but it felt like a lifetime to Grady. Upon their arrival, an unmarked police car was waiting to take them to the hospital.

Bob had made their pickup arrangements and lodging accommodations the previous evening. After calming Grady as much as he could, he had returned home and called Captain Hall back. The Captain filled him in on Edna's involvement with the shooting at the Pickle Barrel. He felt what she had done was heroic and he wanted to help her out. With the help of a friend, Captain Hall had made lodging arrangements for Bob and Grady to stay as long as they wanted. Bob wouldn't tell Grady about Edna's involvement in the shooting. It was a police matter. He would let Captain Hall give him that information.

Grady sat alone in the back seat of the patrol car, and Bob could see he was in deep thought. *I'm sure he is wondering what he will find when he finally gets to see Edna.* Bob was also worried about Edna and if she would be responsive to Grady when he tried to communicate with her.

By nine AM they were at the hospital information desk inquiring about Edna's location.

The middle aged, strictly business desk clerk asked in a firm voice, "Are you family?"

"I'm her husband, and this is Police Chief Bob Rossman."

"Only immediate family members are allowed to see her. Chief Rossman, you'll have to get special clearance from Captain Hall before you are allowed to see her."

"That's alright. Do you mind if I use your phone to call him?" Bob asked.

"Sure, I have his number right here."

The desk clerk dialed the Captain's number and handed the receiver to Bob. The Captain gave permission for Bob to visit Edna, and both men were given a special pass on a chain. They placed the passes around their necks, walked to the elevators, and pressed the button for the third floor where Edna's room was located.

As they arrived at Edna's room, they saw a police officer standing guard near the doorway. Bob wasn't surprised to see the officer, but he could tell Grady was taken aback. As they started into the room the officer quickly intervened. He stepped in front of Grady and requested to see his pass and some identification. Bob presented his badge and pass to the officer and told him Captain Hall had approved his visit. He pointed at Grady and said, "This is Edna's husband." The officer's professional demeanor instantly changed to one of pleasure.

"I'm pleased to meet you, sir," he said, as he reached to shake Grady's hand. "You have a very brave wife. If there's anything I can do for you, I'll be outside the door. Does the doctor know you have arrived? He's been waiting to speak with you?"

Grady appeared puzzled by the guard's presence and the sudden change in demeanor, but seemed more intent on reaching Edna's bedside. He would probably have many questions later. As he shook the policeman's hand he replied, "It's good to meet you, as well. We came straight up to the room after we picked up our passes. I'm sure the doctor doesn't know I'm here."

"Well, don't worry about it. You go on in to see her. I'll let the doctor know you have arrived."

It appeared they were entering a suite of rooms. There was a separate side room near the entrance which had a sleeper sofa and two overstuffed chairs. Side tables sat beside the sofa and chairs. They saw a small counter with a sink, mini refrigerator, and coffee maker. Two cabinets hung on the wall above the counter.

In one corner of the room a flat screen TV rested inside a wood carved armoire. Colorful paintings hung on the warm beige walls throughout the area. Live plants filled the space and made it feel warm and homey. Edna's room, which had a separate entrance, was located down a short corridor. Floor to ceiling exterior windows covered one wall and natural light flooded the space. It looked like a setup for long-term visiting guests. Grady hoped that wasn't going to be the case for him.

Bob stopped Grady at the entrance to the side room. He said he would wait there while Grady went in to see Edna.

Grady continued the walk down the corridor toward Edna's room. He eased the door open and saw her lying in a large bed. She looked so small and helpless lying there with the IV fluids hooked up to her. He was powerless to help her.

As he approached her bedside, tears flooded his face. With shaking hands he picked up Edna's hand without the IV and brought it up to his lips. He kissed it gently. When he settled down from crying and was able to speak, he said, "Swart, are you awake? (*Swart was Edna's pet name Grady had borrowed from his grandfather. His grandfather had a speech impediment, and when he called his grandmother sweetheart, it came out sounding like "Swart".*) I'm here to take you home." Edna didn't respond to his words, or to his touch; which troubled him greatly. In all the years he had known her, he had never seen her like this. She had always been lively, in control, and had always responded to his touch. He released her hand and gently touched her shoulder in an effort to wake her.

"Swart, this is Grady. Wake up, Swart; it's time to go home." Still, there was no response from her. Grady became more frightened. He pulled her lifeless body, the love of his life, into his arms. Then he broke down and wept into the shoulder length hair that was so familiar to him.

Bob and the doctor approached the bedside where Grady sat holding Edna in his arms. He had cried himself out and was savoring every moment of her warm, still body being next to him.

"Grady, the doctor is here to see you," Bob said softly while leaning in close to him.

Grady lovingly eased Edna's unresponsive body back onto the pillow. Then he turned to speak with the doctor.

"I'm Dr. Peters. It's a pleasure to meet you, Grady. I'm so sorry we have to meet under these conditions."

"I'm pleased to meet you, Dr. Peters. How is she doing? What has happened to her?"

"Let's go sit in the other room. We can talk better there. Do you mind if Bob joins us?"

"I don't mind at all; he's more than welcome."

Bob had made a pot of coffee earlier, and before they sat down to talk he offered the two men a cup. While they drank their coffee, Dr. Peters filled them in on Edna's condition when she arrived at the hospital.

"It appears the events which took place at the Pickle Barrel and her involvement were more than her mind could comprehend. She's in deep shock," said the doctor.

"What do you mean by *her involvement?*" Grady shouted. "She didn't have anything to do with the shooting at the Pickle Barrel. She's scared to death of guns; I even had a hard time getting her to attend a gun permit class. She couldn't have possibly been involved with that awful massacre."

"Grady, I'm so sorry. I thought someone had already told you what she did. If it hadn't been for Edna, perhaps everyone in the Pickle Barrel would have been killed that day."

"What are you saying; Edna stopped this madman that was on a rampage? How could she stop such a crazy man?"

"That's exactly what I'm saying. Edna shot and killed the man with her little gun."

Dr. Peters became concerned when Grady fell silent and his face suddenly turned white. "Are you alright, Grady?" he asked.

"Just give him a moment to absorb all this," Bob suggested to the doctor.

"Bob, I'm really concerned about him. Are you going to be around to keep him company for a while?"

"I can be, if he needs me."

"It wouldn't hurt for a day or so, if you can work it out."

"That's why the police are outside her door, isn't it?" Grady said with a trembling voice.

"Are they going to arrest her? What's going to happen to her when she wakes up?"

Grady, this is just normal procedure," Bob said. "The officer is there for Edna's protection until things are cleared up. I'm sure she'll have to give her statement about what happened. But, I don't believe they'll arrest her. She saved a lot of lives. It was self defense. I don't think you have to worry about that."

"My poor, sweet Edna—no wonder she's in shock. She couldn't hurt a fly. Now she has killed someone. That had to have been very traumatic for her. She hates guns, you know. We just bought the Beretta right before she left for her trip to Mississippi; she only shot it once at the range. It must have been awfully frightening for her to load that little gun and fire it at another person. I wish now that I had gone on this trip with her. Maybe we would've gone somewhere else to eat and she wouldn't be here now."

"Grady, you can't think that way. None of this is your fault, or hers. She was in the wrong place at the right time. A lot of people have Edna and that little Beretta to thank for their lives. What's done is done. You have to be here for her now. She's going to need your positive support when she wakes up," Bob said.

"That's right," said Dr. Peters. "She'll need you more than ever when she awakens. You need to keep yourself calm and in control for her sake.

"Dr. Peters, do you have any idea when she'll wake up?"

"I know you want answers from me, Grady, but in cases like this, we just don't know. It could be any moment or days. But, when she does wake up, you need to be at her bedside, because she won't know where she is. And seeing a familiar face will help. We placed her in this suite so that you could be close to her. The sofa pulls out into a bed. You can use the bathroom facilities in Edna's room."

"Where will Bob stay?" asked Grady.

"Oh, don't worry about me. I have somewhere to stay. You stay here with Edna. I have some business to take care of in this area while I'm here. I'll be in and out to check on you." He really didn't have any business in the area, but he didn't want Grady to worry about him.

〰〰

"There's one more thing I need to tell you, Grady," Dr. Peters said. "Edna will most likely be in a very delicate state of mind when she wakes up. She probably won't remember anything about the incident. She may not even remember being at the Pickle Barrel. You see, our brains have a way of shutting out the things we have trouble accepting. What a person can accept and not accept is unique to each person. No one knows how much, or even if, tragedies like this will affect a person's ability to comprehend and live with such an experience. Edna's case has an added tragedy because of her involvement in killing another person. This goes against all she has ever been taught or believed in."

"Doc, what are you trying to tell me? Are you saying Edna may not wake up, or she may not be all there when she awakens?"

"No, I'm not saying that, Grady. I just want you to know, she may not be the same after this. Let's hope she'll wake up soon and remember without causing her further stress. What we don't want is for her to wake up and not remember, and then have some news broadcast jog her memory of her involvement. She may not be able to cope a second time—she could go into shock for a much longer period of time. It could be, she may not recover from a second shock. I'm not saying this will happen. We just have to wait and see what happens."

"Well, what am I expected to do? Keep her locked up from the rest of the world. She's very involved with the community and has a lot of friends she talks to; keeping her away from them won't be easy."

"Let's see what she remembers first. If she remembers nothing of the shooting, then I suggest, until things settle down, keeping her away from all media—that means radio, TV, newspapers. Also, it will be necessary to keep her away from anyone who might tell her of the tragedy. So far, the police have kept her involvement out of the spotlight. But eventually, the news media will find out and it'll become more difficult to hide the truth from her. Hopefully, she'll recall what happened on her own and not through some form of media."

"When do you think she'll be able to travel back home?"

"It depends on when she wakes up. I'm sure Captain Hall wants to question her. He has been calling about her condition ever since she arrived. I have made him aware of her situation and he has agreed not to say anything that might cause her further harm. I see no physical reason why she can't leave when the Captain finishes his questioning, as long as she feels up to it."

"What if she starts asking questions about why she's in the hospital?"

"Tell her the truth…she passed out and is here to find out why. Bob, I understand you're neighbors. Do you think you could inform your neighborhood of the situation? Will that be alright with you, Grady?"

"Yes, that's o.k. with me."

"I see no problem informing the neighbors. I'll call Maggie today and she can get started on it," Bob said.

"Well, I have to see other patients. Remember Grady, I want to know the moment she wakes up. Keep the television off any type of news; she may hear it, even if it's in the other room."

"But, Doctor Peters, she's unconscious. Do you think she can hear what I say, or hear a TV?"

"I have talked with people who have awakened after being unconscious. They were able to repeat and describe what happened in their range of hearing while they were unconscious. I can't say firsthand, but let's don't take any chances and let her hear any bad news."

The doctor left the room to tend to other patients. Bob and Grady sat in silence for a moment. Then Bob said, "Will you be o.k. here alone while I take care of some business?" He felt Grady needed some time alone to absorb all this information and he also wanted to check on his accommodations for the night.

"Sure, Bob, I'll be fine. Go ahead and do what you need to do. I'll go back and sit with Edna for a while. She might wake up and need me. I can't thank you enough for being here for me."

"I'm happy to help. I'll bring you some lunch from the cafeteria before I leave. And, how does Chinese sound for dinner?"

"That sounds great."

When Bob returned a short while later, he found Grady curled up beside Edna with his arm around her. He was hard and fast asleep. Bob placed the tray of food on the side table and left them alone.

CHAPTER TWENTY-FOUR

Although Edna was unconscious, her mind wandered in and out. Of course, she was not aware this was happening to her. When she was out of it, her mind was completely turned off. She had no sense of smell, touch, feel, sight, hearing, and she could recall nothing. Also, she couldn't tell if it were day or night...time had no meaning to her. From the time she shot the man and throughout the night and into the next morning, Edna's mind had been in a shutdown mode.

When Edna's mind was in the active state, she could recall events in her life going back as far as her childhood. She could actually hear, smell, and feel things against her skin. But, even during this active state, she couldn't speak or make any movements. Her mind would skip through moments of time. One moment she would be reliving her childhood, and a moment later, she would be on a date with Grady, or on to other past life experiences. This active state didn't occur often and it was brief. Now in the active state, events of Edna's past life flash through her mind.

"Mama, when will my sack be ready?" Edna asked her mother, as she placed a small handful of cotton she had just picked into the ten foot long cotton sack her mother dragged behind her. Edna had been running back and forth with her little hands full of cotton since daybreak. It was almost time for her mother to leave the field to cook

lunch for the family. Edna would be joining her and was looking forward to a break out of the hot Mississippi sun.

"Edna, you have to stop asking me that all the time. I told you, all the flour has to be used up first, and then the fabric has to be washed and sewn."

"Well, when will all the flour be used up? Can you make a big pan of biscuits for lunch and supper and use it all up?"

"I guess I can do that. Now come here. Take Dickey to the end of the row and wait there with the babies. I need to pack the cotton down in my sack. I'll finish out this row, and then we'll go make lunch."

Edna picked her two year old brother up from where he had been sleeping on the end of her mother's long cotton sack. He was still half asleep and laid his head against her small shoulder. She began to walk toward the end of the row. Still wanting a more definite answer to her question, she turned back to face her mother.

"Will the flour sack be empty if you make two big pans of biscuits for lunch and supper?"

"Now Edna, I won't tell you again to stop asking about that sack! I'll see how much flour is left in the sack at lunch. If there isn't much, then I'll make a large pan of biscuits for lunch and supper. I can wash the fabric out tonight and let it dry overnight. Since tomorrow is Saturday and we have the afternoon off from the fields, maybe I'll have time to sew the strap on. Now, stop bothering me about that sack and go wait for me at the end of the row."

Edna was overjoyed with the thought of finally getting her own cotton sack. She had been waiting what seemed like forever for this moment. Her older sisters Louise and Marie had gotten their sacks first. Her mother said it was because they were older and could pick more cotton.

"I bet when I get my sack, I can fill it all the way to the top and beat them," she said to Dickey, as she quickly walked across the hot soil as fast as her little five year old bare feet would carry them. She placed Dickey beside the box where the babies lay, and then peeked through the netting at the sleeping two day old boy and girl twins. It *felt strange to her having two new babies in the family. Grateful to be out of the hot sun, she sat under the large cluster of oak trees and watched her mother shake the cotton to the bottom of the long canvas cotton sack.*

She could see her older sisters and brothers picking in the distance. Her oldest brother, James, stood, removed his straw hat, and wiped the sweat from his brow with his bare hand. After glancing up at the sky, he stretched his tall, lanky body, put his hat back on his head, packed the cotton to the bottom of his sack, and then bent over and went back to work. His wife, Fanny, had already left the field to cook lunch at their place next door. She also had to take care of their new baby who arrived not long before her little brother and sister came to live with them. Fanny always had to leave the field before her mother did because she didn't have anyone to help her with her chores. So it took her longer to get things done.

Her daddy was picking the row next to her mother and wasn't far behind her. Ruth, her younger three year old sister, was asleep on his sack. Edna knew Ruth would be joining them when they left to go home for lunch. She would pull Dickey and Ruth from the field in the homemade wooden wagon, and then take care of the four younger ones while her mother made lunch. Everyone else would keep on working. When the meal was ready, Edna ran back to the field to get them.

After lunch, pallets were spread on the floor and everyone napped for an hour. They would return to the cotton fields after their nap and work until nightfall. Just as she had for lunch, her mother would leave the field early, about an hour before dark, to prepare their supper.

Edna was back in the cotton fields the next morning, as she was every morning, except on Sunday's. This was Saturday, and she was excited about the family having a half day off work. Her mother had emptied the flour sack and washed it the night before; she saw it hanging on the line to dry that morning while on her way to the field. Dickey was crawling several feet in front of their mother now and Edna was trying to show him how to pick cotton. "See, Dickey, you can do it," she said. Edna took his little hand in hers, and then placed it on a fluffy white ball of cotton and pulled it from the stalk. She held Dickey's tiny hand with the cotton into the air and shouted, "Look, Mama, I knew he could do it. You're a big boy now, Dickey. We will have to tell everyone you picked cotton. Let's go put it in Mama's sack." She walked him toward her mother and made a game out of placing his little wad of cotton in the sack. Dickey giggled and they laughed with him. Edna and Dickey played the cotton picking game pretty much the whole morning. It was nearly time for lunch, and she had tried hard all morning not to mention her cotton sack to her mother. The excitement was too much for her. She just had to say something.

"Mama, can you make my cotton sack for me today?"

Her mother was bent over at the waist while both hands swiftly picked at two rows of cotton. She picked as if her life depended on every ounce of it being placed in the sack. Her swift movements did not change as she answered Edna's question.

"Well, let me see. After lunch, I need to wash clothes and hang them out to dry—the floors will have to be scrubbed—the outhouse needs to be bleached down—the babies need a good bath—and I need some things from town. If you can help your big sisters, and we get all the chores done, I will work on it tonight. The boys can tend to the livestock, but I want you to collect the eggs from the hen house—the boys always break the eggs.

"Oh goodie, goodie, we can do it. I know we can get it all done," Edna said with excitement.

The children worked hard to complete the chores that were given them, but at the end of the day her mother was too tired to work on her cotton sack. Her brothers and sisters knew how important the little sack was to Edna and expressed their disappointment to her before they laid their tired bodies down that night to rest. They remembered their excitement at her age when it was time for them to receive their first cotton sack. The sack was made especially for them, and it made them feel special…almost like a grown-up.

Everyone in the family knew the value of the fabric the sack was made of. Nearly all the clothes they wore had been handmade from the endless array of colors and patterns of the precious fabric, which once held fifty pounds of flour. There were no commercially made cotton sacks for small children. So, each child at the age of five years old was given a flour sack to be used for their cotton sack. They valued their sacks and took very good care of them. When they reached the age of eight, they graduated to an adult size canvas cotton sack. This also, was another step in their young lives that made them feel special and gave them a sense of importance.

It was Sunday afternoon before Edna's mother sat down to work on her sack. Edna eagerly watched as her mother's hand worked the needle in and out the fabric.

"Edna, honey, you'll have to stand back a little; I'm afraid this needle might poke you in the eye."

"How much longer will it be? Can I take it to work tomorrow?"

"I'm almost finished." She finished sewing the last few stitches. Then she tied a knot in the last stitch.

"It's all done," she said, as she held it up for Edna to see.

Edna stood proudly, as her mother placed the long strap over her small shoulder. She ran to the dresser mirror to see how it looked on her. Her mother smiled, as she watched her small daughter admiring her floral cotton sack in the mirror.

"Oh, Mama, the pink roses are so beautiful! I just love it so much! Can I go show it to Daddy and everyone?"

"Yes, you may. When you have done that, would you like to pick a little cotton to put in your sack from the field at the side of the house?"

"Yes, yes, that would be fun," Edna said, as she ran from the room.

Edna saw her parents watching from a distance as she ran to the cotton field to pick the cotton to put in her new sack. She picked a small handful, slowly parted the opening to the sack, and then she carefully placed the cotton inside. Pride and joy radiated from her smiling face as she reached for another handful of cotton.

"We have seen this many times before…she's just like all the others. She'll never be the same after this," her father said, as he placed a loving arm around his wife.

"Yes, I know; she's another one growing up too fast."

The proud, independent feelings Edna experienced while placing the first handful of cotton in her homemade cotton sack was something she had never forgotten.

CHAPTER TWENTY-FIVE

B ob returned from doing his errands and found that Grady had moved from where he had been laying with Edna on the bed. He sat at the bedside holding her hand. His head rested close to her. The lunch he had left on the side table for him was untouched. Bob sat the Chinese food he had brought back with him beside the untouched tray and quietly approached the bedside. Edna still remained motionless on the bed. To him, she appeared to be napping. Grady sensed his presence and sat up.

"Oh. Hello, Bob. I didn't know you were here. Have you been back long? I'm sorry. I can't seem to stay awake."

"It's alright Grady. I just walked in. I didn't mean to disturb you. I brought Chinese for dinner. You must be starving; I see you haven't eaten in a while."

"I appreciate the lunch, Bob, but I haven't been up long. I knew you were bringing Chinese for dinner, so I didn't eat the lunch. I hope you don't mind. I'm pretty hungry now. Let's go into the other room and eat."

"Have you seen any improvement in Edna today?" Bob asked while they ate their egg drop soup.

"I thought I felt her arm move a couple of times; but, I can't say for sure. She made a small sound once and I thought she was waking up. It wasn't much of a sound. It could've been anything—her stomach growling or something. But, it sounded like a moan or grunt to me. Maybe it was wishful thinking on my part. Bob, do you think she's going to come out of this alright?"

"I've heard of cases similar to this. Most people recover without a lot of permanent damage. Some people have to seek counseling for a short period of time; this helps them adjust to the trauma they experienced so that they can feel safe again. I know this is a pretty big tragedy in which she's involved. But, if I know Edna as well as I think I do, she'll come out of this. She'll more than likely give everyone else hell because it happened in the first place. I do know she won't be happy about missing out on her trip to Mississippi. I guess you know she'll probably still go. Only next time, she'll take you with her," Bob said trying to lighten Grady's mood.

"I'll tell you one thing," Grady laughed. "She won't be going off on any more road trips by herself. I have never seen anyone who could get into more trouble by doing nothing, than Edna; she only has to be present to be affected. It's the same way with her health. She can't have a normal health problem; if a drug has a side effect, then she's surely going to get it. She always tells me... *if the drug didn't have it, I wouldn't get it.* And, I guess she's right about that. In the past she has always rebounded from adversity. And, I'm sure you're right, Bob; she's also going to get through this alright. I can't help but worry, though."

There was a small tap at the door. The two men turned their attention in that direction and saw Dr. Peters standing there.

He took a step inside the room and said. "I'm not interrupting anything, am I?"

"We were just having a little something to eat, but you aren't interrupting. Come in and sit down," Grady said.

"I'd love to, Grady, but I have other patients to see. How was your day with Edna? Has she shown any signs of improvement?"

"Not really. I thought I saw a little movement in her arm, but I can't be sure."

"It was probably a muscle reflex." He had really hoped that Edna would be awake by now. He had stopped by the room earlier and found Grady sleeping beside her. They looked so peaceful that he didn't want to disturb them.

"Well, if you don't mind, I'll go back and check on her. Grady, let me know if there's any change in her. I'll be here all night."

"I should be going, too," Bob said after the doctor left. "You have my number if you need me. So, I'll see you in the morning."

After everyone left the room, Grady went back to check on Edna. As he spoke to her, he could see no response. He had an urge to turn on the TV to watch the evening news but knew he shouldn't use the TV in the room. He felt sure Edna would be alright alone for the short time it would take him to watch the news in the visitors lounge. As Grady left the room, he noticed a different police officer posted outside the door. He introduced himself and told the officer he would be in the lobby watching the news.

Only a few people sat in the small family visitation lounge. He could see the news of the shooting was already on the TV screen.

"Is there anything new with the shooting?" Grady asked the middle-aged man he sat next to. "Did they find out who this guy was?"

"They aren't saying much. From what I can tell, this guy went on a shooting rampage and killed a whole lot of people. They haven't given a number of dead or wounded…it's a lot. The gunman was shot and killed, but not much is being said about how he was shot or who shot him. You know, a lot of the wounded are here in this hospital. I came through the emergency room last night and it was wall-to-wall stretchers."

"Do you know anyone who was involved in the shooting?" asked Grady.

"No. Thank goodness. But, they have been interviewing some of the survivors on TV all day; they described it as a massacre. The people they've interviewed didn't actually see the gunman, but they heard the rapid gunfire from his high powered gun. He was shot by someone there, but no one there seems to know who did it. I'm sure if the media knew who it was, it would be plastered all over every TV screen and newspaper in the country. The police are probably keeping that piece of information quiet for some reason. I can't say that I blame them. If this is connected to some kind of terrorist plot, they may not be happy with the person who killed their countryman. Who knows, they might try to get to them. I wouldn't want to be in their shoes, would you?"

Terrorist! I need to go…I need to get to her. Grady suddenly felt sick. He hadn't thought of a terrorist plot, and couldn't tolerate the idea of his *"Swart"* being pursued by some terrorist. He realized now what danger she might be in. It scared him to death.

"No, I wouldn't want to be in their shoes," said Grady. "Would you excuse me? I need to check on my wife."

Grady ran all the way back to Edna's room nearly knocking the police officer over as he charged through the door.

"Grady, are you alright?" the officer shouted as he recovered his balance. "Your wife is o.k. Nothing has happened to her."

"Yes, I know. I just need to be near her," Grady shouted over his shoulder as he kept walking. "You won't let anyone in this room tonight, will you? If I need anything, I'll call you. I'm going to lock the door. So, knock if you want anything."

"It isn't necessary to lock the door, Grady. I won't allow any unauthorized person to enter. You'll be safe. I promise you." The officer lost sight of Grady as he rounded the corner toward Edna's room. It was obvious that something had upset him. He wondered if it had been something he had seen on TV.

Grady slammed the door closed. He fumbled with the door knob seeking the latch. He stared in disbelief at the knob…*there's no lock here.* His eyes quickly canvassed the room for something he could use to brace the door. Seeing a chair sitting next to the desk, he ran to the other side of the room to get it. After he was satisfied the chair was securely propped under the door knob, he then climbed into bed next to Edna and slept.

CHAPTER TWENTY-SIX

✝

Jenny's first church experience was uplifting. The church was small, and not at all what she had expected. The congregation of one hundred fifty people was very friendly. Everyone was eager to express their condolences to Mrs. Brewer and Gene. The minister also expressed his condolences in front of the congregation before he delivered the sermon. The boys nodded off to sleep halfway through the sermon and continued to sleep when she and Gene picked them up and carried them to the car after the service. Mrs. Brewer stayed behind to talk with friends, while they got the boys settled in their car seats.

"Jenny, before I bring Mother to the car, I'd like to ask you if there's anything you need from your apartment? I'll be glad to take you wherever you need to go this afternoon. The next few days will be pretty well tied up with the funeral, but today will be good for me."

"I don't have a lot of things, but I do need to get them. I'm sure my landlady will want to rent the apartment as soon as she can. My handbag with my entire identification and driver's license is in the locker at the Pickle Barrel. I guess there's no way I'll be getting them today."

"Not today, but I'll check on them for you. So, today will be alright to pick up your things from the apartment?"

"Today will be fine. What shall we do with the children?"

"Our neighbors who live close by have two small children. Do you think the boys would enjoy playing with them? I can see if they'll come to the house. There's a very large playroom on the fourth floor. I'm sure they would love playing up there."

"That sounds great. Let's ask them first before we make any definite plans. It may upset them knowing we are out of sight."

"I see what you mean. Alright then, if they don't want to play with the children we'll take them with us. Oh, there's one more thing; the children need clothing. I got them a few things last night, but I think they need more to wear. Would you mind if we went shopping while we're in the city?" he asked.

"I don't mind at all. It was nice of you to think of that. And, Gene, thank you for what you've already done for us."

Gene, looking into her upturned face, dropped his upper body into a low bow and said, "It was my pleasure, madam. Now, I'm afraid I must leave you and rescue Mother from her friends. I'm sure Mary Ann will have a great hot lunch awaiting our arrival, and I know all of us could use it right now."

Jenny stood beside the open door of the car and watched him walk away. She couldn't help but notice his tall muscular body, as he took long strides across the parking lot. Her mind was taking her places she had never been before. Her heart began to race out of control when she realized she had never been alone with a man. And now, she would be in a car with one all afternoon. All kinds of thoughts ran through her mind: *How shall I act? What will we talk about? Maybe Mary Ann can go with him and shop for the boys. But, I have to get my things from the apartment.* Her mind was racing now as fast as her heart. She could feel her face burning against the crisp, autumn air. Beads of perspiration began to form on her forehead. *What's happening to me? It isn't as if I have never*

seen a man before. *I'm sure we can think of something to talk about
along the way. After all, there are a lot of things I'd like to know
about Gene and his family. I'm sure everything will work out just
fine.* She glanced up and saw Gene and his mother approaching,
and they were halfway across the parking lot. "Oh, get yourself
together, Jenny," she said, as she quickly slid in the back seat next
to the children.

The ride back to the ranch was pleasant. The children continued
to sleep. Gene and his mother spoke softly as they talked about the
morning service with Jenny. The boys woke up when they arrived
at the ranch and began to complain about being hungry.

"Don't worry big guys," Gene said while helping the children
from the back seat. "I'm sure Miss Mary Ann has our lunch all
ready for us. I bet I can beat both of you to the kitchen. I'm
starving—let's see who can eat the most." All three of them took
off racing toward the kitchen.

"Well, Pauline, it looks like it's you and me." Jenny extended
her hand. "Here, let me help you out of the car."

"It's such a joy to see children running and laughing around
here again. I feel just like them. I'm so hungry I could eat a bear
right now, but I sure can't run like one. Are you hungry, Jenny?"

"After that big breakfast, you'd think I wouldn't be, but I
could also eat a bear." Both women laughed.

They could hear the laughter long before they made it to the
kitchen. Gene and the boys were laughing and bickering back and
forth about who the real winner was.

Mary Ann stood next to the table where she was placing food
and shook her head at all the commotion. She wondered what
had brought all this on, but knowing Gene...nothing he did
surprised her.

Mary Ann did not fail to meet their expectations for lunch.
She had set the table with blue and white stoneware and flatware
with wooden handles. A large tureen of hot three-bean soup sat in
the center of the table. Fresh-baked bread sat on a wood cutting
board at the side of the table. A platter of sliced roast beef, ham,

a variety of cold cuts, and another platter with lettuce, tomatoes, and various other vegetables were ready to be devoured by the hungry group.

Jenny noticed a freshly baked applesauce cake on the side buffet with a pot of coffee and a pitcher of cold milk sitting next to it. *What a perfect lunch*, Jenny thought. Mary Ann had thought of everything.

As they sat around the lunch table holding hands, Gene asked the blessing. Jenny couldn't help but quietly add a few thanks of her own. This was another new experience for her. She had never had the luxury of enjoying a meal with a real family. This was a feeling she had always longed for but never thought she would ever experience. She still felt as if she were in another world; and for her, she was.

Jenny had never enjoyed the experiences other children had with their parents. The closest thing to a real meal she could remember having with her mother occurred one summer afternoon. She and her mother had worked in the kitchen preparing fried chicken, whipped potatoes, green beans, and yeast rolls. Actually, it was Jenny who did the better part of the cooking, while her mother sat at the small kitchen table smoking and drinking her favorite whiskey. Jenny pretended her mother played a big part in the preparation of the meal, so she could feel like a real family. When Jenny sat the food on the small table, her mother was so drunk she couldn't hold her head up long enough to eat a bite. Jenny was nine years old at the time. Now that she thought about it, she couldn't remember a meal her mother had cooked.

Gene could see the boys were almost finished eating their lunch and thought it would be a good time to bring up the subject of the playroom. "How would you guys like to check out the playroom upstairs after lunch?" He said casually.

"Yes, yes that would be fun," they both said at the same time.

"Do you have a train set, Mr. Gene?" Danny was wide-eyed with excitement.

"I should say there is a train set up there. It runs all along the floor, up the wall and overhead all around the room. The whistle blows every time it comes to a crossroad and when it stops at the station. I think you'll like it."

"Can I turn it on by myself?" asked Rossie.

"It's very easy to turn on and off. I'll show you how. There's something else up there you'll enjoy, but you'll have to wait until night to see it."

Danny said, "What is it, Mr. Gene?"

"It's a telescope. Do you know what a telescope is?"

They shook their heads from side to side.

"Well, it's something you look through to see the stars and planets when they come out at night."

"Can we see them tonight?" Rossie eagerly said.

"You sure can. Oh, I wanted to ask you. Would you like to meet the neighbor children who live nearby? I'm sure they would love to play with you this afternoon if you want to."

Both boys suddenly became quiet. They looked troubled.

"It's okay. It'll only be for a little while. Jenny and I need to go by her apartment and pick up her things. We also need to shop for some clothes for you this afternoon. Would you mind playing with the other children while we're gone? We won't be gone long. I promise."

Mary Ann overheard the conversation Gene was having with the children. She knew it wouldn't go over well with them; so she spoke up. "I tell you what guys. Why don't we invite the other children over and we'll go for a pony ride around the pasture. Afterwards, we can check out that playroom upstairs? Mr. Gene and Miss Jenny can take care of business, while we stay here and have all the fun. When they get back, all of us will have a big picnic in the attic. How does that sound? Would you like that? We'll watch the stars when it gets dark."

"Yes, yes that will be fun," they shouted.

Danny asked, "Can we go now and ride the pony?"

Mary Ann knew she had won them over. "Let's call the other children first, and you need to change out of your church clothes before we do that."

She took the children by the hand and led them from the room. She turned at the doorway and gave Gene and Jenny a wink and smiled.

"What a clever woman she is," Jenny said when they were out of hearing distance.

"That she is. She always knew when to speak-up on my behalf when I was growing up, and I've never forgotten it."

"Yes, I recall some of those occasions. If I were you, I'd get moving before they change their minds." Pauline yawned while saying, "I feel like a nap...see you later." She left Gene and Jenny standing alone in the kitchen.

Jenny started to follow the children. "I should tell them goodbye."

Gene laughed and reached for her hand to stop her. "I think Mary Ann has everything under control. Let's not push our luck by saying goodbye."

The ride to the city with Gene was much more enjoyable than Jenny had anticipated. Neither of them had a problem finding something to talk about. The subjects just kept coming. They talked nonstop all the way to Jenny's apartment, and arrived sooner than Jenny thought they would.

"Would you like me to come in with you, Jenny?" Gene asked, as he parked the car in the driveway beside the rundown Victorian home.

"She isn't going to be happy with me, you know. It might take a while for me to gather my things, but, you're welcome to come inside, if you want to."

Although Jenny had a key to the place, she rang the doorbell. The landlady opened the door with a smirk on her face. She seemed surprised to see a well-dressed, handsome young man standing there with Jenny. She glanced out at her driveway and saw the fancy sports car parked there, and then she stepped aside and allowed Jenny and Gene to enter the house.

"Where have you been? I thought you had been killed at the Pickle Barrel. I was about to call Goodwill to pick up your things. I guess you don't have a job now. I'm sorry about what happened, but I still need the rent you owe me."

As Jenny swiftly passed by the landlady heading for her room, the old woman blurted out everything she wanted to say in order for Jenny to hear before she got out of hearing distance.

When Jenny could get a word in edgewise, she shouted over her shoulder, "Well, as you can see, I'm not dead and I'm here to pick up my things. I don't have a job yet, but when I get one, I'll see that you get your rent money."

Gene was now standing alone in the living room with the landlady.

"Excuse me," Gene said to the landlady when Jenny was out of sight. "I couldn't help but overhear. Do you mind if I ask how much the young lady owes you?"

The landlady looked Gene up and down and said in a matter-of-fact tone, "She owes me for last month's rent and most of this month. It comes to one hundred fifty dollars. I hope she pays it. I have bills to pay, you know."

"Yes. I'm sure you do. Let me take care of this for her." He took five one hundred dollar bills from his wallet and gently placed it in her hand.

The landlady stared at the bills in disbelief. "This is too much, sir."

When she looked up at him again, Gene noticed tears had pooled up in her aging eyes. "I know it's more than she owes you, but it's alright," he said. "I'm sure you can use it, can't you?"

With a shaking hand, she carefully placed the money deep inside the pocket of her dirty apron. "Thank you, sir," she softly choked out, and then she turned and walked out of the room leaving him standing alone.

It didn't take long for Jenny to gather her things, and then they were on the road again.

"Gene, where will we shop for clothing for the children? I'm not familiar with children's apparel."

"I have a friend who owns a children's clothing shop. I talked with her last night about the children needing clothes for a while. She has some casual and church outfits selected for them. She wasn't quite sure about their shoe size. You might want to help her in that department. You can look at the things she has selected and see if it meets with your approval. Please feel free to add anything you think they might need or want. I hope you don't mind that I asked her to select the clothing. I thought it would save us some time. I want to make one other stop after we leave the children's shop."

"I don't mind at all. I'm grateful for the help. I wasn't really sure what to select for two young boys to wear. Thank you so much for thinking of them and me. I'm sure what she has picked out will be just fine."

"I'll introduce Fran to you; I know you'll like her."

Gene was right; she did like Fran. Jenny couldn't believe the rack of clothing Fran had selected for the children. It looked like more clothes than she had ever owned in her whole lifetime. Gene had no problem with the selections and kept encouraging her to add more. There must have been a small fortune on the rack. Yet, it didn't seem to bother him. Gene had already bought dress shoes the night before, so she helped Fran select a pair of sneakers for each of the boys.

Gene was busy playing around in the western wear department. He held a small pair of western boots in the air and shouted across the room, "Jenny, let's take them some cowboy boots. They can wear them when we go horseback riding. Would you like to get them some cowboy hats to go with the boots?"

Jenny could see the happy smile on his face as he picked up boots and hats and placed them next to western style shirts and jeans to see how they looked together.

"I'm sure they would love that," she shouted back at him. After their exchange of words, she slowly worked her way across the room so Fran wouldn't notice anything suspicious. She walked up next to Gene and whispered, "Are you sure? All this is really adding up."

"It's alright, Jenny. It's only money and the children's happiness is all that matters now. Who knows what's in store for them in the next few days? Let's keep them happy for now."

"This is very thoughtful and generous of you, Gene." She picked up a western hat made of straw and studied the style and size. She said, "I can't wait to see them dressed like little cowboys chasing after the farm animals in the barnyard. Do you think they would like a hat like this?"

At that time, Fran approached them and said, "Gene, it looks like it's going to take a while to pack all these things up. I know you have more important things to do this afternoon. So, why don't I have these delivered to your place? They'll probably be there before you get back."

"Thank you, Fran. That'll work out great for us. I appreciate you thinking of that. Oh, here, add these hats to the order." He took the hat from Jenny's hand and picked up another one from the hat rack and handed it to Fran.

"I have one more stop to make, Jenny," Gene said after they returned to the car.

He drove a mile or two through the streets of the city, and then pulled up to the curbside and stopped in front of a chic, very tastefully painted lavender building. A trellis with ivy woven through it, along with roses and wild flowers were painted on the front of the building. A white brick sidewalk led to the small porch with a "Welcome to Lavender and Lace" sign above the door. A high back rocking chair with a floral throw draped across the back was located at the right hand corner of the porch. A white wicker side table and lamp sat next to the rocker. It was like something you would see in the pages of "House and Gardens" magazine. Jenny wasn't sure what kind of place this was, or what they were doing there.

"Is this where you wanted to come?" she asked.

"Yes, Jenny. My friend Allie owns this shop. It's a lady's apparel shop. Allie helped me with your clothing last night. It was late and everything was closed, so she met me here and we selected your church clothing for today. Jenny, I hope you don't think I'm being too forward, but I would like for you to go inside and select some outfits for yourself. If you need help, Allie is very helpful. She opened the shop today just for you. You can buy anything you want, Jenny. I don't want you to worry about how much things cost. It's alright."

Jenny felt her face flush. She was having a hard time finding a voice to speak. *This can't be true—this can't be happening—I must be dreaming.* She reached over and pinched her arm to see if she could feel it. Her heart was racing, and she could hardly think.

"Why...why are you doing this? You don't owe me anything and I don't expect anything from you. I only want to help the children until their parents are located, and then I have to find a job and support myself. I don't deserve this." She hadn't realized it, but tears were rolling down her cheeks.

Gene reached over and took her hands in his and said, "Jenny, I didn't mean to upset you. Mother and I have seen how you care and do for others. And, we just wanted to do something nice for you. After all, you did save my mother's life. Would you make us happy and accept our gift? We don't expect anything in return. We only want you to be happy. Would you do this for us? Go inside and let Allie help you pick out the biggest wardrobe you've ever seen. Buy anything you want and think nothing of it. That'll make Mom and me happy."

"I must be dreaming. Gene, I don't know how to act in a place like this." Tears were rolling down her face now. She wiped at the tears with the back of her hands and took a few short breaths as she struggled to speak. "You...you and your mother are too good to me. How could I ever thank you enough?"

Gene could only imagine what Jenny was feeling at this moment. He had been born into wealth and had never lacked for anything. But, the things he had seen during his many years in law enforcement had taught him a lot about people and poverty. He knew a good, honest person when he saw one, and Jenny was at the top of the list.

"Just be who you are, Jenny. That's thanks enough. So, here take this handkerchief and dry your eyes, and then go inside and have a good time. I'll go check out what's happening at the precinct and see if I can retrieve your things from the Pickle Barrel locker, if that's o.k. with you. Is two hours enough time for you to select a wardrobe?"

"Yes, that will be plenty of time. Thank you, Gene."

They went inside and Gene introduced her to Allie.

CHAPTER TWENTY-SEVEN

L arry rang the doorbell for the third time. "What do you think, Captain—you think anyone's in there?"

"I don't know. But, we have a search warrant and we'll break the door down if we have to. Oh...it sounds like someone's coming. Get your gun ready, Larry...just in case." Captain Hall knew the house was surrounded and wasn't concerned that anyone inside might escape. He could hear someone fumbling with the door locks.

A voice came from inside, "Okay, okay, I'm coming. You don't have to knock the door down."

The door slowly opened and a man about thirty-five years old stood before them. The bright sunlight hit him in the face, and he squinted and held his hand up to shield his eyes. His hair stuck up all over his head and he wore pajama bottoms. It was obvious to everyone that he had just gotten out of bed.

When Butrus's eyes had adjusted to the sunlight he then focused in on the two police officers. They had a badge practically stuck in his face. His heart fell to his feet. He tried to think back for something he might have done to cause the police to show up at his door.

"What do you want?" Butrus tried not to show how anxious he was feeling.

"I'm Captain Hall. I need to ask you some questions." He didn't wait for a response. "Do you have a roommate? Is he here?"

"Yes, I have a roommate. He works at night. I worked the ball game last night and didn't get in until late. I went straight to bed and didn't hear him come in this morning. Is he alright?" Butrus knew full well that Ahmed was in a rage when he left him the day before and had no idea what he could have gotten himself into.

Captain Hall pulled the search warrant from his shirt pocket and held it up for Butrus to see. "I have a warrant. Do you mind if we have a look around?"

Butrus began to sweat. His heart was going crazy. He tried to conceal his feelings and thought he might try and talk them out of the search.

"What are you looking for? Maybe I can help you. I'm sure my roommate will be back soon. I'll call you as soon as he arrives." In spite of him trying to appear calm the sweat trickled down his forehead.

"That won't be necessary," Larry said. "He's in the morgue. We'll just have a little look around."

Butrus was shocked at the news of Ahmed's death. And now, panic-stricken at the possibility of his cell being discovered, he charged through the living room, down the hallway and out the kitchen door into the arms of two uniformed officers.

"Put him in cuffs and take him to the station," Captain Hall shouted over the commotion taking place outside. "We'll question him after we've finished up here. Call the other officers in, Larry; let's take this place apart."

It wasn't long before the search revealed the arsenal in the attic. "I'll have the team tag all this stuff and bring it back to headquarters," Larry told the Captain while visually surveying all the weapons surrounding them.

"Okay, Larry. When you're finished, let's get back to the office. I have a few loose ends to piece together. Then, I believe this case will be wrapped up."

"Do you think this guy had anything to do with the shooting at the Pickle Barrel?"

"I kind of doubt it, Larry. But, I can almost guarantee you; he's deeply involved with other illegal activities—starting with all this weaponry in the attic. And, I intend to get answers to a lot more questions I have for him."

Monday morning, the well rested Captain Hall was back in his office. He had taken off work a few hours early the day before and went home for a long hot bath and a full nights rest. He was eager to get started on tying up the loose ends on the Pickle Barrel shooting. The governor, mayor and press reporters were driving him crazy for answers. He knew it wouldn't be long before he could tell the public the case was wrapped up.

After extensive questioning at the station, Butrus told them about the vendetta Ahmed had against President Bush and confessed to the assassination attempt against the Bush families. He finally cracked after being told about all the evidence against him—the bomb found in the trunk of Ahmed's car matched materials found in his attic, and fingerprints of both men were found on the bomb and the backpack. Butrus had told them how the bomb attack had gone awry and how upset Ahmed had been when he last saw him. Butrus realized he couldn't escape the charges he was facing, but his loyalty to his cause would prevent him from giving up any information about his sleeper cell, no matter what the police said, or did, to him.

Dee gave a little knock at the door, and then walked in. "I hope I'm not disturbing you, Captain. I have a few messages for you, and the results of the fingerprints you've been waiting for are back."

"Alright, Dee, will you just read the messages to me? I don't want to stop what I'm doing right now."

"Of course, I don't have to tell you that the media, the mayor, and governor have been calling about the progress of the investigation. They especially want to know who killed the Pickle Barrel shooter. Also, Gene came by yesterday after you left the office. He wanted to know how the investigation was going and he said something about Jenny and the children being alright. He asked when it would be o.k. to get her things from the employee's locker. Also, Mr. Bob Rossman came by to see you last night."

"Did Bob say anything about Edna's condition?"

"He said Edna was still resting in the hospital and that he would be in touch with you sometime this morning."

A knock at the door startled them. They turned to see Larry standing there.

"Am I disturbing anything?" Larry had poked his head inside the door.

"No, no come on in Larry," said the Captain. "Was that all you had for me, Dee?"

"That's all for now." She walked from the room and closed the door behind her.

"Did you get some rest last night, Captain?" Larry knew he had taken off early the day before.

"I slept for a full eight hours. I can't remember the last time I slept that long. I was about to look at the fingerprint results that just came in. Are you interested?"

"Sure am."

The Captain opened the envelope containing the results. He stood frozen, staring at them in disbelief.

Larry saw the strange look on the Captain's face and asked him what was wrong.

"Larry, hand me that wanted poster book on the shelf over there. I believe we've stumbled onto something very big here."

He took the book from the shelf and gave it to the Captain. They sat down beside each other at the desk and began to thumb through the pages.

"Check to see if you can find these names in the book, Larry: Ahmed bin Hamzah and Butrus bin Fareed."

It didn't take long for Larry to locate the photos of the two men. Both men had been on the most wanted list for years. And, after all this time, they had been pretty much given up for dead.

"Look at this Captain. Apparently, they both have very large rewards on their heads. Do you think they're still in effect?"

"We don't have any official paperwork that says the rewards have been canceled, but, I'll check it out."

"It appears Ms. Edna will end up being a very rich woman if these rewards are still in effect."

"Larry, there are a couple more things I need to check out. I want to see Ahmed's and Butrus's cell phone records again. There are a few more numbers on it that I think we need to check out. It could be that these two guys were part of a terrorist cell, and these phone numbers may lead us to them. I don't know of any other reason why these jokers would be here in this country. If this is a sleeper cell, then I'd like to see that all of them are put behind bars. We may need to get Homeland Security involved."

A few hours later Captain Hall had found the information he was seeking from the phone records. And after notifying Homeland Security, an operation was set up to bring in the two men who lived in Tampa and Miami, along with two other men who lived in Alabama. Their residences were to be rushed all at the same time, so that they wouldn't have time to tip one another off about the police coming after them. In addition, their phone records would be checked for any new numbers the police didn't already have, making it possible to arrest even more cell members.

Captain Hall checked the most wanted records to see if the rewards were still in effect for Ahmed and Butrus, and found that they were. At the moment, he wouldn't release any information regarding these rewards. There could be pending arrests of the four men who were to be picked up later that evening. They may have bounties on them, as well. He especially, didn't want the media to know Edna was about to be awarded a great deal of money. Her fate was still in question and news like this, while good, could be damaging. Yes, he would keep this bit of information under his hat for the time being.

Later that day, Larry dropped by the precinct. He wanted to be there with Captain Hall when the pending arrests were made.

"Larry, come in. You're just the person I wanted to see. Are you going to stay around until the pickups are made?"

"Yah, I thought I'd stick around and keep you company."

"What time are the pickups taking place?"

"I thought we'd give them time to get home from their jobs and have a nice dinner. That way the departments won't have to feed them after they take them in. I thought, eight o'clock sounded good; they should be well settled in by then."

"That sounds reasonable to me. If I were home, I'm sure I'd be settled in by that time."

"That gives us enough time to eat something ourselves. Would you like to join me at the corner café?"

"I'd love to join you, Captain."

"Oh. Larry, I have to ask you to keep quiet about the reward money that Edna will be receiving. I don't want this getting out just yet."

"No problem. What do you think she'll do with all that money?"

"I know what I'd do with it; no one would see me for a long time. I'd be basking in the sun on a long lost beach somewhere far away, while my every wish was being granted by someone else."

"Somehow, I can't see you in that type of setting. You seem to be more the sailboat type. You know, sailing around the world type," said Larry.

"You're probably right…we'll never know. Besides, I couldn't stay away from the action here long enough to sail around the world. Heck, I can't stay away long enough for a two week vacation. Dee, we'll be at the café if you need us," Captain Hall said, as he passed her desk.

Dinner was enjoyable and unrushed. They were back at the office now awaiting the news of the arrests that was to take place at any moment.

"What are the plans for these guys after they're picked up?" Larry asked.

"They'll be questioned and their phone records checked, and then we'll see if they're wanted for anything. I really think they are part of a cell here in the United States. If they are, the Fed's will take control of them."

Dee said through the doorway, "Mr. Rossman is on line two for you, Captain."

He reached for the phone. "Hello Bob, I'm sorry I wasn't here when you stopped by last night. Are you settled in at the guest house?"

"Oh, yes. Everything's great. Thanks for setting this up for me. It's a very nice place. I'm calling because of Grady's strange behavior this morning."

"What's going on with Grady?"

"When I arrived at the hospital, I found Grady locked in Edna's room. He wouldn't leave her to even walk outside the door."

"Grady actually locked himself in the hospital room? Did he say why?"

"The officer, who was guarding the room last night, said Grady went to the lounge to watch the news. He ran past him shortly afterwards as if something had scared him to death. He wouldn't tell the officer what had happened. But, he said he was going to lock Edna's door and to knock if he needed anything."

"But, nothing about Edna's involvement in the shooting has been on the news."

"Yes, I know. Grady finally opened the door to let me in. I never really found out what happened in the lounge, but he told me he was afraid some terrorist might try to harm Edna because she shot the guy at the Pickle Barrel. Do you know anything about a terrorist cell or someone who might want to harm her?"

"There are a lot of wild stories out there about what happened. It's enough to disturb anybody. Maybe Grady saw something in the lounge or someone could have said something to upset him."

"He didn't give me any details, but he's very protective of Edna and still has the door locked."

"Bob, since you're a police officer and I know you, I'm going to tell you something that we don't want to get out just yet. Homeland Security is in the process of apprehending, what we suspect, are cell members here in Florida and Alabama. We have already identified the shooter and his roommate as wanted terrorists."

"Well, you don't think there's a chance that Edna and Grady could be in danger from these terrorists, do you?"

"We have already arrested the shooter's roommate. And at the moment, we are waiting for the feds to pickup the others that we know about. We have their addresses, and they'll soon be in custody."

"I'm sure Grady will be relieved to know Edna is in no immediate danger."

"I feel sure this was a small cell and we'll have them locked up soon. Please tell Grady, he has nothing to worry about. There's no need for him to lock himself inside the room. I'll release all this information as soon as all arrests and charges have been made. Edna's name will be kept out of it for as long as I can hold out. Has there been any change in her condition?"

"There hasn't been much change. Grady is with her all the time. He said she whimpers and there are slight movements in her arms and legs, but she hasn't regained consciousness. Well, I appreciate the information and I'll let Grady know he doesn't have to worry about a terrorist."

"You have a long distance call from Alabama on line two," Dee said, as Captain Hall was hanging up the phone with Bob. He listened as the agent on the phone went into details about the arrest of the two men in Alabama. It had gone down without a hitch.

The agent also told him they had fingerprints of both men and were checking them against all their data bases. Their phone records had already been checked and there were no new numbers the police department didn't already have.

"That's great news. Thanks for your help and congratulations on taking down these two bad guys." Captain Hall hung the phone up.

"We should be hearing from Tampa and Miami at any time," Larry stated. "While we're waiting for the phone calls, I have the number of casualties from the Pickle Barrel shooting. Would you like to hear them?"

"Sure, give me the bad news. By the way, have the parents to those two little boys Gene took home with him been located?"

"No one has come forward looking for the missing boys. Since they don't know their last names, it's difficult for us to identify them and place them with their parents. The boy's first names or a picture of them has not been found in any of the wallets or purses that were collected at the crime scene. We may have to wait until someone reports them missing."

"Okay, give me the casualty report."

"Forty-three killed and thirty-nine wounded. If Edna hadn't put an end to the shooting, casualties may have been much higher."

"Yes, I know. She deserves every penny of that reward money and I'm going to see that she gets it. Speaking of rewards...check the wanted list, Larry. Let's see if those two in Alabama have rewards on their heads."

Larry picked up the wanted poster book and thumbed through the pages until he found the names. "Wow! Listen to this Captain. It says here, this Husam is a ring leader and extremely dangerous. There's a five hundred thousand dollar reward for him. Let me see here," he continued turning the pages. "His partner...looks like he's also a pretty bad guy. There's a three hundred thousand dollar price on his head. So, Captain, will Ms. Edna receive all these rewards?"

"Yes, she will. She's entitled to the rewards, because she brought down the person who led to the arrest of the others. When the other two are brought in, we may find out they have rewards as well."

"Captain, its ten o'clock and I'm a little worried about the Tampa and Miami pickups. Do you think there's a problem?"

"I'm a little concerned, but you know how traffic is in those areas. Maybe they got held up. They're probably running prints and want to make sure they have all the facts before they call us. I'll call them if we don't hear from them soon."

Moments later the phone rang. Dee had gone home for the evening, so Captain Hall answered the call. Tampa was calling to confirm the arrest of the man there and to verify his identity. His phone records, like the others, didn't give any new leads.

At ten-thirty when the information came in from Miami, the news was the same as the others. The arrests had been made and Homeland Security was in the process of questioning all the suspects.

Larry said, as he looked over all the facts at hand, "These guys lived a pretty quiet life. A normal person would have numerous phone numbers that they'd call almost daily. These guys only called one another. It appears they had no friends outside of their small group."

Out of curiosity, Larry opened the most wanted folder to see if the two names from Tampa and Miami were there. They were. Both men had a fifty thousand dollar reward on them. With a big grin on his face he said, "Captain, Ms. Edna just got richer—another one hundred thousand dollars for these two. I'm so happy for her. I hope she wakes up in time to enjoy every cent of it. How long do you think it'll take to get the money to her? You don't think they'll try to renege on the rewards, do you?"

"No. They can't renege on the rewards. Reward monies are secure, and it shouldn't take long to claim it. The guys are in custody, the fingerprints have been verified, and the rewards state that it's for information leading to the arrest, not the conviction.

I'd say Ms. Edna did a little more than give information. She'll get what she deserves. I'll see to that."

"You like her, don't you, Captain?"

"I've never met her, but I like what she has done. It couldn't have been easy for her to take a life—being afraid of guns and all. I admire her husband for caring for her safety enough to insist that she get a concealed weapons permit. And, I'm grateful that she had a gun with her in that big yellow purse. I'm sure she must have thought she would never have to use it against another person. I can just see her trembling hand reaching in that bloody yellow purse trying to locate that gun. Who knows how all this will affect her health and future? She may not be in any frame of mind to enjoy one cent of the reward money. I hope that isn't the case. Do you realize, Larry, if it hadn't been for Edna and her little gun, a lot more people would be dead today and this country would be in an uproar? Yes, as far as I'm concerned, she's a very big hero."

"I hear what you're saying, and I feel the same way. When are you going to tell them about the money?"

"I'll probably tell Grady while I'm at the hospital in the morning. I want to stop by there to check on Edna. Right now, I could sleep on a rock. Let's go home and get some rest. It has been a big day and tomorrow will be just as busy. Will you help me with a press release? I'll have to call the governor and mayor tomorrow and fill them in on all that's happened today."

"Alright, Captain, we'll get it all together in the morning. Are you going to let Gregory Lowe, the Public Information Officer, deliver the press release?"

"I'll fill him in on everything that's happened, but I think I'll inform the public initially. I'm sure there will be a lot of questions to be answered in the days to come; he'll be busy enough with that. At the moment, sleep sounds good to me. Let's get out of here."

CHAPTER TWENTY-EIGHT

E dna lay motionless on the hospital bed. Her mind still wandered as bits and pieces of her life experiences flashed before her. The flashes were coming more often now, and although she wasn't aware of it, her senses were beginning to awaken.

"Edna, I told you to come away from that pen. That old bull will ram his horns in you, if you make him mad."

"But mama, the little duck is in there. I want to hold him." Edna had her face pressed against the chicken-wire fence which surrounded the barnyard. She had never seen anything more beautiful than the green-headed mallard drake. The duck was very tame and she had been holding and petting it ever since her arrival three days ago. Her Tennessee teenage great cousins had teased her all weekend about giving her the duck if she would stay with them. The two families were all outside saying their last goodbyes to one another. Her older brothers and sisters were loading up into the back of the much used homemade camper truck for the trip back to their Mississippi home. To get to her cousin's home her daddy had driven the old truck off the main road for an hour through the back woods. The "road" he

drove on was really a dirt pathway, and along the way, they dodged low-hanging tree limbs and the occasional boulder in their path.

"Come on Edna, get in the truck. It's time to go," her mother called to her. "Don't make me have to tell you again."

"No! I want to stay with the duck. He wants me to stay with him."

Her mother walked across the yard, picked her little four year old body up, and placed her kicking and screaming in the camper with the rest of the children and closed the door.

"NO! NO! I don't want to go! I want to stay with my duck; let me out; I don't want to go!" Trying not to lose sight of her precious duck, Edna pressed her face against the small window of the camper. Her father retraced the route through the woods; back to civilization.

ANOTHER FLASH:

The Mississippi sun was blazing hot on Edna's body. She didn't own a hat, and the sun was glaring in her eyes. Her uncovered face and arms were already burned by the hot rays of the sun. The strap from the cotton sack felt as if it were embedded in her left shoulder from the weight of the cotton she had picked that morning. The strap to her overalls had slipped down her right shoulder and she reached over and pulled it back up. She stopped picking cotton and stood up just long enough to wipe the sweat from her face and to stretch her back and arms. She longed for a cool breeze…or any kind of a breeze…she squinted against the glaring sun as she glanced up at the sky, hoping to see some clouds. There wasn't a cloud in sight. She prayed for a large black, fluffy cloud to come and stop over her head to block the sun and give her some relief from the heat. Better yet, let it rain for a week; that way everyone can stay home and out of the sun for awhile. Not one raindrop had fallen in the whole state for nearly three months. All the vegetation looked withered and dry. The cotton stalks had already turned brown and brittle from the lack of water.

The air was still and hot. The eight foot long sack she dragged behind her was almost full and she dreaded the thought of having to take the heavy sack to the scales to be weighed. She glanced down at her bare feet. The fact that the soil she was standing on was hard, dried up, and about one hundred degrees, didn't concern her. The soles of her feet were tough as leather, so the hot, parched ground affected her very little. But, the small left toe she had rammed into a misplaced bench on her way to use the night-jar sometime in the early morning hours was turning black and swollen. She bent over, gave the toe a rub, and then went back to work.

She really didn't like school. But, she wished now that cotton season was over, so that she could be in her third grade class room, rather than the cotton fields. Maybe today I'll get to go home and cook lunch for everyone, she thought. Her older sisters were on a rotation to leave the field and prepare lunch, but not her. Her mother said she wasn't old enough and didn't have enough experience to cook a meal alone. This was always the explanation her mother gave when she didn't want her to do something. And, she was tired of hearing that she wasn't old enough to do things. Her oldest sister, Elsie, had been teaching her to cook and she had accompanied her a couple times from the field to see how it was done. It wasn't that she enjoyed cooking, but cooking would get her out of the field for a short while. That was her wish at the moment. Edna felt confident she could prepare a meal without her sister, but she was afraid to light the burners on the old broken-down gas cook stove. Lighting the oven was the worst; it always made a big poof when she put the long match to the burner... this frightened her.

"Edna...Edna," she could hear her mother calling from across the field.

Edna stood straight up so that she could see her mother. "Yes, I hear you," she shouted back.

"Go weigh your cotton. Then come get the baby and make lunch today."

She couldn't believe the newly found energy she had. She ignored the aching toe. And, in record time the cotton was weighed, the *baby was cradled in her arms, and she was jumping row after row of cotton; beating a path toward the house to cook her first meal by herself.*

ANOTHER FLASH:

The air was crisp and smelled like heaven. The sun was about to clear the horizon and melt the frost which covered the strawberry field. Edna always enjoyed the mornings in the fields. Her bare hands and feet were cold now, but she knew by ten o'clock the frost would be gone and the sun would be hot and glaring. It was still better than that blistering, hot, Mississippi sun in the cotton fields. Thank goodness her daddy stopped sharecropping in Mississippi. It didn't pay enough money for the time and labor it required. There was nothing like the summers in Michigan. She loved picking strawberries, blueberries, cherries, peaches, and anything else that was there to eat.

"Are we still going to do it today, Edna?" her younger brother, Dickey quietly asked. He walked next to her lugging two empty strawberry carriers. Most of the children had gotten together the night before and decided to race to see who could pick the most. The idea was to race against their parents without their parents knowing about it. They were always playing little challenging games such as this; it kept their energy up for a full day's hard work.

"I'm still on…and I bet I can beat all of you," Edna answered Dickey's silly question. He knew darn well the race was still on. After all, everyone agreed to it the night before. And, once everyone agreed to a secret race such as this, it was not openly talked about again. Dickey knew the rule. She sensed he was up to something. Dickey had never been able to win against her in any race they ever had and she was confident he wasn't going to win this time. However, he did make her work hard for her victories. But, she would never let him know this.

"I don't know about that...I'm pretty fast," Dickey said. "If you let me win, I won't tell everybody that Roy likes you."

So, he wants me to let him win, she thought. "I know just how fast you are Dickey. I also know Roy doesn't like me. And besides, I don't like him. You can tell anything you like...I'm not going to let you win." Did you forget, Dickey that the race isn't against me? It's against Mama and Daddy. She wouldn't allow him to beat her no matter who the race was against. But, she knew because of him, she would have to work twice as hard today.

Both of them took off running to the field to claim a row next to their brothers and sisters and eagerly began the race. They worked all day without taking their usual breaks. A trip to the outhouse was done only when absolutely necessary, and it was done faster than usual. When they took their carriers filled with berries to the shed and picked up empty ones, it was done quickly. They returned to the field without the usual heel dragging. At the end of the day, almost all of them had out-picked their parents. Edna had out-picked Dickey by five quarts. After supper, while the sun dropped in the horizon, all the children lay exhausted under an apple tree far out into the orchard and laughed about their victory.

"Do you want to race again tomorrow?" Louise asked, while laughing as hard as she could.

"NO's"...came from all directions.

"We had better be careful, they may start expecting us to do this well all the time," Ruth added.

A few more days of working like we did today, they'll have to dig a hole to put our tired, dead, bodies in," said Edna.

Johnny, an older brother, and Dickey jumped from where they had been laying on the ground and climbed the apple tree. They dropped to the ground large red apples for everyone below to eat. As they lounged under the apple tree and ate their apples, darkness fell upon them.

CHAPTER TWENTY-NINE

G rady had Bob locked in Edna's hospital room with him, but Bob wanted to talk to him outside the room and said, "Let's step outside for a moment, Grady. I need to give you a message Captain Hall gave me last night. I don't want to talk where Edna might hear."

They stepped outside the door and Grady listened while Bob repeated the message from Captain Hall. "Are you telling me, Bob, this guy Edna shot was connected to some kind of terrorist cell here in Florida? And they say they have all of them under arrest. How do they know they have all of them?"

"There are things that Captain Hall can't tell publicly at this time, but he assured me they have all of them. There's no danger to Edna, or you. He said there's no reason for you to be afraid and barricade yourself in your room. You have been closed up in here too long, Grady. Why don't you let me stay here with Edna while you go out and get some fresh air? Get something to eat while you're out. I promise I won't leave her bedside."

"Will you keep the door locked while I'm gone? When I get back, I won't lock it again. I won't be gone long."

"Take all the time you want. Go for a walk and get some fresh air. Everything's under control here."

Grady walked the hospital grounds. The cool autumn breeze felt refreshing against his face. The walk had been a good idea. His head was full of Edna and what her fate might be. What would happen to her, and to him, if she didn't come out of this? It frightened him to think about it. He really needed to talk with family. Then it occurred to him. He hadn't called Edna's family to let them know about her condition. He pulled his cell phone from his pants pocket and dialed Edna's sister, Ruth.

After talking with family members and eating a quiet meal in the small family owned café, located across the street from the hospital, he returned to Edna's room. He tapped at the door to let Bob know he was back.

"Do you feel better?" Bob asked, as Grady entered the room.

"I feel a whole lot better. Thanks for suggesting the walk; it was just what I needed. Here, I brought you a big slice of homemade coconut cake. I know how much you love coconut cake. The café across the street makes everything fresh. Maybe we'll have a chance to go back there to eat before we leave."

"Thanks, Grady. You just made my day. Do you mind if I eat it now? I made a pot of coffee a little while ago. Would you like to join me in the other room for a cup?"

"Thanks, I believe I will."

Both men sat in silence and drank their coffee, while Bob ate his cake. The silence was broken when Dr. Peters entered the room.

"Is there any good news from Edna today?" he asked.

"Not much, just the usual grunts and twitches of hands and legs," Grady said. "I saw some movement in her eyes this afternoon. At first, I thought she was waking up, but she became still again."

"Those are good signs. I'll go back and check on her. Have a good evening."

"Grady, I'll stay nearby if you want to go to the lobby and watch the news. I know you don't like missing the news."

"I appreciate the offer, Bob, but I think I'll stay away from the news for a bit. The last time I tried watching the news, it was disturbing enough to make me want to forgo news for a while."

"So, will you be alright tonight? I can sleep here on the sofa if you want me nearby. I know you're going to sleep with Edna anyway."

"Now that I know the bad guys are in jail, I'm fine. Bob, I know you need to get back home to your job. You have already done far too much for me. I don't know what I would have done without your company. All I can do now is sit and wait for Edna to wake up. I'll be okay here until she does. I can't express my gratitude enough for all you have done."

"I tell you what Grady; let's see how she does tomorrow. If there's still no change, then I'll go home. So, call my cell number if you need anything. I'll see you in the morning. How would you like to join me for breakfast in the cafeteria? I'm sure Edna will be alright long enough for you to eat."

"Okay, I guess I can break away for a little while."

He was alone now with Edna and thought he would try once again to coax her to wake up. "Swart, can you hear me?" he said. "I know you're in there somewhere. I want you to come back to me. It's awfully lonely here without you. I miss talking with you and hearing your stories about all your favorite ducks. Those ducks truly love you, you know. I talk with Dixie every morning, and she tells me they keep looking for you. She said Stud Lee (Edna's favorite duck) won't eat the spaghetti from her hand. I know you're troubled right now, but everything's alright. You're in a safe place and nothing is going to hurt you. Please come back to me, Swart. I need you to come back." Tears rolled down his face. He climbed in bed beside her and took her into his arms, and eventually drifted off to sleep.

CHAPTER THIRTY

*W*hat's that smell? I know that smell from somewhere. Is that Grady? It smells like Grady. I thought I heard his voice...though it sounded far away. Where did the sound come from? Did he need me for something? It sounded like he was talking about the ducks...something about coming back. What did he mean...come back from where? I need to find him and see what he needs. I must be dreaming...I feel his arms around me. Are we in bed? We never cuddle in bed. I'll just wake up and tell him to get off me. She opened her eyes and focused in on an unfamiliar lamp burning in the darkness. She glanced down at her side and saw Grady's arm draped over her body. However, it took a long moment for her to realize...they were not in their bedroom.

Still wrapped in Grady's arms, Edna said in a loud voice, "Where are we, Grady? I don't remember coming here. And, why are you cuddled up with me?"

Grady heard her voice and sat straight up in bed. He couldn't believe she was awake and as spirited as always.

"Oh! Swart, you're back!" He reached across her body and gave her a big hug. "I'm so glad you're back. I knew you would come back to me."

"Where was I? Where are we? You have some explaining to do mister. Did you drug me and bring me to some fancy hotel?" She sat up in bed, looked around the room, then she saw the IV in her wrist. *Puzzled...*she stared at the IV. *"What's this?"*

"I wish I had drugged you, Swart. But, you're in the hospital in Tallahassee."

"What's the matter with me? I feel fine. How did I get here?"

"Tell me the last thing you remember." He was reluctant to answer any of her questions until he knew what she remembered.

"I was on interstate 10; on my way to visit Linda Ann. I was looking for a place to have lunch. That's the last thing I remember. What happened? Why am I in the hospital?"

"You passed out and the ambulance brought you here. You have been out for a few days. The doctors have done all kinds of tests to see what may have caused you to pass out. They haven't found much. Your red blood count was low and your blood pressure was also low. They have been feeding you by IV and everything seems to be back to normal. The doctor thinks you need to stay quiet and rest for a few weeks. I thought since you didn't make it to Mississippi, maybe the two of us could go somewhere quiet for a while. How does that sound to you? And don't worry about anything at home—Dixie is taking care of everything there."

"Did you call Linda and explain everything to her?"

"Yes. She knows and so does all the family."

"What did you have in mind...leaving from the hospital?"

"Sure, why not?" Grady said.

"So, the doctor thinks I need to get away. Well, if you want to do that, it's alright with me. Do you have some place in mind?"

He didn't have a clue. "Yes, as a matter a fact, I do. It'll be a surprise. But for now, Dr. Peters said to call him the instant you opened your eyes." He gave her a big kiss on the lips. "Welcome back, Swart."

"But, Grady isn't it too late to disturb the doctor?"

"He was quite forceful in his request. I think I should call him now." He pressed the nurse call button.

"Grady, do you need something?" the nurse's voice could be heard on the intercom beside the bed.

"Yes. Would you tell Dr. Peters my *wife* would like to speak with him?"

"I'll tell him right away," the nurse said with excitement in her voice.

Within minutes Dr. Peters was at Edna's bedside talking as if they were old friends. "Welcome back, Edna. Did you have a nice rest? How do you feel? I'm Dr. Peters, by the way."

"Yes, I know. Grady told me about you. It sounds like I had a very long rest. What would cause me to blackout like that? There isn't anything seriously wrong with me, is there?"

"Not a thing. Believe me, we have checked everything. So, you're feeling alright; no pain of any kind?" he asked, as he checked her eyes, listened to her heart and took her blood pressure.

"I'm stiff as a board. I feel like I need to walk ten miles to get all the kinks out; aside from that, I feel great."

"I'm glad to hear that. I still think you need to take it easy for a while. Maybe you should go somewhere quiet."

"Yes. Grady said that's what you thought. So, when do you think I can be released?"

"Let's give it another day, and then I see no reason why you can't leave."

"Then, I guess you'll be removing all these tubes so I can eat some real food. I'm starving."

"You can eat something light for now. I'll have a tray sent up right away, but I want the IV to stay until tomorrow. If you're still okay in the morning, then you can eat whatever you like. Grady, would you like to have a tray sent up for you?" Dr. Peters said, as he started toward the door to leave.

"Thanks, but I'm still full from the big meal I ate earlier today."

Dr. Peters called Captain Hall as soon as he left Edna's bedside.

"I thought you would like to know Edna is awake. She remembers nothing of the shooting. She has been told that she passed out on interstate 10, and was then brought into the hospital. I'm concerned about you questioning her. She might get suspicious if a police officer shows up at her bedside asking questions. Also, do you think it's still necessary to have the police officer guarding her room?"

"I'll have the officer pulled right away. Doc, I can't tell you how happy I am that she's awake. I have been concerned about her. How will it affect her if she finds out through the media what actually happened?"

"I really can't say what affect it'll have. Everyone's different. There could be another setback. I hope we won't have to deal with that. My hopes are that Grady will take her somewhere quiet for a few weeks. Somewhere away from all media and from anyone who might mention the shooting to her…but, I don't know where that would be."

"Let me handle that Doc. I know someone who owns a small island off the east coast of Florida. He's gone most of the time and really only goes there a couple weeks every year. It's a nice, quiet place and has no TV reception or phones. The place is well maintained and has a generator for the lights and air conditioning. It's just a two bedroom bungalow, but I think they'll like it. I stayed there once for a week with my wife and didn't want to come back to the mainland. Do you think they would go for that?"

"I would. I'll pull Grady to the side in the morning and present it to him. After Edna has some quiet time, maybe she'll remember what took place on her own. I believe she'll be able to cope with it better that way."

"Let me know as soon as you get Grady's o.k. and I'll see that the house is stocked with food and everything they'll need for a few weeks. The owner has a nice boat at the marina nearby they can use. It's about a thirty minutes ride to the island. But, it isn't hard to find. Tell Grady not to worry about paying for the trip. My friend lets me use the place anytime I want. He prefers it when someone's there to make the place look occupied."

"You didn't answer my concerns about questioning Edna."

"Why don't I stop by in the morning and play it by ear? You know, ask a few casual questions; nothing that will cause her to become suspicious. I have some important news to give Grady before he leaves. Also, I'm sure Edna will need her yellow purse. I had it cleaned...I didn't want her to know it had been covered in blood. I can mention the island getaway to them while I'm there if you want me to."

"Yes, that will be great, since you'll have all the details. Do you mind if I ask you a question?"

"I don't mind at all. What is it?"

"Isn't her purse evidence or something? Don't you need to keep it?"

"Her purse wasn't used to kill the man...her gun was. I'll have to keep the gun for the time being. I'm sure Grady can find some excuse to tell her why the gun isn't in her purse."

"Sounds like you've thought of everything. Edna is very lucky you are on her side."

"I'm the lucky one, Doc; she's the one that made my job a lot easier."

"How's the investigation coming along?"

"Well, Doc, it's all wrapped up. I have a press conference scheduled tomorrow to make the announcement."

"That's great news, Captain. Let me be the first to congratulate you and your officers. I look forward to hearing the announcement."

Bob exited the elevator on Edna's floor early the next morning and walked the long hallway toward her room. Along the way he saw Captain Hall standing at the nurse's station talking with Dr. Peters. Bob approached the two men and they shook hands.

"How are things going?" Bob asked them.

Dr. Peters said, "You're just the person I had hoped to see this morning, Bob. I wanted to tell you, Edna woke up last night and doesn't remember a thing about the shooting. She's going to want to know why you're here. I'm sure you can think of something that won't tip her off about the Pickle Barrel shooting. I have suggested they go somewhere quiet for a few weeks. Maybe Edna will recall what happened on her own while they're away. Captain Hall has a place in mind for them to go. Do you think you could see that things are taken care of at their place while they're gone? I don't want them to have anything to worry about."

"This is great news…I'm so glad to hear that she's awake. I was really worried about her. I'm happy to do anything I can to help out, Dr. Peters. Consider it done. I had planned to have breakfast with Grady this morning. Will Edna be released today?"

"Go ahead and have breakfast. Maybe Edna would like to join you. However, I do plan to keep her in the hospital another night. They'll be free to leave in the morning for the island retreat. Captain Hall needs a little more time to set things up before they get there, and this will give him the time he needs."

"Thanks for thinking of that, Doc," Captain Hall said. "The additional time will be helpful. I talked with the owner of the island earlier this morning and he knew about the shooting at the Pickle Barrel. He said Grady and Edna were welcome to stay there as long as they wanted."

"That's a very nice thing you're doing for them, Captain," Bob said. "I know they'll appreciate it. Do either of you need to talk with them before we go for breakfast?"

"I have other patients to see this morning and I'm sure Captain Hall has things he needs to get back to," said Dr. Peters. "So, if you don't mind, I think I'll ask Grady to join us in my office before I take care of the other patients. I don't want to take the chance that Edna might overhear our conversation. Bob, can you give us about fifteen minutes?"

"Sure, that's okay with me. I'll just go and have my first cup of coffee in the lobby."

Dr. Peters could hear faint laughter as soon as he entered Edna's suite. He walked down the short hallway and tapped on the door. The laughter stopped as Grady came to the door.

"Hello, Dr. Peters…come in. We were just laughing at one of Edna's duck tales."

They stepped inside the room. Dr. Peters saw Edna sitting up in bed looking as if she had never been sick a day in her life. "It's good to see you up and laughing, Edna. Are you feeling alright this morning?"

"I feel like I have been born again, Doc."

"Well, I see your IV has been removed…you feel like joining Bob and Grady for breakfast in the cafeteria? I saw him in the hall a few minutes ago. He'll be in shortly. For now, I'd like to talk with Grady in my office for a few minutes."

Grady had already informed her of Bob's presence at the hospital. She now looked forward to visiting with him over breakfast.

"Is there something wrong, Dr. Peters?" Edna was curious why Grady was being asked to his office.

"Things couldn't be better, Edna. I just need him to sign some discharge papers for your release in the morning. I won't be here tomorrow to take care of the paperwork. Since I won't be here when you're released, I'll say goodbye to you now, Edna. The circumstances of our meeting weren't all that great, but I'm glad we met. I want you to take it easy for a while, and call me if you need me."

Later, in his private office, Dr. Peters introduced Grady to Captain Hall. "Captain Hall has something he wants to present to you."

The two men shook hands, and then sat in chairs opposite where the doctor sat.

"Grady, I understand you plan to take Edna somewhere quiet for a while. Do you have some place in mind?" Captain Hall asked.

"I have no idea. But, I had better find some place before she's released in the morning."

"Well, I hope I haven't overstepped by bounds here, but I have something set up for you, if you're interested."

"Yes, of course I'm interested."

Grady listened intently while Captain Hall described the place and covered all the plans that had been made for their arrival.

"That's amazing, Captain Hall. Why would someone do something like that for us? I really don't know what to say. It sounds too good to be true. I know Edna would love a place like that."

"We realize Edna needs to stay out of the limelight for a while. You may not know this Grady, but she did a great service by killing that madman. Now, the directions are in this package," he handed Grady a large envelope, "and all the necessary information you'll need. All you need are some swimwear and shorts. I'll have your automobile cleaned and here waiting for you in the morning."

"Captain Hall, I don't know how to thank you. I really appreciate all this. Dr. Peters, is there anything else you need me to do; are there any special instructions for Edna?"

"Just keep her from the media. Allow her to relax and maybe she'll recall the shooting in her own time. Call me anytime day or night if you need to talk. Just go have fun." He shook Grady's hand and the three men walked to the door to leave.

When Dr. Peters was out of sight, Captain Hall said, "Grady, can you spare another few minutes? I need to speak with you privately before you go back to Edna." Captain Hall led Grady into a small chapel a few doors down the hallway.

Grady had been relaxed and happy, but now he was becoming uneasy by the Captain's request to speak with him in private. "There isn't anything wrong, is there?" asked Grady.

"No, there isn't anything wrong. Have a seat. I have something to tell you that I hope will be good news to you." He gave Grady time to get settled in his chair. "This terrorist cell we have just arrested came about because of the man Edna shot at the Pickle Barrel. Not only did she save a lot of lives…killing him led to information which allowed us to track other cell members. There's no telling what they were plotting to do in this country. We found out during the investigation that this guy and his friends had plotted to bomb the president and his family at the football game the other night. He wasn't happy when his plan went awry, so he took his frustrations out on the people at the Pickle Barrel."

"Why would they want to harm our President?"

"The shooter's family had been killed in the Baghdad bombing raids, and he was out to get our president for ordering those raids. That's why this guy went nuts.

Every one of these cell members infiltrated the United States. And, some of them had been living and working amongst us for years. All of them were on the most wanted list and had large rewards on their heads. Since Edna killed one of the cell members which led to the arrest of the others, she's entitled to all of the reward money."

"Captain, are…are you saying…Edna will be receiving a reward for killing this man?"

"I'm saying, she'll be receiving six rewards, which amounts to one million one hundred thousand dollars."

"You can't be serious!" Grady raised his voice louder than he should have.

"I'm very serious. But, Grady, you can't tell Edna about the rewards until she gets her memory back. No one knows how this news will affect her."

"Yes. I understand. I won't tell her until the time is right."

"I don't believe it'll take very long to get the money. I have all the necessary papers ready to submit. I just need to get some information from you before you leave. So, maybe by the time you get back from the island, it'll be in your bank account. Oh, by the way, no charges will be brought against Edna. I also wanted to tell you I'm giving a press release this afternoon to let everyone know about the arrest of this terrorist group. I plan to keep Edna's name out of it. I won't mention anything about the rewards. At some point the media will find out who killed this guy, and I want you to be prepared for a big influx of media at your doorstep. You know how the media can get. So, if it gets to be too much for you, call me and I'll see that you get away until things die down. Now, I've kept you long enough. Bob and Edna are waiting on you for breakfast."

"I can't thank you enough," Grady said, as he stood and shook the Captain's hand.

When Grady went back to join Edna he saw Bob standing in the hallway in front of her room. He greeted him with a big smile. "Are you hungry, Bob? I could eat a bear. Let's get Edna and go get some breakfast."

"You're in a good mood. Did you get some good news or something? And, yes, I'm hungry."

"Everything's just fine, Bob. I guess Dr. Peters told you about our plans to get away for a while."

"Yes, he told me, and I'm glad to see that Edna is doing better and you have a place to take her so she can continue to improve. Since you no longer need my help, I think I'll fly home after breakfast."

"Of course, Bob, you need to get back to your family. I really appreciated your company. I don't know what I would've done without you. I guess you know we won't be coming home right away. There are no phones where we'll be so we'll be out of touch for a while. I'll contact you, however, when I feel Edna is ready to return."

They entered Edna's room expecting her to be dressed to join them for breakfast. She was sitting up in the bed still in her hospital gown.

"Why aren't you dressed for breakfast, Edna?" Grady asked.

"I would love to be dressed if I had something to be dressed in," she replied.

Her response seemed to hang in the air for a second, and then the three of them burst out into spontaneous laughter.

After the laughter subsided, Grady said, "Will you join us if I locate a robe for you? I'll get your clothes from the Suburban in the morning before we leave."

"I tell you what, Grady, why don't the two of you go without me. You know I'm not big on breakfast anyway. But, don't eat too much, because you'll have to have lunch with me." A big smile flashed across her face.

"If you aren't going with us, Edna, then I'll say goodbye for now," Bob said. "I plan to fly back home after breakfast. You guys enjoy your trip and I'll see you when you get back home." He gave her a big hug and a kiss on the cheek. "I'm glad you are back to your old self."

"Thanks for being here, Bob, and tell Margaret I'll make up for the kindness when I get back. Now, the two of you get out of here so that I can rest."

The next morning the sparkling clean Suburban sat in front of the hospital. Edna was happy to be out of hospital attire and dressed in her own clothing. Grady had explained to her where they were going the night before, and now she was anxious to begin their trip to the island retreat. She was also pleased to see her yellow carry-everything purse sitting on the front seat of the truck.

CHAPTER THIRTY-ONE

The day dawned bright and clear as people assembled in the small community church for Mr. Brewer's funeral services. As Gene greeted people at the entrance, Captain Hall approached and expressed his condolences once again. The two men exchanged a few words about the investigation, and then Captain Hall moved along.

Following the services Mr. Brewer was laid to rest in the family cemetery located on the ranch. After the graveside rites the mourners gathered back at the house for lunch. Everyone seemed to have a favorite story or remembrance about Mr. Brewer, and the lunch turned into a celebration of a wonderful man's very eventful life.

Gene was amazed at the number of friends his parents had. They had come from all over the country to attend the services and express their condolences. Most of them had become friends by way of his family's very well-known horse breeding services. These services had produced quite a number of champions for many of the people present. The Brewer family, over the years, had owned several champion race horses of their own. As a result of their success at grooming and siring champions, a big demand had developed for the stud services of their stallions.

Mary Ann and several other women were busy setting food on tables, passing hors d'oeuvre trays, and taking drink requests. Although the house was crowded, Gene could still see Jenny gracefully wandering in and out through the crowd offering something she was carrying on a tray. She seemed to stand out from the crowd in her black, flowing, thigh length, silk dress. Her shoulder length black hair hung straight against her exposed neckline. Her neck looked soft and white, as if it had never seen sunlight. *She has wonderful taste in clothing; wow, she really looks great.* He felt himself staring. His face began to feel hot. He quickly looked around to see if anyone had noticed him admiring her.

Just at that moment, Captain Hall came up beside him, "Gene, I was just wondering about the children—how are they doing?"

"We have to reassure them every day that their parents will be coming soon," Gene said. "Are you making any progress on locating them?"

"Everyone has been accounted for and their families notified. However, we can't verify who the children belong to. They haven't been reported missing by anyone. We found nothing on the dead bodies, or in any automobile, that could identify them. The children had to have been with someone who was killed. I'm sure someone will be contacting us when the family receives the bad news about the death of the person they were with. My office will be the first place they'll call. I'll let you know as soon as that happens. Have the boys had an opportunity to play with any of the animals out back? I always loved being around the horses."

"Yeah, they've been out there. It's such a joy to be around them—especially in the barnyard. Mary Ann let them ride the ponies the other day while Jenny and I were in Tallahassee. They had a ball. And, later that night, we had a picnic in the attic and watched the stars through the telescope. You should've seen the look on their faces, and I've never heard so many questions coming from two little children. It was a great time for all of us.

But, as I passed by their room that evening, I heard whimpering sounds. Sometimes at night when I bathe them, they frequently cry and ask for their parents. I feel so helpless when that happens. We try to keep them occupied during the day. However, at night when everything slows down, that's when things get bad for them. I hope some family member comes forward soon."

"My heart goes out to those little boys. This tragedy has created a lot of heartache for a lot of people. What do you think will happen to your mother now that your father is gone? Have you thought about leaving the force and taking over here?"

"Mother will adjust in time. As for the ranch, Ron pretty much runs everything here anyway. I haven't given much thought to leaving the force. It's in my blood after all these years, and I love my job. Besides, what would you do without me around to keep you straight?"

"I guess you're right." Captain Hall laughed. Gene, when things settle down around here, your mother and Jenny will need to give their statements about what they witnessed at the shooting. Of course, you already know that. There's no big hurry, though, since the case has already been solved. When you get a chance, check your bedroom. I left Jenny's personal belongings from the Pickle Barrel locker on your bed."

"Thank you. She has asked me about them several times. I'm sure she'll appreciate you bringing them."

"How long does she plan to stay here?"

"She said she would stay until the children's family was located. She has no family, no job and no home to go to. She's the most courageous person I have ever met. I'm sure she has no idea where her next step in life will lead her. But, she's a survivor and I'm sure she'll be just fine.

"She certainly does have a lot of survival instincts," Captain Hall agreed. "Well, I have to get back to the precinct. I'll be in touch with you later."

As Captain Hall walked from the room, he couldn't help recalling the sparkle he had seen in Gene's eyes when he spoke of Jenny.

"There you are, Gene," Mary Ann said. She was carrying a hot tray with pigs-in-the-blanket fresh from the oven. A bowl of spicy mustard sat in the middle of the tray. "These are your favorites. I wanted to make sure you had first dibs. You know how fast these things go." She passed him a small cocktail plate and napkin. "Now, help yourself and don't be shy about it."

"Miss Mary, you're still spoiling me after all these years." He took the plate from her and helped himself to a generous helping. "I really do love your hot pigs-in-the-blanket. I appreciate you thinking of me. By the way, have you seen the boys lately?"

"Oh, you don't have to worry about them. All the teens and children are in the playroom upstairs. They're having another picnic. The boys loved it so much the other night they wanted to do it again."

"We're sure going to miss those two little guys when they leave."

"We sure will. But, I hope their parents are found soon. And, I hope they're alive."

"Their parents have to be alive, Miss Mary. Captain Hall said everyone has been accounted for, except for the boys. Since we know their parents weren't killed, it is a little strange that no one has reported them missing."

"Well, they just didn't wander in off the street. You don't think they were kidnapped, and then the kidnappers got killed at the Pickle Barrel, do you?"

"If they had been kidnapped, there would've been an AMBER alert or missing persons filed. There has been nothing filed indicating the disappearance of these two little boys. Captain Hall feels certain someone will call his office before long, inquiring about them."

"I hope he's right. Well, enjoy your pigs. I'll pass the rest of these out."

As Gene ate his pigs-in-the-blanket, he glanced across the room at the maze of people. He caught sight of Jenny. She appeared to be in deep conversation with Larry. He saw them slowly leave where they stood in the living room and enter the library down the hall. He was surprised by the twinge of jealously he felt. *I'll find out what that was all about later.*

Several out-of-town guests were staying the night in the six bedroom guest house located near the main house. Some had already retired for the night in the cottages on the premises. The weather had a nip in the air, so Gene started a fire in the living room fireplace. He invited their house guests to join him and his mother there. Since it had been some time since their last visit, they all gathered in the cozy, warm living room and talked well into the night.

It had been a long, hard day for everyone. All the kitchen helpers had gone home, so Jenny stayed and helped Mary Ann put the last of the serving platters into the cupboards. She then went upstairs and tucked the children into bed. They had been so tired from the day's busy activities, they didn't even cry for their parents. They were asleep almost before their heads hit the pillow. Jenny felt like doing the same thing. She went back downstairs and said good night to everyone. On her way back upstairs, she thought about Gene and regretted not having the opportunity to spend any time with him that day. *I'll have to make up for that tomorrow.*

Jenny had been exhausted when she went to bed and slept much later the next morning than she normally would have. When she finally got up and dressed, she rushed down the hall to check on the children and found they weren't in their room. She figured Gene had them somewhere doing something fun and left their room to go downstairs. As she entered the first floor, the smell of breakfast and coffee was in the air, and suddenly, she felt very hungry.

Mary Ann was alone in the kitchen. She was loading the dishwasher when Jenny entered and hardly heard her soft footsteps.

"Oh! Miss Jenny, did you have a good night's rest?" she said when she looked up and saw Jenny standing in the kitchen. "Breakfast is ready, if you're hungry."

"Good morning, Mary Ann," she said through a big yawn. "Does Gene have the children?"

"No, he doesn't have the children. He and Pauline have gone to the airport to take the guests who had early flights. The guests, who had automobiles, ate breakfast earlier and have already left for their destinations."

Jenny looked out the long kitchen window and saw a strange woman talking with the children. "Who's the woman out back talking with the children?"

Mary Ann didn't bother to look up to see to whom Jenny was referring. "That's Betty. She helps with the household chores a few days a week. She has been visiting family in Texas. This is her first day back and her first time to meet the children. She loves children. Her husband was killed in Vietnam during the war. They had no children and she never remarried. Like me, she has been friends of the Brewer family for years. Betty lives in one of the cottages on the property nearby. Most days, she walks to work. She says it keeps her young and strong. Listen to me, I'm just rambling on. Don't worry about the children—they're in good hands. Sit down at the table and I'll bring you something to eat."

Jenny walked over and sat in her place at the table. She enjoyed her breakfast while Mary Ann picked up around the kitchen and made preparations for lunch. It appeared to her that Mary Ann spends most of her time in the kitchen.

"Mary Ann, do you mind if I ask you a personal question?"

"I don't mind at all, Jenny. You can ask me anything."

"Well, I was wondering if you spend all your time in the kitchen cooking. It has to be awfully tiring for you to cook three large meals a day. It's a wonder Gene and Pauline aren't as big as barrels from eating so much."

"Oh, no, I don't spend all that much time cooking. This is a special time...having you and the children, and Gene here. I want you to eat well while I have you. Not that I don't cook for Pauline while no one else is here...I do. It's just nice to have a large group to cook for. Food is always better when you can cook more of it."

"What do you mean *having Gene here*? Doesn't he live here?"

"I'm sorry, Jenny, I thought you knew. He has a home in Tallahassee and has lived there for years. The main reason he has been here this long is because of his father's death, and because he was forced to take leave from his job. I'm sure he'll be returning to Tallahassee when everything is back in order here."

"I don't know why. I just assumed he lived here and commuted to work. I know it's a long drive, but people do it all the time. Pauline will be lost without her husband, especially when Gene returns to Tallahassee. Oh, I really feel bad for her. I know how it feels to be lonely."

"Don't worry yourself too much about Pauline; she's a survivor. You remind me of her—*survivors, the both of you.* I don't know your story, but I do know a survivor when I see one. What's your story, Jenny? I have a feeling life hasn't always been kind to you."

The conversation had gotten off the subject of Gene and onto her. How did that happen? Jenny could feel tears building in her eyes. She didn't want to cry. *I have a story alright...a story that isn't worth telling or hearing.* The kitchen was quiet now. Mary Ann sat at the table across from her where she could see every shake of her hand and every tear that might fall. *I don't want anyone to know my story. And, I certainly don't need anyone's sympathy.* She had made it alone so far, and when the children's parents were found, she would go back to the way things were. Which wasn't much, she knew, but it was life as she knew it.

"Mary Ann, I don't mean to sound rude, but I don't have much of a story to tell. I just do what I have to do to exist on this earth. You're right; life hasn't always been good to me. But, I'm alive and in good health in spite of my misfortunes. I can't say that I'm unhappy. I'm sure there are a lot of people worse off than me. I feel that everyone has a destiny and everything that happens to us is in the plan somehow. I don't know what life has in store for me, but at this time in my life, I take each day as it comes."

Mary Ann listened in disbelief while the young woman expressed her feelings. She had never seen anyone quite like Jenny. She was so strong and capable, yet she was so fragile. She was smart, but uneducated. She was serious, but fun-loving. Mary Ann really liked Jenny. She saw Jenny was uncomfortable and didn't want to embarrass her any further by asking more personal questions.

"Jenny, since you have finished your breakfast, why don't you go outside and join the children? I'm sure Betty has them involved in something fun and exciting."

Jenny followed the sound of the children's laughter as she walked through the horse stalls into the adjoining animal pen. She found Betty and the children seated on a patch of grass. Each of them was holding a yellow baby duckling. The mother duck, along with four other ducklings, didn't seem to mind the children handling them. When they weren't being picked up, they pecked at the corn Betty had placed on the ground next to their feet.

"Look, Miss Jenny, we have ducks," Danny shouted with excitement when he saw her approaching.

"I see that." She reached down and picked up one of the ducklings. "Mary Ann tells me your name is, Betty. I'm pleased to meet you. Thank you for watching the children," Jenny said, acknowledging Betty sitting on the ground.

"I'm pleased to meet you too, Jenny. We're having a great time. Aren't we guys?"

"Yes, we are having a good time," said Rossi. "We gave the chickens and goats something to eat and they let us pet them."

"Yes...I wasn't afraid of the big goats...was I, Rossi?" Danny spoke out.

"Miss Betty said we could get the eggs from the chickens tonight and we can eat them for breakfast in the morning. Do you want to help us, Jenny? Miss Betty won't care…will you?"

"I don't mind at all. Jenny, you're more than welcome to help gather the eggs."

"I'd love to help. Where are the chickens?"

The boys pointed to a nice size hen house a short distance behind the stables.

"Did you see the hens on their nest this morning?" Jenny asked.

"No. Miss Betty said we can see them tonight…that way, they will be sleepy and won't peck us when we take their eggs from underneath them."

"That's right," Betty said, as she placed the duckling she was holding onto the ground and then stood up. "Jenny, since you're here, I hope you don't mind if I leave you with the children. I have some work to do inside the house. Feel free to wander anywhere you like. The animals are approachable and won't harm you."

After Betty left, the children released the ducklings and were eager to see the big horses. They knew where to go and ran ahead. Jenny caught up with them in the stables. They were looking up with wide-eyed wonder at the largest and most beautiful chestnut color horse she had ever seen.

"He's a world champion," a voice said from behind them. "He never lost a race. No other horse could ever outrun him."

Jenny was startled by the sudden sound of a male's voice behind her. She turned to face the direction the voice had come from and saw the most handsome man she had ever seen. He was tall, had sandy color hair, sky blue eyes, and a muscular body that was golden tan. The sparkle in those blue eyes, and that turned-up crooked smile on his face was enough to make any girl, alive or dead, swoon. He looked as if he had stepped out of *"Play Girl Magazine"*. She felt her heart racing.

"Hey there boys…are ya having a good time?" Betty had introduced the children to him earlier that morning. "Hi, Jenny, my name is Ron." He extended his hand to shake hers. "I saw you yesterday at the funeral. At the time, you were so busy that I felt guilty about interrupting you to introduce myself. I'm glad to see you have slowed down today."

"I…I'm pleased to meet you, Ron," she said, as she accepted his extended hand. She hoped he hadn't noticed her nervous reaction and her blushing face. "Do…do you work here?"

He held her small hand far longer than necessary. "I guess you might say that I play a part here. I oversee the animals—from the chickens to the horses. I make sure the horses are healthy and ready to mate. I decide what horse will mate and when the mating will take place. I'm a veterinarian and my specialty is animal husbandry. This guy here is '*Fantastic Sam*'." He released her hand and walked up to the horse and rubbed his head. "He's here in the holding stall waiting to be bred with a nice little race champion who should be arriving this afternoon."

Jenny was overwhelmed by the large chestnut stallion. She had never been around horses and had so many questions she wanted to ask that she wasn't sure where to start. "He's the most beautiful animal I have ever seen, Ron. Is he too old for racing… has he been retired?"

"He doesn't race anymore, but, he's far from being retired. Sam's our most requested stud."

Danny and Rossi still had their faces pointed upwards, staring at the huge horse. "Can we touch him, Mr. Ron?" Danny asked.

"Sure, I can help you up. But, only one of you can pet him at a time. Who wants to go first?"

They both answered, "Me—me."

"I'll tell you how we can settle this. I'll flip a coin and one of you calls heads and one of you calls tails." Ron took a coin from his pocket and held it up. "Call it, Danny—heads or tails?"

Danny studied his answer in silence for a moment. And then, he said "*Heads.*"

"Alright, Rossi, you have tails."

Ron showed the boys which side of the coin belonged to each of them. Then he flipped the coin, and it landed on the floor. Tails faced up. "Okay, Rossi. You get to go first." He reached behind him and pulled a large orange carrot from his back pocket. "Here, give him this and he'll love you forever."

Rossi held out the carrot for Fantastic Sam and waited for him to take it, and then he cautiously petted his large head.

By the time Ron had sat Danny down from his turn, Rossi was already at the stall next door looking up at another big, jet-black horse. He had a big smile on his face and was pointing his small finger in the direction of the big horse. "Can I touch this one, Mr. Ron?"

Jenny thought this was the sweetest thing she had ever seen. It was a perfect Kodak moment.

"Oh, this is *'Morning Star'*. She's going to have a baby soon. That's why I have her here close to the house where I can keep an eye on her. She really likes children, and I'm sure she wouldn't mind if you gave her a little rub." He gave Rossi another carrot to give the horse, and then lifted him up. "She likes to be scratched behind the ears, like this." Rossi giggled with delight when the horse gave a big whinny as he scratched her ears.

"So, are there a lot of horses on the ranch?" Jenny remembered seeing horses with blankets across their backs on their way to church Sunday morning.

"Actually there's quite a lot," Ron said, as he placed Rossi back on the floor. "You'll see some of them grazing in pastures throughout the ranch. The most sought after and valuable horses are kept in a more protected area surrounded by security cameras. They have quite a good life if you ask me. Remind me sometime and I'll take you to see them."

Jenny was having a hard time concentrating on what Ron was saying. She had been caught up in the sound of his voice, his smell, and his looks, how he communicated with the children, and his overall mannerisms—all these things were very distracting to her. She tried to compose herself. What's happening to me, she thought. I must be coming down with something. But, I don't really feel sick.

A car could be heard rounding the side of the house coming in their direction. But, Jenny hadn't heard the approaching car; she was too busy swooning to notice. The shouts of the children jarred her back to reality.

"Mr. Gene's home!" the boys shouted and ran from the stables to greet him.

Gene was parked and out of the car when he saw the boys running in his direction. He greeted them with open arms, and then picked them both up and swung them around a couple times. "I missed you guys," he said as he swung them. "Have you been having a good time?" He sat them down but kept a hand on each of their small shoulders.

"Oh, yes…we're having a real good time," said Danny. "Mr. Ron showed us the big mama horse and the one that's going to make a baby today. And, tonight, we're going to get the eggs from the chickens."

Gene couldn't help but laugh at Danny's excitement.

Pauline overheard the conversation and rolled with laughter. Oh, the things that children say—it's so good to have little children around again, she thought.

As Gene rounded the other side of the car to help his mother, he couldn't help but see Jenny and Ron slowly walking in his direction. They appeared to be happy about something. The *twinge* in his stomach he had felt on the day of his father's funeral, as he watched Jenny enter the library with Larry, *had returned*.

CHAPTER THIRTY-TWO

G rady had no problem locating the marina where the boat they were going to take to the island was docked. They had made a couple stops along the way to pick up some casual clothing, swimwear, and blueberry crème coffee. Captain Hall assured him that everything they needed was already at the cottage—including food, water, and gas for the boat and generator. The handwritten instructions and map he provided were very helpful. The Captain had thought of everything.

"Are you sure this is the right slip, Grady? Check the number on the information sheet again."

"I'm telling you, Swart, the number on the instruction sheet showed the number seven hundred and that's where we're standing."

Edna looked the big boat up and down and said, "Do you think you can operate a boat this size?"

He did have some concerns about maneuvering such a large boat, but he wouldn't let her know about them. "Now Swart, you remember, you asked that same question when we got our new boat several years ago. And, as you know, I never had a problem operating that one, did I?"

"Yes, but that one was half the size of this one. And as I recall, you were a lot younger at the time."

"Don't worry, Swart. Climb aboard and let the "*Master of the Seas*" show you how it's done." He reached for her hand and helped her aboard the thirty-nine foot cabin cruiser. Edna will never let me live it down, if I crash this thing, he thought.

Grady managed to back the boat out of the slip and maneuver it through the channel into open waters. He felt more at ease now. He wasn't too worried about locating the island. Captain Hall's directions were simple to follow.

There wasn't a cloud in the sky, and Edna relaxed on the sun deck soaking up the sun's rays while she enjoyed the scenery. She was satisfied that Grady knew what he was doing with the boat.

"Look, Swart!" Grady shouted after about twenty-five minutes on the open waters. "I think I see the island. Can you see it? There, just in front of us! We should be there in a few minutes." He couldn't believe how excited he had suddenly become about this island vacation.

Edna stood up from her deck chair and stretched to see with her hands shading the sun from her eyes. "I see it…I see the island, Grady!" As she gazed out across the water at the parcel of land she said, "How long is the island?"

"No one told me. I would guess, just by looking, it's a little more than a mile. It'll make a good walk for us in the mornings and evenings. Just think we'll have a perfect view of the sunrise and the sunset."

"Now Grady, you really don't think we're going to see a sunrise, do you? It has been a long time since we've seen one. Now, the sunsets will be great. I hope we get there soon, because I'm starving. I feel like I could eat a whale and walk the island ten times over."

"Well, it looks like we'll have just enough time to eat, explore the island for a short while, and then watch the sunset."

"Are you sure we'll be the only one's there?"

"That's what I was told. I understand there's only one house on the island, and it's ours for the time being."

Grady docked the boat against the long wooden pier which stretched out into the water. Edna was giddy with joy at the sight of the soft, white sand which seemed to stretch the length of the island. She couldn't wait to sink her feet into it. They couldn't see the cottage from where they stood, but a wide wood plank pathway led through the foliage in that direction. They grabbed their few belongings and followed the pathway through the maze of scrub oaks, sea grapes, palms and mangroves. After a short walk, they entered a clearing and saw it. They stopped in their tracks and took in their surroundings.

They were amazed by the beauty and size of the cottage. It was made of logs and had a wrap-around porch with blue morning glories climbing up and around the eaves. Scattered around the porch were small sitting areas with tables and high back chairs. Rocking chairs of various sizes and styles were also placed around the porch. A porch swing was located on one corner and displayed various shapes and sizes of floral printed pillows. Flower beds were bordered off next to the cottage and planted with creeping juniper which added life and charm to the area. The cottage was shaded by large live oak trees. They could see palm trees scattered in clusters throughout the perimeter. Under one of the clusters, two hammocks rocked in the soft ocean breeze.

"Wow! What a place. How do you think they got all the building materials out here to build this place?" Edna asked with amazement.

"It's beyond me," Grady answered. "Let's check out the inside."

"Let's check out the food situation. I'm hungry."

They felt a warm, welcoming feeling when they discovered the front door had been left open for them. They entered, and then sat the few belongings they had brought with them on the floor. Standing in silence, their eyes traveled around the cozy, tastefully decorated décor of the living room. A stone mantel fireplace was located at the far end of the room. Hanging over the mantel was a large oil painting of a ship with large white sails billowing in the wind on a calm blue sea. The crisp white, overstuffed sofa placed in front of the fireplace looked inviting with fluffy floral pillows. A game table with four chairs sat in a corner near the fireplace. Soft leather chairs were grouped in pairs next to small tables which created reading or conversational areas. On the tables, fresh cut flowers rested inside tall crystal vases. One wall displayed an ornate wood carved cabinet. Behind the glass doors of the cabinet books and other reading materials were neatly arranged. This wasn't the rustic beach house they had expected to see. Edna turned so that she was facing Grady and broke the silence. "How much did this place set us back, Grady?"

He was still dumbfounded by what he was seeing, but, he managed to find the words to speak. "You worry too much, Swart. It isn't costing us anything." She didn't know about Captain Hall and his involvement in all this, and he didn't feel this was the time to explain everything to her. "Dr. Peters arranged this through a friend of his. He told his friend we were looking for a place to stay for a while, and his friend said we could stay here. Apparently, he's always looking for someone to occupy the place when he can't be here. He doesn't want the place to appear abandoned."

"Are you telling me that we're staying here for nothing? That's hard for me to believe. No one's that generous."

"Well, you'll have to believe it this time. You know how it is with people who have a lot of money. Doing something nice like this is nothing to them financially. He helped us out and we helped him. That's the way things happen sometimes. Now, let's find the food." He took her hand and led her in the direction he thought the kitchen would be.

Edna stood in front of the open oversized refrigerator door staring at the large quantity of food neatly arranged on the shelves. "Grady! Come and take a look at this. There's more food in here than we could ever eat in two months. Look at all this beautiful fruit."

Grady peeked around her shoulder into the refrigerator to see what she was talking about. "Wow! I was told there would be food, but I didn't expect anything like this."

"Look!" Edna had opened the freezer compartment and held up a large lobster tail. "This is the largest lobster tail I have ever seen. The freezer is packed with steaks, sea food, chops, burger meat, chicken, desserts, frozen dinners and vegetables of all kinds. Dr. Peters sure has friends in high places."

"Well, since you're the one who's starving, what would you like to have for your first meal here?" Grady asked. He then motioned for her to join him in exploring the rest of the cottage.

As they slowly made their way down the hall, through the office/exercise room, through two bathrooms and two bedrooms, Edna thought about dinner.

"You know what sounds good to me; two of those big lobster tails wrapped in foil with garlic butter and lemon baked on the barbecue grill with baked potatoes and a Caesar salad. Does that appeal to you?"

"I can't wait. I'll get the fire started while you put everything together."

They looked at each other, turned from the master bedroom located in the farthest part of the cottage, and then like two little children, took off racing down the hall into the kitchen. They laughed hysterically while they pulled things from the freezer, refrigerator, stove, and cabinets. At one point, the laughter was so hard, they fell into each others arms and continued laughing as tears rolled down their faces.

"Okay, Swart, we had better settle down and get serious about cooking or we're going to starve to death here in each others arms," Grady said, after he finally settled down a little.

Grady's statement set Edna off on another laughing frenzy. "Yeah, I can see someone coming to the island looking for us because they haven't heard from us in a month. They find two decomposing old farts standing in the kitchen wrapped in each others arms with big smiles on their faces. What do you think their reaction would be?"

Grady was rolling with laughter. It's fun having Edna around, he thought. "I'm sure they'll think that we died laughing."

They were laughing so hard now they had to find a chair to sit on to keep from falling and rolling on the floor.

"Oh, Grady, I do love you," Edna said when she settled down from her laughing frenzy. "I don't know how I thought I could go to Mississippi for two weeks without you. I guess someone was trying to tell me something when I passed out on the road. It wasn't meant for me to leave you. Now, I'm ready to get this show on the road. Crank up the grill, big boy."

They agreed the dinner was the best they had ever had, and the picturesque setting couldn't have been more perfect. They had eaten their dinner at a small white wicker table on the front porch where they could see the ocean through a gap in the mangrove trees.

"Swart, do you still want to go for a walk?" Grady asked after they had placed the dirty dishes in the sink. "The sun is going down and it'll be blacker than tar out here when it does."

"I think we have time for a short walk before it gets too dark. Let me get my walking shoes."

The walk felt good to Edna's stiff body. She only wished it had been longer. I'll make up for my lost walking time tomorrow, she thought. There was very little light from the moon. It was almost pitch dark, but they were near the cottage. If it hadn't been for the porch lights they had left on, they might have passed it up. Grady was right…the night was black as tar out here when the sun went down.

"I want to check to see if the generator has enough gas before I go inside," Grady said. "Do you want to walk with me or go on inside?"

"I think I'll go ahead and start my bath. Do you think you'll need a flashlight? I saw one in the pantry earlier."

"Yes, maybe I should get the flashlight. It looks pretty dark out there. I would hate to encounter a big black bear or something worse," he joked.

"Oh, don't worry, Grady. He'd let you go as soon as he figured out what he had."

"You didn't let me go and you figured out what you had."

"Well, maybe I'm still figuring."

He gave her a love slap across her bottom and then entered the cottage to get the flashlight.

Later that evening as they lay in bed, Grady pulled Edna into his arms and whispered into her freshly shampooed hair. "I love you, Swart. I hope you know that."

"I do…I love you, too."

Wrapped in his arms, Edna slept peacefully all night.

It was very unusual for Edna to rise early in the mornings. However, she was awake, rested, and ready to start the day, so she eased out of bed to keep from waking Grady. Then she proceeded to the kitchen to prepare breakfast.

"Okay sleepy head, wake up. Breakfast is ready," she said while charging across the bedroom floor and landing on the bed next to Grady. She leaned down and gave him a big kiss on the forehead.

Sleepy eyed, he sat up and said, "What are you doing up so early? We're on vacation." He gave his arms a big stretch.

"Even people on vacation have to eat. So, get up lazy-bones. Breakfast is on the patio and its getting cold."

"Alright, let me get a shirt to put on and I'll be right there."

"What do you need a shirt for? There isn't anyone but me around to see you, and I already know what you look like. Besides, I'm wearing what I have on."

He looked at her skimpy, short pajamas and decided to skip the shirt. Then he stepped through the double French doors of the bedroom onto the patio.

The white wicker table looked lovely set with colorful matching china. The china had pink rosebuds with green leaves around the outer edge of the plates. There were matching cups and saucers off to the side of each plate. The china plate rested in a larger green charger plate. This added color to the overall appearance of the table and made the food look even more tempting. The orange juice in the crystal glasses looked cool and refreshing. A crisp rose and green plaid cloth napkin lay beside each place setting. The napkins were made of the same fabric as the table cloth which draped the table. Silver flatware sparkled in the bright early morning light. A fresh, single pink rose stood straight in a green crystal bud-vase in the center of the table. Where did she find that rose? Grady thought.

Edna had made cheese omelets with red Mexican salsa and blueberry muffins. Freshly cut cantaloupe and red strawberries were beautifully placed on the side of their plates next to the omelet. Brewed blueberry crème coffee filled a rose colored china coffee pot.

"This looks wonderful, Swart…almost too good to eat. What time did you get up this morning? It must have taken you a long time to put all this together. Where did you get all this energy? Normally, at home you don't fall out of bed until ten o'clock."

"Now, don't go giving me a hard time. It's just breakfast. You may not get any tomorrow, so you had better eat and enjoy it. I'm eager to finish that walk and put my feet in that gorgeous white sandy beach we saw yesterday."

"But Swart, you have all day…the sun is barely up."

"I know. Maybe before we leave here, we'll see a real sunrise. Right now, I want to enjoy every precious minute of this vacation."

Grady laughed as he pulled out his chair to sit at the table. "With all this newly found energy you have, you probably already have dinner ready for tonight."

Edna was already seated at the table. "Not quite," she said. "But, I was thinking it would be nice to take that big boat out and try our hand at catching our supper. It shouldn't take very long to catch a few fish. What do you think about that?"

"Swart, the freezer's full of fish. Why do you want to take the boat out to fish? We can fish from the bank."

"Well, Grady, it's like this. We're here with all this water surrounding us…there are fish in those waters…there's a big beautiful boat we can use at our convenience…we have all the time in the world with nothing else to do. But, the biggest reason is, I have never had an opportunity to experience something like this, and I want fresh fish for supper."

"I guess that settles it then. When do you want to go fishing?"

"As soon as we finish breakfast and I pack a lunch. I have heard that fish bite best in the mornings, so we had better get moving. We can go for our long walk when we get back."

$$\rightleftharpoons \rightleftharpoons \rightleftharpoons$$

While Grady slowly moved the boat away from the island and into more open waters, Edna readied the fishing gear.

"How about right here, Grady. I have a good feeling about this spot," she shouted over the roar of the engine.

They had traveled about three miles from the small island. The water in this area had a little chop. Fluffy white clouds hung in the sky overhead; *a perfect day for fishing.*

"Do you want to drift or anchor?" Grady asked as he killed the engine.

"Let's drift for awhile. Then if we don't get any strikes, we can anchor. Here, the rods are ready to go." Edna extended her hand with two rods for him. "I see rod holders all around the boat. So, choose your spot and let the race begin."

"Ah, I see...now we're racing. You don't know who you're dealing with here. I once caught the first fish on a deep-sea fishing trip I went on. As it turned out, it was the only fish caught that day. Okay, since we're drifting, I'll set up in the back."

"Well, make room for me, because that's where I want to set up."

Thirty minutes later they were still drifting and hadn't even gotten a nibble. "Alright Grady, I give up. It's time to move somewhere else." Edna began reeling in her line.

"Alright! I wondered when you'd get enough of this. Does this mean the race is off?"

"No. It means we're changing locations. I know there's plenty of fish out here and we're going to have fresh fish for dinner."

Grady moved the boat to a location nearer to the island, but on the opposite side; the current was swifter there. He turned the engine off. "How does this look, Swart? Do you want to anchor or drift?"

"Let's try the anchor this time. While you set the anchor I'll get our lunch ready." She set her rods out, and then she went to the galley kitchen.

They watched their lines while they ate lunch, but were rewarded with only a few nibbles. It was as if something was toying with the bait.

"Do you think that's a fish messing with the lines, Grady?"

"It very well could be." He pulled his line up slightly to see if anything was on it. There was nothing on his hook. "Let's give it another thirty minutes, Swart. If we don't get a bite, then let's go back to the island."

At the end of the thirty minutes there still was no activity.

"Swart, we had better get back to the cottage so that you'll have enough time to let the fish from the freezer defrost."

"Alright, rub it in mister. I know there's fish out here, and I plan to catch at least one of them before I leave this island. We must be doing something wrong. Do you think there's a fishing book in the cottage we can read on *how to catch fish*?"

"We have given it our best shot. So go ahead and pull your lines in. We'll try again in a couple of days."

Edna had brought both of her lines in and was in the process of storing the rods. Grady picked up his last rod and began to reel it in when he felt resistance.

"Oh! What's this! Swart, come here! Come see! I think I have a fish." The fish was giving him a run for his money. He was putting up some fight. "It feels like a big one, Swart. Come help me! Bring the net!"

Edna saw Grady fighting with the fish long before she got there with the net. She said, "I don't believe it! He would have to bite your hook."

"Don't worry about that now, Swart. I need your help. When I bring him in close, you reach down and scoop him up with the net."

The closer the fish came toward them, the larger it looked. "Oh! Grady, he looks so big. I don't know if I can hold him in the net."

"Don't worry about holding him up. Just get the net under him good. I'll keep the line tight so that he can't get loose."

They struggled with the fish a couple more minutes, but finally managed to pull it on board. It was beautiful and very large—much more than they could eat in one meal.

They lay exhausted beside the large fish and laughed about their victory. They rested for a short while and then sat back up to admire the trophy catch.

Edna suddenly became somber. "Put him back in the water, Grady."

"You mean in the holding tank?"

"No, I mean, back in the ocean. *I can't kill him*. And I'm not going to eat him."

"But, Swart, you wanted fresh fish for dinner. I'll clean him and get him ready to cook. Just pretend he came from the freezer."

"No! *I won't be the cause of his death*! I won't eat him! I want you to put him back where he belongs. Look at him...he must have been living in these waters for a long time to get that large. We can't *kill* him now."

He noticed her mood had suddenly changed. "Alright, I'll release him. But you can't weasel out of it...I still won the race!" he teased, hoping to lighten her mood.

"That you did, fair and square. And what a prize he is. We'll have a real fish tale to talk about for years to come. Thank you for doing this for me. Now let's get back to the cottage and take some steaks out of the freezer."

It had been a fun-filled day. The steak dinners were delicious. The walk along the sandy beach was relaxing. Edna and Grady were now involved in a hot and heavy game of gin rummy. They were very competitive and hated losing...even to one another.

"Gin!" Grady shouted while laying all his cards on the table.

"I don't believe it! Not again! How do you do that? You must be cheating somehow." Edna said, pretending to be upset.

"I'll tell you my secret for winning, if you'll give me a little kiss." He placed his face near hers and puckered his lips.

She looked him square in the face and said, "Go kiss yourself in the mirror, Grady. You can't bribe me. And you can keep your secret. I'm not playing gin with you again."

"Well, we'll see about that. It's late. Are you ready to go to bed?"

"Yes, I'm ready. It has been a long day."

"So, do you want to go fishing again in the morning?" he joked.

She gave him "*The Look*", and then she walked toward the bedroom.

Grady followed along behind her with a big grin on his face. He switched off lights as he walked. "Oh, come on, Swart. You aren't really mad at me, are you?"

She wasn't upset with him but she would let him think she was a little while longer. Besides, he knew they never went to bed angry. She didn't answer him and kept walking.

Later, Grady crawled in bed beside her and drew her into his arms. He kissed her tenderly on the cheek. Did you enjoy the day, Swart?"

"It was a great day. I wouldn't trade it for anything. But I enjoyed being with you most of all. She turned toward him and gave him a long loving kiss on the lips. "I love you, you know."

"I know...I love you, too. Sleep well, my Swart," he said.

Grady was awakened in the wee hours of the morning by Edna's moans and whimpers. He could feel her arms and legs twitch and jerk. He knew she was having a bad dream. Her memory of the shooting must be coming back. Maybe she'll tell me about it later when she gets up, he thought.

Edna didn't rise early and prepare breakfast like she had the morning before. Grady slipped out of bed and allowed her to sleep as long as she needed. He had breakfast waiting on the patio when she woke up. Of course, the breakfast wasn't as elaborate as Edna's. He was sitting on the patio having a cup of coffee and enjoying the view when she appeared.

"Good morning sleepy-head," he said with a smile when he saw her. "Did you sleep well?" He knew she hadn't.

"Good morning." She yawned and gave her arms a big stretch high into the air. "I can't believe I slept so late. I feel like I have been in an all night wrestling match. I'm sore all over. I think I need a long walk. Oh! Grady, I see you made breakfast. Would you pour me a cup of coffee? I need coffee."

"Why don't you stay in today and rest? We were pretty busy yesterday. You probably overdid it. You just got out of the hospital, you know."

"I feel like I need to do something to work this soreness out. Do you mind if we walk the length of the island a few times this morning while the weather is cool? What time is it anyway?"

"It's ten o'clock. So take your time and eat your breakfast. We can walk when you're ready."

"Oh, Grady, it's past time for the Brattman's radio program. Would you find a radio so that I can listen to him?"

"Swart, have you forgotten, we're on an island. There's no reception out here. Besides, news doesn't change that much. I'm sure you can pick up where you left off when we get back."

"That's right…I forgot about that. I just miss listening to him, that's all. It seems like forever since I heard his programs. Well, I guess we'll just have to use the time to play on the beach again. I take it that there are no cell towers nearby, as well. I'd love to call Dixie to see how things are with Chatty and the ducks."

"I checked with her just before we left and everything was fine. We haven't been gone that long, and I'm sure nothing has changed at home." He knew he wasn't totally truthful with her. Reporters were probably camped out all over their lawn.

The rest of the day was quiet and restful. They leisurely walked the island from end to end for the first time since their arrival. They had followed the wide winding pathways and would stop occasionally to study an unusual plant, or to watch a rabbit hop past. How did a rabbit get out here? Grady thought at the time. Park benches had been placed along the paths where you could sit and admire the scenic views. At one end of the island, families of dolphins played in the water. Edna and Grady sat on a bench nearby and watched the dolphins while they drank the water they had brought with them. A group of white pelicans tussled over a dead fish on the sand close by, and didn't seem to notice that they were being watched.

Grady had been faithful about checking the generator every day to be sure it had plenty of gas. It was usually dark when he checked it, so he could never see what was stored inside the large wooden shelter. Today, it was still daylight when he checked the generator. He could now see two long kayaks lying across the back wall of the building. They had two kayaks at home and loved to take them out on all-day adventures. He would be sure to tell Edna about them tonight.

Grady was in the restroom involved in his forty-five minute nightly ritual of brushing his teeth when Edna entered and began her own nightly ritual at the other sink. He thought it would be a good time to bring up the kayaks.

"Guess what I found outside in the shed earlier?" He didn't give her a chance to respond. "I found two kayaks. Would you like to go venturing tomorrow?" He knew she would be pleased with the news.

"*Kayaks*...I can't believe we've been here all this time and didn't know there were kayaks in the shed. If the moon was full, we could go for a moonlight paddle. Do you remember the last time we went moonlight paddling with the kayak club? We saw hundreds of alligator eyes glowing in the light of our headlamps along the water's edge? You don't think gators are way out here, do you?"

"I'm pretty sure there aren't any alligators out this far. And, it'll be a while before the moon's full. Besides, we have all day to kayak, which should be more than enough kayaking time. We won't have to kayak at night and run the risk of running into thousands of eyes glowing in the dark."

That night Edna was very restless. She tossed and turned, moaned and whimpered. Grady had never heard her talk aloud in her sleep, until now. He was becoming increasingly worried about her health and knew he couldn't question her about her restless nights.

The next morning Edna awoke groggy and with a slight headache. She made her way from the bedroom onto the patio and sat at the table where Grady was having coffee and enjoying the cool morning ocean breeze. Placed on the table mat in front of her was a bowl of freshly sliced assorted fruits and yogurt.

"Good morning, Swart." Grady could see she wasn't her usual happy, spirited self. "How did you sleep? I thought you might like a light breakfast this morning. Can I get some coffee for you?"

"Thanks, Grady. A light breakfast sounds great, but a cup of strong black coffee in each eye sounds even better." She placed her hands over her closed eyes and groaned.

"Did you have a rough night?" He studied her carefully. "You want to talk about it?"

"It's the dream…I don't know what's happening to me. I keep having the same dream but nothing ever comes together. It never makes sense. I feel it's something bad, but, like I said, I don't know what it is. When I'm dreaming, it feels so real, but I can't remember anything when I wake up. I'm just left with a strange, scared feeling. This has happened a couple nights now. You don't think I'm losing it, do you?"

"You aren't losing anything, Swart. Remember, Dr. Peters said you needed rest. Everyone has bad dreams occasionally. If you aren't up to kayaking today, why don't we take a blanket down to the end of the island and lie around and read all day? I'll pack a picnic. Maybe we can take a few fish from the freezer and toss pieces to those white pelicans and see how close they'll come to us."

"Oh, I'm alright. I'm sure a couple of aspirins will take care of my slight headache. Let's take the kayaks for a spin around the island for a little while. Maybe, when we return, we can walk back and feed the pelicans. We can see if they're still there while we're kayaking in that area."

The kayak trip around the island was enjoyable. Edna forgot all about her headache after she picked up her kayak paddle and got in the water. The dolphins were in the same area as the day before, and they swam all around the kayaks. Edna was delighted with the interaction they experienced with the dolphins and wanted to go back to see them again the next day. The white pelicans were in the same spot and rested quietly on the sand. After the kayak venture, they walked the island. They eventually made it back to feed the pelicans and managed to entice them to eat out of their hands. The day's adventure was tiring for both of them, so they went to bed earlier than usual.

$$\rightleftharpoons \quad \rightleftharpoons \quad \rightleftharpoons$$

Grady sat straight up in bed when he heard Edna's scream. He didn't take the time to switch on the bedside lamp. He pulled her into his arms in an effort to console her. He thought she was dreaming, but she was fully awake and wouldn't stop screaming.

"Swart…Swart…look at me, what is it? You're dreaming… you just had a bad dream, that's all. Everything's alright now… you're safe."

She stopped screaming but continued to cry. Her uncontrollable shakes frightened him. He had never seen her so disturbed. He held her tight and kept reassuring her that she was safe. After a few minutes, she settled down enough so that she could speak.

"Grady, it…it was so real. I…I can't believe such a horrible thing could ever really happen."

"Swart, it was just a dream. Just lie back down and rest. Try to forget about it. It was only a bad dream." He knew it wasn't just a dream and hated that the person he loved more than life itself was suffering so badly. He couldn't even imagine the fear she must have felt at the Pickle Barrel.

"I don't want to lie back down, Grady. You go back to sleep. I'll go sit on the front porch and let the cool breeze blow in my face for a little while."

Grady glanced at the clock on the night stand and saw it was almost five o'clock. It was getting light outside, so he threw the sheet off and stood beside the bed.

"I think I'll get up, too. We have talked about seeing a sunrise. This is a good time to do just that. Why don't I brew a pot of your favorite coffee and make a couple fried egg sandwiches real quick? We can walk to the end of the island and eat while we watch the sun come up. Would you like to do that, Swart?" He knew the walk wouldn't take her mind off the dream, but hoped it would help to settle her down a little.

"That sounds like a good idea. I just need to get outside for a while. I'll get a robe and put on my walking shoes."

While the coffee was brewing, Grady made the sandwiches, and then changed into jeans and put on his walking shoes.

The dream was still fresh in Edna's mind as she walked in silence toward the island's end. She was puzzled why she would have dreamt such a horrible dream. She had never experienced such fear. *I could never do anything as horrible as that. However, I can smell the blood, as if it had just happened…it's sickening.*

Grady spread the blanket he had brought with him onto a flat grassy area, and then helped Edna settle herself on the ground. The sky was becoming brighter and large streaks of the sun's rays radiated off a cluster of low-hanging clouds in the distance, but the sun wasn't quite ready to peek over the horizon. He sat close to Edna and placed his arm around her shoulder.

"I think I'll have a cup of coffee. Would you care for one?" Edna's favorite coffee always soothed her, and he hoped it would work this time.

"I'd love a cup. Thank you, Grady."

In the early morning twilight they drank their coffee in silence and waited for the sunrise, which wasn't very long. Then the enormous orange ball barely peeked over the ocean's horizon. Rays of orange, yellow and blue streaked the sky and sparked the beginning of a new day. Grady marveled at the glowing orange ball and felt its power and energy. It made him feel so small and insignificant. Grady closed his eyes and silently thanked God for such a glorious event. He felt guilty for missing out on this wonderful gift from God which took place every morning while he slept. *I'll make an effort to change this in the future.* He looked over at Edna. She had her eyes closed with her chin pointing into the air. She looked as if she were being energized by the sun's rays. He could see she was caught up in the moment and didn't want to disturb her by making conversation. They sat this way for some time, and the sun was well over the horizon when Edna broke the silence.

"Thank you for being here for me and for this glorious opportunity. I won't ever forget this. I'm sorry about waking you like I did. It must have frightened you to death. It would have me. I don't know why I had such a bad dream."

"You gave me a fright alright, but I don't mind. That's what I'm here for. You're all I have and I love you and want to protect you. So, feel free to wake me screaming at any time," he said, trying to lighten her mood.

She couldn't help but smile a little at Grady's comment, but the dream was still worrisome to her. She could remember all of it now. It was so vivid in her mind.

"Swart, I can tell something is bothering you. Would it help to talk about it?" He had to be careful about how he approached this subject with her.

"Oh, Grady, it was so bad. I don't think I can get it all out without breaking down again. It's that same dream that's been nagging me every night. I remember the dream now and it feels so real…it's troubling to me."

"Listen Swart, if you want to talk about what's bothering you and get it off your chest, I'm here to listen. If you break down, I have a shoulder you can cry on. Do what you feel is best for you. Don't worry about crying or screaming. No one's around to hear you but me. It might help you to talk about it though." He recalled Dr. Peter's words…*give her time…let her recall on her own time.*

Edna began telling Grady what she had dreamt. She didn't stop until she had told of her every involvement in the Pickle Barrel shooting. She broke out into tears several times during the process. Grady placed his arm around her shoulder and assured her that she was alright and that no harm was going to come to her. It frightened him to hear what she was saying because he knew *it had really happened.* It took all his willpower to keep from falling apart himself. *I have to be strong for her sake.* But, he wasn't sure he would have the strength to tell her that everything she was telling him had really happened.

Edna rested her head against Grady's shoulder while she cried. It gave him a much needed moment to search his mind for the right words to tell her the truth. She was already distressed about the dream. He didn't want to cause her further distress, or worse, another shock. He knew there was no way around it. He had to tell her now. He sat her up so that he could look into her beautiful face. His heart was beating out of his chest. He was scared to death but he had to tell her the truth.

"Swart, I don't want to upset you any further, but I do need to tell you something." He took a deep breath before he spoke. "Look around you, Swart." He took his time and spoke softly. "You are in a nice quiet place and there is nothing or anyone here to harm you. I wouldn't let anything harm you...you know that. Sometimes things happen that's out of our control. I don't know why—it just does. Someone may be in the wrong place at the wrong time, or someone may be in the right place at the wrong time. You were in the wrong place at the right time."

"Grady, I'm not following you." She could see him struggling to get out what he was trying to say, and she had a strange feeling it was something she didn't want to hear. "Stop talking in circles and tell me what you have to say."

He was having a hard time keeping himself together. "I really don't kn—I really don't know how to tell you something that I know will upset you greatly."

She looked away...took a few deep breaths. Then she turned back and looked him straight in the eyes and whispered, "Its true...the dream...it happened."

Grady pulled her into his arms and whispered back. "Yes, Swart…it happened."

Grady held her close while she cried against his chest. Then she pulled away from him and asked, "How much of it really happened?"

"I'm sooo sorry, Swart, but from what I've heard from Captain Hall, and what little I've heard on the news, and now hearing your side of what took place; I believe all of it happened."

Edna suddenly jumped to her feet and began pacing back and forth. She pulled at her hair, and then screamed: "It can't be true! I couldn't have been there and done such an awful thing! I could *NEVER* kill anyone! Tell me it was just a nightmare. Please…tell me…I didn't take another person's life." She was crying so hard, it was difficult for her to breathe. "Please, please, Grady…tell me. Tell me I didn't kill that man," she cried.

Grady rose to his feet to be on her level. He was frightened for Edna's state of mind. He felt powerless to help her now when she needed him more than ever. He gave her a minute to absorb the truth. Then, he brought her into his arms again and whispered into her ear. "I'm so sorry this happened to you. It's all over now. The bad guy is gone and you have nothing to be afraid of. Will you sit down and listen while I fill you in on everything? Please, Swart, I know this is hard for you, but we can't change what has happened. I wish that it hadn't happened, but it did. Now, we have to accept it and go on living. You have done nothing wrong. You did what had to be done. It was the only chance for survival those people in the Pickle Barrel had that day. If you hadn't killed that man, everyone, including you, may have been shot or killed. Let's sit down and talk about it."

After they were settled back on the blanket, Grady added more coffee to their cups. He passed an egg sandwich to Edna. "We need to keep our strength up, Swart. Eat your sandwich while I tell you what I know."

He wasn't looking forward to telling her what he knew. So, he took his time, ate his sandwich, and then took a few sips of his coffee. He saw Edna's hands shake as she took the wrapping off her sandwich, and he wanted to give her a moment to settle down. As he watched her, a light sea breeze lifted a few strands of her shoulder length hair and blew them around her face. He thought how beautiful she still was, even after all the years he had known her. He had never regretted one moment being with her.

They had eaten their sandwiches before Grady began to tell her what he knew about the shooting and the terrorist cell. Tears rolled down Edna's cheeks as she listened to Grady tell about Captain Hall and how he had made the arrangements for them to use the cottage. He continued to tell about Dr. Peters' and Bob's involvement. And how they all had conspired to keep everything from her; hoping she'd recall what had happened in her own time. He told her everything he knew... *ALMOST.*

He wasn't sure how she was going to take this next bit of news, but he would brace himself just in case it didn't go well with her. "Swart, there's one more thing I need to tell you. Captain Hall said you're entitled to the rewards these terrorists had on their heads."

"That's *BLOOD* money!" She jumped to her feet again and began to pace back and forth. She threw her hands into the air, pulled at her hair and shouted, "I won't have any part of it! I won't accept it! I won't spend one cent for killing another person! They can keep it! A lot of people were killed and others are affected by this tragedy and I shouldn't profit from it. I won't take blood money!"

Grady was taken aback by her behavior. He hadn't braced himself enough for this reaction. In all the years he had known her, he had never seen her this way and wasn't sure how to settle her down. Of course, neither of them had ever killed anyone and was offered money as a reward for doing so. His emotions were mixed about accepting the money, as well. The money was the result of the death of another person; however, there were a lot of good things they could do with it. Once again, he stood to meet her and drew her into his arms.

"Swart, you need to settle down now. I know all this has come at you all at once. It's hard to comprehend, I know. But being this upset isn't good for your health. I'm sure when you have the chance to think about all this, you'll figure out the best thing to do about the money." *He figured the money was probably already in their account.* "Come; let's go back to the cottage and take a long hot bath. Then I'll put together a large chef salad for lunch."

"Grady, I'm ready to go home. I want to get our things from the cottage and go home." She began gathering their coffee cups and blanket from the ground to leave.

"This is a lovely get-away. Are you sure you don't want to stay and relax another few days?" he asked while assisting her with the blanket.

She stood still and let her eyes slowly scan out across the ocean, and then around the island. "It is a lovely place, Grady, and I've really enjoyed our time here. If things were different, I'd love to stay here forever. But, I'm ready to go home now."

"You mean, right this minute? You don't want to wait until after lunch?" He wanted to keep her away from the mainland and the news media for a few more days.

"I see no reason why we can't leave as soon as we gather our things."

"Swart, I'm afraid all this is still fresh in the media back home. You know what it'll be like. It'll be all over the television and radio. I don't want this to affect you anymore than it already has. We can stay here a few more days while you adjust to all this."

"I understand your concerns, Grady, and I appreciate all you've done to protect me, but things aren't going to get any better out here on the island. I'll have to accept what has happened…I can't change that. I can, however, stay away from the media. I won't watch TV or listen to the radio."

"That means you'll have to give up Gary and Rusty for a while. Can you do that?" *This will be a great sacrifice for her,* he thought, and it tugged at his heart.

"I'll do what I have to. Let's go home."

CHAPTER THIRTY-THREE

Grady parked the boat in the same slip, and they saw that everything in the boat was put back where they had originally found it. Then, they walked across the parking lot to their Suburban. Edna's mood had lightened somewhat, but in the back of her mind she was still troubled over what she had done. She knew, from this day on, her life would *never* be the same.

"Oh, Swart, Captain Hall wanted me to call him the minute we got back on the mainland. Will you get the phone from the glove box for me?" Grady was busy starting the engine to allow the air conditioning to cool down the inside of the truck.

"When you talk with him, tell him I want to see him," she said, as she passed the phone to him.

He was puzzled by her request. "You mean you want to talk to him?"

"No. I mean I want to see him. And, I want to see him today."

"I thought you wanted to go home, Swart. Tallahassee is a long way from here. If we go, we'll have to spend the night, and then go home tomorrow," he said in an attempt to discourage her from making the long trip. He knew full well, he would do whatever she asked.

"I don't mind going home tomorrow. I need to see Captain Hall today."

"Alright then, I'll let him know," he said as he dialed the number.

Captain Hall had not expected to hear from Grady so soon. His first thought was that something bad had happened to Edna.

"Hello, Grady. How are things with you? Was everything alright at the island?"

"It couldn't have been any better. We had a great time, and I want to thank you for everything. We followed your instructions and left the generator running and closed the door behind us. It's a great place for a getaway."

"I'm glad you had a good time. You're back so soon. Is everything alright with Edna?" He wasn't sure how much he should say, in case she could hear.

"She remembers everything about her involvement in the shooting, and I told her what I know. That's one reason I'm calling. If you have the time, she wants to meet with you today. We should be in Tallahassee around one o'clock."

"I look forward to meeting her. I still need a statement from her for the record. Oh, the money has been put into the account number you gave me before you left. And, another thing, Grady, I hate to be the bearer of bad news, but I had to tell the public who killed the shooter. I held out as long as I could, but the mayor and governor kept insisting. I don't have to tell you what you're up against there with the media. I'm sure you've seen enough news coverage to know what it's like. I hope it won't be too much for you. Have a safe trip and I'll see you in my office when you arrive this afternoon."

They made good time and arrived in Tallahassee at eleven o'clock. Edna was lost in her thoughts about the shooting and did very little talking along the way. She knew she would have to live with this nightmare for the rest of her life and hoped it wouldn't affect her in a negative way.

"We have some time to kill, Swart. Are you hungry? You want to have some lunch?"

"I could eat something. Where would you like to eat?"

"While you were in the hospital, I discovered a quiet little family owned restaurant across the street. They make everything fresh. Would you like to have lunch there? I think you'll like it. It isn't far from here."

"What type of menu do they have?"

"Home cooking the way you like it. You know—fried chicken, chops, meat loaf, Mexican enchiladas, burgers, if you want one, and vegetables of all kinds. They make cakes and pies like you have never seen. It's too early for the lunch crowd, so they may not be very busy."

"You know, I haven't had meat loaf in ages. Let's go. I may splurge and have a slice of pecan pie with ice cream, if I'm not too full after eating a big meal."

"You are a girl after my own heart. I just might join you with a slice of pie of my own."

The lunch was everything they had anticipated. They were so full they couldn't even eat pie; they took it with them.

They arrived at the police department earlier than expected. Captain Hall was there and gave them a warm welcome. He hadn't met Edna when she was in the hospital and he was happy to finally get to do so. She wasn't anything like he had expected. He knew her age and for that reason visualized someone shorter and a lot more fragile. She was tall, slender, and youthful looking. There was a sense of pride and self-confidence about her that he admired. He could tell something was troubling her, though.

"I'm pleased to meet you, Edna," he said, as he shook her delicate hand.

"I'm pleased to meet you, too. I want to thank you for everything you've done for us. The island getaway was a wonderful idea." As they greeted each other, she instantly felt the Captain was a man she would like and admire. His friendly and professional demeanor immediately put her at ease.

"It was my pleasure doing what I could for you. Did Grady tell you that, for the record, I have to take your statement about the shooting? Are you up to it today? I don't want you to do anything that might be too stressful."

"Grady didn't mention anything to me about a statement. I figured it would have to be done at some point. Today will be alright with me, especially, while it's still fresh on my mind; *not that I will ever forget any of it.*"

"Grady, could you give me an hour alone with Edna? Dr. Peters has asked about you every day since you left. Maybe you could call him, or go visit him at the hospital."

"That's a great suggestion. I think I'll stop by to see him. I'll see you in an hour."

He gave Edna a quick goodbye kiss.

Captain Hall listened while Edna gave her statement—which was being recorded. He sat and watched helplessly while the tears rolled down her cheeks as she went into the gory details of the shooting. He thought what a strong and brave woman she was. His admiration was growing more and more every minute, as he listened to her. When she finished her statement, she dried her eyes and drank the water he had placed next to her. Then, she asked that the recorder be turned off.

"I have a request, Captain," Edna said after the recorder was off.

He couldn't imagine what she could want from him, so he asked. "Ms. Edna, I'll do anything I possibly can for you. Tell me what you want."

"Are the names and addresses of everyone present at the Pickle Barrel during the shooting accessible to you?"

"Yes, they are. Why do you ask?"

"Because, I want all the reward money given equally to every family involved."

"Ms. Edna, you can't be serious! It was you who killed this madman and you'll have to live with it for as long as you live. You deserve the money," he said, trying to reason with her.

"Its blood money and I won't have any part of it. Do you think everyone there that day won't carry this with them for the rest of their lives? Do you think that the families who lost loved ones or the ones who were wounded aren't suffering? Sometimes, there are scars that are worse than a gunshot wound. I realize what I have done will haunt me for the rest of my life. But, if I benefit because of it, while everyone else suffers, I know I can't live with that. I want the money given to them. Can you do that?"

"The money is already in your bank account and I can't get it out. I can see that everyone receives an equal share, but, the money will have to be turned over to the department to be disbursed. Are you really sure this is what you want to do? Have you talked with Grady about this?"

"I mentioned it to him this morning. He knows it's my decision to make. I have given it a lot of thought, and this is what I want to do."

He knew he wouldn't change her mind. "When do you want the money disbursed?"

"Now...if you'll allow me to use your phone, I'll transfer the money. You can see that the disbursements are made at your convenience. Do you have the account number where the money can be transferred?"

"Just give me a few minutes while I check with Dee. Would you like something else to drink while I'm up?" He could see she had drunk all her water.

"I would like more water, if you don't mind."

It didn't take long to complete the transfer. Edna signed the necessary paperwork authorizing the disbursement of funds. She crossed her own name off the list of names Captain Hall had placed in front of her.

Captain Hall had never seen anyone like Edna in his whole life. He had one more word to add to the long list he already had to describe her; *GENEROUS*.

Grady was talking with Dee at her desk when Edna and Captain Hall walked from his office. He was delighted to see a smile on her face. It looked like a heavy burden had been lifted from her shoulders. He walked away from Dee's desk to join them.

"Did everything go alright?" he asked, as he took Edna's hand.

"Everything went very well," answered Captain Hall. "You have a very brave wife. Edna, would you mind if I speak privately with Grady for a few minutes?"

"I don't mind at all. Can you point me toward the lady's room? I need to replace my makeup." She walked off in the direction of the lady's room with her yellow carry-everything purse draped over her shoulder.

Captain Hall filled Grady in on everything that had transpired with Edna, including the disbursement of the money. He wanted to be the one to break this news to Grady in case he didn't agree with Edna's decision. His intentions were to spare Edna any more heartache. As it turned out, Grady wasn't at all surprised, and he thought it was an admirable thing for her to do. Captain Hall was touched by Grady's love and concern for his wife. This wasn't something you saw every day.

"Grady, I know you have a long drive back home. Do you plan to leave now, or are you going to spend the night?"

"Edna woke me up screaming at five o'clock this morning. It has been a long, stressful day for both of us. I believe we'll stay the night here. Why do you ask?"

"I was thinking. If you don't already have a place to stay, the place where Bob stayed when he was here is available. You're welcome to stay there."

"We don't have any special plans yet. Are you sure it'll be alright? You have already done so much for us. We wouldn't want to take advantage of your generosity."

"You aren't the kind of people who takes advantage of anything. You're more than welcome to the guest house anytime you want to visit Tallahassee. I want you to know our doors will always be open for you here." He wrote down the address with directions and put them in Grady's hand as he shook it for the last time. "Now we had better get out of here before Edna starts wondering what's going on." Both men walked out of the office laughing like old friends. They could see Edna happily talking with Dee at her desk. Captain Hall caught sight of the loving look in Edna and Grady's eyes as they glanced at each other and couldn't help but feel a little spark of envy.

CHAPTER THIRTY-FOUR

The funeral was over and all the guests had returned home. The large house suddenly felt empty. For dinner that night, Mary Ann served baked fish with curry sauce, roasted garlic potatoes, glazed baby carrots, mixed green salad, and hot apple cobbler with ice cream for dessert. The conversation around the table had been pleasant. The children talked about Miss Betty and Mr. Ron and the things they had done that day with the animals. The trip to the hen house was a big success. Eggs were in a basket on the counter, ready to be cooked by the children the next morning. The children couldn't say enough about the chickens and how they reached under them and took their eggs while they slept.

"It was better than hunting Easter eggs," Danny said with a smile from ear to ear.

Everyone participated in the conversations around the table, and before they had finished eating, they were rolling with laughter. Pauline cherished the happy moment and wished her husband could have been a part of it.

While Mary Ann and Jenny cleared the table, Gene scooped up the boys to take them upstairs for their nightly bath. The women stopped what they were doing and watched him walk across the floor with a giggling child under each strong arm.

"That's a big hunk of a man," said Mary Ann. "He always did have to play tough, but I love him for it."

Jenny just shook her head and smiled.

It had been a long day for Pauline, so she went upstairs to relax in a hot bubble bath. Jenny and Mary Ann finished cleaning the kitchen, and then said good night to one another.

Jenny wanted to check on the children before she retired for the night. She lightly tapped on their door, and then entered the room before anyone had a chance to answer her knock. She could hear them in the bathroom and walked in that direction. Danny was standing beside the bathtub naked as a jaybird; while Gene toweled water off Rossi...they hadn't heard her enter the room. She made a loud coughing sound to alert them that she was present. Danny heard the sound and ran toward her with his arms opened wide.

"Miss Jenny—Miss Jenny," he squealed.

She scooped him up in her arms and placed her face into his small neck. Then, she took a deep breath. "Oh, you smell good enough to eat." She nibbled at his neck and pretended to eat him. He giggled and giggled until she stopped.

Gene walked through the bedroom with Rossi wrapped in a towel. He sat him on the edge of the bed until he could be dressed in his pajamas. "It sounds like you guys are having a good time," he said, as he picked up the pajamas for Rossi.

"I can help get the children ready for bed, if you don't mind."

"That would be helpful. Thank you, Jenny. Danny's pajamas are in the top drawer of the dresser."

They had the children dressed in no time. As they tucked them under the covers, Gene noticed they had become quiet and withdrawn. He had seen them do this before, and it usually was followed by tears for their parents.

"Miss Jenny, can you read us a story?" Rossi said in a low somber voice. "Aunt Debra Kay always reads us a story when we go to bed."

Jenny froze in her tracks. She wasn't sure what she had just heard. She looked at Gene and caught his eye. Without saying a word, Gene eased onto the bed next to Danny. Jenny did the same next to Rossi.

Rossi began to cry and asked when his mommy and daddy were coming to get him? Jenny reached beside her on the nightstand and picked up a fluffy, soft teddy bear and placed it in his arms. He held the bear like it was an old faithful friend. Jenny noticed he paid particular attention to the bear's ears. He kept rubbing the ears with both hands. She didn't question him about this action, but continued to observe.

"His ears looks just like Mickey Mouse ears," Rossi said after a few moments.

Again, Jenny and Gene's eyes gravitated toward one another. They knew this might be a good time to gain important information which could lead them to their parents.

"So, you have seen Mickey Mouse." Gene said.

"Mickey Mouse has big ears; see, like my bear." He held the bear up for them to see.

"Did your mama and daddy take you to see Donald Duck and Cinderella's Castle?" Gene thought he would try to keep this subject alive while he probed for the necessary information he was seeking.

Tears began building in the children's eyes at the mere mention of their mama and daddy. Gene was unsure about pushing them any farther—then Danny spoke.

"Aunt Debra Kay took us to see Cinderella," he said. "We went on a boat in the water under a building and saw, *It's a Small World*". Aunt Debra Kay said it was her favorite and we got to ride again. We had cotton candy and it got all over our face. It tickled my nose." Tears were still wet on the little boy's face as he spoke.

"Ah, yes. *Cotton candy*—sounds good. Now that I think about it, *It's a Small World*" is my favorite ride, too," said Jenny. *She had never been to Disney World.* "Do you live near Aunt Debra Kay? Is that why she took you to Disney World?"

"We came on the plane and Aunt Debra Kay took us," said Rossi.

"Oh! So, you got to fly on a big airplane. That must have been fun for you. Where did you fly from?"

"Danny had a puzzled look on his face, as if he didn't know how to answer. Then he said, *"Home."*

Jenny caught Gene's eye once again. They held eye contact for a few seconds.

"Did you fly by yourself on the big plane?" Gene continued to question.

"Mama and daddy came with us on the plane. Daddy let us watch a cartoon on the little TV and we looked out the window at the clouds."

"The plane made a real big loud noise when we went off the ground," Rossi interjected.

Gene's heart was racing. He felt he was close to getting the answers he needed to locate the parents.

He asked, "Did your mama and daddy fly back home?"

"Aunt Debra Kay took them to the airport and we waved to them when the plane was in the sky."

"I bet they were waving back at you through the window of the plane," said Jenny.

Tears started rolling down Rossi's face as he asked about his parents once again. Danny's flood of tears followed seconds later. Gene and Jenny drew the boys into their arms and tried to reassure them that everything was alright.

"Are you ready for me to read a story?" Jenny asked in an effort to get their minds onto something else and hopefully calm them down.

Rossi pulled away from Jenny's hold and said, "Yes, I want to hear the story, Miss Jenny."

They laid the children's heads back onto their pillows and dried the tears from their eyes. When they were well settled under the covers, Jenny picked up the storybook and began to read. Gene kissed the children good night, and then left the room to call Captain Hall.

Captain Hall was still in his office when Gene called with the new information he had gotten from the children. "So, they didn't have a last name for their aunt, nor did they know where she lived." said the Captain.

"No, they didn't seem to understand about last names. I thought you could check the casualty list to see if there was someone with the name Debra Kay. I know all the families have been notified, but still no one has reported the children missing. Maybe she was single and the children were staying with her for a while. She may be from Tallahassee, or nearby. According to what the children said, the parents are from out-of-state somewhere. They may not know about her death yet."

"I see what you're getting at, Gene. Give me a little time to check the casualty list and I'll call you right back."

Thirty minutes later Captain Hall called back with positive information concerning Debra Kay.

"We really have something to go on now," he told Gene. "Her name was on the casualty list alright. She lived in the Orlando area. I called the chief of police there to see what I could find out about her. I wanted to know if the family had been notified and if they knew of any living relatives. He told me they sent an officer to the address to let someone know about her death, but there was no one home. She had her mail put on hold for thirty days and didn't leave a forwarding address. Her neighbors said she hadn't lived there long, and no one knew her whereabouts. A couple neighbors remembered seeing two little boys playing in her front yard one day. Her car hadn't been claimed from the Pickle Barrel parking lot, so it was towed to the city lot, awaiting pickup. Notifications have been sent to her address without any response. I guess with all the turmoil around here in the past several days, no one thought to track her family down. From the information I have, she wasn't married.

"Has her body been claimed from the morgue?" Gene asked.

"I just called the morgue, and she's still there."

"So, what happens now?"

"I'm sure by tomorrow we'll have someone in her family located…maybe even the parents."

"That's good to hear, Captain. I'd like to ask you a favor, if you don't mind."

"Sure, Gene, what can I do for you?"

"When you locate them, will you give them my phone number and ask them to call me? I was thinking it might be nice to get to know them a little. Maybe they'd be willing to come here to pick up the boys."

"That's a nice, thoughtful thing to do. I'm sure they'd like that. I'll be glad to give them your phone number."

"Thanks, Captain. We'll talk again tomorrow."

Gene wanted to check on the children once more before he went to bed. He walked down the hallway to their room and eased the door open. He saw Jenny lying hard and fast asleep next to Rossi; the storybook still rested in her hands. He quietly walked up to her and removed the book, and then placed it back on the nightstand. He stood there admiring the scene much longer than necessary. They looked so peaceful. Suddenly, he wanted to a part of this peaceful scene. He walked to the other side of the bed, removed his shoes, and slipped into bed next to Danny.

Jenny could always feel when it was daylight long before she opened her eyes. But, at the moment, something other than sunshine softly touched her face. She slowly opened one eye and was amazed to see two little blue eyes looking back at her. Rossi lay nose to nose with her. She could even feel his breath on her face. The palms of his small hands rested softly on her cheeks as he looked deep into her eyes, studying her intently. She was touched by this action and realized for the first time in her life, *she felt love.* Next to them, Danny changed positions in bed and disrupted their tender moment. Jenny glanced in his direction and saw Gene lying on the other side of Danny.

Gene opened his eyes only to see Jenny and Rossi looking back at him. He couldn't help but laugh at the situation. This set off a chain reaction of laughter that woke Danny. Then, he joined in the laughter; although, he didn't know what he was laughing at. He just wanted to be part of whatever everybody else was doing.

"What are you doing here?" Jenny asked Gene when she finally stopped laughing.

"I might ask you the same thing," he replied.

"Alright, alright, I give up. Who's hungry?"

Danny and Rossi threw their covers off, jumped up, and shouted; "*Eggs*! We get to cook our eggs. Miss Mary Ann said we can cook our own eggs today," said Rossi excitedly.

"Can we walk down the big stairs by ourselves? We know how to find the kitchen," Danny said.

"Are you sure you can find the kitchen? You know you're three floors up. You'll have to walk down two sets of stairs…that's a long way," Gene reminded them.

"We can do it, Mr. Gene. Miss Betty showed us the way."

"Okay then, but you'll have to get dressed first."

Danny said, "Can we wear our cowboy pants and shirt an…?"

"Can we wear our cowboy hats?" Rossi interjected.

Jenny and Gene watched from the top of the stairs as the two little cowboys dressed in their western duds made their way downward.

"We're going to miss them around here," Gene commented when they were down the first flight of stairs and out of their sight. "It shouldn't be much longer before their parents are located."

"How do you know that?" Jenny said. "Don't get me wrong. I want the parents to be found, but it sounds like you think it'll be soon."

"Sit here on the step, Jenny, and let's talk a minute." He took her hand and helped her to be seated. "Last night when I left you in the bed with the children, I called Captain Hall. I told him what the children had said about their aunt Debra Kay. He did some checking and found her. She was killed in the shooting. Her body's in the morgue and hasn't been claimed by anyone. Captain Hall feels sure he'll have someone in her family located today."

Tears began to stream down her face. She was happy. She was sad. Mixed emotions were coming at her from all directions. The children belonged with their parents; she knew that. But she loved them and hated to part with them. She had felt like part of a family for the first time in her life. She wondered what would happen to her now. It was as if she were losing the only family she ever had.

Gene placed his arm around her shoulder. "I thought you would be happy for the children. Why does this news affect you like this? Why are you crying, Jenny?"

"I'm so sorry for acting this way. It's just that I love those little boys and I'll miss them. But, I also know they need to be with their parents, and I'm glad they'll see them again soon."

"I know you'll miss the children. So will I, but just imagine for a moment if you were in the situation these parents are in. If these were your children, and the person you entrusted them with were to be killed suddenly, wouldn't you want them returned to you as soon as possible? Also, think about the children. What happened to them at the Pickle Barrel was bad enough, but to lose your aunt and then not have your parents to comfort you and dry your tears, that would be the worst thing of all."

"I understand what you're saying, Gene." She suddenly felt selfish for wanting to keep them longer. "I know you're right. It'll take me a little while to adjust to the good news, that's all."

"Do you think you'll be adjusted by the time we walk all these stairs to the first floor?" He wanted to lighten her mood.

She wiped the tears from her face with the palm of one hand and then stood up. "I have about one hundred steps to pull myself together, so I guess I'd better get started."

"That's my girl," Gene said, as he fell into step beside her.

When they entered the kitchen, they saw the children standing on step stools at the kitchen island cracking the eggs they had gathered the day before. Mary Ann had doubled over aprons and tied them high around their bodies to protect their cowboy clothing. They still wore the straw cowboy hats.

"Look, Miss Jenny! We're cooking our eggs," Rossi said with a big smile on his face when he saw them enter. Splatters of egg ran down the front of his apron.

"How many do you want us to cook for you?" Danny asked, as he picked up the whisk to beat his bowl of eggs.

Jenny and Gene leaned over their small shoulders to see how many eggs were in the bowls. They were full.

"It looks like you have just enough there," Gene chuckled.

"Well, you sit down at the table. And me and Rossi will bring you some when we cook them on the stove."

They both laughed as they looked down into the innocent faces of two little, egg-splattered cowboys.

Mary Ann had the rest of the breakfast already sitting on the table. So, they sat in their places and waited for the children to bring the eggs.

Pauline entered the kitchen wearing a robe over her nightgown and bedroom slippers. She looked rested and chipper. "I see we have two new cooks, Mary Ann," she said when she saw the children wrapped in aprons scrambling eggs. "Looks like two handsome cowboy cooks to me." She peeked in their bowls. "What's cooking, big boys?" She gave them a big hug and kissed their cheeks.

"Chickens eggs," they announced in a loud voice, and giggled.

Breakfast was enjoyable. The eggs were cooked to perfection, thanks to Mary Ann assisting the *cowboy cooks*. The boys reveled in the attention everyone gave them over their cooking. They'd break out into a big grin every time they saw someone take a bite of their eggs.

"Since you cowboys cooked breakfast this morning, I think you should choose what you want to do today." Gene figured it might be their last day with them and he wanted them to enjoy whatever they wanted to do. "What do you say, boys? Do you want to do something special?"

"I want to go horseback riding!" Danny shouted.

"Yes! Me, too…I want to ride a horse, too," Rossi shouted with excitement.

"Horseback riding it is then. What do you say, Jenny? Would you like to go horseback riding?

"I've never been on a horse. I don't know if I could ride, but I'd love to learn. You'll help me, won't you, Gene?"

"It's like riding a bike," he laughed. "Don't worry. I have a horse you can ride; she'll follow me anywhere. So all you have to do is sit on her back, and I'll take the lead."

"Then I'm all for it. Let's go."

"Would you like to take a picnic lunch on your journey?" Mary Ann knew how much the boys loved picnics.

The boys jumped up and down with joy at the mere mention of the word "*picnic*".

"It's decided then. Jenny, it looks like you and I need to get on our riding duds. Why don't we change, and then meet in the stables out back?"

Pauline was enjoying the conversation around her and said very little. She knew it wouldn't be long before Gene and Jenny would be back in the city and the children would be back with their parents. She dreaded the thought of the house being empty again. It was a big house, and it needed children in it. But, at the moment, she didn't want to think bad thoughts; she wanted to enjoy everyone while she had them. "Well, while you young folks are riding, I think I'll write some thank-you notes."

"I'll have the picnic basket ready by the time you come back down," added Mary Ann.

"Thank you for suggesting a picnic, Mary Ann." Gene gave her a quick kiss on the cheek and left the room to get dressed.

By the time Jenny got dressed and entered the stables, Gene already had the horses saddled and everything ready to go.

Gene watched her as she entered the stables. Her long legs were accentuated by the tight jeans she was wearing, and it was all he could do to keep from staring. She appeared confident and graceful as she made her way across the floor. Her black hair was tied back into a ponytail underneath his mother's old worn-out Stetson hat.

"Look what we have here, boys," he said, as she came closer. "It looks like we have a cowgirl riding with us today. Which of you lucky boys will have the pleasure of riding on the saddle with her?"

Both boys ran up to her and threw their arms around her legs and said, "I will! I will!"

Gene just stood back and watched with a big smile on his face. "Alright then boys, who wants to ride the *big* horse with me?"

Without saying a word, Danny turned loose of Jenny's leg and ran to Gene. He was eager to ride the *big* horse.

"It looks like we have the answer to that question," said Gene.

He brought the small brown and white Appaloosa closer to Jenny. "Her name is, "*Shadow*". You don't have to worry about a thing. Just sit on her and she'll follow me. I grew up with her. When I was a little boy and she was a foal, we went everywhere together—*hence her name became—Shadow*. She followed me like a dog." He gave Shadow a pat on the head. "She's old now, but we're still best friends. Aren't we, girl? You'll be alright, Jenny... she's very gentle. Here, let me help you up on her back." Gene extended his hand.

Jenny slipped Shadow a carrot she had brought with her from the house. She gave her a pat on the nose. "I know we're going to get along just fine. Aren't we, girl?" Jenny said before she allowed Gene to assist her up into the saddle. He then lifted Rossi up in front of her.

Gene and Danny took the lead on the big snow-white stallion named, "*Klondike*". Shadow fell in step behind him just as Gene said she would. It was a great day for horseback riding. The sun's glare was softened by white fluffy clouds which floated effortlessly in the sky. A light autumn breeze made the tall grass in the pastures bend and sway.

As they wandered aimlessly through pastures of tall green grass, the children were eager to point out the cows and horses grazing in the distance. They traveled for some time on pathways through heavily wooded forest and along creek beds. At one point they stopped to let the horses rest and drink water from the flowing creek. While they waited, the children removed their boots and waded in the stream. Jenny pointed toward a beautiful cottage off in the distance and asked Gene who it belonged to?

"That's part of the ranch. Betty lives there. Mary Ann also stays there when she feels like it."

"I understand Betty walks to the main house on the days she works...she has a long walk."

"I know. She loves it, though. She could drive if she wanted to, but she says the walk keeps her young. You know, she's a very good horsewoman. There was a time when she would ride a horse everywhere she went. Then one day she said the horse was the only one getting exercise, so she started walking everywhere. I've never seen anyone quite like her."

They rode for another ten minutes when they rounded the crest of a hill and Jenny gazed down on a truly breathtaking view; a large tree-lined lake stretched out in front of them. The sun's rays sparkled on the crystal blue water and gave the appearance of a field of diamonds. A cool, gentle breeze blew through the long limbs of palms trees and weeping willows. The back and forth motion was almost hypnotic. Large branches of the mighty live oak trees extended beyond the banks and over the water, providing a deep cool shade along the water's edge.

Gene stopped at the top of the hill to take in the view. It had been a long time since he had admired this scene. He wondered if Jenny was experiencing the same feelings he always felt when he came to this spot.

"We made it, partners," he said, as he turned back in his saddle and looked in Jenny's direction.

"Oh, Gene, this is so beautiful. I never thought something like this would be out here."

"I thought you might like it. This place has always been special to me." He dismounted the horse, and then brought Danny down and gently sat him on the ground.

"Would you like to have your picnic now, or would you rather play around the lake first?" Gene said, as he made his way over to help Jenny and Rossi off the horse.

"I'm hungry. Can we picnic first?" said Danny.

Rossi echoed his brother's words as Gene reached up to take him from Jenny's saddle.

Jenny smiled and voted to eat now.

With both boys safely on the ground, Gene turned to assist Jenny from the saddle. He placed his hands around her small waist, supporting her slender body as she dismounted. She seemed to glide out of the saddle. Before her feet were planted on the ground, she was incredibly close to being in his arms. He could smell the fresh clean scent of her bath soap. He inhaled deeply to savor the smell. The longing to pull her into his arms was strong. It had been a very long time since he had had feelings like this for anyone and knew he had to stop them before it was too late. He was ten years older than Jenny, and he suspected she had lived a very sheltered life. He realized he had only met Jenny a short time ago and knew very little about her. What he did know about her, he liked. But, one thing he did know was that she was strong-willed and had the determination to live and do the right things in life more than anyone he had ever met. She gives all of herself, yet, she asks for nothing. *This is what I admire about her.* But he also felt he could see through to her fragile soul…deep into that inner core of innocence. Her whole life lay before her, and she would have many new opportunities and experiences to look forward to. He wasn't sure he could, or should, be a part of them. Slowly, he released his hold on her and returned to his horse for the picnic basket.

After they ate the lovely lunch Mary Ann had packed, they stretched out across the king size blanket Gene had brought with him to rest for a while. While they slumbered, they listened with interest as Gene told the story about playing and swimming on the lake with Ron and Larry as a child. He told how they had tied a rope to a limb of a large oak tree which stretched over the water's edge. They'd swing out into the water and see who could land the farthest from the bank. He talked about fishing, and how one time, they built a fire on the bank to cooked two fish they had caught that day. The funny part was none of them could eat the fish because they hadn't removed the scales. They also didn't know enough to clean the insides out of the fish. They were only eight years old, but at the time, they thought they knew exactly how to cook a fish. After that, they never tried their fish-cooking skills again.

When Gene finished telling the story he jumped to his feet and walked toward his saddle, which was now lying on the ground. He had let the horses loose to graze in the pasture. He said, "Would you guys like to go fishing? Come on, I'll show you how." He removed two folded fishing poles then unfolded them. Laughing, he held one of the poles high into the air and shouted, "This pole brought in one of the fish we cooked over the fire." He was still laughing when the boys ran up to him and took the poles from his hands.

Jenny fell back on the blanket and laughed hysterically. Later, she joined Gene at the water's edge and watched as he demonstrated to the boys how to cast the line.

He explained to them how to tell if there was a fish on the line. Of course, he knew that wasn't going to happen because he had taken the hooks off before they left the stables. However, he had left a small weight and bobber on the line. They watched the children cast their lines repeatedly into the water. It looked like they were getting the hang of it, so he and Jenny went back and sat on the blanket and continued to observe from there.

Gene noticed Jenny's eyes were fixed on the boys, and she had become unusually quiet; it was as if she had slipped into another world. "Jenny, are you alright?" he asked. "You appear to be in deep thought. Is something bothering you?"

"I'm sorry, Gene. I didn't mean to be rude. I was thinking about the children leaving soon. I just had a moment there where I was missing them. Do you think Captain Hall has located their parents yet?"

"He seemed confident they would track them down today. Let's not think about all that right now. Let's just enjoy them while we have them. Ask me something else; something I can answer this time."

"Well, there are a lot of things I'd like to know about you and your family. I really don't know where to begin. One thing I'm curious about, if I'm not being too nosey, is how your family acquired all this property? And, why did they want a stud farm?"

"Now, I can answer that. And, you aren't being nosey. I don't mind telling you the story, but it's pretty long. Are you sure you want to hear it?"

"Well, the children are busy fishing; we aren't going anywhere. I'm all ears...so, tell away."

"Mind you, I'm only repeating the story I've heard, which has been passed down from one generation to the next. There's no telling how much of it has been exaggerated or down right made up through the years. But, by the time it reached my ears as a little boy, it made a pretty good story. This is your last chance to back out if you don't want to hear generations of past history," he teased.

She slapped his arm. "Just get on with it."

"Alright...you asked for it."

$$\sim\!\!\sim\quad\sim\!\!\sim\quad\sim\!\!\sim$$
$$\sim\!\!\sim\quad\sim\!\!\sim\quad\sim\!\!\sim$$

"My *great-great grandfather* and his wild mustang wandered the countryside for weeks at a time. He would stay here and there for a day or two, paying particular attention not to stay in any one place too long. His horse, I believe his name was Max, was his best and *only* friend. Well, my grandfather and Max had been traveling aimlessly through the wilderness for days and they were hot, hungry and their water supply had run out the day before. When he came over that hill over there and saw this big blue lake surrounded by shade trees, he coaxed Max into a full run and charged into the water. He thought it would be a good place to rest for a couple of nights, maybe shoot a rabbit for a meal, cook a pot of beans, let Max graze on the soft green grass, and stock up on water for their next journey to wherever. It was late in the day and he was tired. So, he didn't bother with trying to find something to cook. While Max was having a feast on the lush grass nearby, grandfather made himself a bad cup of coffee from the coffee grounds he'd used the day before. Then from his shirt pocket, he pulled out his last strip of dried beef jerky, savored every morsel, and then he went to bed hungry. When he woke up the next morning, he was surrounded by hundreds of wild horses. They were drinking water from the bank. Now, grandfather loved capturing and breaking wild horses. Nobody was any better at it than he was.

Max didn't look like much of a horse, but he was the fastest-running horse grandfather had ever seen. During his travels, when he needed a few dollars for supplies, he'd often find a sucker who would foolishly bet him on a race. When they saw my grandfather's little horse, they thought the race was already won and gladly plopped down their money. Max always left a trail of dust behind for the other horses to follow. He never lost a race, so I'm told.

Anyway, as he watched the wild horses drink that morning, he saw an opportunity to make a few easy bucks. He'd just set up camp for a couple weeks, build a temporary corral and capture and break a few of them. His plan was to take the horses with him to sell as he traveled through towns. With an abundant amount of trees in the area, he built a corral by nightfall. After eating the only fish he was able to catch that day, he tied Max to a tree. Then, he crawled inside his bedroll and slept under the stars. He was worn out from the full day's hard work.

The next morning he awoke to find the wild horses had not returned to drink from the lake. Also, Max was gone. He didn't know how he could've gotten untied. Grandfather was beginning to wonder if perhaps Max had learned how to pull on the rope and untie himself. He called and called for him, but he didn't come. He was nowhere in sight, which wasn't like Max. Maybe Max had taken a liking to one of the female wild horses and was out chasing after her, grandfather thought. It was about one o'clock in the afternoon when grandfather finished building his makeshift camp. He heard a whinny in the distance and saw Max running like the wind toward him.

That night before he went to sleep he put Max in the corral he had built the day before. The next morning, the gate was wide open and Max was gone again. He thought, maybe Max had pulled the rope which held the gate closed. For him to go through all that trouble, he must have really liked that little filly. At midday, Max could be seen racing across the field toward the camp. The third night, he made sure Max was tightly tied to a tree near him. This time, he decided to stay awake so that he could see how Max was getting loose. The next morning, Max was gone. He had fallen asleep sometime during the night and missed out on the great escape. When Max came charging back this time, a handful of Indians could be seen far in the distance, chasing after him. My grandfather realized then, he was sitting in *Indian country*. They were stealing his horse. When Max ran away from the Indians for the third time, they didn't bother to steal him again. After that, they didn't bother my grandfather, either; but he could see them off in the distance watching his comings and goings.

It didn't take him long to locate the wild herd of horses. He managed to capture three of them the same day he located the herd. And, after he had captured ten, he went to work day and night breaking them. It wasn't long before all ten horses were eating out of his hands. All the while, the Indians were watching.

The way I understood it, the Indians wanted broken horses. They were pretty good at capturing wild horses by corralling them inside canyons. Problem was, they didn't have anyone who could break a wild horse. After many days observing my grandfather breaking the wild horses he had captured, the Indian Chief approached him to make a deal. The Chief offered to trade furs and hides for trained horses. He also vowed not to interfere with his safety, or his comings and goings on the land. My grandfather knew an opportunity when he saw one. He knew he could trade the hides and furs for money and goods. It didn't take long for him to figure out that this was what he wanted to do for the rest of his life. So, he decided to settle down and stake out his homestead. He stayed on this land for years while he trained horses for the Indians. It all started right here in this spot where we are today. After he staked his claim for this land, he built a more permanent structure to live in. His ingenuity and hard work resulted in the enormous amount of land we have today.

News spread quickly about my grandfather's expertise at breaking wild horses. Everyone wanted broken horse back then. They paid good money for them, too. The house we passed on the way here, the one Betty lives in now, was bought with money made from the sale of his broken horses. It was the first house built on the property.

My *great grandfather* built the second house. That is where Ron now lives. It's located in a secluded area further back on the property; this is the area where the thoroughbred horses are kept. I'll take you there sometime soon. My great grandfather wasn't into training wild horses, like my great, great grandfather. But, he had a lot of horses on the ranch who were descendants of the wild horses his father had trained. He farmed the land and supplied most of the farms in the area with grain and hay. He raised corn and vegetables of all kinds, and was very successful with his farming enterprise. When he saved enough money, he built the third house, which is now the guest house next door to the main house. By this time, the ranch had grown so large, field help was needed. The hired ranch hands needed living accommodations. So, ten separate small cottages were built. They're scattered throughout the ranch. Grandfather made sure they were equipped with all the modern conveniences available at the time. He wanted his ranch hands to be healthy and happy. He felt happy workers were more dependable and productive."

Gene paused from his storytelling and called to the boys to see if they were alright. They shouted back that they weren't catching any fish.

"Well, just keep trying. There's a lot of fish out there," he shouted back. "I'm sorry for the interruption, Jenny. Do you want me to continue, or have you had enough?"

"Oh, no, I'm enjoying the story. Please continue."

"Alright, you asked for it. Where did I leave off?"

"Your great grandfather built ten cottages for the hired help. So, when did the stud business start? And, why did they name the ranch *Lucky Boy Stud Farm*?"

"Oh. *My dad's father* wasn't into farming the land, although he did continue to grow and supply grain and hay for the local farmers. His passion was thoroughbred horses; he bought, sold, bred, and raced them. The thoroughbred stallions he raced quickly gained the reputation for being the best and fastest in the country. My grandfather noticed everyone associated with racing wanted their mares bred with his fast stallions. It didn't take him long to see the lucrative side of breeding horses. While he continued to have great success racing his stallions...breeding them, became his real passion."

Gene lay back and stretched out on the blanket beside Jenny. He studied the white fluffy clouds passing overhead as he continued to tell the story.

"The first time my grandfather brought his big stallion out to mate with a mare, the owner of the mare slapped the stallion across the rump and said, *"Lucky Boy"*. Grandfather noticed after numerous breeding sessions, most of the owners would slap the stallion across the rump in this same manner and say the same thing. It became a tradition, which was still going on as my father grew up and began learning the business. It was my father's father who built the large house we live in today. I'd say the stud business was very lucrative. *My father* loved the stud business. He also loved to grow things on the land. That's why we grow a number of different kinds of crops today.

When I was twelve years old, my father decided to put up the large wrought iron front gate. You know the one we came through when you first arrived. He took a lot of time working out different designs until he found the one he liked. But coming up with a name for the ranch to be placed on it was the one thing that troubled him the most. I don't know if you know this, Jenny, but Ron's father lived here on the ranch. His name was Hobert. He took care of the horses and livestock. He, also, was my father's best friend. So, anyway, the gate had been up for some time with no name on it. Still, my father couldn't come up with a name he liked for the ranch. One day, he and Hobert were planting trees and laying out flower beds around the gate, when they decided to take a break. While they rested under a nearby oak tree, they began joking back and forth about a name to be placed on the arch of the gate. Suddenly, Hobert shouted out, *"Lucky Boy Stud Farm"*.

Instantly, my father loved the name. The very next day he had the massive gate dismantled so that the name could be added."

$$\sim\!\!\sim\ \sim\!\!\sim\ \sim\!\!\sim$$
$$\sim\!\!\sim\ \sim\!\!\sim\ \sim\!\!\sim$$

"Now you know the history of the ranch and where the name came from. I told you it was a long story."

"Ah! But what a history lesson it was. I enjoyed every minute of it. How fortunate you are to know so much about your family's history and to have been born and raised on this wonderful land. What will happen to it now that your father isn't here anymore? Have you thought about running the ranch? I hope this heritage doesn't stop with you, Gene."

Jenny's statement cut him to the core. He loved the ranch and knew everything about running it. But, he also loved his law enforcement job. He knew he would inherit the ranch when his mother passed away, but hadn't given a lot of thought about what he would do when that time came. *I can't think about my dear mother's death,* thought Gene.

His thoughts were disrupted by sudden screams from the direction of the lake. Thinking something awful had happened to the children; Gene jumped up and ran toward them. Jenny ran close behind. When they got there, they saw Danny had a three inch fish on his line. The boys were screaming with delight. They had never seen a live fish. They stood over the fish with their little heads down, cautiously watching it flop around on the ground.

"I caught it, Mr. Gene!" Danny shouted. "Just like you said—the lake is full of fish and I got one! Look, Miss Jenny. See my fish!"

"That's a big fish, Danny," Gene said. *Puzzled,* he picked the fish up in his hands to inspect it. *How in the world did he catch a fish without a hook on the line?* He saw the line hanging from the closed mouth of the fish and gave it a little tug. The line didn't pull out of the mouth. He opened the mouth and discovered the fish had swallowed the small lead weight. Gene was amazed that this had happened, but he wouldn't say anything about the hooks to anyone just yet…maybe later.

Gene held out the small fish and asked the boys if they wanted to touch him?

They were reluctant at first, but with a little encouragement they gave in. As they ran their fingers over the scales of the small fish, they'd jerk their fingers back and giggle.

"He feels funny," Rossi said. "Can we take him home and put him in a jar?"

"We can keep him in our room," Danny added.

"I don't think that's a good idea, cowboys. You see, we have no way to get him home; he needs water to live. You wouldn't want him to die, would you? Why don't we put him back in the lake to grow into a real big fish? We'll come back some day and catch him again."

"How long will it take him to get real big, Mr. Gene?"

"I don't know, Rossi. But, I bet by the time you come back again, he'll be big enough to eat."

After the fish was released, Gene whistled for the horses, and then he saddled them up. Everyone looked forward to getting back in the saddle for the ride back home.

CHAPTER THIRTY-FIVE

As they drove into the three car garage, Edna said, "Oh, Grady! It feels so good to be home again. Did you notice the neighborhood seemed unusually quiet for this time of the day...I wonder why?"

Grady knew why. But, he wouldn't bother her with the reason. Before they left Tallahassee to return home, he had called Dixie to see if any reporters were in the area. According to her, the neighborhood had been full of news media a few days ago. They had gone house to house trying to get any kind of information they could about Edna. But, Margaret and Bob had already informed all the neighbors about Edna's involvement in the shooting and about her health issues. So when the reporters came knocking at their doors, none of them would answer it. Dixie said all of the neighbors had taped cardboard over their door bells with a note that read "Out Of Order". Grady was petty well sure the neighbors were staying inside their homes because they didn't want to take the chance at being accosted by reporters canvassing the neighborhood.

Dixie had told him a newspaper reporter just happened to catch her early one morning as she crossed his yard to feed the ducks and fish on the lake. She didn't want to appear rude to the reporter, so she made small talk and answered a few simple questions he had asked. The questions were mostly about the ducks and fish, and how Edna had become interested in them. She casually mentioned that the neighbors had nicknamed Edna, "*Mama Duck*", because she always took in any sick or injured duck that found its way to her back yard. She told the reporter that Edna kept the sick and injured ducks in the walk-in shower of her guest bathroom, and how she would nurse them until they were well enough to be released.

The next morning's newspaper headline read—***PICKLE BARREL HERO—KNOWN AS MAMA DUCK TO NEIGHBORS—HAS NOT BEEN SEEN SINCE INCIDENT.***

"I'm sorry about the publicity I've caused, Grady," Dixie had said. "I had no idea when I was talking with that reporter he would put something so insignificant on the front page of the paper. I refused to talk with any of them after that. And when it was obvious you weren't home and they couldn't get any information from the neighbors, the reporters left. I have seen television trucks and newspaper reporters slowly driving by your place several times a day. I'm sure they're waiting for you to come home, or looking for another neighbor to pester like they did me."

"There's no need to apologize, Dixie," he had told her. "I know how the media can get. I'm just sorry you were subjected to all this. We appreciate you being here for us and for all you've done. Could I ask you to do one more thing? We should be arriving there around five o'clock. If you see any media at that time, would you call me on my cell phone and let me know?"

"I'll call if I see anyone. I can't wait to see you."

Now, safely at home, Grady was grateful they had managed to avoid the media. He had dreaded the thought of arriving home to a yard full of reporters. As soon as he unlocked the door to enter the house, Edna made a path straight to the answering machine to check the messages. This was a common practice for her whenever they were away from home for any length of time. Only this time, he was still in his protective mode and didn't want her to listen to the messages.

"Grady, I can't believe this! There're sixty-five messages on the answering machine," Edna shouted through the doorway as he brought the luggage inside. "We have never had so many messages before. Do you think the news media has been calling here?"

"More than likely they have. Why don't you let me listen to them, and I'll save the ones we want to call back. Do you want to call Dixie and let her know we're home? I know she has missed talking with you."

Their first night back home was quiet and peaceful except for Edna's inability to sleep peacefully. Grady noticed Edna had become more and more restless at night. The whimpering sounds she had made in her sleep two nights ago had now turned into broken speech. He knew she was still burdened by the shooting and he wasn't sure what to do to help her.

At seven o'clock the following morning they were awakened by the ringing phone.

"Who is it, Grady?" Edna asked, as she rolled over on her side to face him.

He sat up and checked the caller ID on the phone which sat on the nightstand next to him. "It looks like the newspaper. The answering machine can pick it up. I'm going back to sleep."

Thirty minutes later the phone rang again. This time it was the TV media. Once again, Grady allowed the answering machine to take the message. The phone rang four more times before eight o'clock.

"Swart, we aren't going to get any more sleep unless we unplug the phone. Are you ready to get up or do I disconnect?"

Edna lifted her night mask from her eyes. She squinted from the bright morning light that glared through the uncovered transom windows in the bedroom. "Oh, let's just get up, Grady. I can't sleep anymore, anyway. How would you like to have some pecan waffles for breakfast? I could really use some. And, go ahead and unplug the phone when you get up. No one's calling but the media. I don't know why they'd want to talk with us. And, we certainly don't want to talk to them. Our friends and family have our cell number if they want to contact us."

"I'll unplug it, but you know they won't stop until you tell them what they want to hear. And, I don't think you're up to talking publicly about what happened to you at the Pickle Barrel."

"Why can't they just leave things alone? Does every tragic thing that happens to a person have to be publicized? You're right; I'm not up to it. It's none of their business that I had to kill a man. I'm not some kind of hero. I'm not looking for fame because I did what I had to do to survive."

Grady could see she was upset. He rolled over next to her in bed and pulled her into his arms.

"It's alright, Swart. You don't have to talk to anyone if you don't want to. We'll do whatever we can to avoid them. Maybe they'll get tired and leave us alone. Now, did you say something about waffles?"

Moments after they were up and tending to their morning hygiene, the front doorbell rang. Grady reluctantly answered the door wearing only his pajama bottoms. A young, well-dressed TV reporter introduced herself as Kim and asked if she could speak with Edna. He looked out past her and saw that his whole front yard was full of camera crews from all over the state. Grady told Kim that Edna wouldn't be giving a statement to anyone, and to tell her fellow colleagues, who were waiting outside; there would be no statements now or any other time. The young woman continued to press him for information, until he closed the door in her face.

"So, I take it, that was a reporter at the door," Edna said, when he reentered the bathroom.

"Yes. I told her to get lost and for her to tell all her friends outside to do the same."

"Friends?" Edna slowly lowered her toothbrush from her mouth and let it rest in her hand.

"Yes, Swart, our front yard is full of reporters. It didn't take them long to find out we're home."

"Do you think they'll leave since you told them there would be no statement?"

"I wouldn't count on it."

For a week, they felt like prisoners in their own home. Every day it seemed as though more and more media trucks, camera crews, newspaper reporters and onlookers filled their yard and neighborhood. The police had tried to clear them out two times without much success. They left just long enough for the patrol car to get out of sight, then they returned. The neighbors still wouldn't respond to the media's questions, and everyone was growing a little weary of the noise from their communications devices. The heavy traffic parked along the small neighborhood streets, which now spilled out onto the main road leading into the neighborhood, was disruptive for all the residents.

Grady had always enjoyed maintaining his yard. But now, he felt forced to hire someone to mow his grass. He didn't want to be bombarded by reporters like Edna had been when she went outside one day to feed her ducks and fish. She hadn't been outside since. Now, Dixie was coming over twice a day to feed them. The media had become accustomed to Dixie's comings and goings, and after she continually refused to answer their questions, they left her alone.

Grady was becoming increasingly worried about Edna. She was getting very little sleep and the nightmares were worse than ever. He didn't tell Edna, but he had called Dr. Peters the day before and had voiced his concerns about her. The doctor felt the stress of the media was too much for Edna and had suggested they go somewhere quiet so that she could rest. He had also called Captain Hall earlier that morning to ask if they could use the island again. Captain Hall was pretty sure it would be alright, but he would check with his friend and call back soon. Now he had to tell Edna about his plans for returning to the island. Another thing he needed to do was to figure out how they could slip out of their home without being noticed. Edna was busy in the kitchen, where she spent most of her time these days. He thought it might be a good time to approach her about another trip to the island.

Edna was standing at the sink washing a cup when Grady walked up behind her and wrapped her in his arms. He placed his lips against her soft neck and asked how she was feeling.

She lowered the cup back into the dishpan and leaned into his embrace. In all their years of marriage, she had never grown tired of his loving arms around her. "Oh, Grady, you really don't want to know how I feel, do you?"

"Yes, I do." He turned her to face him. "I'm worried about you, Swart. I can tell all this media attention is affecting your health. You aren't resting at night."

"Yes, I know, but I don't want to take sleeping pills. The noise from the media camped on our doorstep is disturbing to me. How much longer do you think they'll hang around? You'd think they'd get the message after awhile."

"To tell you the truth, I thought they'd be gone long before now. It looks like they're going to be here for some time. So, why don't we sneak out and leave them here on our doorstep? They never see us anyway. We can put our lights on timers, and they won't be able to tell if we're here or not."

Edna laughed. "And how do you propose the two of us are going to sneak through that maze of reporters and onlookers? We can't just materialize somewhere else."

"Ah. That's right. But, you should never underestimate the abilities of the one and only Dr. Grady."

"You already have something in mind, don't you? I bet you've been planning this for some time."

"Not for very long. I do have something in mind I think we can pull off, but we'll have to get Dixie involved."

"Even if she could help, where would we go to get away from the media? They'd surely see us leave and someone would follow."

"Have you forgotten about the island already, Swart? I called Captain Hall and asked if we could go there again. He was sure it would be alright but he wanted to check with the owner first. He'll call us back sometime today."

"See! I knew you had this planned. Let's say that it's o.k. How do you plan to leave this neighborhood without being seen by the media? And, when do you plan to pull off this great escape?"

"Now, now, Swart, let's don't get ahead of ourselves. Let's call Dixie and see if she'll help us. If everything works out like I think it will, we can leave in the morning. Do you think you could pack a small suitcase by then? I'll call Bob and let him know what we're up to and where we'll be. We may need his help, as well."

"I'm sure we can be ready to leave by morning. Shall we call Dixie now?"

Grady went into the details of his plan while Dixie and Edna listened on the phone. Feeling confident it could work, they decided to leave the next morning. Shortly after they hung the phone up, Captain Hall called. Grady answered the phone, but Captain Hall insisted on talking with him and Edna at the same time. So Grady called Edna to the speaker phone.

"Are you two sitting down?" Captain Hall asked.

"No. Should we be?" Grady had a feeling the Captain had bad news for them.

"You may want to sit down for this news."

Not knowing what to expect, they sat together on the sofa.

"We're sitting down," said Grady.

"Grady and Edna, you know how much you liked the little island where you stayed recently? Grady, you asked to return there again. Well, when I called the owner of the property to clear your return visit, he wanted to give the island and the boat to you."

They both sat speechless. They weren't sure they had heard the Captain correctly.

"Hello...are you there...Grady—Edna? Can you hear me?"

"Yes, Captain. We hear you. But, what did you say?"

"I said the island belongs to you now. You can use it anytime you want."

"I don't understand. Why would someone give us an island?" said Grady.

"My friend was very impressed with Edna and what she did at the Pickle Barrel. He thinks she's a true hero. He said you don't find true hero's much anymore. And he wanted to do something nice for the two of you. He doesn't use the place much and thought you'd get more use from it. He wants to keep up the maintenance on the place as always, if that's alright with you. The boat is serviced twice a year and he'd like to take care of that, too. Everything will be transferred into your name as soon as you're ready. His only request is that you enjoy it."

"What a generous thing for him to do," Edna said, when she finally got over the initial shock of the great news. "May we have his name so that we can thank him for his generosity?"

"He doesn't want any thanks—he already knows how much you appreciate it. He asked to remain anonymous. I know you'll respect his wishes."

"Of course, we respect his wishes. Would you convey our appreciation to him? We're overwhelmed by this news. Please tell him that the island will get a lot of use from us," Grady said.

"I'll give him your message. So, when will you make your first trip as the new owners?"

"Tomorrow, if we can sneak out of here," said Edna.

Captain Hall gave a big belly laugh. "Good luck with that. I'll talk with you again soon."

Grady and Edna sat for some time on the sofa absorbing the news they had just received.

Dixie made her usual early morning walk across the street to feed the ducks and fish. Only this time she walked toward the driveway and told everyone parked there to move their vehicles because she had to use Grady's Suburban to pick up duck and fish food and she needed the driveway. They had seen her on previous occasions driving her small compact car through the neighborhood and would know her car couldn't hold large bags of grain. The explanation she had given seemed to satisfy them. She stood her ground and watched as each vehicle was moved, and then she went inside to get Edna and Grady.

"How did it go out there?" Grady asked when Dixie entered the side garage door. "They didn't give you a hard time, did they?"

"Not at all, it went quite well, actually," she laughed. "I don't know what I would've done if they hadn't cooperated. I was scared to death. Are you ready for the big get-away?"

"Everything's loaded in the Suburban," said Edna. "Now, Dixie, after we're settled in the back floorboard, will you see that we're covered well by the blanket? The windows have dark tinting, so even if someone glances through them, it'll be hard to see us back there."

"Yes, I know. Those windows are difficult to see through. I don't believe we'll have any problems. Now, let me go over this once more. I'll drop you off on Country Road, where Bob will be waiting to take you to your next stop. I'll then pick up the duck and fish food before returning home."

"That's right. Be sure the reporters see you unloading the grain. That way, they won't get suspicious. Bob's waiting for us at the rendezvous, so let's get going. Dixie, thanks for everything. We could never repay you for all you've done for us." Grady opened his arms wide to give her a big hug.

"We love you girl and we'll miss you while we're away," Edna said, as she hugged Dixie goodbye. "You know there's no phone communications where we'll be. If you need anything, call Bob. And, thanks for taking care of Chatty and looking after everything for us. We really do appreciate it."

"I'm glad I can help," Dixie replied.

As Dixie slowly backed the Suburban out of the garage and drove down the driveway, reporters came running from all directions to catch up with her. They were beating on the windows, asking her to roll the window down to talk. She stopped and rolled the window on the driver's side down just enough for them to see the seats were empty. As they made small talk with one another, Dixie watched their eyes wander around the inside of the automobile. Satisfied no one was inside; they backed away and allowed her to pass.

Bob was waiting on Country Road as planned, and Grady and Edna switched into his automobile for the ride to the boat ramp.

CHAPTER THIRTY-SIX

The picnic and horseback ride was a great success. Danny and Rossi couldn't stop talking about it at the dinner table that night. When Gene told about the fish Danny caught without a hook on his line, there wasn't a dry eye at the table. Mary Ann insisted it was a fish tale they'd made up to impress everyone. "I really did catch a fish, Miss Mary," said Danny. "Mr. Gene said we had to put him back in the water so he wouldn't die."

"Well, boys, the next time we catch the "big one", we'll have to bring it home to prove to the women that we know how to fish."

Pauline laughed so hard. She remembered very well, Gene coming home with all kinds of fish tales when he was a little boy. She also remembered how she thought those fish tales sounded a little too good to be true. But Danny and Rossi were so sincere; she felt this one might just be true.

Their laughter was disrupted when the phone rang. Mary Ann left the table to answer it. "Yes, sir...he's here," she could be heard saying. "We've already finished dinner. We're just sitting around the table talking. No, sir...it isn't any bother. He's right here." She walked across the kitchen floor and handed Gene the phone. "It's Captain Hall," she said.

"I've been expecting this call. Would you ladies excuse me while I take this outside?"

Gene stepped outside the house before he started his conversation. "Hello, Captain, do you have any news about the children's parents?"

"That's why I'm calling. The parents called me a few minutes ago. They'll be arriving from California in the morning. Their first stop will be to claim Debra Kay's body. Then, they'll pick up the children. I told them what you suggested about them picking the children up at your place and I gave them your phone number. I'm sure they'll call you some time soon."

"That's great news. I'm glad you found them and they're alive. I know two little boys who'll be very happy tomorrow. Before you contacted them, did they know about Debra Kay's death?"

"No. They thought the aunt was driving the children across country to California. She had planned to stop and sightsee along the way. The parents said Debra Kay loved spending time with the boys, and she was in no hurry to get them back to California. So, when they hadn't heard from her for a few days they thought it was because they were having such a great time and didn't think it was important to call them. They tried calling Debra Kay's cell phone several times but didn't get an answer. They just thought she was possibly traveling somewhere outside of cell phone range. Needless to say, when the authorities showed up bearing the bad news, they were shocked. They had heard about the shooting at the Pickle Barrel but had no idea their family was involved."

"What a tragic story. But, as a result of this shooting incident, there have been a lot of tragic stories. Thanks for giving me some good news to tell the boys. I'll talk with you soon."

"Oh, Gene, I need to ask you; do you still have that young woman, Jenny, staying there?"

"Yes, she's here. Do you still need her statement?"

"No. We have it already. Larry took it the day of your father's funeral. She's quite extraordinary. I need her address. She didn't put her address on her statement, and I have some correspondence for her. Will she be at your address for a while?"

"I'm not sure what'll happen to her now that the children's parents have been located. She said she would stay until then."

"Alright then, I'll see you soon."

Gene was eager to go back inside and give the good news to everyone, except the children. He thought it would be better to let the children be surprised when they saw their parents tomorrow. He found only his mother in the kitchen when he entered. He asked where everyone had disappeared to.

"Mary Ann's getting the boys ready for bed. When you stepped outside to speak with Captain Hall, Jenny left the house by way of the back entrance. She appeared to be upset about something. What do you think could've happened to her?"

"Mother, Captain Hall called with some very good news. The boy's parents have been found and they'll be here tomorrow to get them."

"Oh, that's great news."

"Yes, it is. But, Jenny knew I was expecting this news. She has grown very close to these little boys, as we all have. But, she's having a hard time letting them go. Also, I'm sure she's worried about a place to live and a new job. I don't believe she has any family. She never talks about them if she does."

"We need to find out if she has family who can help her. But, if she needs a place to live, she has a place here with me—for as long as she wants. We may not be blood related but, after all we have been through, I feel like she's part of our family. In the short time I've known her; I've grown to love her. I don't care where she came from. I only care about where she's going and that she's happy. So, you go find her and get everything straight with her."

"Mother, Jenny's use to the city life, she may not want to stay way out here on the ranch. She said she'd only stay until the children's parents were found."

"That was then and this is now. Maybe she'll change her mind. You go and talk with her; see how she feels. If you can't talk her into staying, then send her to me."

"Alright, I'll talk with her. Will you be going to bed soon?"

"I'm on my way," she said, as she gave him a big kiss on the cheek.

Gene heard Jenny in the garden long before he saw her. She was leaning against a marble statue crying. He walked up behind her and said, "What's the matter, Jenny? Why are you so upset?"

Wiping the tears from her face with her bare hands, she turned to face him. "I feel like my whole world is falling apart."

At that moment, she looked like a little girl to him. He pulled her trembling body into his arms and allowed her to cry. She felt so fragile there in his arms. He wanted to protect her from whatever it was that bothered her so badly. He held her this way for some time before he spoke again.

"Jenny, I'm so sorry you feel this way. Can you tell me why you're so upset? Maybe we can work on it and get your world back together again. Here, take this handkerchief and dry your eyes." He watched her dry the tears from her face. "I have an idea. Why don't I go inside and get a bottle of wine and a couple of glasses. Then, let's walk down to the water garden and talk for a while. Would you like to do that, Jenny?"

She finished drying her eyes then gave Gene back his handkerchief. "I'm sorry you had to see me like this. I don't know what has gotten into me; I never remember crying like this before. I'll go back inside with you and wash my face while you get the wine."

"That's my girl." He placed his arm around her waist as they walked toward the house. He noticed that she didn't shy away from him when he held her earlier, and now, she seemed at ease with his arm around her waist. The night breeze blew a few strands of her long black hair into his face...it brushed his cheek. He was drawn to the fresh clean smell of it. Before he realized it, he had briefly closed his eyes and was leaning close to her… inhaling her wonderful fragrance.

While Jenny was refreshing herself, Gene was busy in the kitchen gathering the wine, glasses, cheese, crackers, and a thermos for hot cocoa. The phone rang, and he stopped what he was doing to answer it.

Moments after he had everything safely packed in a small picnic basket, Jenny entered the kitchen looking refreshed.

"Wow, you look nice and fresh," he said. "I see you put on a warm sweater, which is a great idea. Just give me a second and I'll get one from the closet for myself."

When he returned from the closet he had his sweater and a large blanket draped over his arm.

Jenny saw the sweater and blanket and said, "Are you expecting a freeze while we talk?" Then she saw him pick up the picnic basket. "Oh, now I see…we're having a picnic."

Gene enjoyed her playful manner and teased back. "I thought we would wrap up tight in the blanket and drink cocoa." He made a quick glance around the room, "Now, let's see…have I forgotten anything?"

She laughed. "It looks like you have everything to me. By the way, where's this water garden we plan to visit?"

"It's just a short hike through the back woods. I think you'll like it." He took her by the arm and escorted her outside.

The flat winding pathway made the walk through the woods easy. The light from the full moon and low voltage lighting scattered throughout the greenery was enough to illuminate the pathway before them. After they had walked about ten minutes, Jenny heard water trickling and figured they were getting close to the water garden. The sounds of water became louder as they walked deeper into the woods. Then suddenly, they were in a large clearing. Jenny could see lighted fountains of various shapes and sizes scattered throughout the perimeter. Lush greenery and colorful flowers served as backdrops for each fountain. A small pond with a waterfall was located at the right of the property.

The waterfall was connected to a stream which ran through the garden and trailed out into the natural woods. She noticed a white gazebo glistening in the moonlight near the pond. Curved pathways lay between the well maintained grassy areas. The path they had walked in on led to a small white wooden footbridge that crossed the stream and meandered toward the gazebo. Jenny stood speechless, frozen in her tracks, while she absorbed the beauty of the garden.

Gene stood in silence and watched as Jenny gazed out across the water garden. Whenever he came to visit the garden, he was often spellbound by the beauty of it. Until now, he had never shared this garden with anyone else, and felt honored to be here with Jenny. He gave her a few moments to take it all in before he broke the silence.

"This is the water garden, Jenny. How do you like it?"

"It's paradise. Are you sure this isn't the Garden of Eden? I feel like I'm in heaven."

"It feels like heaven to me sometimes, too. Come, let's walk over that little bridge to the pond and sit under the gazebo. From there you can get a full view of the garden. On a full moon night like this the view is incredible."

They walked in silence until they reached the gazebo. Gene stepped inside the gazebo and placed the basket and blanket on the bench. When he turned back around he saw Jenny leaning against the railing, admiring the magnificent view.

Jenny stood under the gazebo and looked out at the full view of the garden. The beauty was overwhelming, and the sounds from the garden were amazing. She could hear varied tones as the water trickled in the fountains. The sounds seemed to come together to form a sweet melody. She stood silently... *listening*.

Gene came and stood beside her. He could tell she was hearing the fountain's sweet, calming, sounds, just as he had always heard them. He said nothing for a long moment while they listened and admired the view together.

"My father built this garden with his own hands," he said after awhile. "He presented it to my mother on their first wedding anniversary. That's why he put it so far from the house. He didn't want her to know he was building it until their anniversary date. He pulled it off, too. Mother thought all the extra time he spent away from the house was because he was working with the stud horses somewhere on the ranch. She still says it was the best gift she had ever received."

"I believe that," Jenny said. "This was a true labor of love."

Gene pointed at the gazebo bench and said, "This bench might be a little hard to sit on for a lengthy time. Would you like to spread the blanket on the grass near the pond?"

"I'd love that." She reached behind her and picked up the blanket and started walking toward the pond.

Gene followed with the basket.

Later when they were well settled on the blanket and their wine glasses were filled, Gene thought he'd bring up the subject of the children's parents. He hoped she had adjusted to the fact that the children would be leaving soon and wouldn't start crying again when he mentioned it.

"Jenny, I need to talk with you about the children. You probably already know their parents have been located. They'll be here tomorrow to pick them up."

"I figured as much when Captain Hall called earlier. I'm really glad for the children. I'll miss them." She began to tear up...her voice was shaky. "I realize I've become too close to them. I like to pretend they're mine. I feel so close to them, I don't want to see them go." She felt as if her heart was being ripped from her body. The emptiness, which had been such a familiar part of her life, had returned.

"I know how you feel, Jenny. Maybe you need a few more days with them while you adjust to the fact that they have to leave."

"Their parents are coming tomorrow. How can I have more time than that with them?"

"While I was getting the wine earlier, they called. I asked them to stay for a few days, so that we can get to know them. They have to be in Florida anyway to arrange Debra Kay's funeral and to settle her estate. They were reluctant to accept the invitation at first, especially since they didn't know us. But, once I pointed out that we have already been taking care of the children, that they are happy here and would have a safe place to stay while they settled their affairs, they accepted the invitation."

Jenny held her half-filled wine glass up in the air, and then flew across the blanket. She was so happy; she threw her arms around his neck and planted a big kiss on his lips. She hadn't given any forethought to her actions, but now that it was done all kinds of thoughts were running through her mind. She had never kissed anyone on the lips before and, although it was quick, she was pleasantly surprised at how much she enjoyed it. She had felt Gene's arms wrap around her waist and he had pulled her closer to him. An unfamiliar, sinking feeling in the pit of her stomach was all she could feel now. Suddenly, she wanted his strong, loving arms around her and longed for his lips against hers...but, she slowly backed away from him. She said, "I'm sorry, Gene, I shouldn't have done that."

Gene was taken by surprise when Jenny flew across the blanket and kissed him. He had wanted to kiss her since the first moment he saw her sitting on the floor at the Pickle Barrel. Now that she was in his arms, he realized the age difference between them was no longer important to him. He wanted her, but he didn't want to rush her. He removed his hands from her waist and brought them up to cradle her face. And, forgetting about all the things that had held him back before, he looked deep into her beautiful blue eyes and—*he kissed her.*

The kiss was long and tender. She melted into him and felt as if they had become one. Her body was awakening for the first time in her life. Feelings were there she never knew existed. She savored the taste of his kiss, his essence, his every movement. She felt alive…her heart raced…*she couldn't breathe.* She broke the kiss and backed away from him while she caught her breath.

Gene could see her struggling to breathe and said, "Are you alright, Jenny? I didn't mean to upset you."

"Oh! No, no, you didn't upset me. I…I just couldn't breathe." She took deep breaths in and out…in and out.

"Are you saying I take your breath away?" he teased.

"You did that…and more. Do you kiss all your female friends like that?"

He laughed. "I don't kiss any of my female friends."

"Okay then, how about girlfriends?"

"I don't have any girlfriends—unless you're available."

She suddenly became serious. Looking him straight in the eye she said, "What are you saying, Gene?"

"Jenny, from the first moment I saw you at the Pickle Barrel, I've wanted to be near you. I want to know all about you. I want to take you places and do fun things with you. I want to move beyond being friends—I want to be able to kiss you like that anytime I want." He pulled her close and kissed her on the forehead. "I want you, Jenny."

"Why me?" she whispered softly. "You really don't know anything about me or where I come from. I could be wanted for murder for all you know. Besides, I don't deserve someone like you."

"Jenny, I don't want to ever again hear you say that you don't deserve anything. You deserve everything that life has to offer. It doesn't matter to me where you're from. I'd like to know everything about you, but only if you want to tell me. Oh, by the way, did you forget I'm a police officer? I know you aren't wanted for murder."

They both laughed.

She settled in closer to him, took his hands in hers and held tight. She had trouble speaking at first, but she wanted to tell him about her uneventful life. Then, if he still wanted a relationship, she would consider it.

"I have never spoken about my life to anyone," she began. "No one has ever been interested enough to ask about my meager existence, but I want to tell you about myself. Life has been a struggle for me. I pretty much raised myself in a rundown one bedroom apartment near the Tallahassee slums. The rent was paid by the welfare department. I saw my mother between her drug and alcohol rehab visits. She never was there when the welfare authorities came knocking at our door, so I'd lie and tell them she was at work…she could never keep a job. In spite of the scarcity of food at home, I never really went hungry, thanks mainly to the school lunch program. I'd take on little jobs at school to cover the cost of my school supplies. When I turned sixteen, I got a job after school and on weekends. With high hopes of escaping the slums one day, I saved as much money as I could. But when I turned eighteen, welfare would no longer pay for the apartment. So, I had to find somewhere else to live. I was out of high school then and had found full-time work at a local diner. The small amount of money I had managed to save had been used up on my living expenses. Am I boring you to death with my uneventful life's story?" she stopped telling the story and asked.

"You don't bore me, Jenny. I want to know about your life no matter how good or bad it has been for you. Please continue; I want to hear more. Would you care for a refill on your wine before you get started?"

"I'd love that. Thank you, Gene."

After Gene refilled her glass, she took a sip then continued her story.

"The only relative I ever knew was an elderly great-aunt who kept me as an infant. I'm not sure she's still alive, as I haven't seen or heard from her in years. If I have other relatives, I was never told about them. My mother often disappeared for weeks at a time. I never really found out where she went during those times. She was on one of those long absences when I was forced to leave the apartment. Returning to find an empty apartment had to have been very frightening for her. I'm sure she had no idea where to start looking for me, and I had no way to find her. I returned to the apartment several times, hoping to find her there. You pretty much know the rest; I worked at the Pickle Barrel for three years and lived with a crabby old lady. I have never had a boyfriend or a girlfriend…didn't have time for either. For me, a social life was nonexistent because I've always been too busy trying to make ends meet. So, there you have it—my life story."

Gene placed his arm around her shoulder, and then he leaned in and pressed his face into her hair. He inhaled deeply to take in the fresh scent. "That's quite a story. You've spent pretty much all of your life on your own. How could a mother do something like that to a child?" He softly said into her ear.

"Oh, Gene, I can't blame her too much for what she did. I'm not saying the way she treated me was right, and I don't want to leave you with a bad impression of her…she was a good person. On my last visit with my great-aunt, she sat me down and told me about my mother."

Gene could tell Jenny's mood had turned solemn and wondered if what she was about to tell him troubled her. He said, "If it makes you uncomfortable, Jenny, you don't have to talk about it. I understand."

"It's just that it has been so long since I've thought about it. I had almost forgotten what a tragic young life my mother had. I really don't mind talking to you about it."

"Circumstances overwhelmed my mother at a very young age. She was a young girl in trouble with no one to help her. You see, it all happened when she was a senior in high school. Like a lot of other high school seniors; she lived happily in a middle-class home with two loving parents, and was looking forward to attending college. *Instantly*, her life changed forever. As she walked home from school one day, a black van pulled up beside her and two men forced her inside. A classmate walking two blocks behind her saw the van and reported the incident to the police. The next day they located the stolen van with my unconscious mother inside. They never caught the men who attacked her. She lay in a coma for three months after the rape. When she woke up, she was three months pregnant. Added to that, her parents had been killed by a drunk driver one week before she came out of the coma. She moved in with her aunt until I was born. After that, she got into drugs and alcohol. I guess I was too much of a reminder of what had happened to her. Now, do you still want to date me?"

"More than ever," he said, as he turned her face toward his and gently kissed her.

"Gene, do you mind if I ask a favor of you?" she said when they broke the kiss.

"Your wish is my command. What can I do for you, milady?"

"This may not be the most appropriate time to ask you this, but I need to ask if you know someone who could help me find a job?" I could also use some help finding a place to live."

He was shocked into reality by her question. It had totally slipped his mind that she might leave.

"What do you mean?"

"I'm going to need a new place to live, remember…I lost my room. I can see if the Pickle Barrel will transfer me to another area, but I really want to do something else. The boys won't need me after their parents arrive tomorrow. So, I thought I had better start thinking about moving on. I'm sure we can make arrangements to see each other…can't we?"

"Jenny, I don't mind helping you in any way I can, but you know I have to go back to my job soon. I'm really worried about leaving Mother. I know she won't be alone out here, but she's very fond of you and likes having you here. She and I have talked about having you make this your home, if it's alright with you."

She lifted a brow and shook her head. It had never occurred to her that she could live in such a wonderful place. "You mean move in…make this my home? Are you sure Pauline wants me to move here?"

"We both want you to stay. Mother said if I couldn't talk you into staying, she wanted me to send you to her. Jenny, you'll always be welcome here. This could be your home. You'll have the freedom to come and go as you please and there are plenty of cars and horses to get you there."

"Shall I get a job in this area then, so that I can pay rent?"

"You can get a job, if you want one; but, not to pay rent. Like I said, this will be your home, not a rental place. You can have the rooms you're currently in, or you can move to the guesthouse out back. There's another empty cottage on the property, but it's a distance from the house. You can have it if that's what you prefer. Mother and I just want you to be happy wherever you are."

"I'm overwhelmed, Gene. You don't need my answer right now, do you? I'd like to think about it and talk with your mother before I make such an important decision."

"Take your time, Jenny. Decide what it is that *you* really want to do. Now, would you like to have a little late-night snack and hot cocoa?"

They sat beside the pond talking and drinking wine and cocoa until two AM.

After they returned to the house, Jenny wanted to check on the children. Knowing their nights were limited with the boys, Gene decided to join her. As they stood at the foot of the bed looking down at them, Jenny became emotional again. Tears began to run down her face.

"This is so hard for me, Gene," she whispered to keep from waking the children. "I'm going to miss them so much."

"I'll miss them, too. But don't forget, we'll have them for a few more days."

Jenny walked to the bedside, kicked her shoes off and crawled in beside Rossi. Without another word, Gene went to the other side, removed his shoes and crawled in beside Danny.

CHAPTER THIRTY-SEVEN

B right and early the next morning Danny and Rossi bounced up and down on the bed next to Jenny and Gene.

Danny landed on Gene's chest as he said, "Wake up, Mr. Gene. I want to cook some eggs."

Rossi stopped bouncing and settled down next to Jenny. He placed his small hands on her face, looked at her closed eyes and said, "You're pretty."

Jenny heard his comment and peeked out of one eye. She saw his sweet little face close to hers. Before he could move she grabbed him and began tickling his ribs. He screamed with delight. This quickly turned into a tickling frenzy, with Gene and Danny eagerly joining in on the fun.

After Danny and Rossi cooked their eggs and everyone had eaten breakfast, they went to the stables to see the pregnant horse, Morning Star.

Peering inside her stall, Rossi said, "She didn't get her baby yet, Mr. Gene."

"I see that, Rossi. It shouldn't be much longer before the baby arrives." He saw Danny stretching his small arm toward Morning Star; trying to pet her. "You need some help there, big guy?" He held Danny up so that he could pet Morning Star's head.

While Danny was busy with Morning Star, Jenny followed after Rossi as he chased the snow-white Peking ducks through the barnyard. She stopped by the corn bin and picked up a handful of grain to entice the ducks. She caught up with him and put the corn in his hands. "Okay, Rossi, let's sit here on the grass. Hold out your hands and they'll come and eat the corn." He did as she instructed, and moments later the ducks were all around him. The ducks gobbled up the corn in no time. Jenny enjoyed watching him interact with the ducks and wondered what it would be like to have a little boy of her own.

As Gene and Danny talked to Morning Star, Gene suddenly became aware an automobile was approaching. He sat Danny back onto the floor, and asked him to go see what Jenny and Rossi were doing in the barnyard. As Danny raced away, Gene walked outside the stables to see who was driving up.

Gene saw a sheriff's car and another car following close behind. He knew at once it was Captain Hall and the children's parents and walked toward the driveway to greet them.

After everyone exited their automobiles, Captain Hall introduced Daniel and Ashley to Gene.

They were a young couple, about his age. They looked tired. "I'm pleased to meet you," Gene said, as they shook hands. "I'm sorry about Debra Kay and all you're going through. It's nice to have you here, even under these circumstances. I'm sure the first thing you want to do now, though, is to see your children. After you see them we'll get you settled, in either the guest house, or with us in the main house. The kids are in the barnyard, which is through the stables right over there. I didn't tell them you were coming. I wanted it to be a surprise."

"Gene, we can't thank you enough for all you've done for the children, and for us. I know this must be a difficult time for you and your family, given your father's passing and all that has happened, and we're truly grateful for your kindness. I hope we'll have time to talk later so we can express our appreciation more fully," Daniel said as the four of them walked toward the barnyard.

Danny and Rossi were holding a large pan of corn for a goat to eat when their parents entered the barnyard. Rossi glanced up and saw them in the distance. He let go of his side of the pan and ran toward them screaming, "Mama! Daddy!" Danny dropped the pan and followed, hot on Rossi's heels. Both boys were instantly up in their parent's arms. Jenny stood motionless, as she watched the happy reunion. It was a touching moment, and tears of joy filled everyone's eyes.

♎

After everyone went inside the house and all introductions had been made, Captain Hall asked Jenny to take a walk with him. They made small talk as they walked in the direction of one of the beautiful, shaded flower gardens. After they entered the garden and wandered around for a few minutes, Captain Hall spotted a garden bench. He took hold of Jenny's elbow and guided her over to sit with him. She had no idea why she was there.

"Captain, you didn't bring me for a stroll in the garden to make small talk. Do you have some bad news for me or something?"

"No. I didn't bring you here for small talk, Jenny. But I did want to talk with you alone." He settled in next to her on the bench. "Remember in your statement regarding the shooting, you mentioned a woman you were holding a table for? You stated she had been carrying a large yellow purse."

"Yes, I remember her. She came in all sweaty and out of breath. I thought at the time she looked as if she had been jogging. She asked me to hold her table while she went to the restroom to wash her hands. After the shooting started in the gift shop, I heard her shout for people in the dining area to move toward the kitchen. I assumed it was to keep the confused crowd from entering the gift shop where the shooting was taking place. Why are you asking me about her? She isn't in any trouble for something she did at the Pickle Barrel, is she?"

"No, she isn't in any trouble. But, what I'm about to tell you is something that needs to be kept quiet for now, Jenny. It's alright that Gene and his mother know. However, I don't want the media to find out just yet. Do you think you can do that?"

"I have no problem keeping quiet about anything you tell me."

"You may have seen on the news or read in the papers about a woman who shot the gunman. Well, it was the woman you were describing. Her name is Edna."

"Captain Hall, since I left the Pickle Barrel that day, I haven't seen any news. I have no idea who shot the gunman, nor, have I heard anything about the shooter. I only know what I saw...*that will be with me forever.*"

"I'm sorry, Jenny. I didn't mean to bring back bad memories for you, but I think there are a couple things you need to know. This kind lady, who stopped in for lunch that day, happened to have a gun in that big yellow purse. What I don't want you to tell anyone is that the man she shot had a very large reward on his head. He was associated with five other men who also had large rewards. Using information we obtained after the attack, we managed to track them down and arrest them. Because Edna was responsible for us getting this information, she received all the reward monies, which amounted to a very large sum."

"Well good for her. Did she survive the shooting? I didn't see her when I was looking through the gift shop for survivors, and the only person I saw with a gun was the shooter. At the time it didn't occur to me to look for the person who had shot him. I was just glad the shooting had stopped. I felt sure everyone there was going to die that day. But, if there was only one shooter at the Pickle Barrel, then who are the other five men you mentioned?"

They were a terrorist cell, which we successfully broke up, thank heavens. And, Edna did, in fact, survive, which is partly why I'm here. I came here to tell you she refused to accept the reward money. She wanted it equally divided among everyone who was there that day. I have your share," he said as he pulled an envelope from his jacket pocket and handed it to her.

"What's this?" she said as she took the envelope from his hand. "I didn't do anything to deserve any money. This belongs to Edna. She's the one who killed that man. She saved our lives."

"Believe me, Jenny; I did my best to convince her to keep the money. She wanted you to have it, so take it. Do something good for yourself. It'll be a way to thank her." He would never tell anyone, but Pauline had requested that her share be added to Jenny's.

This young woman must be very special to Pauline, he had thought at the time Pauline had made the request. Now, after having this talk with Jenny, he understood why Pauline had such a fondness for her.

"Well, may I have her address and phone number, so that I can at least thank her personally?"

"I wish I could give it to you, but she doesn't want any thank-you messages. She's having a very hard time adjusting to the fact that she has taken someone's life. It wouldn't be helpful to her to be receiving a lot of thank-you mail. When I talk with her again, I'll tell her how much you appreciated the money."

"I do appreciate it, Captain. Having no money of my own, I was looking at having to find another job and somewhere to live. The money would've been very helpful for that, but Gene and Pauline have asked me to stay here."

He noticed a sparkle in her eyes when she spoke of Gene and Pauline. "That's great, Jenny. I hope you're going to take them up on it. I've known Pauline and her family for years. They're wonderful people, and I know you'll love it here."

"I haven't accepted their offer yet, but I'm going to. In the short time I've been here, I've grown and changed in so many ways. But, more importantly, I've grown to love this family. So instead of using this money for rent, I'm going to see what college has to offer."

"That's wonderful, Jenny. I'm sure Edna would love to hear the money is being put to good use. Now, I must get back to Tallahassee. I'll walk with you back to the house. I want to say goodbye to everyone." He stood and then reached for her hand.

Ω

Jenny hadn't mentioned the reward money to anyone until late that afternoon when she and Gene walked the path back to the water garden. They didn't take a picnic basket or blanket this time. They just wanted to walk and talk. She had had her talk with Pauline earlier that day about moving in, and was convinced Pauline really wanted her to stay. Jenny had accepted the offer, but she had waited until now to tell Gene about accepting the offer and the reward money.

"That's quite a story you just told about Edna giving the reward money away. What a generous and fascinating person she must be," Gene had said when she told him about the money. "Isn't it something how one thing leads to another? Who would've thought out of this horrible massacre such a positive thing could happen? Now that you have all this money, do you plan to go off to college—maybe do something big and famous?" He was really afraid she would go off and he'd never see her again.

Smiling at his comment, she stopped in her tracks. She looked him straight in the face for a brief moment, and then she said in an optimistic tone, "I plan to do something big and famous alright. And, I plan to do it right here on this ranch."

"What! Are you moving in, Jenny?"

"Yes! I'm moving in. Your mother and I talked it over this afternoon and everything has been worked out. I'm here to stay."

Before Jenny knew it, he had her locked in his arms swinging her around and around. After a few rounds, he lowered her back to her feet, but continued to hold her close to him. He lowered his mouth to hers. This time the kiss wasn't soft and gentle like it had been the night before. His mouth was hard and demanding.

Jenny felt the passion in his kiss and eagerly responded to it. She responded with all the passion she had bottled up inside her. Her hands wound around his neck as he softly touched her in places a man had never touched before. Then she felt his hands move under her shirt, touching her warm skin. The unfamiliar sensation startled her, and she found herself jumping back from him.

"I'm sorry, Jenny, I didn't mean to frighten you." He was puzzled by her sudden reaction.

She struggled to breathe. "No…no. You…you didn't frighten me. It's just—I have never been kissed like that before—*actually, she had never been kissed by anyone*—and no one has ever touched my body. It just surprised me, that's all."

He knew he was moving too fast for her, but he was finding it harder and harder to be around her without touching her. It had been a long time since he had felt this way about another person. He had to find a way to express his true feelings for her without driving her away.

He stepped close to her, took her hands in his, and looked her straight in the face. "I really care for you, Jenny. I'd never do anything that you didn't approve of. I hope you know that. Now, I may have gotten too carried away just then because I wanted you so much, but I'll never hurt you."

"I wasn't afraid of you hurting me, Gene. I was afraid of *my* feelings. Hugging and kissing has never been a part of my life. But, I guess if I'm going to be around you, I'd better get use to it."

This response broke the tension of the moment and they broke out into laughter.

He drew her into his arms and tenderly kissed her forehead. "You'd better learn to like it, because I'm a hugging, kissing maniac. You'll have a hard time escaping my long arms and puckered-up lips."

As she struggled to contain her laughter, she said, "Yeah, I can see us fifty years from now. You're shuffling down the long hallway, chasing after me for a kiss with your long outstretched arms and your lips hanging down to your chin. Of course, I won't be that hard to catch as I hobble the halls."

He laughed so hard tears rolled from his eyes. "Where did you get your sense of humor, *Jenny Three Stars?*"

She stopped laughing and looked up at him. "What did you call me?"

"Oh! It just slipped out. I hope you don't mind. I called you, *Jenny Three Stars*, because of the stars on your Pickle Barrel apron. When I first saw you, I wanted to know your name. When I saw your name under the stars, I immediately thought—*Jenny Three Stars.*"

"I really don't mind. Actually, it has a certain charm to it. I guess you'll be going around calling me Jenny Three Stars now."

He grinned from ear to ear, revealing snow white teeth that glistened next to his suntanned face. He said, "I'll try to refrain, but don't be surprised if it slips out from time to time."

Before they knew it they had wandered into the water garden. It was Jenny's first time to see it in the daylight. She marveled at the colorful flowers and greenery which surrounded the fountains and stretched along the perimeter of the garden. She could see quaint sitting areas with small benches scattered along pathways and nestled next to gentle flowing fountains. The garden had a romantic, whimsical feel to it. A white wooden bench surrounded by a stand of red camellias near a three-tier fountain caught Jenny's eye. She took Gene's hand and pulled him in that direction.

"I'd like to sit on this bench, if you don't mind."

"That's my favorite bench," he said. "Let's sit and talk so that I can learn more about you."

"You already know all about me. Now it's my turn to learn about you."

"I thought you already knew everything about me. Remember, I told you my history the day we rode the horses to the lake."

"That's family history. You haven't told me anything personal about yourself."

"Okay. Ask me something personal and I'll tell you what I want you to hear."

"Stop joking. I told you about my pathetic life. Now you have to tell me what I want to know about yours."

"Alright, alright, go ahead, ask me anything." He leaned back on the bench and prepared himself for her questions.

"You're a very handsome man with a great career. You have a wonderful loving personality. I'm curious to know why you aren't married. Every single woman in this county should be after you."

Out of all the questions in the world she could've asked, why did she choose to ask this one? He didn't want to talk about this part of his life. But, he knew he was falling for her and didn't want any secrets between them.

He said, "Jenny, this isn't a subject I like talking about, not even with my closest friends and family. But, because you have asked and I want to be up-front and honest with you, I'll tell you. I was married once. After I completed my police training I married my high school sweetheart. We had been married six months when she died suddenly of a brain aneurysm. I never really got over it. It was too painful to talk about. I've dated a little but never found anyone I could love like I did her—*until now*."

Hearing what he had to say made Jenny feel awful. She regretted ever asking him that question. She fell into his arms and said, "I'm so sorry I asked you that. I had no idea you had been married and that it had such a tragic ending. I'm sorry I made you talk about something that upsets you so. I hope you know I'd never intentionally hurt you."

He gently sat her upright and said, "It's alright, Jenny, I'm not upset. I would've told you about the marriage soon, anyway, because this is something you should know. So, don't apologize. You haven't upset me."

His cell phone rang and interrupted their conversation. Gene checked the caller ID and saw it was Ron. "Jenny, I really should answer this call. Do you mind?"

"I don't mind at all." She got up from the bench to give him some privacy, walked a few feet to the three-tier fountain, and ran her hands through the water. She tried not to eavesdrop, even though she was still within hearing distance. After a few moments of concentrating on the cool water she was playing in, she glanced over at Gene sitting on the bench. From his facial expressions she could tell he was concerned about something.

He put his phone away and came to stand beside her. "I hate to cut our outing short, Jenny, but I have to go. Ron said Morning Star is down. She's having a hard time delivering the foal. This same thing happened with her mother and we almost lost her and the foal."

Gene continued to talk as they swiftly walked the path back to meet Ron. "It was touch and go for the mare until dawn the next day. Ron's father, Hobert, had a great deal of experience with horses and was able to help deliver Morning Star and save both horses. Hobert and my father were both exhausted by the time the foal finally arrived and stood on her own. Once they were sure the two horses were okay, they stepped outside the stall for some fresh air. As they enjoyed the fresh morning air, they talked about a name for the new filly. They had tossed a few names around when Hobert glanced up and saw the last star hanging brightly in the sky. He shouted, "Morning Star". It wasn't clear whether he had been just pointing out the star, or if he had suggested a name for the foal. Either way, my father liked the name Morning Star. That's how she got her name. Let's just hope we don't have another Morning Star on our hands this time—maybe we'll have a Midnight or Evening Star," he joked.

"Hobert was good at naming things, wasn't he? As I recall, he named the ranch, as well. Do you think Morning Star is in real danger? You really don't think she'll die, do you?" Jenny asked.

"I hope not. But there's always that chance in a case like this. However, Ron's a very good doctor, and he's dealt with this kind of thing before. I do worry about Morning Star suffering, though."

They could hear Morning Star's loud whinny long before they arrived at the stables. "Maybe you shouldn't come in with me, Jenny. Bringing a foal into the world isn't a pretty sight, and this could take some time"

"If you don't mind I'd like to come in for a little while. If it gets to be too much for me, I'll leave. Maybe there'll be something I can do to help...bring you coffee or cocoa, maybe. Listen Gene; if I plan to make this my home, I need to know what goes on around here. I want to be a part of the ranch, and if this is something that happens here, I need to learn to deal with it. Dealing with difficulties has always been a big part of my life... this is another part of my life.

"Lady, you drive a hard bargain. Don't say I didn't warn you, though. You may want to go change into some old clothes if you're going to help bring a foal into the world. I'm sure Mother can help you with that. I have some old clothes in the barn I can jump into."

Morning Star's labor lasted for hours, and she was becoming weaker by the minute. Ron had done all he could for her and all they could do now was wait. Jenny sat on the floor holding the horse's head in her lap while she whispered soft words into her ears. Morning Star seemed to respond to her soft, soothing voice and lay quietly between contractions.

"You're putting her to sleep," Ron said. He had never seen anything quite like this before.

Suddenly, Morning Star jerked her head up. She cried out one last time, and then the foal lay on the floor. Everyone practically shouted with joy when they saw the little black foal flounder about trying to rise to her feet.

"She looks good and healthy to me," Gene said. "What about Morning Star, you think she'll be alright, Ron?"

"Oh, yes. She's tired, but she'll recover soon."

Jenny gave the new mother a big hug, and then she kissed her between the eyes. "You did great, Morning Star. I'm proud of you," she said.

A little before midnight the newborn foal was standing on all four lanky legs. Shortly after she stood everyone came from the house to see her. The children were especially excited to see the newly born foal.

"What is her name, Mr. Gene?" Danny asked.

Picking a name for the new foal hadn't been difficult for him. He had known for some time what he would name the foal if it had been born a filly. "Danny, I have a very special name in mind for her...*Jenny Three Stars*." As he said the name he glanced at Jenny and saw her lovely face, frozen with surprise.

Rossi reached out to touch the foal. "I like that name. It's like Miss Jenny's."

"Come on children. Let's go back inside," Ashley said. She turned to face Gene. "Thank you for including us in this glorious occasion. It's something we'll remember for a long time."

"This was certainly a new experience for me," said Daniel. "I really appreciate you waking us up to be a part of it. I know I'll never forget this."

"It's something I won't forget, either. Good night guys," said Gene. He stood for a long moment and watched them return to the guest house.

Later when everyone had left the stables, Jenny stood at the stall admiring the new mother and her foal. Gene had finished cleaning up and came to stand beside her.

"They're magnificent animals, aren't they, Gene? Thank you for allowing me to be a part of this. Why did you give the foal my nickname? Don't get me wrong—I'm honored beyond belief. But, why did you do that?"

"Well, don't you think she looks like you?" he said jokingly. "Look at her; she's jet black. You have jet black hair. She has long lanky legs; you have long lanky legs."

"Alright, alright, I get it. And, I want you to know, I don't have lanky legs, they're just long. But really, why did you name her, Jenny Three Stars?"

"I can't think of a better name for such a beautiful animal." He pulled her close and kissed her. As he held tightly to her, she seemed to melt into his embrace. Her lips parted as they kissed, and his tongue softly explored her sensuous lips. He felt her passion growing as she responded to his every move. She pressed tightly against him and scraped her fingernails up and down his back like a wild animal. Gene could feel desire spreading throughout his body. He wanted to devour her, and he could tell she felt the same.

Morning Star's loud whinny from the stall interrupted the moment. As they broke the passionate kiss and turned to see what was happening, they saw Morning Star struggling to get on her feet.

"Shall we help her, Gene? I'm afraid she may hurt herself struggling like that."

"I don't know, Jenny. Horses usually figure these things out for themselves. But, if it makes you feel better, we can see if she'll let us help her."

"It'll make me feel better...thanks."

They stepped inside the stall and approached the horse. Morning Star lay still and allowed them to move around her.

"Let's see if we can give the little mother a hand," Gene softly said, as he took the bridle in his hand. He told Jenny to support the neck. "When I say go, you push up on her neck. I'll pull the bridle at the same time. Gene waited until Jenny had a good hold on the horse's neck. "Do you want to get up, Morning Star?" he said while scratching her between the ears. "Come on girl. We're here to help you." He tugged a little on the bridle and watched the mare's response. "I believe she's ready, Jenny. Go."

She pushed, while he pulled, then Morning Star rose slowly to her feet. Once she had her feet under her, the new mother walked across the stall to join her baby. Upon seeing her mother approach, the hungry foal eagerly nuzzled her and then began to nurse.

Jenny asked, "Will they be alright by themselves tonight?"

"I'm sure they'll be alright. You know, horses have babies all the time in the wild."

She laughed. "Oh! So, I'm to believe you are an expert on horse birthing now."

"That's right. I've been around horses all my life...know quite a lot about their traits and breeding habits. I know a little something about the wild ones, too—like you."

"So—now I'm wild," Jenny said playfully.

"You were a few minutes ago," he smiled and winked at her, remembering the moment.

Jenny's face turned red. She was suddenly embarrassed by her behavior earlier.

Gene could see Jenny's face had suddenly turned red. He knew he had embarrassed her, and reached for her hands. "Jenny, sweetheart, please don't be embarrassed about your true feelings. This is what happens when two people care for one another. I loved kissing you. I loved the way you kissed me back. You make me feel alive. It has been a long time since I've felt this way, and I don't want that feeling to go away. I don't want you to feel embarrassed because you're capable of loving someone. You do care for me, don't you, Jenny? I hope I'm not being presumptuous, but I do think you are attracted to me."

"I'm not sure what love is, Gene. I've never really been loved by anyone. I only know I have feelings like I've never experienced when I'm with you—in your arms. I have strong urges running up and down my body when you kiss me. I lose all self-control. I feel I can't get enough of you, and I want to devour you. These feelings are new and frightening, and I don't know what to do about them. If these feelings are called caring, then I care for you. If they are love, then I love you. This is all so new to me." Tears pooled up in her eyes and she began to tremble.

He wrapped his arms around her trembling body and allowed her to deal with her emotions. He was touched by what she had said. He needed a moment himself to absorb it all.

She pulled away and dried her tears. "You must think I cry all the time. I don't remember ever crying much before. Maybe when I was little, I cried a lot for my mother. I've noticed after the shooting at the Pickle Barrel, I cry at the drop of a hat. I've changed somehow, and I believe it's because I have feelings for someone for the first time in my life. I feel like I have a real family now, and I finally understand what it means to actually have a life. I owe this to you and your mother. I won't ever go back to the way I was. I thought I was living, but I know now I was hollow and empty inside. I loved no one…no one loved me. I just existed." She turned her back to him and faced the stall.

He stepped up beside her and said, "Jenny, you're dealing with a lot of unfamiliar feelings right now. The tears will stop when you find someone to love. When you feel loved, Jenny, you'll want to give love in return. You'll be so happy, you couldn't cry if you wanted to. I just want you to know, I don't want to rush you into feeling anything for me. You need to know your own heart. Don't let me influence you. Just because I need and want you, doesn't mean that you need and want me. Follow your heart. I may not like what it tells you, but I'll accept it. I only want you to be happy, Jenny."

She flew into his arms and said, "I have never been happier in my life than I am right now. And, Gene, this is my heart speaking. I realize I'm no good at expressing my feelings. I can only say, I do need and want you. I knew this when you called me over to speak with you at the Pickle Barrel. At the time I didn't know what to do about my feelings. Now I can't imagine life without you in it and I do love kissin-----

His mouth was on hers as he pulled her into a tight embrace.

Her nails dug into his back, and she pulled at his hair and groaned. She released all the emotions she had pent up inside as she melted into him. All the love she had held and never been able to share poured out of Jenny. She now had someone to share that love with, and she wanted Gene to know exactly how she felt. She wanted him and only him.

Gene felt her love and passion as she moved inside his arms and kissed him. She was like a madwoman. He was like a madman. They were all over one another. He had never felt such love and passion for another person—not even with his first wife. Her body was calling him and he wanted her more than anything. But he didn't want her first love-making experience to be in a stable. He wanted the best for her; a quaint little beach bungalow nestled under tall palm trees on a romantic island somewhere far away. He respected her enough to wait until the time and the place was right.

He softened his kiss and then slowly pulled away. "Wow! That was some kiss," he said. "We'll have to do that more often. A kiss like that could get you in big trouble, and I don't want to get you in trouble, sweet Jenny. If we decide to take that step, I want it to be somewhere special. I won't take advantage of you. You mean too much to me."

Her heart was still racing. She hadn't fully settled down from the passionate kiss. She understood what Gene was saying, but her *body* was saying something else. Desire and intellect were at war in Jenny and desire was a little ahead at the moment. These intense emotions were a little disturbing for her.

"Gene, I'm afraid my emotions are getting the better of me, and suddenly, I'm very tired. If you don't mind, let's say good night and see what tomorrow brings. Although, I do want to say one thing before we part—I love you."

CHAPTER THIRTY-EIGHT

With the exception of clean linens on the bed and fresh perishables in the refrigerator, the island was just as Edna and Grady had left it. A large colorful fresh floral arrangement and a bottle of wine sat on the dining room table. The card sitting beside them simply read: To the new owners.

As they walked side by side through the cottage, Edna admired every little object. She was seeing it for the first time as an owner. "Grady, I still can't believe all this belongs to us. I don't know how to act. Here, pinch me," she extended her arm toward him. "I need to know if I'm dreaming again. Am I going to wake up and find all of this gone?"

He took her arm and placed it in the crook of his bent arm. "Well, if you're dreaming, so am I. It's hard to believe that someone would give away something like this. However, I don't believe Captain Hall would've told us the island belonged to us if it weren't true. Besides, the papers are being drawn up as we speak."

"I really don't believe Captain Hall would ever mislead us. I'm still trying to absorb the reality of it, that's all."

After dinner that night they made a fire in the fireplace to take the chill out of the air. They each had a glass of the wine from the bottle that had been left in the cabin for them. As they sat cuddled on the sofa watching the fire, Edna seemed more relaxed than Grady had seen her since the shooting. *Returning to the island was a good idea.*

After taking a few sips of her wine, Edna asked, "What do you think will happen when we go back home again? I don't think I could take a yard full of reporters again.

He pulled her a little closer to him and softly said, "I don't think much will change, Swart. As soon as the media finds out we're back in town they'll be back, hounding us just like before."

"So in order for them to leave us alone, I'll have to go public with what happened to me. I guess that means television, newspapers, and radio."

"I'm sure all of them will want a piece of the action. How do you feel about all the publicity? Are you up to it?"

She drank the last of the wine in her glass, reached for the bottle, and refilled it. Grady's glass was nearly empty, so she topped his off. After she had settled back into her comfortable spot she said, "I'm not up to running all over the country repeating this tragic story to everyone. I want all those reporters out of our neighborhood, and I want our quiet, boring life back. I think I'll do one television interview. Then I won't talk about it again. I'll make that clear to everyone. Maybe then, they'll get the message and leave us alone. Otherwise, we're going to move out here and live on this island."

"Move to the island…that's something to think about," Grady teased. "Do you think the person supplying the food out here will continue, if we move here permanently?"

"Get serious, Grady. We need to figure out what to do about this."

"You need to figure it out, Swart. This decision has to be yours, since you're the one who'll have to do the talking. There are lots of television shows that would love to have you as a guest. You just need to decide where you'd feel most comfortable telling your story?"

"Well, if I'm only going to be on one program, I want it to be the *Gary Brattman Show*. I also want you with me wherever I end up. I can't do this alone."

"Do you think Gary will cover your story? His show usually has a political theme and is aimed at national issues. The attack at the Pickle Barrel might be considered more of a local matter, and might not be the type of thing he would report."

"Well, from the size of all the reporters in our neighborhood, I'd say this is a story that already has plenty of public attention. It's obvious to me; for whatever reason, people want to hear about my experience. There were many others involved in this tragic incident. So, I'm not really sure why the media has singled me out to pursue?"

"I don't know, maybe it's because you were the one who shot the man. I think you should call Gary and see if he wants the story. If he doesn't, I'm sure someone else will air it. When would you like to do this?"

She leaned her head back on the sofa and took a deep breath. "Oh, I hate being in the public eye, but I might as well get it over with. We won't have any peace until I do. I'll call Gary tomorrow to see if he's interested."

After a restful night's sleep and a good breakfast, they were in the boat crossing the waters toward the mainland. Edna sat in the lower deck out of the cool, early morning air. She was busy jotting a few notes on a notepad in case she got to talk with Gary. The boat engine suddenly cut off and the boat glided to a stop. Edna knew they hadn't traveled long enough to be on shore. She placed the notepad on the side table and listened carefully. Not hearing any immediate problem, she walked to the upper deck to see why Grady had stopped the boat. She was on the top step of the upper deck when she saw him running in her direction.

"Swart, come with me." His tone sounded urgent. "You have to see this." He took her hand and slowly and quietly brought her toward the bow of the boat. "Look. Keep your eyes on that area." He pointed in an area nearby.

She focused on the area just for a moment. The water was flat and still. Then she saw a large spray of water shoot high into the air. She saw another one and then another. "Whales!" she shouted. "How many are there? I've never seen whales in these waters. What are they doing here?"

"Keep looking, Swart. I counted ten before I killed the engine. Do you think they're sperm whales? Maybe they're a family— migrating."

"I'm not sure. It looks like they have several babies with them. Oh! What a sight to see. I wish everyone could see this."

Moments later, they were out of sight. Having lost sight of the whales, Grady fired up the engines and continued the trip toward the mainland as Edna, reluctantly, went back to work on her notes.

By eleven o'clock Edna was on the phone with Gary and arrangements were being made for their appearance on his show in New York City. Grady paced up and down the marina parking lot anxiously awaiting the news about the show. He saw Edna close her cell phone and walk down the boat ramp to him.

"Well, what did he say? Does he want you on his show? Did you get to talk with Gary?" he eagerly asked.

"Slow down, Grady. Let's go back inside the boat. I'll tell you everything while we have lunch." She turned back and started walking in the direction of the boat.

As Edna prepared a sandwich for lunch, Grady hovered at her side, eager to find out everything.

"Alright, Swart, I've waited long enough," he said, as she placed the food on the table. "Now tell me everything before I go crazy."

"Go ahead and sit down, Grady. Eat your lunch." She gave him time to settle in his seat, and then she sat in the booth across from him and began to tell what had happened. "It took a few minutes for Gary to come to the phone. He was busy with his radio program. I really didn't expect to talk with him. I thought maybe someone would call me back or something. When I said my name, the man who answered the phone asked me to hold while he went for Gary. I can't believe I really got to talk with him."

"Swart, stop rambling…tell me what happened."

"Oh well, like I said, he came to the phone during a commercial break. He talked as if he already knew who I was. I told him I wanted to tell my story on his program and nowhere else. He seemed very surprised, but pleased, that I asked him to air this story. He said he would love to have both of us. Then he had to leave and go back to his broadcasting. I heard him tell someone to take care of me and to schedule us as soon as possible."

"So when did they schedule us?"

"They wanted us tomorrow, but I told them it was too soon. We leave in two days. The hotel reservations are being arranged, and a plane will be sent to pick us up at the airport."

"Are they sending a private plane to pick us up?"

"They didn't want us traveling with the public. Somehow, they knew we were having a hard time with the media. Oh, they wanted us to come the day before the show so that we could rest and meet with Gary. The show will be in three days."

"Let's call Dixie and tell her. She can tell the neighbors so they can watch the program. Maybe she'll leak this news to those reporters who are still camped out on our lawn. I would love to see their faces when they find out they've been outsmarted by two old farts." They chuckled merrily at the thought of the exasperated looks on the faces of all those journalists.

"Also, I'd like to call Captain Hall. I'm sure he'd like to know."

CHAPTER THIRTY-NINE

The ranch seemed empty now that Danny and Rossi were back in California and Gene was back at work in Tallahassee. They talked with the children almost every day on the phone. Yet, Pauline still felt lonely without all the people around. She missed all the activity. Jenny had settled in at the ranch and was able to help make up for some of the loss. She was especially glad Jenny had decided to stay in the main house instead of the guest house. She really liked having her near. Meals were enjoyable—always one of the highlights of her day. She looked forward to having everyone around the table and the engaging conversation that followed. They especially enjoyed the gourmet meals Jenny prepared, with a little coaching from Mary Ann. Jenny was quickly becoming a very good cook. Pauline and Jenny often sat for long periods of time talking at the table with Mary Ann and Betty after they had eaten. Sometimes the four of them would get so involved in a card game they'd be up into the early morning hours without realizing how late it was.

On days when she was up to it, Jenny would walk with her to the barnyard to visit the foal, Jenny Three Stars. She hadn't been surprised when she heard Gene had named the foal after Jenny. From the moment she saw Gene with Jenny at the hospital, she saw something between them. It had been a long time since she'd seen that sparkle in her son's eyes. She suspected they had become very close. It wouldn't surprise her if they were romantically involved. They were both pretty closed mouth about it if they were. Nevertheless, they couldn't hide that sparkle in their eyes from her. *I've been there myself. I know the look.* They seemed to get along well. She had been impressed with the way they had cared for the boys. *Oh, what I would give to see Gene happily married with children of his own.*

Now as she sat looking out across one of the many flower gardens her loving husband had built for her, she couldn't help remembering her life with him and how their life together had begun, and *how quickly it had ended.*

"Oh, there you are," Jenny said, as she walked up behind Pauline, breathless from all the running around. "I thought you had left town or something. I've been looking all over for you."

"I'm sorry, Jenny, I didn't know you were looking for me. I needed some fresh air and thought the garden was a good place to get it." Pauline patted the seat next to her, inviting Jenny to sit there. "Is there something wrong?"

Jenny took the seat. "No...no nothing's wrong. I wanted to tell you Gene called. He took the afternoon off and will be here earlier than his usual late Friday evenings. But, there's something I need to talk to you about though. He wants to take me out for dinner and to see a play. We'll be out quite late, since we have to drive back to Tallahassee. I'm afraid he won't have much time with you tonight. But, he'll be here all weekend. Do you mind spending the evening without his company?"

"Mind! Good heavens child. It's about time he took you somewhere. I don't know why he has waited so long. You two go and enjoy yourselves. When does he expect to arrive?"

"He had just finished having breakfast with Ron and was on his way when he called around eleven. He should be here by lunchtime. Pauline, may I ask you something else?"

"Jenny, you know you can ask me anything."

Jenny felt awkward and out of place. Her head hung low as she spoke. "I've never been on a date. What do you wear to dinner and a play? I want to look nice for my first date."

The love Pauline felt for Jenny at that moment was almost more than she could stand. She had never seen anyone like her. She wanted to fold her arms around her and protect her from all harm. "Do you remember that blue outfit Gene picked out for you to wear to church? I believe that will be perfect. If you don't mind wearing them, I have a beautiful blue sapphire pendant and earrings."

Jenny was touched by the generous offer of the jewelry. Pauline felt like the mother she had never had. "It will be an honor to wear them. I'm sure they'll look beautiful with that outfit. But, are you sure you want to loan out your expensive jewels?"

"No. I don't want to loan them out. I want you to have them—as a reminder of this first date with my son."

"Oh! Pauline. You don't have to do that. I'll never forget this date and how you have helped me. You keep your jewelry."

"I want you to have them, Jenny. You're young and have many years ahead of you to wear them. I enjoyed wearing jewelry when I was young. But, I'm afraid; my jewelry wearing days are over. The arthritis in my hands is so bad; I can't even wear my wedding rings." She held out her left hand for Jenny to see. "Besides, an old woman like me would look foolish wearing jewels. Now if you don't mind helping an old lady inside, I'll get the sapphires for you before Gene arrives." Pauline didn't mention the fact that her beloved husband had given the sapphires to her as a reminder of their first date.

Jenny leaned next to Pauline as they sat there on the bench and gave her a big hug and kissed her on the cheek. "How will I ever thank you for all you've done for me? I love you," she said.

"You just did," Pauline replied.

Jenny felt like Cinderella dressed in her blue suit with the sapphires draped around her neck. The matching earrings glistened on her ears. This was a new and very exciting experience for her.

Elegance was all around her, and she was beginning to relax and enjoy the surroundings. A princess could not have been any happier than she was at the moment.

She loved the dark navy blue pinstriped suit and crisp white French cuff shirt Gene wore. The red silk tie had a matching kerchief which peeked from the jacket pocket. Jenny felt he was definitely her prince, and the shiny white sports car he had driven was their carriage.

They dined at a quaint upscale family owned French restaurant. They didn't feel rushed and no one was in a hurry to leave. The tables were draped to the floor with white linen table cloths. Fine white china plates trimmed in gold were stacked in layers at each place setting. Resting beside each place setting was beautifully carved gold flatware. Gold rimmed, crystal stemware sparkled in the candle light. Soft, romantic music played in the background, and couples could be seen holding hands while speaking softly with their heads together.

Gene was captivated by the romantic feel of the restaurant and by Jenny's beauty and charm. He enjoyed watching the way she moved her hands and the way she tilted her head as she spoke. Her beautiful blue eyes seemed to pierce his soul when she looked at him. He wanted to skip dinner and take her to his place and explore every inch of her; although, he knew he would never do that to her and tried to get his mind off such thoughts.

"Gene, is there something wrong? For a moment there it looked as if you were somewhere else. Am I boring you with all my small talk?"

She never missed the slightest movement, he thought. Now he was convinced she could see through to his very soul. "Nothing you could ever say would bore me. I didn't want to lose track of time and was wondering what time it was." He checked his watch. "We have a little while before we have to be at the theater." He had stretched the truth a little. But, he had also been wondering about the time.

"I've never seen a professional stage play. Thank you, for asking me to join you tonight. May I ask the name of the show?"

"I'm so sorry, Jenny. I don't know why I didn't tell you. I guess I was too captivated by your beauty to think about anything else."

She blushed. She wasn't accustomed to complimentary remarks…but she liked it.

He saw the sparkle in her eyes and knew she had enjoyed the compliment. "The show is called "In the Beginning". I believe it's about the beginning of mankind, and Adam and Eve in the Garden of Eden. It reminds me of us in the water garden. We had our first long talk and got to know one another better there. You might say it was the beginning for us, as well." He took her hand which rested on the table and brought it up to his lips.

Her eyes locked with his and held for a long moment. The sensation of his lips on her hand ran up her arm—into the deepest core of her body. She wanted to fly across the table and ravish him. "It—it sounds wonderful," she stuttered.

He lowered her hand from his lips but continued to hold it. "In order to arrive at the theater on time, maybe we should leave now."

After the play they were back in the car driving down the interstate toward the ranch. They had traveled several miles with only brief snippets of conversation. The lack of conversation was mainly because Jenny was replaying the evening and the play in her mind. She broke the lull in the conversation by saying, "The play was all I thought it would be. You were right. It did remind me of our time in the water garden. Gene, I'll always remember this special night, and the wonderful man I shared it with."

He couldn't stand it another second. He pulled the car to the side of the road…screeching to a sudden stop. He reached across the seat and in a matter of seconds he had Jenny locked into a hard, passionate kiss. He could tell she was into the kiss as much as he was. After a moment he pulled away from her. "I just had to do that, Jenny. I don't think I could've made it home without kissing you at least once. I don't know what will happen another five miles up the road. Just be ready for anything."

They both laughed.

She sat up straight, smoothed her hair, took a deep breath and tried to settle down. "That was a pleasant surprise alright. If we keep this up, we won't make it back to the ranch before daybreak."

He took a couple of deep slow breaths. "It's a good thing we don't have much farther to go. I'd hate for one of my co-workers to catch us making out here on the side of the road in this small sports car. I'll try to control my emotions for the rest of the trip," he said, as he drove the car back onto the highway.

Later when they arrived at the ranch, Gene asked Jenny to walk with him to the water garden. "I want to talk with you a little longer," he said.

The timer had gone off on the lights to the pathway and water garden. So, he stepped inside the back door of the house and turned them back on. While there, he pulled a blanket from the closet shelf and got a coat for Jenny.

He placed his arm around her waist as they walked toward the water garden. The late night air felt damp and cool against his face. It invigorated him. He wasn't tired or sleepy and felt he could talk all night with Jenny. He wanted to get to know everything he could about her.

"It seems to be more beautiful every time I see it," Jenny said when they entered the garden. "The grounds are always so manicured. Who maintains them?"

"There are several gardeners on the payroll. They each have specific jobs around the ranch. They really are professionals and always seem to know what to do and when to do it. Would you like to sit on the blanket or wrap up in it?" They had made their way to the far end of the garden next to the pond.

"I'd like to sit and wrap up with you in it," she smiled and winked.

After they were wrapped up and settled comfortably on the ground, he said, "Wrapped up together was a good idea, Jenny. Tell me, how are your college courses coming along? Have you decided what career path you want to take?"

"I think I know what I want to do. But I don't see how a college degree will help in the profession I'm considering. I'm taking a couple business courses this term while I figure out if college is the route I want to take."

"So what is this profession you desire?"

"I've developed a fondness for horses. I want to train them; maybe get into the racing end of it someday. What do you think, Gene? You think you could help me out in this area? I hear you have a few horses."

"Boy! That's not what I expected to hear. I thought you might say you wanted to be a pilot, doctor, nurse, scientist or something. A horse trainer...I don't know," he joked. "I have faith you can do anything you set your mind to. So if you want to train horses, I'll start you out on your first project; Jenny Three Stars is yours. You can train her, feed, groom, and see to her well-being. While you are doing that, I have a few unruly horses you can try your talents on. So, exactly when would you like to get started?"

"I'm serious, Gene. You aren't making fun of my desire to train horses are you?"

"I would never underestimate anything you wanted to do. I think you're great with animals. Especially, after I saw the way you were with Morning Star during the delivery of her foal. You had her so relaxed. I'm sure that's why she delivered as quickly as she did. I believe you'll make a wonderful trainer. I meant what I said...Jenny Three Stars belongs to you. I'll do whatever I can to help you achieve your goals. And, for your information, there are a lot of unruly horses on the ranch that I'd love to see trained to do various things."

Before he could say another word she had her arms thrown around him, causing them to become off balance and fall backwards onto the ground. She felt so good lying there in his arms. Neither of them made a move to sit back up. He pulled her even closer and kissed her softly on the neck, the collarbone, her forehead, and then her lips—her sweet lips. Their bodies were pressed together as they lay under the blanket. He wanted to touch and explore every inch of her. She whispered his name. He whispered hers. He knew in his heart she was the one for him. He wanted to tell her.

"I love you, Jenny," he whispered into her ear.

"I love you, too. More than I could ever express."

They lay facing each other. He kissed her forehead. He inhaled the scent of her perfume and the scent of her silky clean hair. "Sweet Jenny, I have something I want to tell you."

She backed away from him so that she could have a full view of his face. "You can tell me anything."

"I resigned from the police force. Today was my last day at work."

Knowing how much Gene loved his law enforcement job, Jenny was shocked by this news.

"Why did you do that, Gene? You love your job."

"I did love my job. However, I have been on the force long enough. Now that father is no longer here, I feel I need to spend more time with Mother while I have her. She would never say so, but I believe she needs me here on the ranch. And, besides, I can't stay away from you any longer. I thought I would go crazy these past few weeks because I couldn't see you. Our talks on the phone every day was the only thing that got me through the notice period I gave the department. I want you, Jenny. I want you to be my wife. Will you marry me?"

She sat straight up. Her heart was racing and felt as if it were going to jump out of her chest. Shock and disbelief overpowered her. Tears of joy pooled up in her eyes. She had never expected a proposal of marriage. She threw her arms around his neck and said. "Oh, my darling Gene, I love you more than life itself. I wouldn't want to live in a world without you by my side. I would love to be your wife. Are you sure you want to marry me?"

"I'm very sure. I love you, Jenny."

They held each other briefly, and then Gene pulled away and said, "Oh! Jenny, I just realized that I've just proposed to you without a ring. I'm so sorry. Do you mind if we go tomorrow and pick one out? I guess I got overly excited and couldn't wait to ask you." He gave her a gentle kiss on the lips.

"I don't mind, Gene. The important thing is the proposal, not the ring. I'm in no hurry for a ring. Have you given any thought to when you want to get married?"

"That's really up to you. I'm ready now…right this second." He had a broad smile on his face.

Jenny took his hand in hers and said, "Gene, I don't know anything about weddings. I've never even been to one. The closest I've ever been to a wedding is to watch them on television." As she contemplated a wedding, Jenny suddenly felt a little lost.

"I'm sure mother would be a big help to you in that area. She'll probably want the whole county to attend. Would you like to have the ceremony at our little church in town?"

"Would you mind if we have it here in the garden? This is a very special place for us."

"What a wonderful suggestion. I wish I had thought of that. I'm sure Mother will be honored. Do you have a special date in mind?"

"Not really. Why don't we talk it over with your mother and see how soon we can put together a small ceremony? It's very easy for my side of the family. I have no one to invite."

"Is there no one to walk you down the aisle…except, in this case, it will be down the path?"

Eyes casting downward she softly said, "There's no one."

"Do you know who has great admiration for you and would consider it an honor to walk you down the path?"

"Who would that be?"

"Captain Hall."

"I really like Captain Hall, and he has been very kind to me. Do you think he would do that for me?"

"I know so. Let's ask him tomorrow. I'm sure Betty and Mary Ann will be glad to stand with you, if you don't have anyone else." He knew she didn't.

"I would love to have them stand with me."

"Well, I'll get Ron and Larry to stand with me. Then we'll be on the road to having our wedding planned." He kissed her again. "Let's go inside and get some rest. We can tell everyone our plans to be married in the morning at breakfast."

Breakfast was ready and waiting by the time Gene and Jenny came down stairs. Pauline and Betty were sitting around the island talking. Mary Ann brought the orange juice and milk from the refrigerator and sat them on the table next to the platters of food already sitting there. The moment Pauline saw Gene and Jenny; she knew that something had happened between them the night before.

"Good morning," she said. "How was your date last night?" Oh yes. The sparkle she had seen in their eyes yesterday was still there, Pauline thought.

Jenny came to her and kissed her cheek. "Unforgettable, thank you, she said "Dinner was lovely, the show was outstanding, but the company was the best of all." She caught Gene's eye and smiled. Jenny could tell they were eager to hear all about their date.

"I see breakfast is ready. Is everyone ready to eat?" Gene said in order to change the subject and get Jenny off the hook.

Pauline noticed Gene didn't sit in his usual place at the table. He sat beside Jenny. Seeing the two of them together sparked memories of the loving relationship she once had with her darling husband. Her son had not loved another woman since his first wife died. She longed for a loving relationship for him—*one like she once had.*

"Mother, Jenny and I have something we want to ask you. Betty and Mary Ann, we want you to hear this as well," Gene said after everyone had eaten their breakfast. "We would like to know how long it would take to put together a small wedding." He said nothing else and waited for their reaction. He reached for Jenny's hand.

It took a moment for them to realize what he had said.

"A wedding! Did you say, *wedding*?" said Mary Ann. "Gene, are you and Jenny getting married? I don't believe you are marrying our sweet Jenny. What a glorious day this is." She rounded the table in a flash and gave them one big hug.

Betty shortly joined the group hug. Pauline would have been there first but she couldn't get out of the chair and move across the floor fast enough.

"Oh, Gene! Jenny, this is indeed great news," Pauline said, as she embraced them. "Why don't we all sit back down and make some arrangements for this wedding?"

"Let me see your ring," Betty said, as she lifted Jenny's left hand from where it rested on the chair arm. Seeing there was no ring on her finger, she slowly replaced her hand. "Oh…I'm sorry," said Betty with embarrassment. I though---

"I thought it best that Jenny pick out her rings," Gene interjected. "We're going to the jewelers today. Mother, if you don't mind, we would like to be married in your water garden."

"Oh! What an honor that would be to your father. If only he could be here to see this." Tears began to pool in her eyes.

Gene saw her teary eyes and reached for his mother's hand. "Now, Mother, this is supposed to be a happy occasion. I'm sure father will be there that day. He'll be watching every move we make in that garden. He would want you to enjoy this time."

"He would…wouldn't he. Let's get back to planning the wedding." She picked up the pen and notepad she had placed in front of her earlier. "Do you have anything special in mind?"

"Nothing other than, we don't want anything elaborate, and we only want just a few friends. Mother, that doesn't mean the whole county."

Pauline just smiled and said, "I think we can handle that, can't we girls," indicating Mary Ann and Betty.

"Don't worry about a thing. You'll have the *most beautiful* wedding ever. How about your wedding dress, Jenny? Do you know what you want?" Mary Ann was eager to get started.

"I...I don't have anything in mind. I was thinking maybe you and Betty could help me select a dress. Also, I have no friends or family of my own to ask so would you be my bride's maids?"

"It would be an honor," said Mary Ann.

"I would love to be your bride's maid," Betty added.

In no time at all the wedding plans were finalized.

"Well, now that everything has been settled with the bride's maids. I need to call Captain Hall and the groomsmen to see if these plans suit their schedules. We have a lot to do in three weeks," Gene said, as he stood from the table to leave.

"Gene, I'd like to talk with you for a few minutes before you do that. Will you take a walk with me outside?" Pauline proceeded to scoot her chair from the table.

"Of course I will, Mother." He assisted her with the chair. Then they walked toward the door.

Later that afternoon, Gene met Jenny in the water garden to look over the area for the placement of the wedding party. After mere moments of observing the area, they both agreed the gazebo would be the perfect location. He directed her toward a nearby bench which faced the pond. "Let's sit for a moment. I'd like to talk with you about something."

Jenny settled herself on the bench. She noticed Gene had a melancholy look on his face and she said, "Is there something wrong?"

"Oh, no…everything's perfect. I can't believe how smoothly our plans are falling into place. I wanted to ask you; have you given any thought about the kind of wedding rings you want?"

"The only ring I've ever owned was my high school class ring. I bought it with the money I saved from my part time jobs. I know very little about rings and nothing about diamonds. I'm not particular, Gene. I'll be happy with anything. *You* are all I *really* want." She softly kissed his lips.

He pulled her into his arms and kissed her with all the love and passion he had in him. His hands were all over her—under her blouse, touching the soft skin of her waist and her back. She didn't pull away from him this time and he could feel her responding to his touch. He wanted more and more, but he knew he wouldn't take everything he wanted until they were married. He eased up on the kiss, and then slowly pulled apart.

"Suddenly, three weeks is a long time away," he said. "It's getting harder and harder for me to keep my hands off you, Jenny."

Her eyes were closed as she rested her head against his shoulder. She couldn't believe the love one person could feel for another.

"I know how you feel," she said softly. "At times, I feel as if I want to jump inside you so that we can be as close as we can get to one another."

"Jenny, I need to talk with you about your rings." He drew her face up so that he could look into her eyes. "I don't want you to think I don't want to buy your rings. I'll buy you the biggest and most expensive rings you could ever want if that's what you want. What I'm trying to say is Mother wants you to have her wedding rings. They were passed down from my grandmother to her. She thought it would be nice to pass them to you. You don't have to accept them as a wedding set. I'm more than willing to buy your rings. You can just have them to wear when you want to." He took the small sterling silver box from his jacket pocket and held it up for her to see.

Jenny stared at the beautiful silver box and admired the small carvings that adorned it. The word "Love" was simply carved on the box top. "What a wonderful heirloom, Gene. I feel honored to be asked to wear such a precious heirloom and to be a part of such heritage. This is so thoughtful of you and your mother. Thank you, Gene. I'll be sure to thank Pauline for thinking of this wonderful gift."

"But you haven't seen the rings yet," he teased.

"It doesn't matter what the rings look like. It's the thought and heritage that matters. I truly feel honored to be a part of it." She drew near to him and kissed him lightly on the lips.

He removed the engagement ring from the box and slowly ran it up her long slender fingers until it rested in the proper position. It was a perfect fit. This was meant to be, he thought.

Jenny held her hand up to get a good look at the ring. Nestled between six long aquamarine baguettes was a three carat aquamarine stone. The sunlight bounced off the stones causing them to sparkle. The ring was more beautiful than she could have ever imagined.

"It...it's so beautiful. How can I wear something so beautiful with all the work I plan to do every day? I'm afraid I might damage or lose it."

He took her hands, which now rested in her lap, and held them tenderly in his. He said, "Don't worry about that sweetheart. Wear your rings...enjoy them. If you lose them, I'll see that they're replaced. No matter what my mother and grandmother were involved in around here, they wore those rings. I saw my mother one day up to her chin in blood as she delivered a calf that was having a difficult time coming into the world. She didn't bother to take her rings off. She got down and dirty quite often on the ranch. I'm sure from what I hear about my grandmother, she was in the thick of things, as well."

"The rings are so beautiful and shiny. It's hard to believe they've been through so much wear and tear. They have a *real* history." She raised his hands to her lips and kissed them. "Do you mind if we go back to the house now? I'd like to thank your mother for being so thoughtful. And, thank you, Gene. What about a ring for yourself? We can go to the jewelers today and buy one for you."

"I'm glad you brought that up," he said. I'd like to wear my father's ring, if it's alright with you. It was also passed down from my grandfather to him."

"Oh how wonderful. I don't mind at all that you want to wear your father's ring."

Once again, they tenderly kissed, and then walked back to the house to find Pauline.

CHAPTER FORTY

෧෧෧

While they were on the mainland, Edna and Grady had called friends and family to inform them of their upcoming appearance on the *Brattman's* television program. The trip had taken the better part of the day. They were weary from the day's events, and neither of them felt like walking or doing anything else. After an early dinner of soup and salad, they went to bed.

In the wee hours of the morning, Grady turned in the bed, and as he did, his arm fell over onto Edna's side. His eyes were still closed as he felt around for her. He was surprised to find she wasn't in bed, so he sat up and looked around the room for her. She wasn't in the bedroom, or anywhere else in the cottage. He eventually found her sitting on the porch swing. Not wanting to startle her, he made a slight noise with the screen door before he approached where she was sitting.

"Oh, Grady, I didn't wake you, did I?" Edna said when she saw him coming in her direction.

"You didn't wake me. I turned in bed and you weren't there. What's the matter? Can't you sleep?"

"I'm having a hard time dealing with the fact that I took another person's life. I did what had to be done…I had no choice…I know that. But, I can't stop thinking about his family and what they must be going through. Do you think his family knows he was in the United States, and what happened to him?"

He placed his arm around her shoulder and pulled her close. "I know this is hard for you, but you must not let this affect you like this. It isn't good for your health. You aren't resting at night, and I have noticed your appetite isn't what it used to be. You have to realize, Swart, this was a *very bad* man. He was connected to other bad men who wanted to harm this country and our people. I don't believe you really realize the importance of what you've done by killing this man. The radical Islamic terrorist cell he was a part of had planned to assassinate the entire Bush family at the football game the night that you killed him?"

"How do you know that? No one ever told me that!" Edna was shocked to discover the man she had shot was a terrorist. "I thought he was just upset with someone at the Pickle Barrel about something they might have said or done to him. It never occurred to me to ask why there was such a large reward for him."

"I'm sorry, Swart. I didn't tell you at the time because I thought you had enough to deal with. Captain Hall told me about it when he told me about the reward money. It was before you were released from the hospital. He said after questioning the roommate for some time, he confessed everything about their assassination plans that had gone awry. Apparently, the guy you killed was very distraught over the failed assassination attempt and took his frustrations out on everyone at the Pickle Barrel. Police officers found a bomb in the trunk of his car capable of making a very large dent in the stadium. It would have taken a lot of lives."

"Oh my, Grady! "What do you think would've happened if I hadn't been there with my gun? Do you think he would've gotten away with killing all those people? I could have been one of those fatalities. It makes me ill just thinking about it."

"We can't think about all that now, Swart. What's done is done. All I know is, if you hadn't shot that madman, a lot more people might've been killed or wounded. In spite of what happened to you, I hope you realize you were there at that time for a reason. There's a reason for everything we do in life…even if we don't understand the reasons why. You took another person's life…I know that's hard for you to accept, but you have to believe it was a good thing.

"While we're on this subject, I haven't seen my gun. Do you know where it is?"

"Oh, I almost forgot…your gun. Captain Hall had to keep it as evidence, but he'll return it to you as soon as he can."

"I'm so glad you're here to talk with me." She cuddled close to him. "I love you so much. Having you here to lean on makes me wonder what will happen to this man's family now that he's dead. I feel sorry for them, having to deal with the loss of a loved one. What would drive a man to leave his family to murder innocent people in another country? I will never understand."

"Captain Hall said his entire family had been killed in the Baghdad bombing raids. This was the reason he was here in the United States…to get revenge against the Bush family."

"Oh, I had no idea. I guess he felt he had nothing to live for. What a tragedy all this has turned out to be."

Edna noticed the sky was becoming lighter and, she wanted to walk to their favorite spot and watch the sunrise. *Watching the sunrise was quickly becoming their favorite pastime.* Grady, would you like to go and watch the sunrise?" she asked.

He was glad to see her mood had lightened. "Sounds like a good idea to me. Do you want to take coffee and something to eat?"

"Let's just stroll down and watch the sunrise. I'll make breakfast after we get back."

They had been sitting on the porch swing wearing only their pajamas and Edna was chilly from the damp air. "I think I'll get my heavy robe and shoes…you want yours?"

As they sat on the park bench watching the sunrise, the conversation turned to their ownership of the island and its fate when they both passed away; especially since they had no children to leave it to. They tossed around a few ideas but quickly ruled them out. Edna was in deep thought about how they had acquired the island when a great idea came to her.

"Let me run this idea past you, Grady. We acquired this island because someone thought I was a real hero. Wouldn't it be nice if we returned the favor by putting it in a trust to another real hero, who also might need a hideaway? Then, they can leave it to another real hero."

"Swart, I don't know where you come up with some of your ideas. But, I'll have to say, this one sounds like a pretty good one. Let's run it by Captain Hall and see what he thinks about your idea. While we're discussing ideas, maybe we should give the island a name. It can't be an official island without a name."

She closed her eyes against the early morning rays and thought for a moment, "How does *Hero Island* sound?"

"How did you come up with that name?"

"Think about it. In the future, only *heroes* will be allowed to stay here. Once the island is placed in trust, it'll be passed down from one hero to another hero."

"I think we should put up a big sign with that name on it at the end of the dock," he suggested.

It was two days before their appearance on Gary's show, and they spent them leisurely playing around the island. The dolphins had become accustomed to them. They swam all around their kayaks and even allowed Edna and Grady to pet them. During all their play time Edna never mentioned fishing again, she didn't dare: especially since Grady had caught…"*the big one*"…the one she made him put back into the water. Nor, did she talk about, or even mention, the tragic shooting.

Edna was now rifling through the meager wardrobe they had brought from home for something to wear on Gary Brattman's television program.

"Grady, we only have a few casual clothes here; nothing suitable to wear in front of the whole country. If I had known before we left home we would be appearing on national television, I would've packed better."

"You worry too much, Swart. I'm sure Gary doesn't care what you wear. The story is what he's interested in. Besides, we're going to be there a day before the show. I'm sure we can find time to shop for something to wear."

"You always have an answer for everything, don't you? It's a good thing someone in this family worries. You're likely to go off in your underwear and not care at all that the world might see you," she teased. "I'd probably get the blame for not seeing that my husband was properly dressed before he left home."

"Well, I guess I'll have to wear proper underwear then."

"Alright, I give up. We have nothing here that's worth taking. Let's don't bother with packing anything. We can buy what we need when we get there." She stashed the small suitcase back in the closet.

Bright and early the next morning they were on the water headed for the mainland. The plane was to be at the local airport in two hours to pick them up. As they traveled closer to the mainland, Edna became increasingly apprehensive about appearing on Gary's show.

Someone approached them the moment they entered through the doors at the air terminal. From the man's friendly demeanor, you would've thought they were the best of friends. The man didn't appear to have any problem picking them out of the crowd of people who were coming and going. This made Edna wonder how he knew what they looked like.

They were escorted straight to the plane. A very friendly hostess introduced herself as Rachel, showed them to their seats, and offered them a choice of drinks. They gave her their drink choices and watched her walk off toward the rear of the plane. While they waited for the drinks, they sat in silence and visually surveyed the beautiful cherry wood décor of the cabin. Moments later, Rachel returned and sat the drinks on the side table next to Edna and Grady.

"We have clearance for takeoff, and we should be airborne shortly. Please be sure your seat belts are fastened before we begin to taxi. Also, a nice lunch has been prepared for you, and once we have reached our cruising altitude, I will be happy to serve you. The restrooms are down the hallway, and if there's anything else I can do for you, please press the call button." Once Rachel had given them this information she turned and returned back in the direction from whence she had come.

"Can you believe this, Grady? I feel like I'm in *"high cotton"*. Edna said when Rachel was out of sight. "Look at this cherry wood décor…it's so shiny and sleek. During our travels in the military, we flew in many types of planes, but *this one*…it's something else." She sipped her drink. "So, this is how the rich get around." Her eyes wandered around the plane. "I could get accustomed to traveling like this."

"It's a nice way of getting around, alright," Grady commented while glancing around the plane. He looked at the time on his wristwatch. If we had been traveling commercially, we would probably be just now taking our shoes off in the security line."

They both laughed.

It didn't take long for the plane to reach cruising altitude and level out. Rachel reappeared from the rear of the plane and offered them wine with their lunch. Moments later, she brought out a tray with their lunch beautifully displayed and sat it before them.

"This is all so beautiful. I don't know whether to eat it or take a picture of it," Edna said after Rachel left the cabin.

The four inch square slice of pink salmon, lightly covered in dill sauce, lay next to long dark green strips of steamed asparagus. Red-skinned, parsley potatoes looked colorful against the delicate snow-white china plate. A cream cheese stuffed pear salad, garnished with pecans and topped with a cherry, rested in a matching salad plate.

Grady said, "You can take a picture if you want to, but I intend to eat every bit of it. The light breakfast I had this morning is long gone." He picked up his fork and began to eat.

Edna admired the food one last time before she picked up her fork.

The two hour flight passed rather quickly. Upon landing Edna and Grady were escorted quickly through the airport and into a waiting car. They made good time from the airport through the light afternoon traffic, and were soon walking into the building housing Gary Bratt's broadcast studio. They were given a tour of the studio and were told what they could expect the next day during the broadcast. After the tour they were taken to Gary's office to finally meet one of their favorite political commentators.

Gary was in his glass-enclosed office going over that night's program with his producers when he saw Calvin (Cal) escorting Grady and Edna. Their pictures and a description of what had happened at the Pickle Barrel had been plastered all over the news for weeks. Because of that, he already knew something about them and what they looked like. He had been surprised, but honored, when Edna called and asked to tell her story on his television program. Every news agency in the country had sought her out for an interview. During their brief talk on the phone she had told him she would only discuss her experience publicly one time, and she wanted to do it on his show. He quickly gained a great admiration for her courage and how she was dealing with the aftermath of this tragedy. He excused himself and walked outside the office door to greet them.

The tour of the studio was more than Grady and Edna had expected. They hadn't realized all that went on behind the scenes. Edna felt as if she were old friends with Cal, the executive producer of Gary's show, and was honored to have him escort them through the studio. She had listened to Cal and Gary kid back and forth on the radio nearly every day for some time. She saw Gary step outside the door of his office and walk in their direction. Suddenly, her heart stopped. She was speechless. She felt as if she were in a dream and would awaken to find herself at home in her bed. She was still in her dreamlike state as Gary shook her hand and said, *"Hello, Edna."*

"I'm so glad to meet both of you," Gary said, as he shook their hands. "I hope the trip to New York was enjoyable for you. Have you been briefed on what to expect on tomorrow's show?"

"Yes—yes," Edna managed to get out.

"Your staff has been very helpful," Grady said. "I believe we're ready. We have really enjoyed the tour of the studio. There're a lot of behind-the-scenes activities that we weren't aware of."

"Yes, there is. So, is there anything you need before the show? Hotel accommodations have been made for you. A nice restaurant is located in the hotel. The network will be glad to provide your meals if you wish to eat there."

"Thank you very much. Everyone has been so nice to us, and please be sure to thank the network for us. There is one other thing you might help us with. We came without any clothes to wear on the show. Since we aren't familiar with the city, could you recommend somewhere we can shop for something to wear?"

Gary knew they had come from the sunny state of Florida and noticed they had on lightweight casual clothing. Their clothing wasn't suitable for the frigid New York winter weather. "Do you have *coats* with you?" he asked.

Grady laughed. "To be honest with you, Gary, we brought nothing with us. We escaped from our neighborhood the other day by hiding in the floorboard of our Suburban. Our neighbor drove us past the media that was camped out on our lawn, so we didn't have an opportunity to take much with us. We have been staying on a remote island off the coast of Florida, and didn't need much in the way of clothing, only casual beachwear. Besides, at the time of our escape, we had no idea we would be appearing on your show."

Gary couldn't believe what he was hearing. He had no idea these people had to flee their home in order to get some peace and quiet. Yet, they seemed to be happy and could even joke about the predicament they were in. However, he did notice Edna was very quiet, and he was *concerned* about that.

"I know the perfect place for you to pick up something to wear, and I'll have the driver take you there when you leave the studio. I want you to pick out anything you want. I'll call Tom and have him put your things on my account. Oh, don't forget to include winter coats. You may have noticed, *its cold out there*," he said jokingly, as he wrapped his arms around himself and pretended to shiver.

"That's a very generous offer, Gary. But you don't have to buy our clothes. You and the network have done more than enough for us. We don't expect anything like this from you."

"Please, I want to do this for both of you. Now, Grady, if you don't mind, I'd like to speak with Edna for a few minutes. You can have something to drink in the lounge while you wait, if you want." Gary reached for Edna's hand. "Would you join me in my office, Edna?"

Edna was still in her dreamlike state. "Su-Sure," she stammered. She took his hand and walked with him to his office. *Am I really holding Gary Bratt's hand?*

"Would you care for something to drink, Edna?" Gary asked, after she was seated. He could see that she was uneasy and wanted to give her a minute to settle down.

"A glass of water would be nice. Thank you."

He brought the water to her and then sat in the chair across from her. "You're very quiet, Edna. Is everything alright? Are you having second thoughts about appearing on the show?"

"Oh, Gary, I can't believe I'm here talking with you. I listen to you every day on the radio, and I watch your television show every night. I never would have dreamed in a million years I'd be here…on your show. I'm sorry, I'm just overwhelmed," she said as she drank some water. "But, I'm not having second thoughts about appearing on your show. So much has happened to me lately that I have a hard time figuring out what's real and what's a dream. This is *real*, isn't it?"

Gary could tell Edna was having some trouble dealing with her experience. Usually, he would go over what the guest on his program would have to say before the program. However, he didn't want to put Edna through any more stress by making her discuss it now, and then have to repeat it again on his show. He would hear her story for the first time along with the rest of the world.

"Yes, Edna, this is all real. You don't have to be concerned about anything. You and I are sitting here having a normal conversation, and that's just how it'll be tomorrow. All you'll have to do is to tell what happened to you at the Pickle Barrel. Is there anything special you want me to say before I bring you on the air?"

"Yes. I'd like for you to make it clear to the media that this is the ONLY interview I intend to give. Tell them to *leave us alone*. We want, and need, our privacy back. I also want everyone off our front lawn so that we can go back home."

"I'll be happy to convey that message. Now, let me have the honor of treating you and Grady to a big shopping spree at my favorite shopping spot. You have a nice dinner and a good night's rest, and try to be back at the studio an hour before the show tomorrow." Gary walked her to the lounge to meet up with Grady.

The next morning on his radio program, Gary announced the pending interview with Edna for that night's television program. As per Edna's request, he stressed that this would be the ONLY interview given by her. He encouraged everyone to listen as he was dedicating the entire program to her story.

∿∿ ∿∿ ∿∿
∿∿ ∿∿ ∿∿

In his opening monologue that evening, Gary made the same announcement he had made on the radio program that morning. He gave Edna's request for the media to stop hounding them and to leave their neighborhood so that they could have some peace and quiet. He explained how Edna had gone into shock after the shooting and had been hospitalized for several days before regaining consciousness. He described how emotionally distraught and fragile Edna still was, even now. The media, trying to uncover everything about the woman involved in this tragedy, was affecting her rest and recovery from this very tragic event. The harassment had become so intrusive that they had to flee their home seeking peace, and that was when Edna had sought his help. Gary explained that he personally knew very little about Edna's involvement in the shooting, except that she had killed the gunman. He only knew what the news media had reported, which included all manner of speculation concerning Edna and what had happened at the Pickle Barrel. But, tonight all speculation would be put to rest because Edna would, for the first time, tell her story to the public. Gary then turned and introduced Edna and Grady to the watching audience.

Gary watched them walk hand-in-hand across the stage. Grady looked confident and relaxed, dressed in a dark brown blazer, tan slacks, white shirt and red tie. Edna looked more like a mature fashion model, dressed in a burgundy and gray tweed tailored suit. The matching four inch gray high heels she wore made her look tall and slender. Her posture was straight and she held her head high as she gracefully walked across the stage. Tonight she appeared to be in total control. She looked *nothing* like she had the day before at the interview.

Gary listened without interruption while Edna gave details of her dreadful experience at the Pickle Barrel. When she got to the point where she had held the trigger down and the gun would fire no more, he had to interrupt her.

"Excuse me, Edna, I don't mean to interrupt your story, but, are you saying you emptied your gun into the shooter?"

"Yes…how could I ever forget such a horrible thing? I was so afraid. When I finally got the courage to pull the trigger…I didn't stop. I kept firing until there was silence. I saw the man jerk several times before he fell to the floor, and that was the last thing I remember at the Pickle Barrel. The next thing I remember was waking up in the hospital several days later."

"Have you not read any newspapers or seen any television coverage about this tragedy?"

"Let me answer that for her, Gary," said Grady. "For several days after the shooting, Edna was unconscious. The doctors couldn't say when she would wake up, nor could they predict what her state of mind would be when she awakened. As it turned out, she remembered nothing about the shooting when she came to. Her doctor felt it best to keep her from finding out through the media that she had shot and killed a man. He had hoped she would recall what had happened in her own time. When she was released from the hospital, we went to a quiet place for a few days where she could rest and hopefully remember. During that time, it all came back to her. But, given her fragile state of mind, we felt it best not to subject her to all the stories in the media. We didn't want to risk any further shock to her system. And, because of our attempt to protect Edna, neither of us have seen nor read any form of news since Edna's hospital stay."

Gary was having a hard time believing they didn't know about all the publicity surrounding them. Everyday there had been new headlines about the shooting and Edna's whereabouts. The media hounds had dug up everything they could find on her and plastered it all over the news. It was good that Grady had kept her from all of it, he thought. He wanted to talk off camera with her for a moment, so he announced a commercial break.

"Edna, are you holding up alright? Do you need something to drink?" he asked during the break.

"I wouldn't mind having a little drink of water. Otherwise, I'm alright. I'm not as frightened as I thought I would be."

"That's good. I'm glad to hear that, Edna. Do you need something to drink, Grady?"

"No, I'm okay, Gary."

Someone brought the water to Edna, and then informed Gary that the phones wouldn't stop ringing and the e-mails were a mile long. This story had garnered a great deal of public interest, and everyone was happy to finally meet the woman that had stopped a terrorist. Edna's story was compelling, and she was receiving numerous notes of support and sympathy.

While she sipped at her water, Gary said, "Edna, we'll be back on air in just a few moments. But, before we go back on air I have something I need to tell you that you aren't aware of. I don't want you to be upset when I give you this news…it isn't bad news. I just don't have time during this break to fill you in on it. Are you o.k. with this?"

"If it isn't bad news, I think I can handle it."

The cameras were on again and Gary welcomed his audience back and continued his coverage.

"Grady, you said earlier in this program that you and Edna haven't seen or heard any form of media news since before Edna was released from the hospital. So, you probably aren't aware of the phrase "*The Divine Shot*".

"No. I don't think I've ever heard the phrase. Have you, Edna?" Grady asked.

"I've never heard that phrase. What does it mean?"

"Edna, you said you emptied your gun into the gunman when you shot him," Gary stated.

"I'm sure I emptied the gun into him," she interjected.

"Do you remember loading the gun, Edna?"

"I remember being so frightened that I shook all over. I had bloody tears in my eyes which made it difficult to see. At first, I struggled with the shell as I attempted to load the barrel, but I finally got the shell into the chamber. At that point the man began firing rapidly again, and bullets suddenly started flying overhead. I was so afraid at that moment—I'm not sure what happened next. The gun was new and, I wasn't really all that familiar with it. I remember aiming the gun at the man's back. I didn't want to be looking into his face when I pulled the trigger. While I held the trigger down, I saw him jerk several times as he fell to the floor. Then, there was silence. I knew I had shot him."

Gary could see that tears had begun to pool up in Edna's eyes. He couldn't believe what he was hearing. Chills ran up and down his body. The details he was about to expose to her had been the talk of the media for some time. Yet, she and Grady weren't aware of everything that had happened at the Pickle Barrel.

"*The Divine Shot*" is the name that has been given to the lone bullet which penetrated the heart of the gunman. You see, Edna, the shell you placed inside the barrel was the *only* shell in the gun. You hadn't loaded the clip in your little Beretta. It was found lying beside you on the floor, and all the shells were still in it. Everything had to have happened just right in order for that single small caliber shell to penetrate his heart and kill him. Everyone in this country feels God must have guided your hand that day. I know you don't want to hear this, Edna. But what you did was heroic. It couldn't have been easy for you to take another person's life. I hope you can take comfort in knowing a lot of other lives were spared because of your brave actions."

Gary could see Edna had become withdrawn again. A single tear escaped her eye and rolled down her cheek. She sat still… staring into space. Gary was afraid he had lost her. Her face looked pale, and he became very concerned for her. Grady didn't look much better. Gary pulled his chair next to Edna's and took her hand in his.

"Listen Edna...Grady...this has been a nightmare for both of you. You must believe, Edna, God put you there to do His will. He also put Grady in your life to help you through this. You will overcome this someday. Are you alright?"

Edna was still trying to comprehend everything Gary had said. *"The Divine Shot"—single shell—gun not loaded—shot through heart—God guiding her hand.* She quickly replayed the events of the shooting that day in her mind. She was sure she had used all the shells in the gun. Most importantly, she now remembered asking God to guide her hand and to do His will. For the first time, she realized she couldn't have done what she did...*alone.* God was with me that day, she thought. She suddenly felt as if a very large burden had been lifted from her shoulders. She remembered feeling this way in the Pickle Barrel after she had asked for God's help in dealing with the gunman.

"Gary, I'll be alright," she said. "I now know that God was with me that day. I want to thank you for reminding me of that fact and for allowing me this opportunity to air this story on your program."

He noticed the sudden change in her, but only replied, "The pleasure was all mine." Then he went to a commercial break.

During the commercial break Edna and Grady left the set. Before they left Gary asked them to stay and join him for dinner after the program.

In his closing remarks he made another plea to the media to spare Edna and Grady from any more publicity.

∿∿ ∿∿ ∿∿
∿∿ ∿∿ ∿∿

Gary was making dinner plans with Grady and Edna, when his producer approached him with an urgent phone call. He took the phone from the producer's hand and was surprised to hear it was someone from the office of the President of the United States.

They had been trying to locate Edna for some time. Apparently, no one they had talked with knew where she was.

"She's standing right here," he said after a few moments of conversation. "Would you like to speak with her?" He gave the phone to Edna and told her it was from the President's office.

"What do they want with me?" she said, as she took the phone from Gary's hand.

"I'm not sure," he said.

She stepped aside to talk in private, and then moments later she hung up and gave the phone back to Gary.

"Well, what did they want?" Grady asked.

"They want to present me with an award of some kind at the White House next week. I don't want any awards."

"That's wonderful, Edna!" Gary said. "You should be honored. Your bravery should be recognized."

"Bravery had nothing to do with it. I did what I had to do to survive…I don't need a medal for that."

"What did you tell the White House about attending, Swart?"

"I told them I would talk it over with you and get back with them."

"Do you mind if I put in my two cents worth?" Gary asked.

"We value your opinion," Grady said. "Please feel free to speak your mind."

"This truly is an honor, Edna. I think you should go and accept this award. And, if you aren't in any hurry to get back home to Florida, why not spend the few days while you wait, here in the city? You can continue to stay in the hotel where you are, then do some sightseeing until you have to be in D.C."

"I wouldn't mind seeing the city, Swart. Would you like to stay here while we wait?"

"I'll think about it over dinner." *I really wouldn't mind seeing the city*, she thought.

Voices could be heard coming down the hallway toward where they stood in the studio. The three of them turned to see who was approaching. They were shocked to see Rusty Howard heading in their direction.

"It's good to see you, Rusty," Gary said, as they shook hands. "You don't often pay visits to my studio. What are you doing here?"

By this time he was busy shaking Edna's hand. "I wanted to see a *real hero* in person," Rusty said, as he continued to hold her hand and look into her eyes.

"Th…th…thank you," was all Edna could manage to say. She couldn't believe Rusty was really holding her hand. He actually came to see me, she thought.

"We're going out for dinner. Would you like to join us, Rusty?" Gary asked.

"I would consider it an honor to dine with you," Rusty said.

CHAPTER FORTY-ONE

Jenny and Gene were happy with the decisions they had made for the wedding arrangements in the water garden. They were almost back home when they saw Mary Ann running toward them, waving the phone back and forth high in the air. She had a frantic look on her face. Thinking it was a big emergency, they ran to meet her.

Nearly out of breath, sweat running down her face, Mary Ann said, as she passed the Jenny the phone, "Jenny, Jenny, it...it's...I don't believe it. They want to talk with you. It's the President's office."

Jenny put her hand over the receiver and whispered to Mary Ann, "What do they want with me?"

Mary Ann shook her head from side to side. "I don't know," she mouthed back.

Jenny answered the phone with a soft *hello*. Then she listened to what they had to say. "Why me?" she said. Then she listened again. "Yes sir, I understand...I'll be there." Jenny hung up and gave the phone back to Mary Ann.

Gene could see her face was very pale. She seemed stunned. "Jenny, did something bad happen? Are you feeling alright?" Afraid she might collapse; he held her by the waist and pulled her closer to him.

Concerned, Mary Ann asked, "What's the matter, Jenny?"

"Th…the President wants to give me an award for bravery. What shall I do, Gene? I didn't do anything that required bravery. Anyone could've done what I did."

"Yes, but no one else did what you did. Don't minimize your part in helping those people at the Pickle Barrel. I know Mother and those two little boys appreciated your help. Who knows what would've happened to them if you hadn't been there. You also managed to keep a panicked crowd under control, probably keeping many of them from being hurt. You deserve to be recognized. So, when do they want to present the award to you?"

"Oh Jenny, I'm so happy for you. I believe you deserve the award, too. Can we all go to see you receive your award?" Mary Ann said with excitement.

"I hope this won't interfere with our wedding plans. They want me there next week. Gene, do you think all of us could go? They said I could bring as many guests as I want and that accommodations would be provided for us. I was told there would also be a dinner banquet following the awards ceremony."

"It sounds like we have a lot of shopping to do before then." Gene said. "You'll need something to wear to the awards ceremony and something very special to wear to the banquet. Let's go and give the good news to Mother and Betty. I bet Captain Hall would love to be there with us."

Mary Ann took Jenny's hand. "All of us girls can go shopping tomorrow. And while we're at it, we can stop by the bridal shop. It's going to be so much fun, Jenny." A big smile crossed Mary Ann's face when she noticed Jenny was wearing Pauline's engagement ring.

CHAPTER FORTY-TWO

Jenny stood in front of the floor length mirror admiring the new pastel pink chiffon dress she was wearing. She was in the holding room awaiting her time to appear on stage to receive her award. The closed circuit television was on and, even though the sound was on, she wasn't paying any attention to what was happening on stage. She was very nervous about being the center of attention in front of a large group of strangers. She needed to get her mind off it, so her thoughts wandered from one thing to another. Her thoughts were now on the beautiful wedding dress she had bought earlier that week. She went over in her mind every little detail of the dress, and imagined herself walking through the water garden wearing it. *I hope Gene likes it.* She never would have believed her life could have changed so drastically in such a short period of time. As she gazed in the mirror, she wondered if this was really happening. She felt blessed to have friends, whom she loved so dearly, sitting in the audience waiting to see her receive the award. She wished that her mother could have been there and wondered where she was. A knock at the door startled her.

"You have one minute, Jenny," said the stage manager.

She took a deep breath, inspected herself in the mirror one last time, and then she stepped outside the door.

Edna stood on stage while the speaker spoke of her heroism and display of courage. She felt out of place and wanted to leave. Seeing her dear friends Bob, Margaret and Dixie sitting next to Grady in the audience was what kept her from falling apart where she stood. Then she saw entering the stage, the waitress who had held the table for her on the day of the shooting. *This girl is the real hero. If I recall correctly, her name is Jenny.* She looked so young and innocent. Edna instantly lost track of what the speaker was saying as she caught the young woman's eye. They began to run toward one another with their arms outstretched. They met in the middle of the stage and fell into each others arms, weeping.

The large room became so silent one could've heard a pin drop as the audience watched the two women on the stage. The speaker stopped talking and waited for them to regain their composure. The members of the audience were also caught up in the emotional scene, and soon there wasn't a dry eye in the room. The women eventually pulled apart and returned to their places on stage. But, they continued to hold tightly to each other's hands while the speaker spoke of Jenny's heroic deeds.

"Mr. President, if I could ask you to present the awards to these two brave women," the speaker said. President Bush walked over and embraced each of them. After making brief congratulatory remarks he presented their awards. As the President presented the awards the audience jumped to their feet with thunderous applause.

After the ceremony, they spent a little more time backstage visiting with President and Mrs. Bush. Then they worked their way through the crowd looking for their invited guests. They were stopped every few minutes by people asking them questions about the shooting. Both women were eager to escape the crowd, but were gracious to anyone that approached them. "Just think, Jenny, we have this to look forward to again tonight."

"That's right, Edna. But tonight I'm not letting Gene out of my sight." Jenny had been scanning the room hoping to see him.

"Oh, I see Grady!" Edna shouted over the noise of the room. "He's standing by the drink table. Come with me, Jenny. I want you to meet him." She took Jenny's hand and pulled her in the general direction of the drink table.

Moments after Edna had introduced Grady, Dixie, Bob and Margaret, Jenny felt a tap on her shoulder. She turned to see Gene standing there. "Oh, Gene, I have been looking all over for you. How did you find me? Edna and I have been looking for someone in our party since we left backstage. Everyone, this is my husband-to-be, Gene." She reached up and kissed him on the cheek. "Gene, this is Edna and her husband Grady, and these are their friends, Dixie, Margaret and Bob."

"I'm pleased to meet all of you," Gene said as he shook hands with them. "Edna, I've heard a lot about you. I'm glad to finally get to meet you." He then introduced his mother, Betty and Marry Ann.

"So, this is where everyone has gathered...in front of the drink table," Captain Hall said, as he approached the small group of people. "I don't see any drinks in your hands. Can I get anyone a drink? Has everyone been introduced?"

Edna smiled and said, "We have been introduced. But, I don't believe you've met our friend, Dixie." Edna had already been told that Captain Hall and Bob and Margaret were old friends.

Captain Hall shook Dixie's hand and said what a pleasure it was to meet her. "How would you folks like to go somewhere quiet so that we can talk and get to know one another better before our big outing tonight?" he added.

"That's a great idea, Captain," Gene said. "I saw a quiet little lounge on the second floor while I was wandering the building earlier. Will that be o.k. with everyone?"

The dinner banquet was elegant. A large round table had been reserved up front for Edna and Jenny and their guests. After their long visit in the lounge earlier that day they all felt like old friends.

Captain Hall sat back in his chair and looked out across the large table at everyone sitting there laughing and talking. He couldn't help thinking to himself how much their lives had changed in such a short time. It amazed him how new beginnings could come from a tragic event. He was glad to have been a part of it. It was moments like this that made him realize how much he loved his job.

Before everyone departed for home the next day they exchanged addresses and phone numbers, and promised to keep in touch. Gene and Jenny extended an invitation for everyone to attend their upcoming wedding.

CHAPTER FORTY-THREE

The ranch was buzzing with activity now that everyone was back from Washington and the wedding was only a few days away. The wedding coordinator Pauline had hired was in the kitchen issuing orders to the florist and caterer. Since there would be no rehearsal, the wedding party had been given their simple instructions earlier that morning. It was going to be a small wedding. Gene had to restrain his mother—she wanted to invite everyone in the county...*just as he thought she would.* They narrowed the guest list down to seventy-five people. A luncheon was to take place in the formal dining room following the mid-day ceremony in the water garden.

Gene leaned against the wooden fence rail that surrounded the pasture and admired Jenny from a distance as she slowly pulled the brush through Jenny Three Star's jet black coat. She looked as if she had always belonged there. The bottom part of the tight fitting jeans she wore was tucked inside of her tall leather boots. Her long sleeve white shirt was rolled up to her elbow, showing only the lower portion of her slender arm as she moved the brush back and forth. His mother's old Stetson hat rested on mounds of black curls which had been pinned up underneath.

She talked softly to the young filly and appeared to be enjoying the moment. The filly responded to Jenny's touch as if she were her mother. Morning Star didn't seem to mind that Jenny was brushing her foal…she was grazing in the pasture. He had been watching Jenny for some time before she noticed he was there. When she saw him, she squealed, dropped the brush to the ground, and then ran toward him with her arms open wide.

"I didn't see you standing there," she said, as she embraced him. "I missed you this morning. Pauline said you had to go into Tallahassee to see Captain Hall. I would have gone along to keep you company if you had gotten me out of bed. I hope everything's alright."

Gene smiled broadly and looked deep into her sky-blue eyes. "I appreciate that, sweetheart. But, I left very early and I didn't want to disturb your beauty rest."

"But, I wouldn't have minded getting up for you."

"You looked as if you were enjoying yourself out there with Jenny Three Stars. I enjoyed watching the two of you. You're going to spoil that horse rotten if you aren't careful." He glanced down and saw Jenny Three Stars standing right beside her. "See…she thinks you're her mother."

The horse nudged Jenny's side, which caused Gene to laugh out loud. "I told you. Why don't you walk her over to her *real* mother? I want to talk to you for a moment." He stayed where he was and watched her walk the filly back to where Morning Star was grazing. They really do look like mother and daughter, he thought, as he watched them walk side-by-side across the pasture. Moments later, Jenny was back standing beside him, holding the brush she had dropped in her hand.

"You said you wanted to talk to me," she said.

He took her hand. "Yes, I do. Do you mind if we walk while we talk?"

He looked serious. Suddenly she felt uneasy. "I don't mind at all. Is everything alright?"

"I hope so, Jenny. I have done something that I hope will not upset you. The morning after we made our wedding plans I called Captain Hall and asked him to try and locate your mother."

She abruptly dropped his hand and stepped away from him. "You and Captain Hall have been looking for my mother all this time without telling me. Why did you do that? Did you not feel it important enough to inform me before you went probing into my private life? I'm not some little kid, you know. I've been making my own decisions all my life. Did you think I would disapprove or something? Or did you want to find my mother to see what she's *really* like? Maybe you don't want to get mixed up with a family such as mine." She wanted to cry, but she stood firm and refused to let even one tear fall.

"Jenny, I don't think you're being fair to me. I didn't mention it to you because I wasn't sure we could locate her. I didn't want to get your hopes up, and then disappoint you. You have already had enough disappointments in your life. I've told you before; it doesn't matter to me where you're from, or what kind of family you have. I love you…that's all I care about. I thought you might like to have your mother at the wedding. Every girl needs to have her mother at her wedding. I'm sorry if I overstepped my bounds. I thought you would be happy to know that Captain Hall has located her."

Jenny flew into his arms, and the tears she had been holding back began to flow freely. "I'm so sorry. I don't know why I said all those bad things. It's just that I had given up all hope of ever seeing her. I was beginning to think *I didn't care* to ever see her again. This just took me by surprise. Please forgive me for being so nasty to you. I really do appreciate what you've done. And, I do want my mother at our wedding."

"Jenny, I want you to know, you're free to speak your mind no matter how you think it sounds. You should always say what you feel. I don't want you tiptoeing around my feelings thinking you might hurt me. That's not the kind of relationship I want for us. Perhaps I should have consulted you before we began looking for your mother. I thought it would save you some heartache if we couldn't find her...and it would be a nice surprise if we did. I'm the one who needs your forgiveness. I'll try not to make that mistake again."

She pulled away from him and dried her eyes with the long sleeve of her shirt. "Alright, alright, we forgive each other. Now what can you tell me about my mother?"

He couldn't help but smile at her little-girl mannerism. "Well, I went by to see her this morning."

"See her...you didn't tell me you saw her."

"Yes, I know, but I'm telling you now. She really looks good. You'll be pleased to know she has been clean for four years. I guess losing you was a wake-up call for her. She works full time in this quaint little family-owned restaurant across the street from the hospital in Tallahassee."

"We were in that hospital not long ago," Jenny interjected. "My mother works across the street from the hospital? This is so hard for me to believe. I was so close to her and didn't even know it."

"She's the cook in the restaurant and lives in an apartment over the place."

"I guess she learned to cook after all," Jenny said.

"From the looks of the pies and cakes on display there, I'd say she learned quite well. Would you like to go see her? We can go any time you're ready."

"It has been a long time since we saw each other. She may not recognize me. Maybe she straightened out her life because I wasn't in it as a reminder of what happened to her. Do you think she even wants to see me?"

"You mustn't think that way, Jenny. Your mother has been through a lot. But I don't think she would ever forget what you look like or think of you as some kind of reminder of the past.

She has experienced a lot of heartaches in her lifetime. Maybe you can help her enjoy life for a change."

"I'd like that...I really would. Did you talk with her while you were there? Did you tell her who you are...about us?"

"I just made small talk with her. I didn't tell her about you or about us. She's a very nice lady. I think you'll be proud of the changes she has made in her life."

"Give me time to take a quick shower and change from my work clothes. Then I'll be ready to go. It should take me about thirty minutes. Can we leave then?"

"I'll have the car waiting for you," Gene said, as he kissed her lightly on the lips. "I do love you, Jenny Three Stars."

"I love you too, Gene. Your love has opened new doors for me, and now I look forward to beginning a new life with you and my new family."

∧∧∧ ∧∧∧ ∧∧∧
∧∧∧ ∧∧∧ ∧∧∧

EPILOGUE

The news media cleared out of Grady and Edna's neighborhood after their appearance on the Brattman Show. However, talk of her interview with Gary dominated the airwaves for days afterwards.

Edna and Grady went back to their small island after the awards banquet for a little R and R. Edna wiped the dust off a leather-bound bible she had found on the bookshelf in the cottage. She and Grady read it as they waited every morning for that *glorious gift from God* to peek over the horizon.

They often spoke of the dinner they had shared with Gary and Rusty while they were in New York. They still had a good laugh now and then when they recalled the embarrassment Rusty exhibited after he mistakenly said something which alerted them to the fact he had been the one who had given them the island. Rusty liked the name they had chosen for the island. He was especially thrilled with their idea to pass *"Hero Island"* down to other hero's by way of a trust. Although the trust was set up under Edna and Grady's names, Rusty offered his legal service to set up and manage it. He also insisted upon providing the future financial support for the upkeep of the island. A large sign displaying the name *"Hero Island"* now stood proudly at the end of the dock. It wasn't as if a lot of people would ever see the sign…

very few people knew of the island's existence. The sign was meant to give a semblance of importance to the simple secluded island retreat. It would be seen and appreciated by the future heroes who would follow in Edna's footsteps.

The media returned to Edna and Grady's doorstep not long after their return from the island. Their previous departure had been short. Word had gotten out about the reward money and the fact that Edna had *given it all away.* This was another story the media wanted. Overwhelmed by this new media influx, Edna once again solicited help from Gary and Rusty. She wanted them to announce on their programs her reasons for not accepting the reward monies. It was their statements that played a big part in clearing the media from their neighborhood once again. However, the phone calls requesting book rights were relentless. She knew she would never have any peace or quiet until everything was out there for everyone to see. So, she asked Gary if he would help her publish her story. He put Edna in touch with a publishing company he knew and trusted, and with the help of their very good editors, the book was published.

Edna had hoped her life would settle down when the book was released, but it was more hectic than ever. Book sales were off the charts. She was sought after more now than she ever was before. Nearly all the talk show hosts wanted her to appear on their programs. Requests for book signings were numerous. Movie producers began pursuing her. Edna wanted no part of it and avoided publicity as much as she could. Yet, she was still sought after and her book kept selling as fast as the publisher could print them. As soon as the royalty checks came in, Edna passed the funds to family members for their personal needs. After all her family's needs were met, she then used the funds to help her friends with their needs. Edna still felt somehow, this money was...*Blood Money.* Grady finally convinced her otherwise, after he pointed out all the good things she had done for everyone she knew. Everyone, that is, except him. Now he was really looking forward to buying *his new Suburban.*

☆ ☆ ☆

Jenny Three Stars was quickly becoming the number one race horse in the country. Her owner/trainer was also gaining a very favorable reputation in the horse training arena. After their wedding and honeymoon, Jenny settled in at the ranch and began learning all she could about horse training...racing...breeding... and tending to the health needs of the farm animals. Gene had put her in contact with the best horse trainers so she could gain the knowledge she needed. She learned quickly and in no time at all she had Jenny Three Stars running like the wind around the track. In addition to the hours Jenny spent training horses; she had carried a full load of college courses at night, and had earned her business degree in record time. She felt a business degree would help her better understand the business end of operating the ranch.

Jenny's mother was thrilled to, at last, be back with her daughter. She was particularly happy to have been a part of Jenny's wedding. Shortly after the wedding she moved into one of the vacant cottages on the ranch. She came to be very good friends with Pauline, Betty and Mary Ann. Often, her mother and Mary Ann would cook gourmet meals in the kitchen together. Everyone noticed their waistlines had inched up since there were so many good cooks in the kitchen. Her mother loved riding horses, and she and Betty spent hours at a time on horseback exploring the ranch.

Daniel and Ashley brought Danny and Rossi back to the ranch every summer for a visit. The boys spent their vacations learning to ride horses and romping through the pastures. They were developing an interest in the various vegetable crops which were grown on the ranch, and were eager to learn how they grew. Often they made trips to visit the lake and tried their best to catch the big fish they had once caught and then released. The Pickle Barrel incident didn't seem to affect them much. As time passed, the crying stopped and the nightmares went away. They were back to being two happy little boys.

It was a happy time for everyone when the children were around. Edna and Grady also came every summer while the children were there. It felt like a family reunion to all of them.

This was a special time in Pauline's life. The ranch was alive again and filled with activity. However, this summer would be very special. A new person would be joining the ranch and the reunion. Gene and Jenny were expecting their first child. Pauline looked forward to the day she could hold her first grandchild in her arms.

Summer was near...so was a new beginning.

ACKNOWLEDGEMENTS

This book came to me in a dream. I was tormented day and night for weeks by this dream. It made a story that kept growing daily and resulted in the publication of this book. While this book came about as a result of a dream, there were, however, people involved who supported and encouraged me to write this story, which I was so reluctant to write.

I owe a large debt of gratitude to my dear friend Dixie Barnette who initiated the book idea. Without her driving force and continual support from the beginning to the end, this book would not have materialized. She shared her editing abilities with countless hours of reading and editing this book. The many hours of her personal time she gave to help me with my endeavor are greatly appreciated.

My husband Joe, who has always supported me, went the additional mile this time with his patience and support. His male point of view regarding certain characters in this book and his editing skills were very helpful. He showed patience when it was needed. He listened when I needed to talk. He gave a helping hand when I needed help. For all these reasons I give to him my undying love and appreciation.

Some of the names I used in this publication are real. These people know who they are. I want to express my gratitude to them. It was a pleasure for me to bring their fictional characters to life.

My nephews Danny and Rossi drowned together at the age of ten and eleven in 1971. I used their names in this book as a memorial to their young lives. They have long passed from this life, but their memory will always remain in our hearts.

The information I received from Corporal Eugene Brewer, Law Enforcement Investigator, Florida Highway Patrol, gave me a better understanding of police protocol and procedures used during a crisis.

Ted Kleinschnitz, at Action Gun Outfitters, Inc. Melbourne, Florida, was very helpful in explaining to me the differences in various types of high powered weapons. He didn't demonstrate an AK-47 to me, but he did show me one.